Tiina Nunnally

Maija

A NOVEL

Fjord Press
Seattle

♋ *With special thanks to my first readers, Steve Murray and Susan Scott, whose encouragement kept me writing.*

Published and distributed by:
Fjord Press, PO Box 16349, Seattle, WA 98116
tel (206) 935-7376 / fax (206) 938-1991 / email: fjordpress@aol.com

Editor: Steven T. Murray
Cover design: Jane Fleming
Design & typography: Fjord Press
Cover painting: "Moonlight" by Edvard Munch (1895), 93 x 110 cm.
    Used by permission of Nasjonalgalleriet, Oslo, Norway.
Back cover photo: Steven T. Murray

Excerpt from *The Kalevala*, translated by Keith Bosley (copyright © 1990), used by permission of Oxford University Press, Oxford, England.

Excerpt from "Future's Shadow," from *Love & Solitude: Selected Poems 1916–1923* by Edith Södergran, translated by Stina Katchadourian (copyright © 1981, 1985, 1992), used by permission of Fjord Press, Seattle.

Printed by McNaughton & Gunn, Saline, Michigan

Library of Congress Cataloging in Publication Data:
Nunnally, Tiina, 1952–
    Maija : a novel / Tiina Nunnally.
        p.   cm.
    ISBN 0-940242-68-0 (pbk.)
    1. Finnish American women—Fiction. 2. Family—United States—
Fiction. 3. Death—Fiction. I. Title.
PS3564.U53M35   1995
813'.54—dc20   95-17033
                                                                CIP

Printed in the United States of America
First edition, 1995

For Eeva and Elam

Maija

I have a good mind
take into my head
to start off singing
begin reciting
reeling off a tale of kin
and singing a tale of kind.
The words unfreeze in my mouth
and the phrases are tumbling
upon my tongue they scramble
along my teeth they scatter.

The Kalevala
translated by Keith Bosley

One

When Leena Martin's sister Maija died suddenly in the middle of April, everyone expected Leena to fall apart. The two sisters had been close friends. Not that they actually saw much of each other, since one lived in Milwaukee and the other in Seattle. A week's visit every few years was all they could manage, and even less often now that they were in their seventies. And they weren't much on letter-writing either, since they both refused to write in Finnish, their native language—they were stubborn about being American. But neither one had ever truly mastered the idiosyncrasies of written English. They had been in the United States almost forty-seven years, but the vast differences in the two languages had proved insurmountable for both Leena and Maija.

Their spoken English was fluent enough, though neither could rid herself of a strong accent that showed up in the heavy, rolled "r's" and the extra stress on long vowels. And certain words were never conquered: "blanket" was always pronounced "planket," and a "sweater" was a "sveather." Their kids teased them mercilessly, even after growing up and discovering for themselves the embarrassment of struggling with an unfamiliar language in a foreign country.

But it was in writing that all the fine points of the language completely deserted the two sisters, though in a different way for each of them. Maija wrote a perfectly correct English, but that was exactly the problem. It was much too correct, it sounded stiff and unnatural, and nothing of herself ever penetrated the rules. Leena, on the other hand, had never managed to switch from Finnish grammar to English. She left out articles, she used the wrong prepositions or put them in the wrong place, and her spelling was as close to spoken pronunciation as she could make it. Her bewilderment was so complete that she took to ending her sentences with rows of exclamation points, as if trying to shout her message from the intractable page. So the two sisters seldom sent letters to each other.

But they did talk on the phone once a month. Over the years it had become a set ritual, never formally discussed or agreed upon, but expected, anticipated, a reliable marking off of the months. When they first came to America and needed each other most, long-distance calls were an extravagance neither could afford. Later, they each decided in private that the phone calls were worth the expense. It was their one indulgence. On the first Saturday of each month one of the sisters would call the other around nine in the morning, and they would talk for exactly an hour. Leena began the year's calls in January and they alternated after that.

Maija was the older one and more sedate. She was thin, tall, and angular with a big nose and beauty-shop hair, carefully coiffed. She always wore a dress. She was conservative and proper but dignified, befitting an old-fashioned kindergarten teacher who wished to set the right example for her charges. Courtesy and manners were part of her curriculum. She had no patience for the American custom of using first names or other informal means of address. She surrendered her first name to strangers only reluctantly, offended by forced familiarity and bold advances. She believed in formality. It was essential to her view of the social order, to establishing the proper alliances.

Emigrating had made Maija more Finnish than any Finn back home. She meticulously observed the old customs, she remembered in detail the old places that had long since vanished. And her native language, when she did speak it on occasion, had not changed in forty-seven years—it had been stopped in time, mummified; it was a colloquial throwback, a linguistic museum piece. And beneath her proper façade she was gloomier than any other Finn. She was a worrier and a grumbler. She brooded, she was full of foreboding, and she firmly believed in omens.

She was a forest person trapped in a city landscape. Seattle was the only place in the States where Maija felt happy. Its looming fir trees and gray skies suited her. At twenty-eight she had married Pentti Lahtinen, a Finnish-American man with an equally dark temperament, and they had one daughter. Then, after only five years of marriage, her husband died. Maija became a kindergarten teacher at Queen Anne Elementary, supporting herself and her daughter Briitta, and she never looked for or wanted another man. She simply closed off that part of herself for good. She taught school for thirty-two years. A decade ago she retired, and now she was dead.

Leena got the news in a telegram delivered to the door at ten in the morning. She was home alone.

Her husband Robert had left at eight to work on his lecture

notes before his weekly graduate seminar started at eleven. It was his favorite course: Psychology 805, "Flight from the Nuclear Family," a title borrowed from a painting given to him years ago by his younger daughter Elly.

Created with all the fury of her seventeen years, the painting showed a figure in flames, its face hooded and dark, fleeing off the right side of the canvas, leaving behind a hazy group of people huddled in the upper left corner. The painting had at first cut Robert to the heart. He felt incriminated, caught, found out. He knew she was having a hard time at school, but he had been blind to her unhappiness at home. Here he was, Professor Robert Martin, acclaimed author of two textbooks on family therapy and a successful marriage counselor, but he didn't know his own daughter was in trouble. A classic case of tunnel vision. And he was stunned.

It took a full week after Elly gave him the painting for Robert to bring himself to ask her what was wrong. Not directly, of course. In spite of all his training, the communication techniques he had mastered proved ludicrously inadequate in his own home. The few times he had tried to draw on his expertise to deal with a Martin family crisis, the cold appraising eyes of his children had leveled his professional aplomb within seconds. He was reduced to the faltering, fumbling attempts of most fathers and husbands faced with a problem of an emotional nature, and it made him all the more flustered and confused. Leena found this side of Robert particularly endearing, but his children frequently thought him weak and hypocritical.

On this occasion, the painting came as a jarring reminder that he was not paying close enough attention at home. His career was skyrocketing, he loved his university life, and he was excited about the research he was doing with a team of colleagues (all much younger than he was). But the painting stopped him cold, and for once Robert listened to the warning of his heart, and after a week of worry and cowardice, he sat down to talk with Elly.

That conversation changed him in a way he could never have foreseen. It changed them all. Years later he asked Elly if he could use the title of her painting for a course on the modern American family, and she had consented with a wry but pleased smile. She knew that in his own way he meant to honor her. And Psychology 805 had quickly become one of the most popular graduate seminars in his department.

This was now Robert's last year at the university, and he was actually looking forward to being professor emeritus so he could finally write the three books he had been planning for years. The research was done but he just never had time for the writing. The three cardboard boxes full of notes in the closet were haunting him, and he was starting to feel an urgency and anxiety that he could only ascribe to a new sense of mortality. He'd lived a long life, but he seldom thought of it that way. Usually when he stopped to think about the passage of time, his twenty-five-year-old self—energetic, full of plans, brash, and political—would step forward and say, "Come on, stop worrying; there's plenty of time." But lately he had begun to feel closer to his real age. He was seventy-two, after all, and he could no longer put off anything of importance. He had to write those books.

Leena was washing the breakfast dishes when the doorbell rang. Her kids had been trying to buy her a dishwasher for a long time, but she always firmly refused their offer. She liked washing dishes. It was her time to think. It was an old habit, not really needed anymore now that the kids were gone, but she didn't feel like giving it up. She could turn her back to the kitchen, the house, the family, and the world—to all the noise and demands and complaints. She found it soothing and meditative. She liked to plunge her hands into the warm soap suds, with the hot water running in a steady stream next to the dishpan. And she paid no attention to her kids' groans about saving water. She knew that it took all day for women living in remote parts of Alaska to haul home the twenty gallons of water that she used up every time she did the dishes. (Her daughter Kirsti was always reporting such facts in the hope of "educating" her.) She knew it was wasteful, but she didn't care. The sound of the running water was part of her escape, part of her daydreaming. She needed it, she craved it. It was her time alone, and she was not going to change.

When Leena washed dishes she was not a Milwaukee housewife with three grown children and a professor husband who was well respected in his field. She was not seventy years old with a stocky body and graying hair that she had finally decided to stop dying blonde. In the fifteen or twenty minutes it took her to wash dishes she was thin, young, and always married to an artist: a world-famous painter, or a sculptor. Like Leonard Beal, for instance, who had rented the upstairs apartment for six months when they lived in the house on Murray Avenue. When he suddenly moved away, he left behind a mold for a bronze horse under the elm tree in the back yard. It was covered with a sheet of plywood that warped and buckled in the fall rains. Every so often one of the kids would lift up the plywood and stare at the horse-shaped indentation. When they moved to Prospect Avenue, the mold and the plywood were still under the elm.

More often, though, Leena daydreamed she was the envied wife of a concert pianist. They had a fancy apartment in Helsinki and a comfortable summer house on a secluded lake with their own sauna and a rowboat painted with blue and red flowers. Every June they would drive out to the country to open the house for the first time after the long winter months. Leena would open the door and step inside, and her eyes always filled with tears. She was overwhelmed by the smell of summer—last summer's heat and wood smoke, closed up and now released. And all her summer memories came flooding back—the smell of freshly cut birch branches, the taste of sausages smoked in the searing heat of the sauna rafters, the scent of wild blueberries picked from scrubby plants on the forest floor, the sting of nettles brushing against a bare leg, leaving tiny white blisters on her skin. And the sleepless nights bathed in the glow of the sun that never went down completely.

When the doorbell rang, Leena was just picturing herself stepping into the rowboat with the blue and red flowers as Pär tentatively dipped the oars into the water. (Of course her concert pianist had to have a *Swedish* name, signifying his aristocratic lineage.) They were going to row out to the little uninhabited island for afternoon coffee. Leena had packed a basket with cheese and butter and *limpa*, that aromatic dark Swedish rye pierced with bits of orange rind. The copper coffeepot was in the basket too, and they would build a fire on the shore and stay the whole afternoon. They never really did much of anything on the island—talked a little, or dozed in the heat, sitting on cushions on the uneven terrain of the shore. On rare occasions they would move back into the woods, out of sight, and make love in the shade of the birches.

Sometimes Pär would hum through a new composition and ask Leena what she thought of it. He liked to hear her opinion because she envisioned music so differently. For Pär, music was pure mathematics in the highest, most profound sense. Listening to music was like dreaming in elegant equations, a recognition of pristine and complex mathematical relationships. He was shocked to learn that Leena did not experience music the same way. For Leena, music was all colors and shapes. Bold, strong, and vibrant. Or soft, pastel, and full of nuances, all depending on the piece of music. And she wasn't shy about telling Pär what sort of images and colors were swirling through her mind, once she realized that he wasn't going to scoff at her fantasies. And he never scoffed.

But on most of those hot afternoons on the lake, they didn't say much at all. They would simply sit and stare at the rippling water and listen to the mesmerizing lapping of the waves against the shore.

The dull clang of the doorbell startled Leena, pulling her out of her reverie, wrenching her away from her Finnish interlude. She blinked rapidly and her shoulders hunched as a little shudder raced down her spine. She hated coming back before she was ready. She turned off the water and reached for a paper towel to dry her hands. Another example of her wastefulness, according to Kirsti, but she just couldn't imagine using a damp and grubby dishtowel hanging from the refrigerator door. It wasn't sanitary. And besides, it looked so untidy.

The doorbell rang again. "I'm coming, I'm coming," said Leena as she hurried through the dining room and then stopped to straighten a cushion on the living room couch before opening the front door.

"Telegram for Mrs. Robert Martin," mumbled the teenager standing on the porch with a Western Union patch safety-pinned to his shirt pocket. "Sign here," he said, pointing to an "X" on line 15 of the form attached to the clipboard, which he handed to Leena along with a ballpoint pen.

She wrote her tiny, cramped signature without a word, her normal effusiveness with strangers cut off by the sight of the yellow telegram. She knew it was bad news. It was always bad news. Her father's death had been announced this way. And her mother's too. She shut the door with a muted "Thank you," and stood in the front hall with the telegram burning in her left hand.

Her mind was still focused on that Western Union patch pinned to the boy's rumpled shirt, and she wondered why he didn't have a proper uniform. For an instant, the image of her son Joel flashed before her, the way he had looked at seven years old, standing on the doorstep with his shirt torn, his shoelaces untied, and his nose bloodied again by a bigger boy's fist. He had a way of looking up at her with his doleful, apologetic brown eyes that made her want to sweep him up into her arms and hug him tight. But she seldom did. Affection was something assumed in the Martin family but all too rarely expressed. Instead, she would take her son's hand, exclaiming, "Not again, Joel!" and lead him to the bathroom to wash his face.

Leena looked down at the envelope she was holding. Slowly she opened it and read the three lines typed on the page. Then she folded the telegram neatly, stuffed it back into the envelope, and put it face down on the dining-room table. Later she would call Robert. Right now she was glad to be alone, and she went into the bedroom and closed the door.

Two

Kirsti Martin found a message from her father on the answering machine when she came home early in the morning from her trip to Århus.

"Kirsti? This is your Dad calling. We had some bad news today. Your mother's sister Maija died, and I thought you'd want to know. Call me back when you get a chance."

Kirsti played the message twice and then glanced up at the clock on the wall. Too late to call now. It was already after midnight in Wisconsin. And she was going to be busy all day with her research, so she couldn't call until evening. If she timed it right, she might be able to catch Robert during his office hours at the university. The logistics of accommodating the seven-hour time difference between Copenhagen and Milwaukee, combined with the exorbitant cost that seemed to double with every tick of the clock, always made her calls home stressful, even under normal circumstances.

Kirsti listened to her other messages, jotted down a few reminders to call people back, and then turned the machine on again so she wouldn't have to answer the phone. She didn't feel like talking to anybody right now. Then she sat down at the kitchen table and leaned back in her chair.

Maija was dead. It seemed so sudden, although she *was* seventy-five, and lately Kirsti had almost gotten used to hearing about the deaths of elderly people that she knew. But the word "elderly" seemed all wrong for Maija. She was imperious and regal, and Kirsti still pictured her as she looked twenty years ago, when the artistic flamboyance of Alan M. Braddock III had lured Kirsti to Seattle, his home town. They had seen Maija fairly often during the first two years of their marriage.

That was back when Alan was still dreaming of fame as a painter, and Kirsti was ardently supporting his pretensions with a regular paycheck from a stultifying office job. That was before his envy of her discipline and drive finally surfaced and he tore up her college degree in a malicious rage; and before Kirsti's resentment of his creative prerogative boiled over one morning and she found herself, dressed in her light gray suit and ready for work, violently kicking the side of the bed as Alan slept on, oblivious. That's when she knew it was over.

But when they first moved to Seattle in 1975, they were still delirious with youthful lust and full of grand schemes for the future—someday they would buy a plot of land on Vashon Island, build a geodesic dome, and live the perfect artistic life. Their present existence was only temporary. They wouldn't be staying long in that dark studio apartment in the basement of a dilapidated building on Capitol Hill, with its damp walls and entrenched mildew that spotted and warped their books, the rampant silverfish that ate the charcoal right off the pages of Alan's sketchbook, and the faulty plumbing and grimy shower stall that no amount of Ajax would ever get clean. And they would soon get rid of all the makeshift furniture scavenged from dumpsters and construction sites: their sofa made from old doors set on top of cinder blocks, their table one of those big wooden spools used for cable, and their bed a three-inch-thick foam mattress in a plywood frame on the floor. Kirsti did her best to brighten up the place with pillows and patchwork quilts stitched on her ancient treadle sewing machine, but it didn't really matter how things looked, because it was all temporary.

In the meantime, money was tight and the $15 a week that Kirsti budgeted for food left them in a constant state of hunger, so the occasional dinner invitation from Maija was always accepted with secret glee.

For one night they would be released from their steady diet of oatmeal, macaroni and cheese, baked potatoes, and popcorn. All cheap, starchy foods designed to convince their stomachs they were getting plenty to eat. A diet appropriate to a bohemian lifestyle and the tradition of poverty and sacrifice for the sake of art. Alan was the cook, and whenever they had a few extra dollars, he liked to buy cheap cuts of meat and make oddly spiced stews with lots of onions.

One day Kirsti bit down on a piece of metal that turned out to be buckshot from the horsemeat that Alan had bought in a fly-by-night butcher shop at the Market. Kirsti looked down at her plate in horror, then gave Alan a murderous glare, jumped up from the table, and locked herself in the bathroom.

Some time later Alan tapped on the bathroom door saying, "I'm sorry, Kirsti. How was I supposed to know there'd be buckshot in the meat?"

"Damn you, Alan Braddock," shouted Kirsti. "Don't you *ever* feed me horsemeat again." And from then on she always asked, to Alan's unending exasperation, "What kind of meat is in the stew *this* time?"

So whenever Maija called to ask them over for dinner, they never turned down her invitation for a decent meal.

Maija would open the door before they even had a chance to ring the bell. She expected them to be prompt, and she had been watching them approach her house from the bus stop at the end of the street. She lived in Ballard, in a neat yellow bungalow with white trim, flanked by rhododendron bushes and two towering Douglas firs that were landmarks in a neighborhood otherwise devoid of trees.

There had been plenty of trees around when Maija and her husband bought the house, but one by one they had fallen to the chainsaw and ax. This was one of the topics that would inevitably come up during dinner, since Maija could not forgive her neighbors their craving for sunlight and space that had compelled them to chop down the trees.

Whenever she was feeling especially gloomy, she would get in her sky-blue 1953 Plymouth (which still ran perfectly, thanks to her Finnish mechanic, Joonas Väinämöinen) and drive out to Lincoln Park in West Seattle. There she would walk for hours through the damp, close woods, breathing in the pungent smell of the evergreens and gazing up through the layered canopy overhead. In cold weather she would stride along the paths in a wool skirt and black rubber boots, with her hands jammed into the deep pockets of her dark green jacket. When it was warmer she wore sturdy walking shoes and a light print dress, with a sweater draped over her shoulders. She never carried a purse or bag, because she wanted to move through the woods unencumbered.

Maija was a familiar figure to the other regulars walking in the park. They would nod or wave, and Maija always politely responded in kind, but she was happiest when she had the paths to herself.

Sometimes she would see the pair of bald eagles that had arrived early one spring and made a nest in the top of the tall fir at the edge of a clearing. The resident crows and gulls screeched and swooped, trying to scare them away, but the eagles were implacable, and every year they returned to the same roost.

Maija simply could not fathom why her neighbors would cut down their trees.

∝

"Welcome," Maija would always say when Kirsti and Alan arrived. "Come in. Let me take your coats." And she would give her niece a little pat on the shoulder and insist on solemnly shaking hands with Alan, a ritual she repeated when they left. He thought this an absurd affectation, but Kirsti told him it was a European custom and he should just be glad that Maija, with her penchant for formality, hadn't decided to address him as "Mr. Braddock."

Five minutes after they walked in the door, dinner was ready to be served, and they would sit down immediately at the dining-room table, always elegantly set with gleaming white dishes on a tablecloth of royal blue or dark cranberry. Alan would launch right into the food, polishing off a full plate while Kirsti's fork was still skirting the edge of her dinner as she listened to Maija's news of her daughter, Briitta, who was a graphic designer in Portland. The customary speed with which Kirsti dispatched one of Alan's meals was never in evidence at Maija's house.

For Kirsti, part of the pleasure was visual. She liked to look at the green peas next to the red beets next to the steaming slab of roast, all individually displayed so vividly against the white china background. Even when Alan splurged on the ingredients, his cooking was always a one-pot concoction, an amorphous mass of browns that might be tasty enough but was visually undistinguished, and Kirsti saw no reason to linger over the food. But Maija's dinners were resplendently simple and colorful, and Kirsti took her time.

The evenings were never dull, in spite of the litany of complaints that Maija couldn't refrain from mentioning—if it wasn't the disappearing trees, it was the city's failure to keep the crosswalks painted, or the steady decline in the quality of produce in the grocery stores. The familiar themes always brought a smirk to Alan's face, and Kirsti would have to give him a stern look, silently begging him to be nice. (She wanted him to make a good impression, in case Maija happened to mention him to Leena in one of their monthly phone calls.) But Maija had a strong interest in art and literature, and her eclectic knowledge never failed to surprise them.

They had assumed that a kindergarten teacher would have a house filled with picture books and cute little drawings from the five-year-olds in her class. They discovered, however, that although Maija staunchly encouraged the creative impulses of her students, she didn't believe in sentimentalizing over children's art. She had framed three of her daughter's childhood paintings that were good enough to hint at the talent that eventually gave

Briitta her career. Otherwise, Maija's house was austerely but tastefully furnished.

Two tall bookcases were filled with art books. Edvard Munch, Marc Chagall, Vilhelm Hammershøj, Emily Carr, Louise Nevelson, and a Finnish painter named Hugo Simberg were Maija's favorites. She had the collected works of Virginia Woolf, the novels of all three Brontë sisters, and several editions of Emily Dickinson's poetry. There were books by Henrik Ibsen, Jonas Lie, Amalie Skram, and many other Scandinavian authors, all in the original languages, which Kirsti could partially decipher, drawing on her good command of German. Maija's prize possession was a first edition of *Landet som icke är* by the poet Edith Södergran, for whom Maija's languorous white cat was named. A dark red *ryijy* rug with a black bramble pattern hung over the gray-striped sofa, glass candleholders of classic Finnish design stood on the oak coffee table, and family photographs in beautiful dark frames covered a good portion of one wall in the living room.

One of the photos immediately caught Kirsti's eye on their first visit to Maija's house. It was an old black-and-white picture, a little out of focus. Two timidly smiling girls, wearing obviously new dresses, were holding hands and staring straight into the camera.

"Who's this?" Kirsti asked Maija, pointing to the photo.

"That's your mother," she said, indicating the younger girl, "and that's me. I was eleven and Leena was six. We were going to our aunt's wedding. It turned out to be a terrible day."

"What do you mean?" asked Kirsti.

But Maija only shook her head somberly.

Kirsti stole a glance at that photo every time they visited. She found it hard to think of the six-year-old as her mother, especially since it was the only childhood picture she had ever seen of Leena. There were piles of Martin family photos thrown randomly into the big red trunk back home. As kids, Kirsti and Elly and Joel had regularly sifted through them on rainy afternoons when they were too bored to do anything else, but there were no early pictures of Leena or her sister from their childhood home in Finland.

After dinner, Kirsti and Alan would sit on the couch and wait for Maija to join them as soon as she had cleared the table and put water on for tea. She always firmly declined any assistance from her guests. Then they would talk for a while, and the conversation usually turned to art.

Maija took a keen interest in Alan's work, and Kirsti was grateful for this, since her parents had made it quite clear that they didn't entirely approve of either her husband or his art. When she brought Alan home for the first time and announced that they were engaged and were planning to move to Seattle, Robert had been tight-lipped and abnormally patriarchal.

"And how will you make a living?" he asked Alan, his voice so full of disdain that Kirsti was genuinely startled.

"Oh, I don't know... I've been thinking of giving painting lessons," drawled Alan, intentionally slumping in his chair. He enjoyed playing the role of the decadent artist who was robbing the famous professor of his brilliant and virginal daughter.

Kirsti missed the rest of the conversation because Leena impatiently pulled her into the kitchen.

"So, where did you two meet?" she asked Kirsti.

"Well, I was standing in line to buy a ticket to the Bergman film festival on campus, and Alan was standing behind me. We started talking, and then we ended up going to see the films together."

"And now you two are bunking together?" Leena asked Kirsti, who felt a surge of hysterical laughter, instantly suppressed, at Leena's choice of phrase. Her mother could never bring herself to discuss anything related to sex, and she usually found all sorts of ways to avoid the topic.

When Kirsti got her first period she was twelve years old, and it happened, much to her distress, right in the middle of choir practice. An odd sensation of nausea and heat sent her dashing to the bathroom as soon as the last song was over. "Oh no," she moaned, stuffing wads of toilet paper into her underpants and taking off her plaid skirt to examine it for stains. When she got home after school, she threw her bloody underwear into the clothes hamper.

That night, as Kirsti did her homework at the desk in the room she shared with her sister, Leena came in with a pink box of Kotex dangling between her thumb and forefinger. "Here," she said, "I think you need this."

When Kirsti started high school, her mother gave her a tedious book on marriage and sex. And that was the extent of Kirsti's sex education at home.

She was lucky that her best friend, Shelley, had an older sister who seemed amazingly well-informed about all sorts of biological matters. And she was only too happy to share what she knew with Shelley and her little friends. Otherwise, Kirsti would have been dismally ignorant.

"Well, yes, Mom, we moved in together a few weeks ago. Alan wants to go back to Seattle, so we're going to get a drive-away and leave after the semester's over."

"What about your studies?"

"Oh, Mom, I'm tired of living in Madison and I'm bored with the university. I can always go back later, but right now I just want to do something different."

Leena was intrigued with the idea that Alan was a painter, but she was not too enthralled with the actual young man. His scraggly dark hair and loose, baggy clothing gave him an unkempt appearance that Leena could not reconcile with her more romantic notion of The Artist. And neither Leena nor Robert could find much of appeal in the scratches and scrawls on the pages in Alan's sketchbook. They didn't want to meddle, so they kept their opinions to themselves, but their unspoken judgments were palpable.

"Doesn't he seem a little immature, dear?" Leena would occasionally venture in her phone calls to Kirsti. Robert would studiously avoid saying anything at all about Alan (Kirsti and her father usually talked politics on the phone), but he always ended his calls with the question: "So... when are you going back to grad school?"

When Kirsti and Alan went down to the courthouse and got married three months after their arrival in Seattle, Leena and Robert sent the newlyweds a set of Teflon cookware and a hundred-dollar check. Neither of them ever mentioned whether they were hurt at not being invited to the wedding, even though it *was* only a civil ceremony.

Alan's parents were not as reticent about their utter disapproval of both their son and his choice of wife.

Kirsti met Sheryl and Alan M. Braddock, Jr. only once, but that encounter was enough for a lifetime. Alan had warned her about his parents. He had been estranged from them for years, and their only communication was an occasional postcard. It was with great reluctance that he agreed to accept the dinner invitation, which arrived by mail after his parents saw the wedding notice in the *Seattle Times*.

Kirsti was curious about meeting her in-laws, and she put on her good blue dress with the silver buttons for the occasion. Alan was glum and morose. He had resigned himself to the visit, but he refused to dress up.

They took the bus to his parents' Laurelhurst home, and Alan was visibly nervous as he rang the bell. His mother opened the door.

"Alan! How are you, honey? And this must be Kristy. Come in, children, come in," Sheryl Braddock gushed as she gave her son the requisite hug and aimed a sharp glance at her daughter-in-law. Alan had said that his mother looked like Elizabeth Taylor, and she did have the dark hair, big eyes, and voluptuous figure. But there was a hard edge to her voice that was nothing like the breathy, little-girl voice of the movie star.

"Hi, Mom. It's Kirsti, not Kristy," said Alan.

"Oh, that's right," she said. "Al, the kids are here!"

Alan's father made his appearance with a glass of red wine in his hand. He was slightly shorter than his son, but the years had not added any extra pounds to the wiry frame that was evidently a family trait. He looked as though he had the same hyper metabolism that allowed Alan to eat huge quantities of whatever he liked, without ever giving a thought to his weight. Mr. Braddock nodded to his son and gave Kirsti a dry little kiss on the cheek as he said hello.

"What would you kids like to drink?" he asked, leading the way into the living room.

"I'll have a glass of wine," said Kirsti.

"A glass of water," said Alan at the same time, and they sat down next to each other on the sofa upholstered in expensive-looking brocade with white and gold flowers. The cushions were so soft that Kirsti was afraid if she leaned all the way back, she'd never be able to get up again. They both perched uneasily on the edge. Kirsti crossed her legs and tried to look casual. Alan was fidgeting with a strand of his hair. His father served the drinks, and then sat down in one of the matching armchairs on the other side of the glass coffee table.

Sheryl Braddock went out to the kitchen to get the hors d'oeuvres: a plate of little pastry shells filled with crab meat and asparagus tips in a glutinous sauce, and a tray of blanched vegetables arranged in a pinwheel around a bowl of dip. Kirsti didn't think she could cope with any of it, but she politely put a carrot stick and some cauliflower on her plate. Alan flatly said, "No, thanks."

"Well, it seems congratulations are in order," said Mr. Braddock without a trace of enthusiasm. "Sheryl and I saw the notice in the paper. How long have you kids known each other, anyway?"

"Six months. Could you cut the 'kids' crap, Dad? We're both twenty-three years old. We're not children anymore."

Oh God, thought Kirsti. This was going to be a lot worse than she expected.

"Are you from Seattle, Kristy?" Mrs. Braddock hurried to

ask, jumping into the icy silence before her husband could respond.

"No, I'm from Wisconsin. I grew up in Milwaukee, but I've been studying at the university in Madison, working on my Master's, and that's where I met Alan," Kirsti said all in one breath.

"Oh? And what are you studying?"

"Comp Lit—I mean, comparative literature. But I'm not studying anymore. I've got an office job now. Downtown in the Smith Tower."

Mrs. Braddock seemed to have nothing more to say. She stared at Kirsti blankly, and then shifted her gaze to the hunched figure of her son, who sat scowling at the floor.

"And what are you doing these days, Alan?" she asked. "Still have the house-painting business with your friend Keith?"

Kirsti couldn't imagine Alan hauling around buckets of house paint and climbing up ladders, and she'd never heard of Keith, but she hid her surprise by taking a bite of her carrot stick.

"No, it didn't work out. We couldn't find enough customers, and then Keith took off for California, so I decided to visit some friends in Madison."

"Then what *are* you doing now?" asked his father coldly.

"I'm doing my artwork. I'm going to be a painter, a real painter. OK? Why do you always have to be so critical? Why do you think everybody has to be a stockbroker or a businessman like you?"

"Why can't you ever get a decent job? If you're so grown-up, why don't you show some responsibility for a change? Are you going to let your *wife* support you for the rest of your life?"

"Now, Al…" said Mrs. Braddock, trying to intervene.

"You keep out of this, Sheryl. I'm sick and tired of hearing about his 'artwork' and watching him waste his time on all kinds of bullshit. If he didn't keep finding all these girls who were willing to pay his rent, maybe he'd actually be earning a living by now."

Kirsti set her wine glass down on the coffee table so sharply that the stem snapped instantly in half. In slow motion she watched the crystal glass topple and the dark red liquid flow over the delicate rim, splash onto the table, and then cascade onto the white shag rug on the floor.

"Oh!" shrieked Mrs. Braddock. "My glass! My rug!"

"Fuck you!" shouted Alan at his father. "You don't know anything about real life. All you care about is money and *things*. You don't give a damn about me and you never have. So go ahead and keep your ritzy house and your spiffy car and your stupid friends. I don't want anything to do with you anymore. Come on, Kirsti, let's go."

And he grabbed Kirsti's hand, pulling her along with him to the front hallway, where he yanked their coats out of the closet, tore open the front door, and then slammed it hard behind them. They raced down the front steps and kept on running all the way to the bus stop. Both of them were breathing hard, and Alan was cursing. Then they looked at each other and burst out laughing. They were still laughing as they got on the bus and rode home.

But neither one of them ever mentioned the aborted dinner again. In her heart, Kirsti felt hurt and confused. And Alan was truly afraid that his fury might consume him.

CB

The last time Alan and Kirsti visited Maija together, it was one of those typical November nights in Seattle, damp and cold, with a menacing sky and occasional bursts of rain. On an impulse, Alan had decided to give Maija one of his paintings, so he wrapped it up in a piece of red plastic and tucked it under his arm as they were rushing out the door to catch the six o'clock bus. The next one didn't come until 6:30, and Maija would be upset if they were late.

This was during Alan's "black period," when he was experimenting with multiple layers of black paint applied to a white-washed canvas. He would scrape away one or more layers, or wipe off some of the paint while it was still wet, but never enough to expose the white undercoat. He created images that were only visible if the light hit the surface at a certain angle. Seen head-on, the paintings were nothing more than solid black rectangles. He had done five or six of them, and he had decided to give Maija the one he called "Portent and Pestilence." In the right light, three winged figures were visible crouched in a swirl of geometric shapes. Alan had hit his thumb with the hammer while stretching the canvas on the frame, and he thought the spattered blood, now invisible under the paint, was particularly significant.

Alan handed the plastic-wrapped package to Maija as soon as they stepped in the door.

"I've brought one of my paintings," he said. "I want you to have it."

"Why, Alan, that's quite a gift," said Maija solemnly, shaking his hand. "Thank you so much. Let me put it in a safe place in the living room so we can open it with the proper ceremony after we've had dinner." And she propped the canvas, still in its wrappings, against the wall next to the sofa.

After dinner, Kirsti and Alan sat down in their usual places on the couch while Maija moved back and forth from dining room to kitchen, going through her normal routine of clearing and rinsing the dishes. Alan picked up a book about Emil Nolde that he found lying on the coffee table, and he was soon absorbed in examining the exquisitely printed color plates of Nolde's paintings.

Kirsti leaned back and let her mind wander. She was feeling comfortable and warm after dinner, and she was still savoring the sight of the dark green shell of the acorn squash holding the orange flesh of the vegetable, topped with a little pool of brown sugar and butter.

For the past few weeks she had been slowly making her way through a book by Victoria Benedictsson with the help of a Swedish-English dictionary. A novel that Maija had recommended about a young girl who dreamt of becoming an artist. Kirsti found it a rather disturbing book, and she wanted to ask Maija if she knew anything about the author's life.

Out of the corner of her eye, Kirsti saw Maija's cat, Edith, saunter out of the guest room, stop to stretch, and then prick up her ears as her attention was caught by something next to the sofa. Alert and tense, Edith crept closer, and Kirsti leaned down to see what she was stalking.

A thin black trickle of oil paint was snaking across the light gray carpet from a small hole in the plastic wrapped around Alan's painting. He had finished it only a few days ago, and it probably hadn't dried completely, and then the rain had leaked under the plastic, and now it was making a permanent stain on Maija's rug.

Kirsti uttered a little gasp and glanced over at Alan, but he was still engrossed in his book, and he didn't even notice when Maija came into the room. She walked right over to Kirsti's end of the sofa, evidently intent on picking up the painting, and then she stood for a long moment, surveying the scene: Edith hunkered down, her tail switching, her wide eyes fixed on the ribbon of paint still inching its way out of the red plastic; and Kirsti's face, white and appalled.

"You know, I think I'll just get rid of this plastic in the kitchen and then we can have a look at the painting," said Maija calmly. And with one hand she picked up the package, while with the other she scooped up Edith, and she carried both of them out of the room. In a few minutes she returned with a damp cloth, which she tossed lightly on top of the miscreant oil paint.

"Shall we look at your painting now, Alan?" she said loudly, giving Kirsti a discreet little smile. Alan pulled himself away from his book, and they all went into the kitchen, where Maija had placed "Portent and Pestilence" on top of the white enameled kitchen table, where "the light was better," she said. The painting didn't seem to be dripping anymore, and neither Kirsti nor Maija mentioned the stain.

ભ

That was their last dinner at Maija's house. Not because she never invited them back, but because three weeks later Alan's incipient frustration with his work began to have a devastating effect on their marriage.

He lost all interest in his black paintings and decided that canvas wasn't an appropriate medium for his art. He started scrounging around for old pieces of junk and hauled home heavy chunks of discarded particleboard from a shop around the corner that assembled kitchen counters. He slathered everything with globs of oil paint and threw handfuls of sand or dirt at the wet surfaces. He stopped taking regular showers and would wear the same t-shirt and drawstring pants until Kirsti cautiously hinted that he might want to change his clothes.

Then for months on end he never even left the apartment, and he refused to answer the phone whenever his friends called. Finally they stopped calling altogether. Kirsti would come home from work to find him sitting in the dark, holding a piece of metal or a scrap of wood in his lap.

"So... what's for dinner, Alan?" she would ask, turning on the lights and hoping to prod him out of his moodiness.

"I'm not hungry," he would say. "You go ahead and eat."

And Kirsti would open a can of soup or cook up a pot of plain spaghetti, and sit down at the table to eat alone. They spent the evenings in silence, Alan sullenly reading a few pages of a tattered biography of Nikos Kazantzakis or leafing through old art magazines. Kirsti read Benedictsson or Kafka or Böll, casting an occasional worried glance at her spouse. After she had gone to bed, unable to wrest more than a few sentences from Alan, she would hear him prowling around in the dark on the other side of the folding screen that separated the bed from the rest of the apartment. The refrigerator light would go on, and Kirsti knew he was taking out whatever leftovers she had put away. She was relieved to know that at least he wasn't trying to starve himself to death.

Eventually, Kirsti bought a used copy of *The Joy of Cooking* and taught herself to make a few easy but nutritious dinners, like baked chicken and tuna casserole, so Alan would have some variety in his late-night foraging in the fridge.

Around one a.m. he would finally come to bed, crawling under the covers with infinite care, avoiding all contact with Kirsti. Then he would fall asleep with his legs tucked up and his back turned toward her. He never touched her anymore. Kirsti would lie awake, missing his touch. Missing the pulse of his fingertips on her shoulder blades that could send shivers of electricity down her spine. Missing the whisper of his lips on her cheek that could made her legs go limp and her toes tingle. But he never wanted to make love anymore.

Kirsti started having the same nightmare over and over again.

She is riding in a bus through a dark, snow-covered landscape. She is the only passenger. She rings the bell and the driver opens the door and lets her off. The bus pulls away and vanishes around a bend in the road. She realizes that she has gotten off at the wrong stop, a desolate crossroads in the countryside miles away from home. There is no moon, there are no stars, but the snow seems to emanate its own icy glow, and Kirsti starts walking toward home. The eerie silhouettes of craggy trees and ramshackle buildings loom up at intervals along the road, and Kirsti is cold and scared. Suddenly she comes upon a young man dressed in black who is viciously kicking a mound of snow. He swings his face around toward her and gives her a leer, saying: "I know where you've hidden the body. I know where the body's buried." And then he returns to kicking the mound in the snow. Kirsti starts running down the road. There is a light in the distance but she never seems to get any closer, and she can still hear the black-clad man taunting her: "I know where you've hidden the body. I know where the body's buried." And then she wakes up.

At exactly 4:11 in the morning her eyes would fly open in terror, her heart pounding loudly in her ears, her throat dry and tight, and she could hardly breathe. Her nightgown was clammy with sweat and waves of nausea washed over her. She couldn't bring herself to get out of bed. She would lie there motionless and pretend to sleep. With every muscle tensed, every fiber of her brain alert, her breathing jagged and shallow, she would lie there in panic until exhaustion finally overcame her. Around six a.m. she would fall asleep. At seven she had to get up for work.

In the morning, Alan was always sound asleep when Kirsti left for the office.

॰८

One day when Kirsti came home, Alan was lying face down on the bare floor, with his hands stretched out over his head. He had nothing on but his Jockey shorts. The air in the apartment was thick with a sickening combination of paint fumes and sandalwood incense.

"My God, Alan, what's wrong?" exclaimed Kirsti.

Alan lifted his head a few inches off the floor and peered up at her vacantly. "What's wrong?" he said. "You want to know what's wrong? I can't paint a goddamned thing anymore. It's all bullshit, just like my father said."

"But Alan, I think you're going to be a great painter. You're just going through a slump right now. Why don't you take a break for a while? Do something else for a change. Why don't you get out of this apartment and see some of your friends? Forget about painting. You'll get back into it later. I know you will."

"What a Pollyanna you are," Alan sneered. "I'm telling you it's all over, I'm never going to paint again."

"Oh, Alan..." sighed Kirsti, sitting down next to him and putting out her hand to stroke his back.

"Don't touch me!" shouted Alan. "Just leave me alone!"

Two days later he ripped Kirsti's college degree off the wall from its place of honor over the sofa where he had proudly pinned it up when they first moved in. He shredded it into a million bits, called her a "smug little bitch," and said she shouldn't think she was better than him just because she had some meaningless piece of paper. Then he broke down completely and apologized in tears.

One morning a week later Kirsti found herself kicking the bed with a venom she didn't know she possessed. She couldn't stand any more of Alan's fits and temper tantrums. He was driving her crazy, and she wasn't getting any sleep. She had been patient, sympathetic, worried, and concerned. But now she was just plain mad. At work she looked up the number for the graduate school at the University of Washington and called to ask for an application. She had them send it to the office, so Alan wouldn't see it. She filled out all the papers, including the financial aid forms, and in July she was notified that she had been accepted. She was going back to grad school in September. And she was leaving Alan.

Kirsti's friend Lydia offered to rent her a small but sunny room in the house she shared with two other women in the U District. Kirsti accepted at once, and on a Friday in the middle of August, she called Maija to ask if she could borrow her car.

"Yes, of course you can," said Maija on the phone. "How are you? I haven't seen you and Alan in such a long time."

"I'm leaving Alan," Kirsti rushed to tell her aunt, feeling a lurch in her stomach as she actually uttered the phrase out loud. "It's over. And now I'm going back to grad school. I haven't told Mom and Dad yet. I wanted to wait until it was all settled."

There was a long pause, and then Maija said, "I'm sorry to hear that, Kirsti. This must be very difficult for you. Can I do anything?"

"I just need to borrow your car for the day so I can move all my stuff," Kirsti said with tears in her eyes, but she was determined not to cry. This was *her* decision, and she knew she had to go through with it.

The next day she took the bus out to Maija's house and rang the bell. Maija answered the door with the car keys in her hand. Silently she gave them to Kirsti, who could only manage a stifled "Thank you. I'll bring the car back by five," before she spun on her heel and got into the sky-blue Plymouth.

A few days earlier, when Kirsti told Alan that she was quitting her office job and going back to school, he didn't realize at first that she meant to leave him.

"But how can we afford it?" he asked, suddenly alert.

"I got a student loan and they gave me a grant to cover tuition," said Kirsti evasively. And then she took a deep breath and plunged right in and told him that she was moving out on Saturday.

"I want a divorce, Alan. We can't go on like this anymore. It's not healthy for either one of us. I need my own life. I need to use my mind again. I'm dying in that office job. I don't belong there. And maybe if I leave, you'll be able to paint. Maybe I'm stopping you from doing your artwork somehow."

White-faced and trembling, Kirsti put out her hand to touch Alan, but he pulled away with a look of sheer hatred.

"Fine," he said. "Go ahead and leave." And without another word he stormed out of the apartment, and he hadn't come back.

It didn't take long to pack up all her possessions in the six cardboard boxes that she had lugged home from the liquor store. The next-door neighbor helped her load the treadle sewing machine into the trunk of the car, and she was just pushing the last box onto the back seat when Alan suddenly appeared on the sidewalk in front of the apartment building. He looked wan and bedraggled, and he seemed honestly perplexed to find her on the verge of departure.

"So you're really going?" he asked Kirsti.

"Yes, I am," she said, putting her hands on his shoulders and looking him straight in the eye. "Take care of yourself, Alan."

And then Kirsti got in the car and pulled away from the curb, leaving Alan standing there with his arms hanging limply at his sides.

She didn't stop crying until she drove up to her new house in the U District.

Late in the afternoon she parked the Plymouth in Maija's driveway and walked up to the house to return the keys. Maija opened the door, gave her a worried look, and then reached out to put her arms around Kirsti. "Are you OK?" she asked.

"I'm fine," said Kirsti, both surprised and touched by Maija's unusually overt expression of concern.

"Come in and have some tea," said Maija.

And Kirsti dropped onto the sofa with a deep sigh of relief as her aunt went into the kitchen. Edith hopped down from her vantage place on the windowsill and stationed herself on the floor in front of Kirsti, giving her one of those penetrating and unblinking feline stares.

"What are you looking at, Edith? Haven't you ever seen a free woman before?" whispered Kirsti, feeling a streak of hilarity flash through her drained and exhausted mind.

∽

That was seventeen years ago, and she had not seen Alan since. The divorce was a simple procedure, handled with an exchange of signatures by mail, and Kirsti's subsequent appearance before a judge, who stamped the papers with a sarcastic flourish. Alan's presence was not required.

Even when Kirsti was going to the U, their paths never crossed, and the few mutual friends they had were eventually forced to declare their allegiance to one or the other ex-spouse. A year after the divorce was final, Kirsti read a review in the paper of Alan's one-man show at a small avant-garde gallery in Pioneer Square. From the description of the show, it seemed he had returned to painting on canvas, and several all-black pieces were even mentioned. But the critic had not been kind. And not long afterwards, Kirsti heard dire rumors that Alan had suffered a total collapse and that a friend had discovered him daubing a canvas with his own excrement. But Kirsti refused to believe such stories. The last news she had heard of Alan was that he had moved to the Bay Area. He was sharing a house with his mysterious friend Keith, and he had taken a temporary job as a waiter in a waffle shop. He had apparently given up painting for good.

ભ

The sharp click of the answering machine and the whirring sound of the tape as it recorded a message abruptly brought Kirsti back to her sublet apartment in Copenhagen.

My God, it was already after ten, and she had an appointment at eleven o'clock with an archivist at the Royal Library. She picked up a green elastic band from the table, pulled her shoulder-length blonde hair into a ponytail, and twisted the elastic around it. Then she stood up and arched her back to stretch out the kinks. She had just enough time for a cup of tea and a piece of bread with cheese.

Kirsti went over to the sink, rinsed out the white china teapot and set it on the drainboard. From the shelf on the wall, she took down the black enamel tea canister with the pink flowers. She pried off the lid, which was always a little stubborn, and lifted out the plastic scoop nestled on top of the loose tea leaves.

And then she stood there, leaning slightly over the sink, with the canister in her left hand, the scoop in her right, and tears flooding down her cheeks. She was overcome by the smoky perfume of Earl Grey tea, the only kind of tea that Maija ever served. And she stood there and wept. She wept for Maija and for her cat Edith. She wept for Alan. And she wept for her own young, naive, and gullible self.

Three

It was Saturday, two days after the telegram arrived, and Leena was sitting on the living-room couch knitting a baby sweater that she had promised for a friend but hadn't worked on for at least three months. Robert was in the kitchen washing dishes. She couldn't remember him ever doing any kind of housework before, but he desperately wanted to do something for her, and she had accepted his offer. He had already come in twice to ask her where to find things—first the dishpan and then the soap. She could hear him clattering the pots from yesterday's curried chicken and rice that she had cooked for dinner.

After sitting motionless in the comforting darkness of their bedroom for several hours on Thursday, she had called Robert at the university, and he had rushed home and taken care of all the necessary phone calls. First to Maija's daughter Briitta, who had sent the telegram, and then to all the kids. The funeral was going to be next Wednesday in Seattle, and Robert had already booked their plane reservations, but they weren't yet sure if any of the children would be able to come.

Robert came into the living room wearing his old barbecue

apron with the ad for Flame-Ready Charcoal on the front. He had found it in the back of the linen closet when he was looking in vain for a dishtowel. Leena explained to him that she didn't believe in dishtowels, and he should just let everything dry in the rack. Now he appeared holding the cast-iron skillet in his hand.

"I can't seem to get this clean, Leena," he said hesitantly.

"Oh, don't worry about it, dear. Just put it in the sink to soak and I'll take care of it later."

"OK," said Robert, giving her a smile and turning back to the kitchen. He was worried about his wife. He knew that losing Maija must be a great blow. He felt the loss himself, and he had shed some tears in the privacy of the bathroom down the hall from his office after Leena called him at work. So he was concerned about Leena's eerie composure. When he came home on Thursday, he found her sitting at the kitchen table reading the *Milwaukee Journal*. As he gently pulled Leena to her feet and folded her into his arms, he noticed that the paper was four days old.

"Oh, Leena. I'm so sorry," he whispered.

And then she clung to him for a moment and cried a little. But she quickly pulled herself together.

"Call Briitta," she said. "Ask her about the funeral. Tell her that we'll be there." And then she gathered up the various sections of the newspaper, tossed them into the garbage can under the sink, and went to the bedroom closet to get out the vacuum cleaner.

Leena spent the rest of that day and all of Friday cleaning the house. She took down the curtains in every single room, washed them, ironed them, and hung them back up. She vacuumed all the carpets and used the special attachment to clean the uphol-stered furniture. She scrubbed the kitchen floor on her hands and knees, rubbing hard on the scuff marks next to the back door that were always so difficult to remove from the linoleum. The blue and white stripes of the linoleum always made Leena laugh a little at herself. They didn't really match the rest of the kitchen, but the blue was the exact blue of the Finnish flag, and Leena knew she had to have that linoleum when she saw it in the store.

She carried a sponge and a bucket of warm soapy water from room to room, wiping down the walls and getting rid of the fingerprints on doorknobs. She opened all the windows and let the cool air blow through the house. She needed air and sun-shine. And she was grateful that it was spring.

Diane Avery was worried about Leena too. She called on Friday to ask Leena to go for a walk.

"Hi, Leena, it's me. Isn't this weather great? Let's go over to Estabrook Park and take a walk."

"Hi, Diane. No, I can't make it today. I have to clean the house."

"But it's such a nice day. You don't want to spend the whole day indoors. The housecleaning can wait."

"No, it can't. I have to clean the house. My sister died yester-day."

"What? Oh, Leena, that's terrible. Why didn't you call me? Shall I come over and keep you company? Do you need any-thing?"

"No. No, thanks, but I'd rather be alone. And I really *do* have to clean the house."

Diane offered a few more words of sympathy and then hung

up. She called Robert at his office, and he told her that Leena seemed to be OK except for her cleaning mania. But he didn't see any real harm in it, and maybe she needed some distraction right now. Then Diane called the florist and ordered a basket of bright spring flowers to be delivered to Leena's house along with a note telling her to call anytime if she needed to talk.

The flowers were now sitting on the coffee table in front of the sofa, and occasionally Leena would look up at them as she knitted the pale yellow sweater.

Diane was a good friend. Leena knew everybody in the neighborhood. She talked to all the shop clerks, and she often struck up conversations with strangers standing at the bus stop next to her. One night at dinner she told Robert that she had met the famous political activist, Father O'Ryan, on Oakland Avenue while she was waiting to cross the street. They got to talking and he told her that he was giving up the priesthood and all his political activities to marry a woman from his church. Robert laughed in disbelief and said she must have been day-dreaming. Two days later the news was on the front page of the *Journal*.

But both Robert and the children knew that in spite of Leena's gregariousness, she did not make friends easily. Her sister Maija was a close friend. And Diane Avery was too.

Leena had met Diane years ago when they were both in their thirties. They had signed up for tennis lessons at Lake Park, and they ended up practicing together at least once a week. Neither of them played tennis anymore, but they still saw each other often, taking long walks or talking over a cup of coffee in Leena's kitchen.

Diane had been the wardrobe mistress for the Milwaukee

Repertory Theater until they moved into their swank new building downtown. Then she decided to retire from theater life because she knew she wouldn't feel comfortable in all that glittery splendor. The stuffy, crowded backstage of their old quarters had suited her fine, and she didn't want it to change.

Over the years, Leena had seen quite a few plays, thanks to the free tickets from Diane, and she got a kick out of recognizing actors who had made the transition from local theater to television.

"Why, that's Graham Davis!" she would tell Robert, pointing at a middle-aged man hyping cough syrup in a commercial break during the evening news, which they always watched together. "I remember when he played one of Puntila's men in that Brecht play at the Rep."

Last night when Robert turned on the CBS news, which still claimed his loyalty even though Dan Rather's wooden demeanor was a sorry replacement for the warm intelligence of Walter Cronkite, Leena jumped up from her customary spot on the couch and announced that she was going to make curried chicken for dinner.

"Why don't we go out, Leena? You've been working hard all day, and there's no reason for you to cook."

But Leena was already halfway to the kitchen, and she didn't seem to hear him at all. Robert could tell from the set of her back that she was determined to make curried chicken. And from years of experience, he knew better than to argue with her Finnish stubbornness.

Every member of the Martin family had felt the force of Leena's will at one time or another, usually at the most unexpected moments. Her stubbornness had become legendary.

Cঙ

Five years ago, Robert and Leena had made a trip back to
Rovaniemi near the Arctic Circle. Robert had been invited to
give a series of lectures at the University of Helsinki during the
month of May, and afterwards they decided to rent a car and
drive north to visit the area where they first met, back in 1947.
They pulled into a gas station outside Rovaniemi at two in the
afternoon, and Leena couldn't resist telling the attendant that
they had helped to build the community health center after
the war.

A big smile spread across the attendant's face as he told them
that his father, Jorma Sirkkala, had worked on the building too.
Robert and Leena didn't remember his father, but that didn't
seem to matter, and before they knew it, Matti Sirkkala had
invited them in for coffee.

The three of them sat down together at a little round table in
the office in the back of the gas station. It looked as if Matti's
wife had had a hand in decorating the room. A blue ceramic
bowl with small yellow apples stood in the middle of the table.
Bright cotton curtains hung at the window, and a basket woven
from birchwood stood on the floor, filled with newspapers and
magazines. There were no greasy rags or pieces of machinery
anywhere—it was the cleanest gas-station office they had ever
seen.

Robert explained, in rusty but understandable Finnish, that
he had come to Finland with an American group after the war to
help rebuild the town when the Germans left it in ruins as they
retreated. He had never been in Europe before, and he knew
virtually nothing about Finland. A few weeks after he arrived in

mid-July, he fell off a ladder and landed in a thicket of prickly bushes, and the nurse had liberally swabbed his scratches with mercurochrome.

Leena laughed and told Matti Sirkkala that when she got off the bus from Helsinki to join the work group a few days later, the first thing she noticed was the man with the bright orange streaks covering his bare chest and one side of his face.

"Who's the guy with the orange paint?" she asked her friend Kaisa, who had already been in Rovaniemi for several weeks.

"That's Robert Martin," she said. "He's American. He fell into a bramble patch."

"Does he speak Finnish?" Leena asked.

"Not much," said her friend.

"*Päivää,*" said Leena with a smile as she passed Robert on her way to the women's dorm.

"*Päivää,*" replied Robert, giving her a startled glance. He didn't recall seeing that cheery-looking young woman with the short blonde hair before.

The next afternoon Leena found herself standing next to the American as they painted shelves and cupboard doors that would eventually be installed in the examining rooms.

"How are your pains?" asked Leena, pointing to Robert's scratches, hoping that her sign language would make up for her faulty English.

"Oh, they don't hurt much at all," said Robert, obviously relieved that he wouldn't have to search for a reply in Finnish. "You speak English?"

"Some," said Leena, with that same bright smile he remembered from the day before. "You are from where?"

"I'm from Tennessee," said Robert. "In the southern part of the United States. How about you?"

"Helsinki," said Leena. "I live with parents and sister in Helsinki."

That night Robert sat down next to Leena as everyone gathered around the campfire to talk and rest after another long day of hard physical labor. He introduced her to his American friends, and then he borrowed a guitar and sang her a folk song in English. Leena was a little embarrassed by the intensity of the gaze he directed at her as he sang. She felt herself blush, and she heard Kaisa snickering beside her. But she was pleased, too. She liked the lanky, lean look of Robert Martin. She liked his soft brown eyes and dark hair, and she liked the sound of his voice. It reminded her of rolling hills—that's what she saw as she sat next to him in the dark and listened to his voice: gently rolling hills.

Leena didn't realize how much time she was spending with Robert and his friends until a few months later, when she took a basket of food to a family who had recently arrived from the east. Like thousands of others displaced from their land when Petsamo, the eastern arm of Finland, was ceded to the Soviet Union after the war, the family had finally made its way to Rovaniemi. There were so few buildings left standing after the Germans torched the town that four or five families were now crowded into every remaining house, while makeshift shelters were hastily being erected. And some people were living in tents.

Leena knocked on the door frame of the single-story building that had once been a small café. There was no door, only a faded curtain that had been tacked up over the doorway and then tied back with a piece of string fastened to a nail. Leena poked her head inside, calling out, "Hello, is anyone home?"

An old woman in a drab brown dress and a frayed apron came out of the back room and greeted Leena with a timid "Hello." She seemed to be the only one there. When Leena introduced herself and handed her the basket of food, the woman asked her to sit down on the bench just inside the doorway. The only other furniture in the room was a straight-backed chair and a rickety table. Then she insisted on offering Leena some bread and butter from the basket of provisions. Leena protested, but the woman was adamant. She was a guest in her house, after all.

So Leena ate a piece of bread as the old woman sat silently on the chair in front of her and gazed down at her lap, slowly massaging the swollen joints of her fingers.

"How are you and your family getting along?" Leena asked the woman. "Is there anything you need?" But the woman only shook her head without a word. Leena filled the silence by chatting about the progress of the construction work in town and about her own family back in Helsinki.

When she finally got up to leave, the woman stood up too, gave her a long look, and said quite clearly, "They say you know the Americans. I don't like foreigners."

So that's why she wouldn't talk to me, thought Leena as she walked back to the work site. And then she realized, with both surprise and a touch of fear, that she had already made up her mind. If Robert asked her to marry him, she would say yes. And she knew that meant she would probably have to leave Finland.

CB

Robert and Leena finished their coffee and thanked Matti for his hospitality. As they stood up to leave, Matti asked them whether they had seen the chapel in the woods that had been built as a war memorial.

"No," said Robert, "we haven't been back here since 1947."

"Oh, you have to see it," said Matti. "It's a beautiful place. I'll take you there. Just let me call my wife."

Matti made a quick phone call, locked up the gas station, and taped a note to the door saying that he'd be back in an hour. Then he jumped into his rattletrap car, yelled "Follow me," and raced off down the road.

Robert quickly turned the key in the ignition of their rental car and stomped hard on the gas pedal to catch up with Matti.

Fifteen minutes later they found themselves driving down a gravel road that seemed to slice through the dense green of the forest. At the end of the road they pulled into a clearing, and there was the chapel. Matti was right—it *was* beautiful. A glass and wood structure with an air of serenity and a sense of grandeur in spite of its small size. And the deep green of the trees made a perfect backdrop.

Robert and Leena got out of the car and walked toward the chapel to join Matti, who was standing in the entrance.

"The town built this chapel as a memorial to the young German soldiers who died during the last days of the war," said Matti. "Many of them had been in Rovaniemi for several years and had made friends with the people here. When the Germans pulled out, thousands of their young boys were killed in the fighting. Many of them are buried here under the chapel floor."

Robert thought it ironic that the people of Rovaniemi would build a memorial to the soldiers who had razed the town, but he kept his views to himself and stepped inside the chapel to look around. "Oh, look at this, Leena," he said, pointing to one of the plaques.

But Leena was still standing on the doorstep with a frozen look on her face.

"Leena?" said Robert. "Aren't you coming inside?"

"No," said Leena, "I'm not."

"Oh, but you have to see this," said Matti. "The architect did such a wonderful job."

"I am *not* going inside that building," said Leena.

Matti looked disappointed, but when he insisted again, Leena stubbornly repeated her refusal. And then he got mad.

"Why won't you go inside? Is there something wrong with honoring young soldiers who died? Don't you have any compassion?"

"Compassion!" spat Leena. "I have no compassion for the Germans. Those soldiers may have been young and they may have been friends with some of the people here, but they were still part of the German army, and that army destroyed this town. I saw what they did myself. I refuse to honor their dead. I will *not* set foot in their chapel."

Matti's friendly face darkened. He sputtered a few unintelligible expletives, said something about "goddamned Americans," and then stalked back to his car and drove off.

Robert and Leena got into their car in silence. When they reached the main road again, Robert glanced over at his wife. She was staring straight ahead, but the stubborn set of her jaw was unmistakable. With a sigh, Robert turned the car south, and they headed back toward Helsinki. He could see that Leena had lost all desire to see any more of Rovaniemi.

CB

"I was thinking of going over to the office for a while," said Robert as he came back into the living room. He had taken off the barbecue apron and put on a clean blue shirt. "I've got some papers to grade, and I'd like to get them all done before we leave for Seattle. Will you be all right while I'm gone?"

"Of course," said Leena. "You go ahead, dear. I'm just going to work on this sweater for a while. Maybe I'll go over to Diane's later this afternoon. Have you heard from Elly yet?"

"No," said Robert, "I guess she didn't get the message I left on her machine. I'll try her again from the university."

Robert bent down to give Leena a light kiss on the cheek, picked up his briefcase from the spot where he always left it next to the hall closet, and went out the front door.

The moment Leena heard the click of the lock, her fingers stopped their rhythmic dance with the knitting needles and her hands sagged into her lap. She leaned her head back against the sofa cushion and closed her eyes. She was thinking about the last of the Saturday phone calls with Maija, only two weeks ago. It had been Maija's turn to call, and she had been upset.

"Leena? Did you hear about the big windstorm we had on Wednesday? Was it on the news?"

"No, there wasn't anything about Seattle on the news. At least not on CBS. Are you OK? You sound a little worried."

"We had 80-mile-an-hour winds and the power was out all over town. The storm pulled up telephone poles and knocked down trees. I thought I was going to lose my Douglas firs, they were whipping back and forth so hard, but they seem to have made it through OK. The roof blew off the house across the street and there were pieces of shingles all over the neighborhood. I had to go out and pick the debris out of my rhododendron bushes."

"Sounds like a real storm," said Leena. "But is anything else wrong?"

"I went over to Lincoln Park yesterday," said Maija. "I just can't get over it, Leena. Giant trees are lying all over the ground. The wind pulled them up by their roots and tossed them a few feet away as if they were toothpicks. Some of them fell down the cliff and smashed onto the beach below—it's more than a hundred-foot drop. Big branches are blocking all the pathways, and it smells like mold and damp sawdust. There are huge clumps of roots just dangling in the air, and some of the trees look like they've been shattered by a bomb. The tall fir in the clearing went down too, and the eagle's nest was gone. Even the park bench where I usually sit had disappeared. There were four square holes in the ground where the legs used to be. But there wasn't a trace of the bench. It was horrible. I have a bad feeling about it. I don't think I can go back."

Leena was used to Maija's complaints and superstitions. She never took them too seriously, because they were such anomalies compared to Maija's otherwise sensible and competent nature. And Leena had always counted on Maija to see her through a crisis, even when they were children back in Finland. Her sister's mild paranoia amused Leena but in no way diminished her respect for Maija's strength.

But this time Leena could hear that Maija was truly upset. She knew that Lincoln Park was her favorite retreat, and giving it up would be a difficult decision. "Maybe you'll change your mind after the parks department has a chance to clean up the wreckage."

"Oh no, I'm never going back. I just can't. First there was the crow, and now the park. I have a very bad feeling about all of this," moaned Maija in her gloomiest voice.

બૂ

Back on the first Saturday in January, when Leena made her monthly call and cheerfully wished her sister "Happy New Year," Maija had responded with a groan.

"Wait till I tell you what happened," said Maija. "I was driving out to Southcenter last Tuesday on 509, and I had the whole freeway to myself. The road was a little icy but the Plymouth was handling it just fine, and I was listening to a Mozart sonata on the radio. I think it was Horowitz playing.

"Anyway, I'm slowing down for the exit, and up ahead I see four crows in the middle of the road. As I get closer, three of them fly off to the right and I'm expecting the fourth one to take off too. But I guess he's a little slow, or at least he doesn't notice me in time, because before I know it, the fourth crow flies straight up over the hood and lands flat against my side of the windshield. One wing is folded under him, and the other is spread out over the glass. The side of his head is pressed against the windshield, and a beady black eye is staring at me. I scream and let go of the steering wheel.

"It seemed like forever, but it was probably only a second before the crow fell off onto the side of the road. I looked back in my rearview mirror, and he seemed to be OK. Just a little wobbly as he hopped along the shoulder. But I was still shaking by the time I got to Southcenter, and I had to rush for the ladies' room on the first floor in Penney's. It's a bad sign, Leena. It's a very bad way to start off the year."

"Now, Maija, things like this happen. I'm sure it wasn't your fault."

But Maija was not to be consoled. And she had made a special point of appeasing the neighborhood crows with scraps of bread, which she scattered in the front yard every morning, even though she didn't much like their raucous cawing over her house. She was convinced they were keeping an eye on her.

♋

"How is Briitta?" asked Leena, hoping to distract Maija from her thoughts of the windstorm and the crow.

"Oh, she's fine. She just designed a cover for a book on Nordic mythology for some big publisher in New York. Knopf, I think. She sent me a color Xerox of it—a little modern for my taste, but Briitta said the editor liked it. Have you heard from Rachel lately?"

"No, I haven't," said Leena, feeling suddenly guilty that she hadn't made an effort to call her granddaughter in the last few months—not since Christmas, now that she thought about it. "But Elly told me that she's the backstage manager for some new club in Denver. A rock club, I think. Elly said something about 'grunge music'; and the fact that Rachel was born in Seattle actually gave her an edge over the other applicants for the job. Did you know that Seattle was such an 'in' place right now?"

"No, I didn't," said Maija, and then she returned to the

subject of the storm. Nothing Leena said could dispel Maija's sense of impending doom, and by the time she hung up, Leena was feeling a little moody herself.

○ઝ

Leena opened her eyes and stared up at the ceiling. She couldn't believe that she would never hear Maija's voice on the phone again. She couldn't believe that their Saturday ritual was over. She couldn't imagine who she would turn to the next time someone in the family was in trouble. She couldn't believe that Maija was dead.

Leena abruptly got up from the couch and went into the bedroom. She pulled open the bottom drawer of her dresser, pushed a couple of blouses aside, and lifted out her button box. It was actually an old wooden silverware box that she had found at a rummage sale when the kids were small. It was already a little scratched and beat-up back then, and the inside slots and compartments for the silverware had been removed, so it could no longer serve its original purpose. But the soft reddish luster of the wood had caught Leena's eye, and she brought it home and had been using it for years as a catch-all for the buttons she collected and other odd mementos.

Leena sat down on the bed with the box in her lap and raised the hinged lid. The box was full to the brim with buttons of all shapes and colors: wooden, pewter, plastic, and cloth-covered buttons; buttons in little paper packets and buttons attached to strips of cardboard; buttons from garments long since discarded; big round coat buttons, and tiny seed-pearl buttons; handmade ceramic buttons she had bought at an art fair, and clear glass buttons with a single dot of color in the middle. And in amongst the buttons were spools of thread, sewing machine bobbins, a Swedish 10-öre coin, an old Timex watch with half of its band missing, a little plastic container of darning needles, and several crochet hooks of varying sizes. There was a pheasant feather that Leena remembered retrieving from the side of the road in Tennessee one summer; and stones collected on the shores of Lake Michigan, dull-looking now, but bright pink and orange when she found them, wet and glistening on the beach. Under the stones was a tiny oval locket made of silver filigree. Coiled up inside was a golden wisp of hair from Joel's first visit to the barbershop when he was two years old.

Leena picked up the locket, put it back, and then turned the whole button box upside-down, spilling out the contents onto the bed. There were two things wedged into the bottom of the box: an elaborate-looking menu and a manila envelope.

Leena pried out the menu with the tips of her fingers and held it in her lap for a moment.

It was from her last night on board the ocean liner that had brought her to America in 1948, sailing from Rotterdam to New York a few months after their wedding in Helsinki. Robert had gone on ahead, and he had already found them a tiny apartment in Milwaukee above a drugstore on Locust Avenue. He was going to finish his doctorate in Psychology while he drove a cab at night to pay the bills. Robert's father had bought Leena a first-class ticket and she had sailed off to her new country in style, more than a little embarrassed by all the luxury.

When she arrived in New York, her father-in-law, William G. Martin, was waiting on the dock to receive her. He whisked her off in a cab to Grand Central Station, where they caught a train to Nashville. Leena was going to join Robert at her in-laws' house for a short visit before heading for Milwaukee. She was so nervous and excited that she remembered almost nothing of the train trip, except for the hours they spent in the smoking car, where Mr. Martin would light up one big cigar after another.

Leena liked her father-in-law. He had a long, creased face and enormous ears. He wore a brown fedora and a vast overcoat with padded shoulders. She liked his easy manner and the way he lounged in his chair as he smoked his cigars. She liked his kind eyes and the way he called her "Sugar" in his soft Tennessee drawl. But she had a much more difficult time learning to like her new mother-in-law.

"Welcome to Nashville, dear," was the first thing Sarah Anne Martin said as Leena climbed out of the cab in front of the Martin family home. The second thing she said, after giving Leena a penetrating look, was, "I know a very good dentist. Why don't I make you an appointment for tomorrow?"

Leena had a hard time holding back the tears as she turned to Robert, who was standing on the sidewalk next to his mother. He gave her a sheepish look, then took her hand, led her into the house, and gave her a big kiss as soon as they reached their room on the second floor.

"Don't mind Mother," he said. "She comes across a little stern, and she can be quite a busybody, but she doesn't mean to be unkind. Oh, Leena, I'm so glad to see you. Don't let Mother spoil the day."

Leena was relieved that Robert had decided to live in the North. She knew that one town would never be big enough for both her and Sarah Anne. (Leena secretly called her "Sam," a plain enough nickname to satisfy Leena's need to defuse her mother-in-law's autocratic power.)

When the Martin kids got a little older, the family often

spent their summer vacations in Tennessee, with Leena and Sarah Anne constantly vying for Robert's attention.

Sarah Anne never could reconcile herself to having a foreigner in the family. Even after Robert and Leena had their third child, she refused to give up hope that the marriage might not last, and she never failed to mention "that nice Jane Dorchester" whenever she talked to Robert on the phone.

"She's still unattached," Sarah Anne would say. "She would make someone such a good wife."

Robert would laugh heartily and change the subject. Leena didn't think it was funny.

But eventually the two women developed a cool respect for each other's tenacity. And they both realized that their fierce love for Robert bound them in a way that nothing else could.

&

Leena smoothed the fraying gold tassels on the edge of the menu. Then she put it down with a sigh and took out the manila envelope from the box. She unfastened the clasp, tipped the envelope, and slid out an old black-and-white photograph.

She held the photo in the palm of her left hand as she put her right hand up to her cheek, as if to touch the cheek of the little girl in the picture. It was the same photo that Maija had hanging on her living-room wall. The two sisters, wearing new dresses, were staring straight ahead at the camera. They were smiling shyly. Maija was eleven and Leena was six. It was the day of their aunt's wedding. And Leena remembered it had turned out to be a terrible day.

Four

The phone was ringing again, and Elly realized she was going to have to get it. That stupid answering machine was always going haywire—they really should buy a new one. She tore off a piece of paper from the notepad she was writing on and stuck the paper in her book to mark her place. Then she shoved back her chair with annoyance, stood up, and reached for the phone on the wall next to the refrigerator.

"Hello," she snapped, tapping her pencil against the kitchen counter and casting an eye at the dirty dishes piled up in the sink. John said he was going to do them before he went out for his run, but he had obviously forgotten again.

"Elly? It's your Dad."

"Oh, hi, Dad. What's up? You don't usually call on a Saturday morning. Is anything wrong?"

"I left a message on your machine. I've been trying to call you for two days."

"Sorry—that machine is a piece of junk. It keeps garbling all the messages. We've got to get a new one. Is something wrong, Dad?"

"I've got some bad news. Maija died on Thursday. I called Briitta and she told us the funeral is next Wednesday in Seattle. Your mother and I were wondering if you might like to be there."

There was such a long silence that Robert thought they had been disconnected. "Elly? Are you still there?"

"Oh my God, I can't believe it," said Elly in a barely audible voice. "I just talked to her last week and she sounded fine. What happened?"

"They think she had a stroke. Briitta was in Seattle on business so she was staying with Maija for a few days. When she woke up at six on Thursday morning, she thought it was odd that Maija wasn't in the kitchen yet. You know how she always gets up at the crack of dawn. Briitta knocked on Maija's door but she didn't answer.

"The minute Briitta stepped into the room, she knew that Maija was gone. The medics came but there was nothing they could do. They said she must have died in her sleep around three. Briitta said she looked perfectly serene."

"How's Mom doing? Is she taking it hard?"

"Your mother has cleaned every room in the house, including the storage room in the basement, and she seems a little too calm. I'm kind of worried about her. She hasn't really cried about it yet. Diane wanted to come over, but Leena said she'd rather be alone. I think she's still in shock. It's probably going to take a while before it sinks in. We're leaving for Seattle on Tuesday night. The funeral is the next day, at two in the afternoon. Do you think you want to come? If it's a matter of money, I'd be happy to get you a plane ticket."

"Of course I'll be there. No, you don't have to buy me a

ticket. Don't be silly. We can afford a ticket to Seattle. I'll bring Rachel too. I'll call you back before I leave and let you know where we're staying. I think we can stay with my friend Denise. Tell Mom that I'll be there." And then Elly hung up.

When John came home from his daily run he found Elly huddled on the bed in tears.

"Elly? What's the matter? Why are you crying?" he asked, sitting down next to her.

"Oh, John. Maija died on Thursday," sobbed Elly.

Without a word, John put his arms around his wife and held her close. He knew there was nothing he could say that would help. Maija was gone, and her absence was going to haunt Elly for a very long time. He knew that Maija was the one who had seen Elly at her worst. Maija was the one who had taken her in; and with her firm, no-nonsense approach, she had set Elly on her feet again.

ca

At the end of February in 1971, Elly put the last touches on her painting and decided suddenly that she would give it to her father. She didn't really know why—Robert rarely paid much attention to her art, and she doubted he would want to hang this particular painting on the wall. It was a lot more extreme than her usual style; a lot angrier too, she had to admit. She called it "Flight from the Nuclear Family."

"Why, thank you, Elly," said Robert with surprise when she handed him the painting the next day. He couldn't recall ever receiving a gift from Elly outside of the usual holidays, and he didn't quite know how to handle the situation.

"Just thought you might like it," said Elly. "It's not really very good." She gave her father a look that was half scowl, half entreaty, and then she turned around and stalked out of the room.

Robert was both perplexed and oddly upset. He didn't know what to make of Elly. She seemed so remote lately. And the title of this painting sounded like some kind of personal affront, a snide gibe at his profession. He mentioned his concern to Leena, but she told him not to take it too seriously.

"Elly's just going through a difficult period right now. She's seventeen, and that's such an awful age. And I think she misses Kirsti. Maybe she's a little jealous too. Going off to college sounds so glamorous. Don't worry, dear. Elly's OK."

But Robert *was* worried.

A week later, when he came down for breakfast on Saturday morning, he found Elly sitting alone at the kitchen table, staring off into space with a piece of cold toast on the plate in front of her. Leena had left earlier for a game of tennis with Diane. So Robert mentally squared his shoulders and decided he had to have a talk with his daughter.

"Morning, Elly. How about another piece of toast? I was just going to fix some for myself."

"No, thanks," mumbled Elly with a skittish glance toward the door.

Robert was afraid she would run off before he had a chance to say anything, so he decided to skip the toast. Instead, he poured himself a cup of coffee from the thermos that Leena left standing on the counter every morning, and then he sat down at the table.

"How's school?" asked Robert.

"It's OK."

"Have you thought about what college you might like to go to? You should be sending off applications about now."

"I don't know... Maybe I won't go to college."

"Do you think you need a year off?" Robert asked cautiously. "Take a little break before you continue your studies?"

"Maybe I won't go to college at all. Maybe I just don't feel like it."

"Now, Elly, you know that your mother and I have always encouraged you to make your own decisions. And I can certainly understand that you might need a little time to yourself. Why don't you get a part-time job and see what the world is like outside of school? But don't rule out college altogether. Keep your options open for the future. A college education is important these days, and your mother and I want you to have that opportunity."

Elly gave her father a seething look. God, he could be such a *professor* sometimes, she thought.

"How about going up to Northfield to visit Kirsti next weekend?" said Robert. "She could show you around Carleton, and the two of you could check out the university in Minneapolis at the same time."

"Carleton! Why should I bother? I don't have the grades to get into a place like that. Why do you always have to compare me to Kirsti, anyway? Little Miss Perfect with her perfect grades and her perfect clothes and her perfect friends."

"Elly, I'm *not* comparing you to your sister."

Robert was appalled to hear her assessment of Kirsti. He had no idea that Elly resented Kirsti's academic success. He always pictured them giggling together in the bedroom they had shared

until they were teenagers. They had always seemed so insepa-
rable.

"You have your own talents, Elly," he said. "You don't need
straight A's to get into college."

"College! God, can't you think about anything else? Not
everybody goes to college. Maybe I don't care about 'opportunities.' Maybe I just want to be like ordinary people for a change.
Lots of people have perfectly happy, normal lives without going
to college. Lots of people get jobs and get married and have
kids—and you don't need a college degree to do that."

Robert didn't know what to say. He had never heard Elly
speak with such anger or fervor before. Her cheeks were bright
red and she was glaring at him so fiercely that he felt an urge to
look away. But he stopped himself, and then he said softly,
"What is it, Elly?"

"Maybe I'm pregnant," she blurted out. And then her face
crumpled. She jumped up from the table, ran out of the kitchen,
and pounded up the stairs to her room.

After a moment of paralyzed shock, Robert stood up and
went out to the front hall. "Elly!" he called, standing at the foot
of the stairway.

A minute later, Elly came running down the stairs, pulling
on the old Navy pea-jacket that she always wore in the winter.
Her face was ashen, and she refused to look at her father as she
raced by him.

"Elly!" said Robert again. And then the front door slammed.

When Leena came home an hour later, she found Robert
sitting motionless at the kitchen table, staring at a half-empty
coffee cup. The absurdly old-fashioned phrase "born out of

wedlock" had been echoing through his mind, and he had been trying in vain to remember the name of the main character in that book by Hawthorne.

"Robert? What's going on?" asked Leena.

"Hester Prynne. That's her name," said Robert, giving his wife a bleak look. "Hester Prynne."

ᚣ

On the first Saturday in March, Leena called Maija and told her the news about Elly.

"We just can't believe it," said Leena. "Robert is trying to stay calm, but I know he's absolutely furious. He has that stony look on his face, and he keeps trying to make Elly tell us who the father is, but she refuses to give his name. Kirsti came home for the weekend, and I think she had a talk with Elly about getting an abortion. Anyway, they ended up having a screaming match about something, and now they won't speak to each other. Robert tried to talk to Elly about giving the baby up for adoption, but she won't listen. She insists that she wants to keep this baby. Everybody's miserable. The whole house has been turned upside down. How could this happen to us? I don't know what we're going to do."

ᚣ

The one thing Leena didn't tell her sister was that she and Robert had had a terrible fight about it all. Robert had a lightning-quick temper that few people outside his family ever saw. Leena did her best not to provoke him because she never could bear to argue. But this time there was nothing she could do to stave off his anger.

"This is all your fault," shouted Robert suddenly as they got into bed a few days after learning Elly's secret. "How could you let her get pregnant? She's only seventeen, for God's sake! Did you know she was sleeping around?"

"I'm sorry about it too, Robert," said Leena with a sigh. "I didn't even know she had a boyfriend. Elly doesn't talk to me anymore. I thought she was just going through some kind of phase. You know how rebellious kids can be at her age."

"But how could she get pregnant? Haven't you told her *anything* about birth control?"

Leena blushed. She knew this was one of her weaknesses. She never could bring herself to have those intimate mother-and-daughter chats that she read so much about in all the women's magazines. She found herself painfully embarrassed by the subject of sex. Her own mother had never once mentioned the topic. When Leena turned twelve, Maija had taken her for a walk in the woods and tersely explained the mechanics of sexual intercourse, closing the lecture with a stern warning about the consequences of sex before marriage.

Robert was the first and only man that Leena had ever slept with. In spite of her shyness about discussing the topic, she was a tender and exuberant partner in bed. Even after twenty-two years of marriage and giving birth to three children, Leena still felt a thrill of intense pleasure whenever she and Robert made love. She loved the touch of his fingers on her breasts, and her whole body ached to take him inside her. When the kids were small and they lived in a tiny apartment, she often had to stuff a corner of the sheet in her mouth to muffle her ecstatic moans.

She loved the comfortable familiarity of Robert's body, and she didn't mind at all the way it had changed over the years. His soft middle and added weight were just as dear to her as his thin form once had been. She loved his smell and his warmth, and she loved holding his hand as they lay in bed at night. She had her fantasies and her daydreams, but they were more about art than sex. She might sometimes wish for a more reckless and impulsive husband, someone less predictable and steady. And yet, when it came right down to it, she really couldn't envision sleeping with any other man.

Her friend Diane once had an affair with a young actor at the Rep, and Leena was enthralled by her daring. She pumped Diane for all the details she was willing to reveal. And Leena tried to imagine herself in the arms of an athletic twenty-year-old. But then she would picture her own middle-aged body, starting to sag and spread, and she decided the temptation of an affair was too big a risk. In Robert's embrace, she never doubted her attractiveness; he made her feel wanted and secure. And his ardor behind closed doors made up for his general diffidence regarding any public display of affection.

But this was all part of a private world that Leena could never discuss with her daughters.

When Kirsti was a freshman in high school, Leena went into a big, anonymous bookstore downtown—she didn't want her local bookseller to see what she was buying—and found a sober-looking text on marriage and sex. She handed it to Kirsti with a nervous smile.

"I think you're old enough to read this now," said Leena. "Why don't you pass it on to Elly when you're done with it."

Kirsti glanced at the book's title and gave her mother a knowing look that made Leena feel even more inadequate. She was often in awe of these two young women she had produced. They both had an independent spirit that was far more daunting than anything she remembered from her own youth. Sometimes she was actually a little afraid of them.

ଔ

"Oh, Robert," whispered Leena as she curled up next to his back, "let's not fight. That won't help matters now. We've both done the best we could as parents. And besides, it's not the end of the world. I think Elly really wants this baby, and we have to respect her decision. Can't you try to accept the situation?"

There was no answer from Robert, but Leena was sure that he wasn't asleep.

ଔ

"Why don't you let Elly come to Seattle?" said Maija over the phone. "She can stay with me and finish her senior year by correspondence. Briitta is away at art school, you know, and there's plenty of room. I'm sure I can find Elly some kind of job, so she won't have too much time on her hands to mope around. It would give everybody a chance to calm down, and by the time the baby is born, maybe we'll all be thinking more rationally."

Leena was skeptical that her daughter would agree to such a plan, but Elly acquiesced at once. She knew she had to get out of the house and away from her parents. She knew it would be unbearable to sit in classes with her belly getting bigger and bigger and with all the other kids staring at her in the hallways. And if Frank ever came back to Milwaukee, she never wanted to see him again. The whole thing had been a mistake. A giant mistake. She would be glad to get as far away as possible.

Elly had been to Seattle only once, when she was four or five, and she remembered virtually nothing about the city. She hadn't seen Maija or Briitta in several years, either. But Maija was a familiar presence in the house because of the monthly phone calls between Elly's mother and aunt. The regular calls were a household institution, a constant of her childhood, and all three Martin children had learned early on never to interrupt their mother when she closed the bedroom door on a Saturday morning to talk to Maija on the phone. And when Elly's older brother Joel was in trouble two years ago, Maija was the one who came up with a solution. Elly had a lot of respect for her aunt because of the way she had helped him.

So Elly agreed to go to Seattle, and a week later Maija met her at the airport.

"How are you, Elly? How was the trip?" asked Maija, giving her niece a pat on the shoulder. "Let me carry one of those bags. How many suitcases did you check?"

"Two," said Elly, a little surprised at Maija's brisk energy. She looked so neat and proper, so prim and lady-like, in her black wool coat and green scarf. And she had one of those strange Finnish Kalevala pins on her coat collar—like the one Elly's mother sometimes wore.

They stepped off the airport subway in the main terminal, took the escalator up one level, and located the carousel where

Elly's luggage was due to arrive. They waited ten minutes but nothing happened. The crowd swelled around them, but the baggage carousel refused to budge, and Maija grew impatient.

"Let's go look at the Louise Nevelson upstairs. By the time we get back, maybe your bags will be here." And she took Elly's arm and steered her toward the elevator.

Elly had no idea what a "Louise Nevelson" was, but in a few minutes she found herself standing in front of a wooden sculpture of black rectangles hidden in a deserted alcove at one end of the terminal.

"Isn't it great?" said Maija enthusiastically. "It's the only piece worth looking at in the whole airport collection. I can't understand why they've stuck it away in this corner."

By the time they had retrieved Elly's luggage and stowed it in the trunk of the sky-blue Plymouth, Maija had run through an entire list of complaints about the inefficiency and poor design of Sea-Tac Airport. Then she abruptly changed the subject and told Elly that she had lined up a job for her at Seattle Community College. Maija knew the head librarian there, and she had agreed to give Elly a job.

"Thanks," said Elly, but inwardly she groaned. It was incredible that she was going to end up working in a college after that whole argument with her father. But she knew she should be grateful, and she had to take the job. Elly didn't want to be a dead weight on her aunt. She wanted to show everybody that she was a responsible person who could take care of herself. And her baby.

⋈

Maija and Elly quickly fell into a routine that suited them both. At five a.m. Maija would get up, take a shower, dress carefully, and then sit down to read the morning paper and go over her teaching plans for the day. She always had two cups of Earl Grey tea, one piece of dry toast, and half a grapefruit for breakfast. Elly stayed in bed until 7:30, which was as long as she could stretch it without being late for work. She would pull on her old striped bathrobe and join Maija for tea at the kitchen table. She was glad that breakfast was always such a spartan affair. The sight of food turned her stomach in the morning, and the mere thought of eggs or bacon could send her rushing to the bathroom.

At eight o'clock Maija would get into the Plymouth and drive off with a wave to her niece, who usually came to the kitchen door to say goodbye. Then Elly would switch on the radio and turn up the volume so she could hear it in the shower. At 8:45 she would run out the door to catch the bus that took her to Capitol Hill.

Elly actually enjoyed her job in the college library. The leisurely pace and friendly atmosphere soothed her frazzled nerves, and no one looked askance when she told them that she was pregnant. Everybody wanted to know when the baby was due, but no one bothered her with embarrassing questions once they heard there was no husband in the picture. And her boss, Sue, didn't mind if she worked on her correspondence courses when things were slow.

By the time warm weather finally arrived in May, Elly was five months pregnant and her regular clothes were all too tight. She had spent every evening since her arrival in Seattle embroidering bright flowers in wild arabesques across the backs and around the buttonholes of cheap blue workshirts. The shirts were soft and roomy, and she could slip on a loose skirt underneath or pants with an elastic waistband. Maija had offered to buy her some maternity dresses, but Elly preferred her baggy cotton shirts.

The regularity of Maija's life, which at first was such a welcome relief after the recent upheaval in the Martin household, eventually began to irritate Elly. She started wishing that her aunt would oversleep, that she would decide to make coffee instead of tea, or that one morning there would be a maraschino cherry in the middle of her grapefruit. Anything to change the unending sameness of the days. Elly began to feel more and more grumpy in the mornings, and by the time she got to the library, she would be downright sullen.

"Hi, Elly. How are you feeling today?" Sue would ask cheerfully. She was a morning person and always annoyingly bright-eyed while Elly was still trying to wake up.

"Just fine, thanks," was Elly's standard reply. And then she would take a cart of books and head into the stacks where she could be alone.

Maija was often out in the evenings, attending PTA meetings or going to one of the book clubs or discussion groups that she belonged to. On weekends she liked to take long walks in the park or on the beach; and she was perfectly content to spend a whole afternoon reading a book with her cat Edith purring on her lap. She listened to classical music and watched specials on PBS. Surprisingly enough, she was also a faithful devotee of "Bonanza." After two months, Elly thought she was going to scream if she had to watch one more melodramatic story about that ridiculous Cartwright family. Maija seemed enamored of "that handsome Ben Cartwright," as she always called him, but Elly couldn't stand the man or his pathetic sons.

"I think I'll go out to the store and get some juice," Elly told Maija one Sunday evening as the familiar theme music flooded the living room.

"All right," said Maija, her eyes fixed on the TV screen in anticipation. She never missed an episode.

Elly grabbed her bag and a floppy blue sweater she had found at a garage sale. It was a man's extra large with leather buttons and big pockets, and she wore it everywhere.

She walked toward the Val-U Supermarket five blocks away, which was open twenty-four hours. She didn't really want any juice, but she needed an excuse to get out of the house. She felt like she was going crazy.

How could she have been so stupid to get herself into this mess? Why did she think that she was the only one who wouldn't get pregnant? Why did she think that she was immune?

She was angry at her parents for their panic and dismay. She was angry at Kirsti for her self-righteous lecturing and pompous advice. She was angry at Joel for his silence and his absence from her life. She was angry at Frank. But mostly she was angry at herself. It was her own damned fault.

გ

When Elly walked into the record store on Downer Avenue last November looking for the Beatles' latest hit "Let It Be," she noticed the guy behind the cash register at once. He had lank blond hair pulled back in a ponytail and tied up with a piece of string. His cheeks and chin were covered with a scanty fuzz that he was trying to pass off as a beard. His ratty-looking black t-shirt had a big hole in one sleeve and an iron-on decal of Mick Jagger on the front. He wore a necklace made from a leather thong threaded through a single shiny red bead. But what Elly noticed most was the way the guy was talking to the customer standing in front of him—one of those suburban-looking kids with too-new clothes, neatly trimmed hair, and a well-scrubbed face. The kid had put a copy of "We've Only Just Begun" by the Carpenters on the counter and was digging some money out of his pocket.

The tall blond clerk gave the kid a look of pure scorn. "Are you really going to pay good money for that pablum?" he mocked.

The kid looked a little cowed but he put a five-dollar bill on the counter without replying.

"I can't believe what shit people listen to," continued the clerk. "Hey Joe," he called to his colleague, "look at this jerk—he's buying another one of those sappy pop tunes."

"Just give me my change," said the kid, putting the 45 protectively under his arm. Two seconds later he was out the door.

Elly was smitten. She lost all interest in the Beatles record—she knew he wouldn't approve. She casually drifted over to the counter.

"Uh... what do you have by the Stones?" she asked with the proper amount of cool indifference.

The guy slapped a 45 onto the counter. Elly read the title: "You Can't Always Get What You Want." The picture sleeve had Jagger in a sailor suit with his arm around a buxom "honky-tonk woman."

"I'll take it," she said.

And then he slowly looked her up and down and said, "How about going to Pete's for a beer?"

As they walked down the block, the record-store guy told Elly that his name was Frank Schaefer and that someday he was going to be a DJ. Elly told him she was a senior in high school, but as soon as she graduated, she was going to be an actress. She didn't know why she said that—the idea had never occurred to her before. And then she told him that her name was Elly Sarovnaya. It sounded more exotic.

They reached the corner and stopped in front of a tavern with a flashing neon sign proclaiming that this was Pete's Place. The door opened and a couple of bleary-eyed men came out, trailing an odor of sweat, stale beer, and cigarette smoke. The place was deserted except for the bartender.

"Hi, Frank," he said. "The usual?"

"Yeah," said Frank, pulling out a bar stool and climbing onto it. "And one for my friend here, too."

The bartender glanced at Elly. "Can I see some ID, honey?"

Elly blushed. She wasn't about to tell Frank that she wasn't eighteen yet, so she mumbled that she'd forgotten her driver's license at home.

"Sorry," said the bartender. "Can't take a chance on getting caught again. If you don't have any ID, you're gonna have to leave."

"Shit," said Frank.

"Want to come over to my place?" he asked Elly as they stood out on the street again. "I've got a six-pack in the fridge."

"OK," said Elly.

Ten minutes later Frank unlocked the door to his apartment

and ushered Elly in with a sardonic bow. The place was a dump. Broken Venetian blinds hung from the two windows in the living room. Patches of a filthy orange shag carpet were visible in between the stacks of old magazines—a haphazard collection of *Rolling Stone*, *Billboard*, *Playboy*, and *MAD*. In the doorway to the kitchen there was a curtain made from hundreds of aluminum beer-can tabs carefully linked together. The beat-up old coffee table was practically smothered with piles of dirty plates, congealed food, and spots of some sticky-looking residue. The plastic ashtrays were overflowing with ancient cigarette butts. Elly had never seen such a pigsty before, and she was impressed.

"Have a seat," said Frank, shoving a pile of clothes off the sofa covered with an Indian bedspread. He went through the linked curtain into the kitchen and came back with a couple of Millers. He handed one to Elly, popped the other one open, and took a long swig. Then he sat down next to her, put his beer can on the floor, and pulled out a joint from a shoebox under the coffee table. He fished a book of matches out of his jeans pocket, lit the joint, and took several deep tokes. He slumped against the lumpy back of the sofa and sprawled there for a moment with his eyes closed, his legs spread wide. The fingers of his left hand drummed against the pouting face of Mick Jagger on his chest. Then he squinted at Elly through the haze of smoke. "Want some?" he asked.

"Sure," said Elly.

Then they listened to the Stones, and after a while Frank put his hand on Elly's arm and then pulled her down on top of him.

"Don't," Elly protested weakly.

"Just a little kiss," said Frank. "A little kiss won't hurt."

"Yes, it will," said Elly, but even *she* wasn't listening to herself anymore.

God, she had been so stupid. And the worst thing of all was that she did it for revenge.

She was sick and tired of her father's admonishments to "sit nice," and "be a lady." She was sick and tired of her mother's tight-lipped reproaches not to use "those kinds of words." She was sick and tired of Kirsti's exasperated reproofs to "stop being so depressed." And she was sick and tired of her own disgusting appearance.

Elly spent hours trying to tame her impossible hair, spraying it with countless bottles of Straight-Set or clamping books to the ends, hoping that gravity would get rid of the curls, which even massive amounts of chemicals couldn't seem to control. She hated her clothes, and every time she bought something new, she ended up taking it right back to the store. The last time she tried to return something, the clerk had refused to accept it, saying there was lipstick on the collar and some kind of stain on the sleeve.

Leena was appalled to learn that Elly had traded her brand-new green dress to her friend Patty for a pair of worn-out bellbottoms.

"But Mom, I looked like shit in that dress," moaned Elly, knowing that she was about to get one of those hurt looks from her mother, who winced at any kind of swearword. Whenever Elly really wanted to make her mad, she would use the word "fuck." She knew it drove Leena crazy.

She was fed up with school, which felt more and more like a prison after they instituted the closed-campus policy and no one was allowed to leave the grounds for lunch. No more pizzas at Mario's, no more driving around and smoking between classes.

Anyone who got caught was suspended, and even Elly didn't think a little bit of freedom was worth all that trouble. She was bored with the smart but wimpy boys who asked her out, their pasty faces blushing at her feigned coarseness. But she wasn't pretty enough in the conventional sense to draw the attention of the jocks. And whenever they opened their mouths, she would remember anyway that good looks were no compensation for dullness.

So her infatuation with Frank was sheer revenge. Revenge for all the boring and insipid people in her life.

She liked driving around with Frank in his clunker VW bus with the cracked windshield and nonexistent brakes. Whenever they headed down a hill, he'd tell her to grab the wheel, and then Elly would steer while Frank bent down and pumped the brakes with his hand. She liked lolling around in his crummy apartment getting stoned, listening to music turned up full-blast. She liked feeling his hands swarming over her naked body, and she didn't mind his caustic remarks about fucking a high-school kid.

Frank was twenty-two and from Chicago. He had dropped out of school and drifted around until he lucked into the job at the record store, which he regarded as a mere stepping stone toward his goal of becoming a DJ. In the meantime, he spent hours making tapes, and someday he'd take a bunch of them down to WOKY and get himself a real job. Someday she'd be hearing him on the radio, and *he'd* be the one to decide what tunes made it big. And of course he'd get rich in the process.

Elly spent more and more time with Frank. Two or three days a week he'd pick her up after school, and they'd drive around for a while and then head over to his apartment. Sometimes they went to a concert, and Elly would stay overnight at his place. She told her mother that she was staying at Patty's. She never brought Frank home, and he never asked her anything about her family. He didn't even know where she lived.

It got harder and harder for Elly to get up in the morning. She started skipping her eight o'clock classes, staying in bed until 7:30, when Leena would pound on her door and ask if she was ever going to get up that day. Elly would drag herself out of bed and trudge off to the bathroom, where she spent half an hour on her makeup and raged at her uncooperative hair. Then she'd throw on a sweater and some jeans, grab her jacket, and run out the door to catch the city bus to school. She had missed the regular school bus by well over an hour. Her breakfast was a Hershey bar. On weekends she slept till noon.

When Elly missed her period in January, she pretended not to notice; when she missed it in February too, she knew she was in big trouble.

She went down to the record store after school to talk to Frank. She dreaded the conversation, but she didn't know what else to do. The guy behind the counter told her that Frank had called that morning to say he was quitting, and he'd already been by to pick up his paycheck.

Elly had a cold and hollow feeling as she walked over to Frank's apartment. He opened the door just as she was about to knock, his arms loaded down with boxes.

"Oh, hi," he said, his eyes glittering with an excitement Elly had never seen in them before. "Guess what? I got a job as a DJ. In Chicago. I sent them a tape a month ago and they called yesterday to say I got the job. I have to be there tomorrow morning. I've got to put all this stuff in the bus. I'll be right back." And he ran down the stairs.

Elly glanced inside Frank's apartment, which was starting to look unusually bare. The stacks of magazines were gone, the top of the coffee table was actually visible, and the linked curtain had been taken down. Elly tore a page out of her notebook, scribbled "Good luck, Frank," and dropped the note in the middle of the sofa. Then she turned around and left by the back stairs.

എ

In the second week of June, Maija's school let out for the summer, and she had a little time off before she started going to the teacher seminars that she usually attended in July and August. She liked keeping up on the latest teaching techniques, she enjoyed meeting new people in her profession, and she was a staunch believer in the healthiness of an active mind. Briitta had decided to stay on at the art school in L.A. for the summer session and wouldn't be back in Seattle until sometime in the fall. Elly was still doggedly going off to work every day, and she had made friends with a music student named Denise, who regularly came to the library. On Thursday nights, at Maija's insistence, Elly went to a childbirth class at the community center in Ballard. But she was still feeling restless and irritable.

One morning Maija looked up from her cup of tea as Elly dropped heavily into her chair at the kitchen table. "My colleague offered me her cabin on Whidbey Island for a week," she said. "It's right on the water, with lots of trees. She says it's a little rustic, but there's electricity and running water and all we have to bring is some bed linen and whatever food we want to eat. It sounds idyllic. Would you like to go?"

Elly stared at Maija glumly for a moment. She wasn't

thrilled about spending a whole week cooped up in some iso-
lated cabin with her aunt. She imagined them getting on each
other's nerves within a matter of hours. And what were they
going to talk about for seven whole days? There'd better be a
radio, or she'd really flip out. But a week away from the library
routine would be a welcome change, and the weather had been
so great lately. She wouldn't mind just sitting out on the beach
for a week.

"I guess so," said Elly. "OK... sure. But I'll have to ask Sue
if I can take a week off. I don't know if she'll let me go."

But Sue was only too happy to give Elly the week off. She
said it would do her good to get out in the fresh air and sunshine.

On Saturday, Maija and Elly packed up the Plymouth and
loaded Edith into the back seat. She promptly hopped up onto
the shelf in the rear window and stayed there for the whole ride,
gazing unperturbed at the passing scenery. She didn't seem to
mind leaving her normal territory behind.

They caught the noon ferry from Mukilteo, and it just happened to be one of the last of the old boats with the dark-wood
interior, the slippery benches lined up along the windows, and
ancient nautical charts peeling off the walls. Maija stationed herself outdoors in the bow of the boat, her face lifted into the wind
and spray, and she launched into a diatribe about the new ferry
boats and their total lack of character. Elly stood silently beside
her and tried to control her wooziness. She was glad it was such
a short crossing.

As they drove away from the dock, Maija put a hand-drawn
map into Elly's lap. "You're the navigator," she said. "Let me
know when we get to Spruce Lane." Then she switched on the
radio and the strains of a symphony filled the car.

"Ah..." sighed Maija, settling comfortably into the worn

seat of the Plymouth, her hands lightly gripping the top of the steering wheel. "How appropriate: *The Karelia Suite* by Sibelius. Do you know it?" she asked Elly.

"No," said Elly with some disdain. Why should she? She never listened to classical music.

"It's a good sign," said Maija. "I think we're going to have a good vacation."

Elly stared straight ahead, wishing she had brought her transistor radio. She didn't know how much of this high-brow stuff she was going to be able to stand.

The cabin turned out to be a simple wooden structure perched on a cliff and surrounded on three sides by tall evergreens. There were two bedrooms, a kitchen, and a living room with a stone fireplace. The rooms were plain, with few decorations aside from pieces of driftwood that someone had collected on the beach. And tacked up on the walls were five or six faded watercolors—obviously the work of an amateur, according to Maija, but not without a certain charm. Everything smelled a little damp and musty, but when Elly opened her bedroom window, she was surprised to see there was no screen to keep out the bugs. She hoped they didn't have the kind of mosquitoes they had in Wisconsin or she was going to be eaten alive. The living room had creaky wicker furniture that had once been painted white, and double glass doors opposite the fireplace opened out onto a large deck with a sweeping view of the water below.

Elly was surprised how easily she adapted to the lazy days on the island. Her aunt was an undemanding companion, and Elly spent most of her time sitting in a lawn chair on the deck, reading one of the trashy novels she found in the bookcase in her room. There was no radio in the cabin, but for some reason she didn't really miss it. In the afternoons she usually walked down the overgrown path to the beach and took a quick swim. The water was too cold to stay in very long, but it felt good to let her heavy body float for a few minutes in the lapping waves. She was starting to feel awkward and clumsy, and she had gained a lot of weight.

Maija always took a long walk in the morning with Edith trotting after her, as faithful as a dog. The weather was perfect, and Maija loved being outdoors. First thing every morning, she would stand on the deck and survey the water and distant shores with a look of pure satisfaction. Then she would call goodbye to Elly, who was usually still in bed, and head off in some new direction into the woods. She found an old bicycle in the tool shed, and in the evenings she often pedaled over to the country store a few miles down the road to get ice cream or some other treat for dessert.

But in the afternoons, Maija sat at the kitchen table and wrote in a blue spiral notebook. Elly asked her one day what she was writing, but Maija laughed lightly and said it was nothing, just some gibberish. When Elly glanced surreptitiously at the page, she couldn't make out a single word. Whatever Maija was writing, it was in Finnish, and the Martin children had never learned more than a few words of their mother's language.

When the children were small, Leena had sung Finnish songs to them and chatted in her native tongue, but as soon as Joel started school, she steadfastly stuck to English. She didn't want to confuse her kids, and above all she wanted them to be American. She had felt the sting of critical glances and unkind remarks because of her less-than-perfect English and her unfamiliarity with American customs. Her kids were not going to grow up being foreigners. This was their country, and there was plenty of time to learn Finnish later on.

And besides, it was convenient for Leena and Robert to have a secret language that the kids couldn't understand. It was their language for adult conversations. Later, when Elly got a little older and started thinking about such matters, she suspected that it was also their language in bed.

But all three Martin children grew up with the music of Finnish indelibly ingrained in their minds. They could instantly identify a Finnish speaker by the rhythm and cadence of his speech, and the language itself had acquired an almost mythic quality for them.

When Elly was nine, the Martin family had spent a whole summer in Finland, a trip financed by a small inheritance that Leena received when her father died. It was the first time Leena and Robert had returned to Finland since their marriage. Elly still remembered with a feeling of awe the way a crowd of excited friends and relatives had closed around her parents when they arrived at the airport in Helsinki. They laughed and shouted and talked on top of each other, leaving the three Martin children huddled around the baggage in uncomprehending silence. After a while they all learned a few rudimentary phrases in Finnish to make themselves understood. But for any real communication, the children would turn to Leena to interpret, and they could see that she enjoyed her unaccustomed role as the more knowledgeable member of the Martin family. In fact, Elly had never seen her mother so animated and at ease.

In high school both Elly and Kirsti took German, but Joel was the real linguistic whiz, and he had tried every language they offered, becoming equally fluent in German, French, and

Russian. He had an ear for the music of each individual language, and could quickly switch from one to the other without the usual stumbling over words and confusion of syntax. But none of the Martin children ever studied Finnish.

All three of them had endured the embarrassment of confronting ignorant teachers who insisted on correcting the spelling of Leena's name. They claimed it had to be either "L-a-y-n-a" or "L-e-n-a." No one had ever seen the Finnish spelling before. And the oddity of Leena's English pronunciation was for years a source of shame for her children, until they grew up and belatedly discovered a sense of pride in their mother's heritage.

As far as Elly knew, Maija had never once been back to Finland since she left the country in 1948.

CB

Three months after Leena sailed from Rotterdam to join Robert in Milwaukee and start her married life, Maija met Pentti Lahtinen standing in front of the pastry display case at the corner bakery. The store was crowded with Saturday morning shoppers jostling to get in line and buy their weekend bread. There were other bakeries in the neighborhood, but this one was the local favorite—the baker put more care into his work, and the store always smelled so heavenly. After the long years of rationing and shortages, everyone craved sugar and butter, and they all splurged shamelessly on bakery goods.

"*Anteeksi,*" said a tall young man standing next to Maija, "but can you tell me what those are called?" and he pointed to a sheet of snail-shaped buns coated with cinnamon and sugar.

"You mean the *pulla*?" said Maija, hiding her surprise. "All of the rolls on that shelf are different kinds of *pulla*. Those ones are called *korvapuustit*." She gave the tall man with the cropped sandy hair a closer look. He spoke fluent Finnish, but with an unusual accent, and it was strange that he didn't know what *pulla* was.

"Thanks," said the man with a grateful look. "People always expect me to know the names of everything when I go into a store just because I speak Finnish. But I grew up in Seattle, and this is actually the first time I've ever been in this country."

"You're American?" asked Maija.

"Yes," said the man, and then he put out his hand as he solemnly introduced himself, "Pentti Lahtinen."

"Maija Saarinen. Pleased to meet you." And they politely shook hands.

Then it was Pentti's turn at the counter and he asked for a dozen of the snail-shaped *pulla*, which the shop girl quickly packed into a white box and handed to him as she impatiently took his money. "Next," she said sharply. There was a long line of customers and she didn't have time for slowpokes.

When Maija came out of the bakery with her loaves of bread, she found the American waiting for her on the sidewalk.

"Would you care to join me for a cup of coffee somewhere, Miss Saarinen?" asked Pentti. He had a way of looking straight into a person's eyes that appealed to Maija. He was direct and confident without being snobbish. And he didn't seem to have that distinctly American habit of smiling excessively at everyone, no matter what the situation. Maija liked his serious demeanor, so she agreed to accept his invitation.

"But I prefer tea," she said. And then they walked down the

street to a little café on Runeberginkatu where Maija frequently went after her classes were over for the day. She had a part-time teaching job at Kivi Elementary, but she was hoping to be hired full-time next semester.

"My sister is married to an American," Maija told Pentti as she poured their tea from the ugly but serviceable brown teapot that seemed to be a trademark of the café. With the amount of business they did, you would think they could afford better china. "She just sailed to New York a few months ago, and now she's living in Milwaukee."

"I have a cousin in Chicago," said Pentti, "but I haven't seen him in a long time. My parents emigrated to America in 1912, and they lived with my uncle and his family in Chicago for about a year. Then they moved out west to Seattle. I've been visiting some of my relatives in Helsinki and Turku, but I'm really over here to do research for a book I'm writing on symbolist painters. I teach art history at Seattle University. Do you know the work of Hugo Simberg?"

Maija looked up from her tea with a startled glance. "Of course," she said. "He's one of my favorites."

"Mine too," said Pentti, giving her a slow smile that seemed to make his gaze all the more solemn.

They sipped their tea in silence for a while, neither of them disposed to small talk or useless chatter. Maija felt unusually comfortable in the company of this quiet, gray-eyed American. At twenty-eight she had had her share of suitors, and she had even been engaged to a young student named Erik before the havoc of war disrupted everyone's plans for the future.

Her fiancé was one of the lucky ones who actually returned from the fighting. Although physically unharmed, Erik was so changed by what he had endured that his engagement seemed inappropriate and wrong. It belonged to another lifetime, a different man, and he had to call it off. Maija was not sad to give back Erik's ring. She too had grown up during the war.

In the fall of 1939, she and her family were evacuated from Viipuri before the devastating Winter War started. They laboriously made their way to Helsinki, leaving behind their home and everything they possessed except for the few odds and ends they managed to carry with them. Maija was dismayed at how little they could take along. She and Leena took books and a few old photographs; their mother refused to be parted from her old copper coffeepot and a fragile glass vase she had inherited from her grandmother; their father loaded his briefcase with customer lists, inventory sheets, and invoices from his stationery shop, as if he were merely going on a business trip and would soon return to take up where he'd left off—even though many of his customers were already dead. When the Saarinen family finally arrived in Helsinki, worn-out and hungry, they found the city in chaos from the Soviet bombs. Maija and her mother went to work in the hospital, Leena sporadically attended classes in a school set up in the basement of a nearby apartment building, and Mr. Saarinen found a menial government job. They all somehow made it through the long years of the war. But Maija could tell that her parents would never recover from the trauma, and she noticed that Leena never told anyone that Viipuri, not Helsinki, was her home town. It was *her* way of coping with the loss.

So when Maija met Erik in Helsinki after the war, she was relieved that he had already decided to break off their engagement. She had been wondering for a long time how she would tell him that she wasn't sure about their relationship anymore.

But now, three years later, she was sitting here in this drab little café with an American man she had only just met, and she had a strange premonition that she would soon be following Leena to the States. She was a reserved person by nature, and it seemed absurd that this stranger could so swiftly and effectively alter her plans for her life. But Maija believed in listening to her inner voices, and she was not afraid to follow where they led.

"Would you like to go the Ateneum tomorrow afternoon?" asked Pentti. "I want to take another look at 'The Wounded Angel' and some of Simberg's other paintings."

"Yes," said Maija. "Thank you. I'd like that very much."

☙

On Saturday night Maija made a special dinner for Elly to mark the end of their Whidbey Island vacation. That afternoon she had gotten into the Plymouth for the first time since they arrived and had driven over to Langley to shop for food. She brought back fresh green beans, a bag of new little potatoes, and a gleaming fillet of dark pink salmon that she bought from a fisherman selling his catch from a boat down at the harbor. For dessert she was planning strawberry shortcake, since she had found some early ripe berries at a roadside stand on her way into town. She was looking forward to a real feast.

Elly offered to help her aunt fix dinner, but Maija sent her back out onto the deck with a wave of her hand. "Oh, no thank you, Elly. There's really not much to do. It's all very simple. Go outside and soak up the last of the sun." And then Maija tied an apron around her waist and started pulling pots and pans out of the cupboard next to the stove.

Elly sat down in her lawn chair and stared out over the water. She picked up her paperback with the gaudy embossed cover (she'd already raced through three others from her bedroom bookcase) but let it fall unopened into her lap. She had to admit, however grudgingly, that she had actually enjoyed this week with Maija. And the episode of the night before had given her new admiration for her aunt's intrepid spirit.

After dinner on Friday night, Maija had made a fire in the stone fireplace, and they had sat down in the sagging wicker chairs facing the flickering blaze. Maija leafed through some new children's books that she was considering using for her class, as Elly leaned her head back and dozed. She seemed to need a lot of sleep lately, and she found herself taking little catnaps whenever she was comfortably settled.

She woke up with a start to find Maija's hand on her shoulder.

"Elly?" whispered Maija. "Wake up. We're going for a walk."

"Now?" said Elly incredulously. "What time is it?"

"It's eleven o'clock," said Maija, "and the moon is perfect. You have to come out and see it. Let's go." And she handed Elly her floppy blue sweater with the leather buttons.

"My God," groaned Elly. "Is this really necessary?"

"Yes," said Maija, steering a sleepy and resistant Elly toward the kitchen door. "You won't regret it."

Maija flicked on a flashlight and led the way to a narrow path in the woods on the left side of the cabin. As they started down the path, she switched off the light.

"Hey!" said Elly. "I can't see a thing."

"Hold on to my sweater," said Maija. "Your eyes will get used to the dark in a minute."

Elly grabbed onto the hem of Maija's gray sweater and stumbled along after her aunt. She looked back and noticed the white blur of a cat a yard or two behind her. This was insane. All three of them fumbling around in the woods in the middle of the night. Maija must be crazy.

But Maija strode along as if it were broad daylight. She seemed to know the way quite well. After a while Elly's vision adjusted to the dim light, and she let go of her aunt's sweater. She began to make out the shapes of individual bushes and trees on either side of the trail. But she was a little scared, and the slightest movement made her jump. She was a city person, and she had never been out in the woods at night before. They walked for a long time. Then the path began to widen, and suddenly they emerged from the trees into a large clearing, illuminated by the bright glow of the moon. Maija moved to the center of the clearing and then stopped to gaze upward.

Wow, thought Elly, this is amazing. She would never have come out here by herself, never in a million years. But Maija was right—she didn't regret it. The dark green clearing flooded with moonlight, the soft sighing of the evergreens, the gentle rustle of the bushes, and the clear sky overhead were simply beautiful. She'd never seen anything like it, and she felt an enormous sense of pleasure and well-being. The knots of anger melted from her shoulders and back, the tense lines of her face relaxed, and for the first time she considered the small life inside her with a tenderness that her defensive attitude had not allowed her to feel. She was going to have this baby, and she was going to find her own way in the world. She didn't know specifically what she would do; she didn't even know what she really wanted. But none of that mattered. She had made a choice, and for the first time she felt strong enough to bear whatever might come.

Elly looked at her aunt standing in the middle of the clearing, ever the proper lady in her cotton dress and gray sweater, her hair immaculately combed, her head tipped back, her face calm, unsmiling, and dignified. She was completely absorbed by the moonlight and the sounds of the forest.

Then Maija lowered her head and her eyes met Elly's.

"You're not scared of the woods, are you?" Elly whispered to her aunt.

"What's there to be afraid of? I feel safer here than in any city. And besides, we Finns have *sisu*."

"What's that?" asked Elly.

"Fortitude, perseverance, and nerve. We don't scare easily. We're survivors, and we don't believe in defeat. Remember that, Elly. You're half Finnish, too." Then Maija picked up Edith, who was rubbing against her leg, and came over to stand next to her niece at the edge of the clearing. She put her hand lightly on Elly's arm. "Let's go back now," Maija said, "and I'll make you some tea."

Five

On Sunday afternoon Robert had two consultations scheduled, so he would be tied up at the office for most of the day. Leena washed the breakfast and lunch dishes in record time, not feeling inclined to linger in the kitchen or daydream. Restless and uneasy, she roamed through the house, smoothing out the covers on their bed, straightening the framed print of a painting by Helena Schjerfbeck which hung in the dining room, and wiping off imaginary dust from the windowsills. She sat down on the couch and picked up her knitting, but she couldn't concentrate on the pattern, and she ended up taking out all three rows she had knit. She didn't usually make so many mistakes. She got up and wandered over to her loom, which she had recently moved into the sunroom. She ran her fingers lightly over the linen warp, but she didn't have the heart to sit down and weave. Finally, she went into Robert's study and called Diane to invite her over for coffee.

"Oh, why don't you come over here, Leena? I can pick you up in fifteen minutes."

"OK," said Leena, "that would be nice." She had never

learned to drive, even though her kids were always urging her to get a license, and she had been saying for years that she was planning to take lessons. But by this time she had no intention of ever getting behind the wheel of a car. She walked everywhere, and in good weather she would climb on her bicycle and pedal for miles, sometimes going all the way out to Bay Shore shopping center if she was feeling especially energetic. And the transit system in Milwaukee was both convenient and reliable, an opinion she didn't mind sharing with anyone standing next to her at the bus stop.

"We're lucky to have such good bus service, don't you think?" Leena would enthusiastically remark. "I take the bus everywhere." And then Leena and the stranger would get to talking, and before the bus ride was over, they would be on a first-name basis, and Leena would know everything about the other person's problems and family affairs. People were always confiding in Leena. Only her children seemed reticent about telling her their worries and secrets.

Occasionally Leena would still have the dream that had plagued her so much when the kids were small.

It's always summertime and she is somewhere out in the country, in the middle of a field of corn that is not yet ripe for harvest. In the midst of the green stalks she sees a child sitting on the ground, crying and bleeding. She picks up the child and rushes out to the road to flag down a car, but there is absolutely no traffic. Parked at the side of the deserted road is an old black car with whitewall tires. Leena yanks open the rear car door and places the child gently on the back seat. Then she climbs into the driver's seat. The key is in the ignition, but Leena has no idea how to drive. She sits there, panic-stricken, listening to the whimpering child.

And then she would wake up, terrified and full of remorse, and she would resolve once again to get that driver's license. But she never did.

Robert was always so willing to chauffeur her wherever she wanted to go. He didn't mind driving her to the store, and he never complained about the amount of time he had to wait while she did her shopping. He would sit in the car or find a chair somewhere in the store and open his book or get out the daily crossword puzzle. When Leena returned a couple of hours later, he would look up with a distracted air and say, "Back so soon?"

Leena secretly considered it a fair trade—she did all the housework and cooking, so it was only right that Robert did all the driving.

A car honked in front of the house. Leena smiled as she grabbed her sweater and purse and checked to make sure the stove was turned off before she headed out the door. Diane had installed one of those funny car horns that actually played a tune when you touched it. Leena didn't recognize the melody (she thought it sounded more like the bleating of a demented sheep), but it made her smile every time she heard it.

Once a week, on Monday afternoons, Diane picked up Leena and they drove downtown to work at the Wisconsin Avenue soup kitchen. Leena had discovered that they needed volunteers after she rescued an old man who had fallen in the middle of the street.

Leena had been on her way over to Boston Store, and she had her thoughts on a lovely glass platter she had seen in the housewares department the week before. She was hoping it was still there. But the minute Leena caught sight of the old man crumpling into a heap in the middle of Wisconsin Avenue, she leaped off the curb and rushed out to help him, waving her arms at the oncoming cars. The drivers all screeched to a stop at the sight of the gray-haired woman in the red jacket flailing around in the street. At first they didn't even notice the old man lying on the ground.

"Are you all right?" asked Leena worriedly.

"Huh?" muttered the old man, squinting up at her with ancient, bloodshot eyes. "What'd ya say?" He was wearing a spotted t-shirt with a Maxell logo on the front, a tattered wool sport coat, and a clear plastic raincoat with big rips around the armholes. Leena also noticed that he had on three pairs of ragged pants, and that the little toe of his right foot was sticking out of a hole in his tennis shoe. He smelled sharply of urine and cheap liquor.

"Come on," said Leena, taking him by the arm. "You have to get out of the street. You're going to get run over." And then she hauled him to his feet and led him back to safety on the sidewalk. As the traffic resumed its frenzied pace, Leena steadied the old man and asked him where he was going.

He seemed incapable of completing a sentence, but he pulled a folded piece of paper out of his raincoat pocket and handed it to Leena with a plaintive look on his face. It was a flyer for a soup kitchen a few blocks away, so Leena took a firm grip on the old man's elbow and escorted him down the street. The crowds of noontime pedestrians parted like magic to allow Leena and her tottering charge to pass, and every face bore a look of utter distaste and scorn.

Leena's eyes narrowed and her jaw lifted in stubborn determination. It made her mad to see the arrogant expressions and lack of sympathy surrounding her and the old man. Who did they think they were, anyway? All these people lucky enough to have a job, lucky enough to have money for lunch, lucky enough to have a home to go to. They didn't realize that they could lose it all in an instant, and they could easily end up just like this sorry old man. They didn't realize how brutally fate could intervene. And you could suddenly find yourself trudging down a muddy road toward an unknown city, leaving all you possessed behind. They didn't know what a fragile line separated fortune from misfortune. They had no idea how lucky they were.

Leena delivered the old man to a hefty, pleasant-looking woman supervising the volunteers who were goodnaturedly dishing out steaming plates of food to a long line of hungry people. There was an atmosphere of subdued camaraderie, and even the hard-core drunks were on their best behavior. The large dining hall was clean and well-lit, and the walls were brightly decorated with scores of children's drawings. Leena was appalled to see how many children were among the ragged throngs seated at the tables. She hadn't realized that so many young families were joining the ranks of the homeless. She decided to volunteer on the spot. And that night she called Diane and persuaded her to come along too.

They had been going to the soup kitchen for over a year now, and they both found it a satisfying though troubling experience.

"Did you see that mother with the four kids?" Leena once asked Diane as they drove home. "She looked like she wasn't more than eighteen, and she already has four children. I don't know how she's going to make it on her own. I think I'll take her some old clothes that I've got up in the attic from when my kids were small."

One day last October Leena was waiting for a bus on Downer Avenue, when a decrepit-looking man dressed in filthy rags approached her and suddenly clamped his clawlike hand onto her arm. She nearly jumped out of her skin, but then she took a good look at the ancient eyes peering up at her. It was the old man she had rescued from the street.

"You brung me to the soup kitchen," croaked the man, smiling crookedly.

"That's right," said Leena. "I remember you too. How are you doing?"

"Pretty good. Thinkin' of headin' south though. Can't stand the cold here in the winter." And then the old man chuckled hoarsely and gave Leena a friendly salute before he slowly moved off down the street.

CŊ

Diane leaned over to unlock the passenger door and then stared up anxiously at her friend as Leena came down the front steps toward the car. She was looking a little haggard, and Diane noticed at once that her socks didn't match. One was dark blue and the other was brown. Leena was usually so careful about her appearance.

She wasn't obsessively fastidious by any means, and her clothes were always rather unconventional, but she dressed with a certain flair. She had a knack for finding one-of-a-kind designer pieces that no one else wanted because the color was out of fashion or the buttons were hideous or there was a small tear in the hem. Leena would snap up the clothes at rock-bottom prices and gleefully take them home, changing the buttons and repairing the holes, and boasting to Diane about what great finds she had made.

Leena loved bright colors, especially various shades of red and orange—colors that few other women her age were bold enough to wear—and she would add a string of silver beads, a bright scarf, or an old Kalevala brooch to finish off the look. She had a style all her own, but her mismatched socks were not a new fashion statement—Diane surmised that they were an indication of her grief. Leena's thoughts were elsewhere, and she couldn't be bothered right now with the trivial things that usually gave her pleasure.

"Hi, Leena," said Diane, patting her friend on the shoulder as she settled into the passenger seat. "How are you holding up?"

"Just fine," said Leena a little too brightly. She busied herself with the seat belt and avoided looking directly at Diane. "Thanks for coming to get me."

And then they drove in companionable silence over to Diane's big three-story house on Lake Drive. They had known each other for so many years that they were completely comfortable with long stretches of silence. Diane could see that Leena was feeling strained and sad, but she was not compelled to force the conversation. If Leena wanted to talk about things, she would. There was no need to pressure her.

Diane had been married to a prominent doctor who had died many years ago and left her financially secure. She didn't really need to work, but she couldn't stand to be idle, so she always found some kind of activity to keep her satisfactorily busy. After she gave up her theater career, she ran through a whole series of jobs, looking in vain for some other work that was compatible with her rowdy and irreverent but compassionate nature. Usually she ended up walking off the job in disgust.

For three months she worked in a big department store, where she was assigned to sell hosiery and lingerie. But she couldn't resist loudly ridiculing the skimpy little garments and binding hardware that passed for modern feminine underwear. She was always trying to persuade her customers to opt for the comfort of cotton instead of the slinky, and unhealthy, nylon that most women seemed to prefer. One day, as she was straightening some packages of pantyhose, she put her hand on top of the long wooden rack and accidentally started off a chain reaction among the display legs perched on top—the taupe leg fell against the mauve leg, which toppled the chartreuse leg, and the domino effect continued down the line, as one by one the dozens of mannequin legs pitched to the floor. Diane was in hysterics, and her customers were too, but the department supervisor was not at all amused.

The next day Diane was transferred to the perfume counter, where she didn't last more than a week. Her new boss caught her making fun of a regular customer who looked like a bulldog and believed in drenching herself with the most potent perfume on the market. Diane was immediately fired, but she wasn't upset in the least. She found retail sales incredibly boring, and she had already been planning to quit.

Then, at the age of sixty, she finally discovered her calling.

She was having trouble with sharp spasms in her back, and no medical doctor seemed able to help her. She had seen all the experts, who had run her through a gamut of mysterious and uncomfortable tests, but she was getting no relief, and everyone seemed stumped by her symptoms.

"I made an appointment to see a massage therapist," Diane told Leena on the phone. "I can't stand this aching pain anymore, and I'm willing to try anything."

"You're going to a massage parlor?" asked Leena in horror, picturing some kind of sleazy dive down by the waterfront next to a disreputable tattoo shop. The Milwaukee streets were regularly flooded with white-clad sailors looking for a good time while on shore leave. The scores of downtown taverns also did a brisk business whenever the big ships pulled into port.

"It's not what you think," said Diane with a laugh. "It's called massage therapy. It's completely above board, and it has nothing to do with sex. I've heard it can work wonders, and this woman is supposed to be very skilled. Nothing else has worked, so I'm willing to give it a try."

Diane was so intrigued by how effectively the massage treatments cured her back pain that she decided to take up the study of massage herself. After two years of intensive training, she had set up a private practice in her home, and she now had a long list of appreciative clients. She had discovered in herself a special talent for the combination of physical strength, anatomical knowledge, and pure empathy that the work demanded.

"Come on in," said Diane as she unlocked the back door. "I turned on the coffeemaker before I left, so the coffee should be ready by now. Let's sit in the kitchen." And she tossed her keys onto the tile counter, picked up the glass Melitta coffeepot, and filled two pink ceramic mugs to the brim. They both took their coffee black, and Leena had taught Diane to make it extra strong. She couldn't stand the way most American coffee was served: tepid, pale, and as thin as dishwater. How could anyone brew coffee that way? And why would anyone bother to drink it? She liked *real* coffee—piping hot and strong.

"Joel called this morning," said Leena as she pulled out a chair and sat down at the round oak table. The chair she was sitting on was painted bright green with pink and purple cats racing up the back and around the seat. Diane's house was filled with a conglomeration of rustic furniture, hand-woven baskets of every size and shape, and unusual examples of folk art, including a spectacular collection of masks.

"He said he's going to drive down from Vancouver on Wednesday for the funeral. And Kirsti is flying over from Copenhagen. I was surprised she would come, because it's so expensive, but she told Robert she wanted to be there. Elly's bringing Rachel with her from Denver. It's turning into a family reunion." Leena's expression was so rueful that Diane reached over and touched her hand.

"Why don't I give you a massage?" she offered. "You won't believe how relaxing it is, and I know it would make you feel better. Your neck muscles are all tensed up." Diane pressed lightly on the back of Leena's neck, evoking a sharp "Ouch" and then a deep sigh from her friend.

"That might be nice," Leena admitted tentatively. Over the years she had heard quite a lot from Diane about the restorative and healing powers of massage, but she had never been willing to try it herself. She couldn't explain her hesitation, since it wasn't a question of personal modesty or embarrassment. She and Diane often went to the local swimming pool together, and they had seen each other naked hundreds of times. They knew all about each other's flaws and assorted aches and pains. And they had had many long conversations about the way their bodies were changing with age. Together they had gone through all the stages of female vanity, impatience, and grim resignation, until they had finally come to a graceful acceptance of the physical manifestation of their long years of life.

Leena thought the deep lines of her friend's face particularly attractive and compelling. She had a wise face, a kind face, but there was an impish sparkle in her eyes that could lead to all manner of escapades and impulsive adventures. Leena never knew what to expect next from her friend.

Diane once called Leena on a Sunday night and told her to pack her bags with hot-weather clothes. She had tickets to Mexico, and the plane left early the following morning. All of Leena's initial objections and protests fell on deaf ears—Diane had made up her mind to go, and she wanted her best friend to come with her. At seven o'clock on Monday morning they were checking in at the airport, and within an hour they were on their way. They both had a wonderful time in Oaxaca.

On other occasions, Diane would call and invite Leena to a play or a concert. And she always knew well in advance what new and exciting exhibits were coming to the Milwaukee Art Museum. Leena often thought herself fortunate to have such a lively and wacky friend. The world was too full of stuffy and unimaginative people who missed out on all the fun. She realized that the daily drudgery of earning a living was what reduced most people to a state of relentless stupor and fatigue. And she knew that, even for her generation of women, she was extremely lucky to have had the freedom not to work at some enervating job. But she still blamed the near catatonic condition of so many people around her on their own lack of imagination and the lethargy-inducing spell of TV.

She had her own favorite TV programs (she almost never missed an episode of "As the World Turns"), but she couldn't believe the number of hours most people spent every day staring vacantly at the tube. She knew it had to be unhealthy. Take all the TVs away for one month, and maybe people would start thinking again. Maybe they would start reading again too.

"Come on," said Diane, pushing back her chair and getting up to lead the way to the massage room. "I'll go get the heat packs while you undress and lie down on the table. You're going to love this. You'll probably want to have a massage every week from now on."

Leena stood up and followed Diane down the hall. She felt tired, slow, and worn out. Maybe the massage would do her good, after all. She didn't want to think about the funeral. And she was worried about Joel. He had sounded nervous and on edge, but she didn't feel she could ask him whether something was wrong. The long years of silence were still having a negative effect on their relationship. And no matter how hard they had tried, neither Joel nor his parents had ever entirely forgiven each other for all those lost years.

☞

In 1969 Joel was a senior in high school, a tall and gangly kid with shaggy blond hair that Leena was always eyeing uneasily. She wished he would get a haircut more often, but she knew he wouldn't listen to her nagging, and she could see that other boys had hair that was even longer. His friend Mike had hair halfway down his back, and sometimes he wore it braided, just like a girl.

Leena sighed. She didn't know what to make of this younger generation. Their choice of clothes, their blaring music, and their profane language mystified her, and she often found them offensive. She wondered if her own parents had been as puzzled by her and her friends. She didn't think so, but those were different times, with war disrupting most of her youth and diverting everyone's thoughts to the basics of survival. She hadn't really had the luxury of being a teenager.

In spite of the current fads, Joel was turning out to be a handsome and charming young man, and Leena was proud of her son. He was not a star student like his sister Kirsti, who was always bringing home prizes for her academic achievements, but Joel's average grades were a reflection of a certain laziness, not a lack of brains.

He had a real ear for languages, but he couldn't be bothered with the boring homework, and he was more interested in taking photographs for the school yearbook than in applying himself to his studies. Joel's engaging manner had always made him popular among his peers, and Leena was secretly a little jealous at the way the girls seemed to flock around her son. She wanted him to be attractive, she wanted him to have girlfriends, but she discovered that she didn't really enjoy sharing his affections. And she was convinced that none of the girls she had seen so far was pretty enough or smart enough for her son.

Leena once confessed to Diane that Joel was her favorite child.

"I know I shouldn't say that," moaned Leena anxiously.

"But I just can't help it. He was my first, and he's always been so easygoing and fun. Even when he got into fights when he was little, he could eventually win over the bullies with his jokes. He doesn't brood about things the way the girls do. Their moodiness really gets to me sometimes. And Kirsti's determination to always be the best is really unnerving—she makes me feel so stupid. The girls are always criticizing me these days. They don't like my clothes or my hair, and yesterday Elly told me I should wear more makeup. I never seem to do anything right, and they give me these withering looks whenever I open my mouth. But I can always depend on Joel to tell me funny stories and make me laugh. He's such a neat kid."

Joel could always make his sisters laugh too. Even Kirsti couldn't help cracking a smile when Joel did his riotous impressions of James Cagney or Ed Sullivan. Behind closed doors he also did an impression of Robert that would send all three Martin children into stifled paroxysms of laughter. And when Joel started in on his assortment of animal noises, Elly would always join him, and the two of them would eventually drive Kirsti from the room with their duet of hoots and snorts and growls.

Joel was always playing harmless tricks on his sisters, and they learned to be on guard whenever he returned from another trip to the magic store downtown. At breakfast they might find a rubber fried egg on their plate. Or when they opened the front door they might shriek at the sight of a gross-looking splatter of plastic vomit strategically placed on the doorstep. Joel once offered Kirsti a bag of chocolate candy, but she got suspicious at the look of glee on his face and refused to eat any. It turned out to be a bag of chocolate-covered ants.

Elly loved her brother's jokes, and she didn't mind his teasing and pranks. When they were kids, he often took her to scary Saturday matinees at the Oriental Theater. The eerie, spotlighted statues of Chinese warriors and folk heroes lining the walls of the cavernous theater made the atmosphere even creepier. And she would sit on the edge of her seat, biting her fingernails, and then bury her head in her sweater during the really scary parts. Joel would poke her in the side and say, "Hey, Elly, you're missing all the good stuff," and she would lift her head just in time to see a gory, mutated figure, dripping with blood, burst into the room of some unsuspecting female. Elly screamed and Joel laughed. They both loved the thrill of cinematic terror.

Kirsti could never be persuaded to come along with them. She said she didn't have time for such dumb movies, but that wasn't the reason at all. She had enough horrifying nightmares of her own, and she didn't need any additional monsters or ghouls keeping her awake at night.

Against her better judgment, she once agreed to watch a few episodes of "The Twilight Zone" with Joel, who was a big fan of the weekly program. But the spooky introductions about stepping into a "fifth dimension," combined with the psychologically terrifying twists at the end of each story, started disrupting her sleep.

Images of menacing talking dolls and man-eating creatures from outer space began haunting her. And certain stories would remain with her for the rest of her life. Like the one about the crotchety old man whose only desire was to read books. By a stroke of luck he ended up the sole survivor of a nuclear war, surrounded by stacks and stacks of library books, enough for the rest of his life. The man was in bliss until he dropped his glasses and broke them, leaving him virtually blind. Kirsti thought this story unbelievably cruel.

She finally refused to watch any more "Twilight Zone" shows after she saw the episode about the little girl who fell through the wall in her bedroom and was trapped in a murky, weightless dimension, unable to get back to the real world. Kirsti couldn't forget the image of the frantic parents blindly reaching their hands through the blank wall, trying to pull their sobbing child back into her bedroom. It gave her goosebumps just thinking about it. Joel teased her about being a scaredy-cat, but she didn't care. She had seen enough horror shows.

When Elly turned six and Joel was eight-and-a-half, the two of them would walk to school together in the mornings. Joel would tell his sister wild stories and get her so worked up that she could barely sit still in class. One day he put a rubbery clump into the palm of her hand and told her that it was alive. Elly's eyes widened as the clump started to quiver and then thin little tendrils broke away from the core and began waving in the air.

"What is it?" she asked Joel with awe in her voice.

"I don't know," he told her, "but I saw it hatch from a red-speckled egg."

Elly carried it solemnly all the way to school and showed it to her friends on the playground. But when they took it to Mr. Riebel, the science teacher, and told him they had found a mysterious living creature, he laughed loudly and said, "That looks like the inside of a golf ball to me."

Even as a teenager, Elly always fell for Joel's jokes, which often took some elaborate planning. One time Elly returned after midnight from a showing of "Planet of the Apes." The house was dark except for a living-room light that her mother had left on for her, and everyone else was already asleep. Elly threw her jacket on the couch, slipped off her shoes, and crept slowly up the stairs. She was tired, and her thoughts were still on the movie. She opened the door to her room, stepped inside, and closed the door behind her before switching on the light.

Elly's screams woke up everyone in the house.

There was a monkey sitting on her bed, blinking at her in the bright light. A real live monkey with round black eyes and little hands that he stretched out toward her so sweetly. Joel had gone to a lot of trouble convincing Mike's big brother, who worked in a pet store, to loan him the monkey for a day. Elly was furious, but after she calmed down, she had to admit it was funny, and later on she could never tell the story without howling with laughter.

But in 1969, two months after his eighteenth birthday and three weeks before graduation, Joel received a letter that put the whole Martin family into a tailspin from which none of them ever fully recovered.

ဢ

Leena remembered the details of that day as if they had been recorded on film. At 4:30 in the afternoon she was standing in the kitchen cooking dinner. She had on a pair of black capri pants and a bright-red Yvonne Sachs sleeveless blouse that she had pulled from the bargain bin in the basement of Gimbel's department store. It had been badly wrinkled and three buttons were missing, but she could tell it was a real gem, and she bought it for a dollar fifty. A little starch and some dime-sized mother-of-pearl buttons had turned it into her favorite blouse. She was also wearing white sandals with silver buckles.

It was a hot and muggy afternoon, and the throbbing in her temples told her that a thunderstorm was on the way. Leena's warning headaches were more reliable than any weather forecast. Before starting out for the beach or a picnic in the park, the kids always asked their mother if it was going to rain. They all joked about her weather predictions, but they took them seriously because Leena was invariably right.

Maija considered her sister's meteorological talent quite similar to her own susceptibility to omens and premonitions, but Leena always laughed at the idea and said it was just a matter of barometric pressure.

Leena hoped the storm would break soon so the rain would clear the air. She loved the aftermath of Milwaukee storms: the dark-green leaves of the tall elm trees glistening with drops of rain, the pavement steaming slightly, and the air momentarily fresh and cool.

That afternoon she had decided to make fried chicken, and the pieces were now sizzling nicely in the electric frying pan plugged into the outlet above the kitchen counter. It was the only Southern dish she had ever learned to make, and it was Robert's favorite. So every now and then she cooked up a big batch of chicken breasts and drumsticks, even though she hated the way the whole house smelled of oil. They usually ate dinner at the kitchen table, but whenever she made fried chicken they sat in the dining room. The smell was just too overwhelming in the kitchen, and she had to open all the windows and doors to air out the room.

She was also planning mashed potatoes and iceberg lettuce with Thousand Island dressing. And she had already filled the copper mold with lime Jell-O and mandarin orange slices and put it in the refrigerator. Robert would be home in an hour, and it looked like everything would be ready just in time.

Joel came into the kitchen with a letter in his hand. He had a strange look on his face, and he didn't say a word as he handed the letter to Leena. She had noticed the official-looking envelope among the dozens of letters and professional journals that Robert received every day. But she had been in a hurry to get to her tennis game with Diane, so she hadn't really looked at it. She assumed it was some official correspondence from the university for Robert.

"What's this, dear?" she said as she unfolded the single sheet of paper. And then she skimmed through the bureaucratic convolutions and gleaned just enough information to make her gasp and look up at her son in horror.

It was from the draft board. The lottery system had just assigned the numbers for Joel's age group. His number was 15. If he didn't get a college deferment or find some other means of escape, Joel was going to be drafted, and there was a good chance that he'd end up in Vietnam.

௵

When Robert came home twenty minutes late for dinner, he found the rest of the Martin family already assembled around the dining-room table.

"Sorry I'm late," said Robert, leaning down to kiss his wife lightly on the cheek. "Sure smells good." And then he sat down at the head of the table and noticed that something was wrong.

They all had a full plate of food in front of them, but no one seemed to be eating. Elly was poking at her mashed potatoes, making rivulets of butter flow down the sides of the lumpy white mound. Kirsti was sitting erect in her chair, her eyes fixed on some indefinable point in the air, her lips set in a tight little frown. Joel had his head in his hands, and Robert couldn't see his face. Leena was fluttering around nervously at the other end of the table, moving the salt and pepper shakers back and forth. She stuck her fork into a morsel of chicken but put it back down on her plate without even attempting to taste the food.

Leena's eyes flitted to Robert's face, and she gave him such a stricken look that he exclaimed, "What on earth is going on here? Did someone die or something?"

Joel lifted his head out of his hands and looked over at his father. "I'm going to be drafted," he said tensely, his eyes glinting with anger.

Robert inhaled sharply and stared at his son in disbelief. "You must be kidding," he couldn't help saying, even though it was quite obvious that this was no joke.

"Oh, right," snapped Joel sarcastically. "I'm just making it all up. Take a look for yourself." And he pulled the draft-board letter out of his shirt pocket and tossed it onto his father's empty plate.

Robert picked up the sheet of paper and quickly scanned the five paragraphs of bureaucratese. Then he looked at his son with an expression that was completely blank. His mind seemed frozen, paralyzed—he had no idea what to say. Robert Martin was a liberal and a Democrat, a man who was proud of his stalwartly left-wing ideas and values, which sometimes put him at odds with the established policies of the university. He had radical friends, Quakers and Catholics, who all actively protested the escalating violence and loss of life in the Vietnam war—the war that the government still steadfastly refused to call a war.

But Robert himself was not an activist by any means. He was not a shouter or a vigorous debater. He didn't make speeches or loudly profess his views, although in small gatherings of his friends he didn't hesitate to make his opinions known. He was against the war, but he didn't feel the need to protest publicly or to join in demonstrations. It was enough for him to condemn the government's policies in private—although on two occasions he had been so outraged by the latest turn of events that he actually wrote letters to the Wisconsin senators. And once he sent a telegram to the White House. But the war in Vietnam was largely outside his professional and personal life. In spite of the daily barrage of reports on the CBS evening news, the war was in some sense abstract, or at least not likely ever to enter his immediate sphere.

Somehow Robert had never thought that his own son might be in jeopardy, that Joel might be ordered to participate in the war.

Robert was not prepared. He had trusted in a benevolent fate. He had assumed that the luck of the draw would fall in Joel's favor, that his son would naturally receive such a high number that there would be no chance of him ever getting drafted. In the back of his mind, he had pictured them all celebrating with a bottle of champagne. He had allowed his own wishful thinking to blind him perilously, and now reality was making him feel the fool. He was simply not prepared.

And then his mind jolted into action. "I'll call Ed," he

announced. "He's an expert on the legal aspects of the draft. He'll know what to do. We just need to get you into some college, and then you can get a deferment, no problem." And Robert jumped up from the table and strode off toward his study to use the phone.

Joel groaned softly and gave his mother a morose look. He was not convinced of his father's power to change the course of events now set in motion by this letter. The brusque and impersonal tone of the communiqué had stunned Joel. For once he had no joke to tell, no wisecrack to make. This time there was nothing to mock or ridicule. The vast machinations of the United States government were light-years beyond the clumsy tactics of all the bullies Joel had had to contend with so far. He felt helpless and lost. And a sense of panic was building up inside him with nauseating speed. The worst part of all was that he felt completely alone. He strongly suspected that his parents were really not capable of finding a solution. He was going to have to do something himself.

Joel abruptly pushed back his chair and got to his feet. "I'm going over to Mike's," he said. "See you later."

"But what about your dinner?" protested Leena with a mournful look on her face.

"I'm not hungry, Mom. Sorry." And then Joel was gone.

There was a sharp clang as Elly dropped her fork onto her plate. Her wedge of lime Jell-O trembled violently, and the last trickles of butter flowed down the sides of the mashed potatoes and flooded around the greasy-looking drumstick. Elly stared at the food in disgust. Then she clenched her right fist and pounded it on the table, chanting, "Shit, shit, shit, shit!"

"Elly!" cried her mother. "You know I don't like you using that kind of language in the house."

Without another word, Elly leaped up from the table and ran out of the room. Kirsti sighed heavily, stood up, and began stacking the dishes to take them into the kitchen.

"I don't think anybody's hungry tonight, Mom," she said quietly. "I'm going to go over to Susan's to do my homework. I'll be back around nine."

Then Kirsti took everyone's plate into the kitchen, leaving only the serving dishes and Robert's place setting untouched. She took her jacket out of the hall closet, picked up a pile of books from the living-room coffee table, and gently pulled the front door shut behind her as she left. Robert was apparently still talking to Ed on the phone, and Leena was left sitting at the dining-room table all alone.

She felt deserted and abandoned. For the last hour her mind had been spinning with worry and concern as she mechanically finished her preparations for the dinner that no one wanted to eat. When she handed the letter back to Joel, he had stood there for a long moment, with an expectant, almost hopeful look on his face. But Leena didn't know what to tell him, and Joel had walked out of the kitchen, crestfallen and depressed.

Leena regretted her silence. She was thoroughly shaken by the instantly envisioned consequences of this cold governmental letter, but she didn't know what to say. She so rarely had serious conversations with her son. In fact, it was usually Joel who offered advice and words of encouragement to his mother, and not the other way around. Leena counted on Joel for his optimism and good humor. She looked forward to their daily sessions of bantering when Joel came home after school. She honestly couldn't remember the last time that she and her son had discussed a serious issue or problem.

Robert was always the one who pulled Joel aside to reprimand him, or to dole out some form of punishment for the minor scrapes that Joel sometimes got himself into. Last year, when an apologetic cop showed up at the front door with an embarrassed Joel in tow—caught walking down the street with two six-packs of beer in hand—Robert had refused to accept any form of leniency.

"What's the normal procedure in cases like this, officer?" he asked.

"Well, we usually take the kids down to the station and fingerprint them. Scares them a bit and teaches them a lesson."

"Then take him down to the station," said Robert, overriding the mild protests of the policeman and ignoring Joel's astonished face.

The incident had provoked a certain tension between father and son that had not diminished with time. And Robert's frequent attempts to give Joel well-meaning advice—advice tempered by his own years of experience—met with a stubborn rancor that was unusual for his son.

Leena remembered one occasion when Robert and Joel actually came close to physical violence. A few months ago she had opened the kitchen door to find them facing each other in fury, both of them frozen in a stance of seething hostility. Their jaws were clenched, their eyes were glaring, and their fists were raised and ready to strike. Leena's sudden appearance broke their focus and concentration, and the two of them immediately retreated to different parts of the house.

"What was *that* all about this afternoon?" Leena asked Robert later that night as they were getting into bed.

"I honestly don't know," Robert told his wife. "One minute we were kidding around, and the next thing I know, we're facing off like a couple of boxers going for the heavyweight title. I just mentioned that I thought Mike was looking a little tired and ragged lately, and I hoped that he wasn't getting involved in any dope-smoking or drugs. Joel flew off the handle and said that just because his friends looked different, it didn't mean they were dopers, and he told me that I was always being suspicious for no good reason.

"That put me on the defensive, and pretty soon we were calling each other names, and then things really got out of hand. I'm not sorry that you interrupted us. I was actually thinking of punching him," said Robert with horror and surprise.

Leena was equally appalled, but she decided it would be unwise to comment.

"Don't you think Joel has changed a lot lately?" Robert continued. "He's not as easygoing as he used to be. He's so restless, and he can't seem to settle down or really apply himself. He's a bright kid, but he's not taking full advantage of all the opportunities open to him. I wish you'd say something to him—he's always talking to you, and maybe he'd listen to *your* advice. He certainly doesn't pay any attention to mine."

There was a wistfulness in Robert's voice that touched Leena. But she still said nothing.

"And the other day Elly let slip that he's not planning to go to the university after all," said Robert, now sounding thoroughly fed up. "She said he's thinking of traveling around for a while. Did you know about this?"

Leena did know about Joel's decision, but she had been afraid to tell Robert that their son had no intention of attending the university, at least not right away. In fact, he never even sent in the application form. Joel had told Leena with a laugh that he wasn't a scholar like his father, and he would probably end up driving a truck for a living. In the meantime, he was planning to hitchhike around the country during the summer, and then find some kind of work in the fall. He had saved up enough cash from his stock-clerk job at Grady's Supermarket to last him three or four months. He had never been east of Ohio or west of the Mississippi, except for one brief trip to Seattle to visit his aunt and cousin many years ago. He was eager to find out first-hand what the rest of the United States looked like.

Leena had complete faith in the intelligence and capabilities of her son. She was positive that someday he would find the right occupation that would enable him to excel. She had no doubt that someday she and Robert would have every reason to be proud of Joel. He just happened to be a late bloomer, and in that way he was much like his mother.

It was only three years earlier that Leena had finally decided to do something about her long-time wish to learn to weave. By now she was already turning out remarkable pieces, several of which the Weaving Guild had accepted for their upcoming show. She would never think of herself as a serious artist, although she liked hearing Robert boast to his friends about "my wife, the weaver." She considered her sense of color and design to be ordinary and commonplace, but she loved the meticulous planning demanded by the craft. And the constant, steady rhythm of the loom's alternating harnesses, lifting and falling, was as soothing to her as the rush of hot water as she did the dishes.

Looking back, Leena couldn't understand what had taken her so long to get started. She had always loved unusual textures and patterns, and the smell of newly-spun wool evoked an emotional response in her that she couldn't explain. It made her feel both melancholy and joyful, and the first time she ventured into Selina's Weaving Shop on Farwell Avenue, she couldn't keep her hands off the dozens of soft, multicolored skeins looped over pegs on one wall of the store. She noticed a blue flyer on the bulletin board announcing Tuesday-night weaving classes, and on impulse she decided to sign up.

She bought herself a simple table loom and spent a year learning basic techniques. Then she bought a second-hand floor loom, and her first real project was a Finnish *ryijy* rug with a black bramble pattern bisecting a deep red background. She had given it to Maija for Christmas, and she was pleased to hear from Briitta that it was hanging over their sofa.

It had taken her over forty years to figure out that weaving was what she enjoyed most. So she was not surprised that, at the age of eighteen, Joel had no idea what he wanted to do with his life. She knew that Robert was exasperated by their son's seeming lack of ambition and direction, but she was perfectly content to allow Joel a great deal of time to find his bearings.

Now everything had changed with the arrival of the letter. In a matter of seconds it had created a critical situation that none of them could ignore. It demanded urgent action.

Diane's young lover from the Repertory Theater had been drafted last year, and shortly afterwards he had shipped out for Vietnam. His letters to Diane were brief and sporadic; in the last six months she hadn't heard from him at all. Leena was afraid to think about the reason for his silence.

CB

Robert strode back into the dining room, sat down at the head of the table, and hungrily piled mashed potatoes, salad, and two pieces of fried chicken onto his plate.

"Ed says not to worry—he'll figure something out," Robert told Leena with a look of relief and elation that she wasn't able to share. She had a bad feeling about this, and for the first time she wondered whether Maija's belief in premonitions was justified after all.

CB

Three weeks later, the entire Martin family sat in the high school auditorium to watch Joel receive his diploma.

Robert had not yet worked out a solution for his son's problem. His colleague Ed had told him that it was too late to file for conscientious objector status. The draft board members no longer gave any credence to last-minute proclamations of religious piety, or "squeamishness," as they called it. They had seen too many cases of sudden conversions prompted by unlucky lottery numbers—conversions designated as "timely" in draft-board lingo. So Robert had been leaning hard on several deans at the university, trying to circumvent the usual red tape and get Joel admitted as a student. After that, a deferment could be arranged. He was optimistic, but the rest of the family seemed steeped in gloom.

Then, on the day of graduation, Joel disappeared.

CB

Two days later, on Saturday, June 7th, Maija called Leena for their usual monthly chat.

"Hi, Leena. How are you? How was the graduation ceremony? Did you have a big party?"

There was no answer from Leena, but Maija could hear something that sounded suspiciously like sobbing on the other end of the line.

"Leena? What's wrong? Tell me what's wrong."

"Oh, Maija, Joel has disappeared. After the ceremony he said he was going to a party with Mike but he'd be home later so we could all celebrate. Robert bought an expensive bottle of French champagne, and I baked a cake, and the girls had decorated the living room with paper streamers and funny signs. But Joel never came home.

"We waited and waited, and finally I called Mike's mother, but she hadn't seen Joel all day—not since she congratulated him after the ceremony. Mike didn't know where he was either. Robert finally called the police, but the officer on duty said there was nothing he could do except file a missing person report. He tried to reassure Robert—told him that teenagers were always disappearing for a few days. He gave Robert a bunch of corny lines about kids 'testing the waters,' and 'sowing wild oats.' Robert got all huffy and said that his son was no ordinary teenager, and he ended up telling the officer to go to hell."

"Why would Joel suddenly disappear?" interjected Maija before her sister could continue.

"He was going to be drafted," wailed Leena. "His number was 15, and he never filed for C.O. status, and now it's too late. We've all been going crazy worrying about what to do. Robert has been trying for weeks to get him into the university, but Joel hadn't planned on going to college right now. He wanted to travel around and then get a job somewhere.

"When he didn't come home by two in the morning, I went into his room and found his backpack and sleeping bag missing from the closet. His hiking boots were gone too. I don't think he's coming back." And then Leena started sobbing again.

Maija was shocked to hear what was going on. She had assumed that the Martin family would have prepared for such an eventuality. She and her sister never discussed politics, but she was fully aware of Robert's liberal views. She had been so certain that he would make plans to protect his son from the draft.

"I'm so sorry about this, Leena. But I'm sure Joel will call you soon. He probably needed to get away for a while to think. I'm sure he'll show up in a couple of weeks. Don't worry too much. He's an intelligent kid, and he knows how to take care of himself."

And then Maija tried to distract Leena's attention by telling her about her own plans for the summer. She had signed up for a couple of seminars, and she was also looking forward to spending some time with Briitta, who would be home for the next few months. She was nineteen now, and she had just finished her first year at art school in L.A. She had a job as a lifeguard at the Ballard pool for the summer.

When the hour was up, Maija offered Leena some more words of reassurance and then said, "Call me as soon as you hear from him."

But several months later it turned out to be Maija, and not Leena, who was the first to hear from Joel.

☙

On a Wednesday in the middle of October, the phone rang at three in the afternoon. Leena dashed into Robert's study and picked it up on the second ring. She'd gotten into the habit of snatching up the phone before anyone else could get to it, hoping against hope to hear Joel's voice on the line at last.

But it wasn't Joel. It was Maija.

"Maija?" said Leena, suddenly confused. She had just talked to her sister a couple of weeks ago, and today couldn't possibly be Saturday since the girls were in school. It was so rare for Maija to call outside of their monthly ritual that Leena felt her heart leap with fear. Something must be wrong. Something must have happened.

"Now don't worry, Leena, there's nothing wrong," Maija hastened to tell her sister, aware that her call might trigger a sense of panic. She knew how tense everyone was since Joel had disappeared. "I'm calling to give you some good news. Joel showed up here on Monday night."

"Oh, thank God," whispered Leena, the color draining from her face. For a moment she could hardly breathe and she felt herself sway slightly, but then she took a firm grip on the phone and said loudly, "Let me talk to him."

"Now, Leena, I think you should sit down and take a deep breath. You're not going to like what I have to tell you. This isn't going to be easy."

"What do you mean?"

"He's not here anymore. I drove him across the border to Canada yesterday afternoon. He'll be safe from the draft there, but he can't come back."

"What? What are you talking about? Why didn't you call me when he showed up? Why did you wait until today? Why didn't you tell Joel to call us? How could you let him leave without talking to me? Do you know where we can reach him?"

"I'm sorry, Leena, but he didn't want to talk to you. I tried to persuade him to call, but he adamantly refused. He told me he wanted to go to Canada, and he asked me for help. Then he made me promise not to call you until he was gone. He seemed very bitter, and I thought it was more important to get him out of the country quickly than to waste time arguing. And I was afraid he would just take off again if I pressed him too hard—then none of us would know where he went."

Maija paused and waited for Leena to say something, but there was only silence on the other end of the line.

"We left around noon," she continued, "and after we got across the border, I drove him to the outskirts of Vancouver and let him off at a gas station. Then I drove the rest of the way into the city and stayed overnight in a downtown hotel. I thought it would look suspicious if I went back across the border the same day.

"I'm sorry, Leena. There isn't much more to tell you. But he promised to send a postcard once he got settled. He looked fine, just a little worn out from all the traveling he's been doing. He said he'd been hitchhiking through the Southwest and then came up the coast to Seattle."

There was still no response.

"Leena? Are you OK?"

Leena was standing rigidly in front of the desk in Robert's study, clutching the phone receiver in her right hand. She had heard every word that Maija said, but she couldn't seem to make sense of it all. Her mind was still fixated on the phrase, "he didn't want to talk to you," and all the words that followed could just as well have been Arabic or Greek.

Suddenly something broke inside of Leena, and all the hurt and anger, dammed up during months of uncertainty and worry, came spilling out.

"What do you mean he didn't want to talk to us? How *dare* he say something like that! He disappears for four months and never even lets us know whether he's dead or alive, and then he shows up in Seattle and he won't *talk* to us? We've all been sick with worry and nobody's been getting any sleep. The other day Robert came down for breakfast and started shouting that the coffee was always cold and he wasn't going to stand for it anymore. And then he actually threw a piece of toast at me. He just went berserk. He's been calling all of Joel's teachers and friends so much that most of them refuse to talk to him anymore. Mike's mother finally told me that if Robert didn't stop pestering her son, she was going to have to call the cops. The police officers down at the station already think Robert's completely nuts, because he keeps bugging them too. He even hired a private detective, but the guy finally told him to stop wasting his money—there was nothing he could do.

"And the girls act as if it's all our fault. They're hardly ever home anymore, and when they *are* here, they go in their rooms and shut the door. They've barely said a word to me since Joel left, and they won't talk to Robert at all. They treat us like lepers, and the other day Kirsti started screaming at me that I was no better than some Greek woman named Medea. I had to look it up in the encyclopedia to find out what she was talking about.

"Who does he think he is, making us all worry like this, and then taking off for Canada without saying a word?

"How could you let him do it?" Leena sputtered, all the fury of her disappointment shifting to her sister. "Don't you know what we've been going through? Don't you know how frantic I've been? Don't you have any sympathy at all?

"How could you let him leave without calling me? How *could* you? My own sister. It's not fair. It's just not fair." And then Leena slammed down the phone.

She had never hung up on Maija before. Over the years they had had disagreements and heated discussions, but never an outright fight. The distance separating the two sisters had made them more tolerant of each other's foibles and faults. They treasured their Saturday conversations too much to spoil them with petty bickering or quarrels. And they needed each other too much to upset the balance by fighting or holding a grudge.

But this time Leena couldn't stop herself. The hurt was too deep, the disappointment too bitter. The swift violence of her action reverberated through her body, leaving her panting for breath, and her eyes stared murderously at the black dial phone on the desk. She wanted to strangle it, she wanted to crush its simple, innocuous form with her iron fists.

Then sorrow welled up inside her and washed away her rage. And she sank down onto Robert's swivel chair, leaned over the desk, and cradled her head in her arms. She wept for a long time.

⋈

Maija sat on her gray-striped sofa holding the dead receiver in her hand until a persistent beeping tone reminded her to hang up the phone. She was a little dazed by Leena's burst of anger, but she wasn't surprised at the way the conversation had gone. She could understand her sister's mixed feelings: relief, shock, disappointment, and then fury. She would probably feel the same way if it was *her* child who had disappeared, although Leena had always been more emotional and quick to react.

Maija sighed heavily and leaned back against the cushions, rubbing her hand wearily over her eyes. She hadn't slept at all last night. The hotel room was much too hot but she couldn't set the thermostat properly, and the windows wouldn't open. She complained to the front desk, but they said there was nothing they could do. She hated these new hermetically sealed buildings and didn't trust any of the propaganda about the wonders of modern temperature control. At five a.m. she finally put on her clothes and went out for a walk.

She loved Vancouver. She had driven up from Seattle many times before, and she knew the downtown area quite well. It reminded her of a European city with all its flower stalls and fruit stands, the displays of bright blossoms and gleaming ripe apples invitingly spread out onto the sidewalks. The city had a cosmopolitan and sophisticated air that homespun Seattle, still clinging to its frontier mentality, would never be able to match.

After strolling for an hour through the streets of the city, which was busily awakening to another work day, Maija headed for her favorite tea shop, "The Empress." It was a popular place, and they always opened early to catch the before-work crowds, but Maija was lucky enough to find a table next to the window. She ordered a pot of Earl Grey tea and two scones with strawberry jam. She was feeling the need to pamper herself after the turmoil of the past two days.

CB

At ten o'clock on Monday night, Maija had been sitting in the living room, deeply absorbed in a new novel by Tove Ditlevsen, a Danish author she had recently discovered when she was browsing through the foreign-language collection at the downtown library. It was a tense and chilling story about a woman writer in the grip of madness, and Maija had just reached the section where the main character discovers, to her horror, that the other patients in the hospital ward all have donkey heads instead of human faces, when the doorbell suddenly rang.

Maija jumped so hard that her book tumbled to the floor, and Edith leaped off her lap in an arc of white fur. Who could be ringing the bell at this time of night? She wasn't expecting anyone.

Maija stood up, grabbed a heavy glass candleholder as a precautionary weapon, and then peered through the tiny peephole in the front door. In the dim glow of the porch light she could see a scruffy-looking young man standing on her doorstep fiddling with the straps of a bulky backpack cutting into his thin shoulders. He was wearing a denim jacket, blue jeans, and a pair of well-worn hiking boots. When he raised his head and looked up at the light, Maija realized that she was staring at her nephew Joel.

"Joel!" cried Maija, setting the candleholder on a nearby bookcase, and then shoving back the deadbolt and throwing open the front door. "Joel! Come in, come in. How are you? We've all been so worried about you."

Joel stepped inside, looking relieved to find his aunt at home. "Hi," he said, smiling tentatively. "I wasn't sure you'd recognize me."

"Of course I do," said Maija, patting his shoulder, acutely

aware of how changed he was from the laughing young man in the last set of Christmas photos that Leena had sent her. "Can I help you get that backpack off? It looks so heavy."

"No, thanks. I can do it," said Joel as he slipped his arms out of the straps and slowly lowered his pack to the floor. Then he stood there for a moment, feeling a little off balance as he was suddenly freed from all that weight on his shoulders.

Before he could object, Maija took a firm grip on the backpack and started lugging it out of the room. "I'll just put it in the guest room," she said over her shoulder.

For a moment, Joel gazed aimlessly around Maija's living room, feeling awkward and ill at ease. Then he knelt down and unlaced his boots, taking them off and setting them next to the front door. He didn't want to track up Maija's carpet. When he noticed how filthy his socks were, he took them off too and stuffed them inside his boots. Edith watched this whole procedure intently and then trotted over to sniff at his feet. Joel bent down and picked her up, and she immediately started to purr.

"She likes you," said Maija, reappearing in the doorway. "Come on into the kitchen and I'll make you some food. I was just about to have a cup of tea myself."

Joel tried to say that he wasn't hungry, but Maija insisted. So he sat down at the kitchen table, holding Edith on his lap, as Maija bustled around, putting together a snack. He turned out to be a lot hungrier than he thought. The greasy burger and fries he'd eaten that afternoon in Portland hadn't really filled him up, but he'd gotten used to a certain hollow feeling in his stomach during the months he'd been on the road. He only allowed himself one real meal a day because he was trying to make his cash last as long as possible.

Maija surreptitiously eyed Joel as he devoured the two turkey sandwiches, the kosher dill pickle, and the slices of apple on his plate. He looked completely worn out, and she felt an urge to smooth back the strands of blond hair that kept falling into his face, but she knew it would injure his pride if she did. And in spite of his fatigue, Joel had an air of resolute determination about him that told her he wouldn't tolerate any coddling or sympathy. She wondered what he had been through these past four months, but she wasn't about to ask.

When Joel pushed back his plate, Maija set a tray of Finnish *pulla* on the table for dessert. She had baked the day before, and the whole house still smelled of cinnamon and cardamom.

The fragrant spices reminded Joel of home. Leena had baked often when the Martin children were small, and Joel remembered how he would sneak into the pantry, lift up the white cloth covering the pale blue bowl, and pinch off a piece of the rising dough and stuff it into his mouth. He loved the yeasty smell and elastic consistency of *pulla* dough. When the rolls came out of the oven—aromatic, crusty, and shiny from the egg and butter that had been brushed on top—Joel and his sisters would crowd around the kitchen table, impatiently waiting for the *pulla* to cool off enough to eat. And for the next few days the whole Martin family would gorge themselves on Leena's wonderful Finnish rolls. But she seldom baked anymore, except at Christmas time.

Joel eagerly reached for a piece of *pulla* filled with raisins, but he set the roll down on his plate without tasting it. He suddenly looked like a bitter old man, full of gloom and resignation.

They sat in silence for a moment, and then Maija said

cautiously, "Wouldn't you like to call your parents? It's almost one in the morning in Milwaukee, but I know they wouldn't mind you calling this late—they're all so anxious to hear from you."

"I don't want to talk to them," muttered Joel, as his shoulders tensed and a frown appeared on his face.

"But they've been so worried about you. You should at least…"

"I'm *not* going to call them," Joel almost shouted. "I can't talk to them. I just can't." And then he picked up the *pulla* and chewed on it glumly, as if it were cardboard.

How could he explain to his aunt that he felt betrayed by his parents? How could he tell her that he blamed *them* for his predicament?

The news of his draft status had struck him like a deadly bolt of lightning—he couldn't understand how it could possibly be true. He knew plenty of guys who had gotten an exemption because they had allergies or flat feet or homosexual tendencies (real or successfully feigned for the occasion). His friend Mike was 4-F just because of a bad knee that he'd injured playing football. And plenty of other guys had received high lottery numbers. Even Bruce Stanton, who was all gung-ho about joining the Marines after he graduated, was in no danger of being drafted; *his* number was 322.

But the United States government had decided that Joel Martin was fit and able-bodied, and any refusal to "serve" was a federal offense punishable by a minimum sentence of two years in prison. Joel started having nightmares filled with jangling keys, resounding footsteps, and slamming, steel-plated doors.

He would see himself standing naked in the middle of a bare and windowless room. Suddenly iron bars would descend from the ceiling and crash down all around him, trapping him in a cage like an animal in the zoo.

Joel kept expecting to wake up from this horrible dream, but every hour that passed only brought him closer to the day he would be drafted.

And it was clear that his parents were not going to be able to save him.

After the arrival of the letter, Leena would greet him every day after school with an anxious look on her face. When he couldn't come up with a joke or funny story to regale her with as usual, she would start chattering about the weather and pour him a glass of juice or chocolate milk, hovering over him as if he were sick with the flu. She seemed determined to avoid any mention of the letter or its likely consequences.

Leena made all of Joel's favorite dishes, but the mere sight of the steaming food on the table sickened him, and he felt as if he were caught in a perpetual remake of "The Last Supper." Eventually he stopped coming home for dinner.

When he sneaked into the house through the back door later in the evening, his mother would be standing at the sink washing dishes, daydreaming as usual, and his father would be sitting in the living room, engrossed in a book. Neither one of them ever noticed him come in.

Robert's frenetic calls and floundering negotiations were even more unbearable to witness than Leena's mutely suppressed panic. He was a whirlwind of activity, calling lawyers, colleagues, and administrative officials at the university. He spent hours on the phone in his study, and then rushed off to appointments downtown, returning home full of warnings and advice. But in reality he was getting nowhere, although he kept professing his optimism to the rest of the family. Secretly, he was thinking of urging Joel to join the coast guard or some other equally inconspicuous branch of the armed services in order to avoid the war. But in all the flurry and commotion, he had not once taken the time to have a serious talk about the whole situation with his son. And this is what Joel resented the most.

It was the same old story. His father always thought he knew best how to handle any family problems. After a great deal of scurrying and lots of false leads, Robert would eventually settle on a solution, which he expected the rest of the family to applaud and accept. He seldom consulted any of them for their opinion or advice. In this case, he never even asked Joel whether he wanted a college deferment at all.

And the truth was, a deferment did not seem that much different from a prison term to Joel. In some ways it was worse, because it was bound to confine him for longer than the minimum two-year sentence. He would have to keep reapplying, and keep on studying, and in the meantime his real plans and dreams would have to be put on hold. He could spend the next four or five years deferring his life just as he deferred his military service.

He couldn't do it. As he saw it, his only alternative was to flee. He was going to have to run away, and that meant heading for Canada. He reached this decision two days after he read the letter, but he didn't tell anyone of his plans, not even Mike or Elly.

During the last weeks before graduation, Joel indifferently let his mother hover in anxious silence as he watched his father fumble in vain for a rational and workable solution. He felt a cold disdain for their confusion and ineptness. He hated them for their impotence and inevitable failure. He secretly raged at them for not warning him, for not telling him that someday he would be trapped and cornered and no amount of joking or bantering would win his release. He blamed them for his own ignorance and blindness.

He would go through the formalities of graduation, but then Joel had made up his mind to leave. He was hoping that his aunt in Seattle would help him. If not, he would try to cross the border himself.

∞

Joel looked up at Maija and said bitterly, "I can't talk to my parents right now. I hate them for what's happened to me. Why didn't they warn me? Why didn't they ever give me any real advice?

"Mom never wants to hear about anything bad. She always expects me to clown around and tell jokes, and she pretends that all the bad things in the world will just go away if you ignore them. She's always mooning around and daydreaming, and she still treats me like a kid.

"Dad thinks he's some kind of superman who can single-handedly solve everybody's problems. He's a perpetual do-gooder who thinks he can change the world. When Martin Luther King was murdered, Dad went to all kinds of meetings on the south side with his liberal friends to discuss the 'rising racial tensions.' He's a hopeless optimist. But he's all talk. He doesn't want to think about the gunfire we could sometimes hear from across the river. Or the riots and curfew and the National Guard trucks rolling through the streets. He's not any better than Mom. They don't ever see what's really happening until it's too late."

Joel sat hunched over the table, his left hand still clutching half of the raisin-filled roll, his face dark with despair. Maija felt so sorry for Joel, but there was nothing she could say to console him.

"I need to get into Canada," Joel continued quietly, his anger now under control. "Otherwise I'm going to be drafted, and I don't want to end up in Vietnam."

"All right," said Maija simply. "I think I can help you." And then they discussed how best to cross the border. There had been lots of newspaper stories about American draft dodgers trying to sneak into Canada, and the border guards had been cracking down lately. Maija was going to have to smuggle her nephew across.

An hour later Joel was sound asleep in the guest room with Edith curled up on the bed beside him. Maija had the distinct impression that it had been a long time since Joel had slept in a real bed, and she decided to let him sleep as long as he liked in the morning. It was only a three-hour drive to the border, and she could use a good night's sleep herself. She wanted to be as rested and relaxed as possible when she faced the border guards in Blaine.

CB

The next afternoon, thirty miles south of the Canadian border, Maija pulled the Plymouth off the highway and drove down a deserted dirt road until a dip in the land blocked the car from view. Then Maija got out and unlocked the trunk. Joel came around to the back of the car and climbed in. She covered him up with a dark wool blanket as best she could and then piled some books and her overnight case in front of him. They had to leave Joel's backpack behind in Seattle because there wasn't enough room for both him and his belongings. After he got settled, Joel was going to send a postcard to his aunt to tell her where to send his things.

Maija gave a few more tugs at the blanket, then closed the trunk, and got back into the driver's seat.

In spite of her calm manner, Maija was worried, and she fervently hoped that she wouldn't be asked to open the trunk. Her amateur attempts to conceal Joel were not going to fool the border guards. She had no doubt that if they opened the trunk, he would be discovered at once.

ോ

When Maija pulled up to the customs and immigration booth at the Canadian border and stopped the car, her heart sank as she caught sight of the surly-looking guard stepping out to approach the Plymouth. His uniform was impeccable, his shoes were superbly polished, and his pen was already poised over his official clipboard with the customs seal emblazoned on the back. He looked like a real stickler for the rules. She wished she had chosen the guard in the other booth—maybe he would have been more friendly—but it was too late now.

Maija rolled down her window and made a point of smiling as she handed the officer her olive-green American passport. A driver's license was usually sufficient, but this time she was taking no chances that the officer might notice her accent and question her citizenship. She didn't want to get caught up in unnecessary questions or lengthy explanations.

"Good afternoon," the officer greeted Maija gruffly, opening her passport and perusing the second page. "And what is the purpose of your trip to Canada today, Mrs. Lahteenen?" he asked, putting the stress on the second syllable. It was a common mistake.

"I'm just going up to Vancouver to do a little shopping, officer. I have a few days off from my job, and I just love your beautiful city." Maija inwardly cringed at the gushing tone of her own voice, but the guard was still staring at her passport, and it was making her nervous.

"Born in Finland?"

"That's right. But I've been a naturalized citizen for almost twenty years, and I'm proud to be an American," said Maija, laying the patriotism on thick.

"I remember reading about Finland after the war," said the guard unexpectedly. "Only country to pay back all its war debts."

Then he snapped Maija's passport shut, handed it back to her through the window, and stepped away from the car as he said, "Have a nice visit."

For a split second Maija gawked at him, but then she nodded, turned the key, and drove smoothly past the raised barrier and into Canada.

Half an hour later, Maija parked the Plymouth behind a boarded-up old gas station and opened the trunk.

"It's OK now," said Maija. "We're in Canada." And when Joel climbed out of the car, his legs stiff and unsteady, Maija couldn't resist giving him a little hug.

"Thank you," said Joel, relief and gratitude evident in his face.

And then they stood there awkwardly for a moment, not quite sure how to say goodbye.

Maija put her hand in her pocket and pulled out something wrapped in a piece of soft leather. She undid the wrappings to reveal an ancient-looking knife with a carved wooden hilt and a sharp-edged blade.

"I want you to have this, Joel. It's my father's *puukko*. He inherited it from *his* father, and it's been in our family now for six generations. It may not look like much, but Isä set great store by it, and it was the only personal treasure he took with him when we fled from Karelia. Right before I left Finland for the United States, Isä gave me the *puukko* and made me promise to take good care of it. He said it would give me strength in my new life. I want you to have it."

And then Maija placed the knife in Joel's hand along with an envelope containing five hundred dollars in cash. She had robbed her emergency fund that she kept hidden in the back of the hall closet in case of an earthquake or a bank failure or a war. And without another word she got into her sky-blue Plymouth and pulled out of the gas station, waving her left hand out of the open window as she drove away. She didn't look back.

Six

Briitta Lahtinen drove up to her mother's neat yellow bungalow in Ballard and parked her coughing and sputtering Toyota in the driveway behind Maija's 1953 Plymouth. She turned off the noisy engine and sat there for a few minutes, staring straight ahead. She couldn't believe that old car was still running. The paint looked as shiny and unblemished as ever, the chrome of the rear bumper gleamed, and only a small patch of rust on the tailpipe revealed any sign of wear at all. She had to admit that the Plymouth actually ran better than her own miserable vehicle, which seemed to spend more time in the shop than on the road. Maija was always admonishing her for owning a Japanese car.

"Why don't you trade in that foreign jalopy and buy yourself a good American car? Look how much trouble it keeps giving you, and it's only eight years old. I've had my Plymouth over forty years, and it still runs perfectly. Detroit was the birthplace of the automobile, not Tokyo. Why give your dollars to the Japanese? We make great cars in this country—you should be driving an American car."

Briitta sat in the driver's seat, smiling at her mother's staunch defense of American industry. Maija wasn't blindly patriotic, but she took pride in the achievements of her adopted country. And she could never understand Leena's initial reluctance and then steadfast refusal to give up her Finnish citizenship.

When Maija arrived in Seattle with her new husband in the fall of 1948, she began studying English in earnest, and she set her mind on becoming an American citizen as soon as possible. Her decision to leave Finland had been a painful one, and the parting with her parents and friends had not been easy. But whatever sorrow, remorse, or trepidation she may have felt in private, she outwardly expressed only cautious optimism and curiosity about her new life in America. She had chosen to marry a foreigner and to live in his country, and she wanted to participate fully in their life together. And her recent experience as a refugee during the war had made her all the more determined to obtain the protection of citizenship. She never wanted to be displaced from her home again—for any reason.

When Pentti died suddenly after only five years of marriage, Maija was glad she had insisted on becoming an American. It gave her greater peace of mind, and it was much easier for her to find a job.

For Maija, the change of citizenship was merely a formality, a way of legitimizing her presence in the United States. It had nothing to do with her perception of herself—at heart she would always be a Finn, and no amount of official documentation could ever take that away from her.

For Leena, however, the matter of citizenship touched the very core of her identity. She knew it was irrational. She knew it was silly to live so many years in America and make it her permanent home, but never formally acknowledge her decision. For years she had to report to the post office for the annual registration of her resident alien status, presenting her original green card, issued in 1948, with the photo of a thin and scared new bride on the front.

And, of course, she didn't have the right to vote. The kids found it odd that Robert would go off to the voting booths without Leena. For a long time the girls thought that voting was strictly a male privilege, just as they associated driving with the male domain. It took Kirsti a long time to overcome her fear of driving—in fact, she didn't get her license until she was in college.

When Kirsti finally decided to take lessons, she ended up with a driving instructor named Mr. Krell, who had been recommended by a friend, but she had her doubts about him from the moment he drove up to the house that she shared with four other students. From the front window she watched him get out of his ugly little car and attach a hand-lettered sign to the back: "Student Driver" it said, with the "er" scrunched onto the right side. Whoever made the sign hadn't planned ahead. Mr. Krell himself was no specimen of neatness or cleanliness, and it took Kirsti only one lesson to decide he was a lush as well. She declined any further association with him, and Robert finally agreed to teach her to drive during summer vacation. But even after Kirsti got her license, she never felt entirely relaxed behind the wheel of a car.

Luckily, the fact that her mother was ineligible to vote didn't affect Kirsti in the same way, and she never neglected to fulfill her civic obligations.

By the time Leena reached her sixtieth birthday, she had to

admit even to herself that she felt more American than Finnish. She and Robert had been back to Finland several times, since Robert's work was highly regarded in Scandinavia, and from time to time he was invited to give lectures and seminars in Helsinki. Leena enjoyed these trips, but she was always relieved to return to their home in Milwaukee. She found the Finns more reserved, less friendly, and even gloomier than she remembered. And she knew she could never live there again. Even so, she stubbornly balked at exchanging her Finnish passport for an American one. It was her one link to the past, to her parents and her childhood, and she just couldn't bear to give it up. But she didn't condemn her sister's decision to do otherwise—in fact, she saw it as a sign of superior wisdom and strength.

In spite of Maija's keen determination to become an American, she was never blithely uncritical of her adopted country. She frequently had harsh things to say about the faults of the U.S. government, and if you got her started, she could go on for hours about the failings of the American education and welfare systems. But she would always end her harangues by saying that America was a young country, and she was willing to give a child the benefit of the doubt while he was still learning.

She was much less sympathetic to the shortcomings of the Europeans. She would reproach them for their bickering and fighting, for their mutual wariness and refusal to work together. She protested that they should know better by this time—after all, they had had centuries to figure out how to live together happily and harmoniously, and they had been through enough devastating wars to teach them the necessity of peaceful cooperation.

But then Maija would contradict her own virtuous condemnation of European chauvinism by letting slip some scathing remark about the Soviet Union. She could never forgive them for taking Karelia. She had left her homeland in the hands of the enemy, and she would never think of the Russians in any other way.

⚬

Down the street a motorcycle started up with a roar, and Briitta's thoughts returned abruptly to the present. She shivered a little and then sighed heavily. She opened the door and got slowly out of her car. It was Monday morning, and she hadn't been back to the house since her mother's death on Thursday. But she couldn't put it off any longer. She needed to come back and finish the preparations for the funeral.

Briitta walked up the path to the back door and then stood on the stoop, rummaging in her Michael Green leather bag for the key. But she couldn't seem to find it, and she finally had to sit down on the top step and dump everything into her lap. She picked up the hodgepodge of items, one by one, and dropped them back into her bag: a small spiral-bound sketchpad; three felt-tip pens; a No. 2 pencil with the eraser bitten off the end (she was embarrassed to admit that she still had that childhood habit); a red-and-black silk scarf; a pair of sunglasses; her brown leather wallet; three crumpled pieces of Kleenex; half a roll of peppermint Lifesavers; a pack of Doublemint gum; two tampons in a plastic holder; a silver tube of Clinique lipstick (her favorite color: raspberry glacé); and a gold barrette that she didn't use anymore, ever since she'd cut her hair.

The left side of her hair now reached just below her ear, while the right side was three inches longer. Max said it made her look mysterious and sexy, and he liked the way a wing of her hair fell slightly over her right eye. Briitta thought it a little severe for her rather sharp features, but she wanted something more bold than her usual, straight, shoulder-length style. She was forty-five, after all, and it was about time that she tried something different. And she had finally come to the conclusion that a conventional or proper appearance was not expected of a successful graphic artist. Even her corporate clients seemed to relish her daring new look.

Maija, on the other hand, had been obviously aghast when she saw Briitta's new haircut for the first time. But maybe it was the touch of henna, lending her brown hair a reddish gloss, that had shocked Maija more than the uneven lengths.

Briitta laughed softly. She had always thought it strange that her mother could be so conservative about clothes and appearance, and yet so open-minded about art.

She found the house key at last, nestled on top of the little black velvet pouch that she always carried with her. Briitta put the key down beside her on the step and then picked up the pouch. She loosened the drawstrings and poured the contents into the palm of her right hand. It was her collection of good-luck charms, small objects that she had acquired over the years, reminders of some propitious occasion or talismans given to her by friends. There were brilliantly colored pebbles, a silver heart-shaped charm, a tiny yellow-striped feather, and a small purple bear with a turquoise heartline—a Zuñi fetish from her drive through New Mexico a few years back. The oldest object was a small gold ring with an oval amethyst stone.

It was a gift from her mother on her twelfth birthday, and even though Briitta had stopped wearing the ring years ago, she still carried it with her wherever she went.

∞

On the morning of January 7th, 1962, Briitta found the little gold ring couched in the white satin of an elegant jewelry-store box sitting next to her plate at breakfast.

"Oh, Äiti," sighed Briitta, reverting to the Finnish word for mother, which she seldom used anymore, now that she was getting older and felt increasingly embarrassed by her mother's foreign accent and eccentricities. "It's so beautiful."

"I'm glad you like it," said Maija, pleased by her daughter's reaction but hiding her own joy behind her perennial reserve. "In Finland, it's customary for girls to receive a gold ring when they're twelve. It's a symbol of womanhood. It will bring you good fortune and happiness. Look at the inscription."

Briitta plucked the ring out of its satin nest and held it up close to her face, peering at the inside of the gold band. In tiny cursive script it said: "*Rakkaus, taide, ja sisu.*"

"What does it mean?" asked Briitta.

"Love, art, and perseverance," Maija told her daughter, giving her a rare look of unveiled affection. Then she brusquely stood up and began making them breakfast.

At Briitta's request, they were having fried eggs, sunny-side up, with bacon and biscuits. There was a frosty glass of Welch's grape juice next to each plate, and a new bottle of Heinz 57 ketchup stood on the table because Briitta liked to add a couple of dollops to her eggs. It was Maija's firm conviction that on your birthday you could have whatever you wanted to eat, no matter how bizarre or unhealthy it might seem. And she promised herself not to complain when Briitta poked at her eggs with a strip of bacon, making the slimy yolks ooze out across her plate, to be sopped up by a doughy biscuit. This habit of Briitta's normally made Maija shudder; on any other occasion she wouldn't have let her get away with it. But a birthday was a day of exceptions, and Briitta always took full advantage of her privileges.

Landmarks in life were never allowed to pass unnoticed and holidays were always faithfully observed in the Lahtinen household, with all the appropriate decorations and foods. As a child, Briitta frequently boasted to her friends about the extra holidays she got to celebrate because of her Finnish heritage. Her favorite was Midsummer, the longest day of the year, when they would drive out to Camano Island or some other place on the water and light a big bonfire on the beach. Maija and her Finnish friends would sing old folksongs, and the kids would pull foil-wrapped *piirakat* out of the coals. Briitta always thought the food tasted better outdoors, especially those traditional, boat-shaped rye pasties, filled with rice and topped with butter and chopped egg.

The chilly Midsummer celebrations were among Briitta's fondest memories. She would sit on an old wool blanket, wearing shorts and a pair of red rubber boots, her hands clasped around her bare legs, the hood of her summer parka pulled up against the inevitable light drizzle. She would watch the water lapping against the shore as the fire crackled, shooting bright sparks into the air. And she would listen to the murmur of voices speaking her mother's incomprehensible language, the familiar cadences flowing around her, soothing and melodic.

Midsummer always made her think of her father, but she wasn't sure why. She was only three when he died, and she remembered very little about him. She knew his face only from the pictures that her mother had hanging on the living-room wall and others pasted into a leather-bound scrapbook. But she remembered holding his hand. He had a big warm hand, and if she closed her eyes she could still feel his fingers closing around her own small fist. Maija told Briitta that when she turned three, Pentti bought her a pair of ice skates. On weekends he would take his daughter to a local rink, where the two of them would skate for hours, holding hands. Briitta didn't remember the outings to the skating rink, but she did remember the touch of his hand.

She was so young when her father died—struck down by a hit-and-run driver on East Madison Street on an inexplicably bright April day—that she didn't know him well enough to mourn him properly. But she always felt the loss of his presence, and she frequently wondered why Maija didn't find her another father.

When Briitta was older and tried to tease her mother about getting a "gentleman caller" (a quaint phrase from a Tennessee Williams play that she'd read in English class), Maija would laugh lightly and promptly change the subject. The one time Briitta insisted on discussing the topic, her mother looked her straight in the eye and said, "I loved your father dearly. I'm not interested in taking another husband." The deep sadness in Maija's face and the tone of finality in her voice told Briitta that this was not a matter for levity or teasing, and she decided not to broach the topic again.

This did not mean that any mention of love or amorous attachments was taboo or off-limits in their house—on the contrary. In spite of her serious demeanor and intellectual pursuits, Maija took a great interest in reports of celebrity marriages and infidelities. She read all the gossip columns in the *Seattle P.I.*, and she always managed to glean the juiciest tidbits of information from the weekly tabloids in the racks next to the check-out stand in the grocery store—although she would never dream of actually paying money for one of those "sleazy rags," as she called them. And she didn't hesitate to tell Briitta her own dire predictions about which newly married couples were not likely to live happily ever after but were headed instead for divorce. Her pronouncements weren't limited to movie stars or famous authors either.

"Didn't I tell you those two wouldn't last?" Maija might say to Briitta at dinner, mentioning a neighborhood girl about to be divorced from her high-school sweetheart, whom she had married only a year before. "I knew it the minute I saw their wedding picture in the paper. There was something about the way she was standing. And he had such a smug look on his face. I could tell that they didn't have a chance."

Briitta grew up with lots of little rituals surrounding the subject of love. Peeling an orange had to be done with the greatest care: using a sharp knife, she had to start at the top and slowly rotate the orange, cutting a spiral all the way to the bottom, and making sure that the peel came off in one piece. Then Maija would tell her to stand in the middle of the room and toss the pungent curlicue over her left shoulder. The peel would land on the floor in some intricate swirl, supposedly forming the first initial of the name of her future boyfriend.

On New Year's Eve, Maija would cover the kitchen table with old newspapers, and then place a bucket of cold water on top. She would get out a big soup ladle used only on that occasion, put a lump of lead into it, and then hold the ladle over the small gas burner on the stove. When the lead was thoroughly melted, she would hand the ladle to Briitta, who would swiftly pour the molten lead into the cold water. Then they would both huddle around the bucket and pull out the metal, now frozen into some weird and fantastical shape. And Maija would interpret Briitta's fortune for the coming year—which inevitably held promises of love.

One year they decided to tell Edith's fortune, and when Briitta pulled the lead out of the cold water, it looked exactly like a big rat with a long, squiggly tail. Briitta laughed so hard that tears came to her eyes, and even Maija couldn't hold back her mirth. For a long time the piece of metal sat on the kitchen windowsill next to a delicate sand dollar and other shells picked up from the beach.

In spite of Maija's little rituals about love, in spite of her interest in titillating gossip and tales of infatuation, she was completely serious when it came to educating her daughter about sex. Even when Briitta was small, Maija would answer her questions about human anatomy with precise detail, explaining the functions of the human body with all the sober forthrightness that came from years of teaching. When Briitta turned eleven, her mother gave her the same formal lecture about the mechanics of sexual intercourse that Leena had received so many years before in Finland—with the same stern warning about premarital sex tacked onto the end. But this time Maija added some practical advice about birth control, realizing that her old-fashioned views were not entirely relevant in 1961. And when Briitta got her first period, Maija solemnly congratulated her on becoming a woman, and then took her out to a fancy restaurant to celebrate.

On Valentine's Day, Briitta would always receive her share of little love notes from boys in her class, and in fourth grade she even found a fifty-cent piece taped to the back of a big lacy Valentine from Bobby Swenson—a true sign of devotion, according to Maija. But Briitta was never very interested in school dances or other social events organized for children her age. She wasn't shy, but she preferred solitude and quiet, and she spent most of her time sketching and painting in her room. Every evening she would curl up with a book in the big armchair next to the window in the living room. She was a voracious reader, going through three or four books a week. By the time she was ten, she'd made her way through everything of interest on the children's shelves at the Ballard Library, and Maija finally convinced the librarian to let Briitta take out books from the adult section.

In high school, Briitta's friends were all a little odd. She naturally gravitated to the misfits and outcasts, the would-be poets, precocious musicians, and genius mathematicians, all loners by virtue of their abnormal intelligence or creativity. But most of them lacked the simple social skills that would smooth their way into an acceptable job or career. And Maija worried that Briitta, with her artistic bent and innate reserve, might spend her life wandering from one unsatisfactory job to another, frustrated and alone. But Maija had underestimated her daughter's sense of steady purpose, which was part Finnish stub-bornness, part American self-confidence. And Briitta had done quite well, moving straight from art school into a challenging job.

When Briitta was twenty-seven and already making a name for herself as one of Portland's most innovative young graphic designers, she finally met a man she could love. It was on a Monday, and she had decided to stop at the Java Jive in Tacoma.

The first time she set eyes on the place, she couldn't resist going inside. The building was an exact, two-story replica of a yellow coffeepot with a red handle and spout. A pink neon sign enticing passersby to "Dine & Dance" flickered over the doorway. The interior turned out to be equally wacky, with an eclectic display of old junk covering the walls, and elaborate cages filled with dozens of exotic birds creating an incredible din. Ever since, she had made a point of stopping in on her way home from visiting her mother in Seattle—even though the coffee was always terrible.

On that overcast Monday afternoon in September, Briitta was the only customer, and she sat at the counter sipping the wretched coffee, thinking about an ad campaign she was working on for Tillamook cheese.

"Could you pass the sugar?" a man's voice shouted over the screeching of the birds.

Briitta turned her head in surprise. She hadn't noticed anyone come in, but there was a pleasant-looking, dark-haired man sitting a few seats away from her. She slid the glass bowl filled with little sugar packets along the counter.

"Thanks," said the man loudly, giving her a charming smile. "Quite a place, isn't it? I'm thinking of using it for a set in a movie."

And for the next ten minutes, they shouted remarks back and forth, before finally agreeing to sit outside where they could have a real conversation in peace and quiet, even though it was a little cold. Max Goldman worked for an upstart production company in Portland, mostly doing offbeat TV commercials, but hoping to make full-length films someday. Briitta told him of her own work with a prominent advertising agency, and her plans to set up business for herself after she got a few more years of experience.

They saw a lot of each other during the next few weeks.

One night, after Max fixed them a stunningly good steak dinner and they'd polished off two bottles of red wine, they fell into Max's bed and spent the rest of the night energetically entwined. Briitta had never met a man who was both unashamedly smart and fun in bed. And she was enormously relieved to find that he sincerely admired her own talents and accomplishments. So many other lovers had disappointed her with their petty jealousy and inane feelings of inferiority, brought on by their insatiable need to compete, even if graphic design wasn't their field. They couldn't stand sharing their bed with a successful woman. At last she had found a man who could be both a tender lover and a real partner.

A week after they moved in together, a package arrived via UPS at their Portland apartment.

"I am sending you my mother's copper coffeepot," said the enclosed note. "Every happy household has one—it's a Finnish tradition. Love, Maija."

Briitta told Max that the battered-looking pot was a family heirloom, and he promptly set it in a place of honor on the mantelpiece. For the next eighteen years the coffeepot accompanied them wherever they went: to Germany when Briitta spent a couple of years working in Hamburg for a high-powered ad agency, and to Greece when Max took on a long-term project, filming a documentary about recent archaeological excavations. Whenever they moved, the coffeepot was meticulously packed and carefully transported to their new home, to be once again prominently displayed. And it was the one possession that Briitta knew she would truly miss if some kind of catastrophe ever left her bereft of all that she owned.

cs

Briitta sat on the steps of her mother's house with the image of Max's familiar face before her. She had sent him a telegram about Maija's death at the same time she sent one to Leena. He was in Sri Lanka directing his first feature-length film, and he wasn't due back for another month. He had called her on Thursday afternoon, while she was still at her mother's house, and offered to fly home for the funeral. He could only stay two days, but he would do it if she needed him.

His voice was full of sorrow and concern. Max had never been close friends with his mother-in-law, but he admired Maija's air of competence and calm authority. He realized early on that her natural reserve precluded any real intimacy, and he respected her wish to remain on a somewhat formal footing. It actually suited him better than trying to force a filial relationship. But they had always gotten on well together.

Maija liked Max's solid equanimity and his dark good looks. She was fascinated by his film work, and they often had long talks about art. Max enjoyed kidding his mother-in-law about her passion for certain paintings, especially the bleak and mournful canvases of Edvard Munch. "I don't know, Maija," he would say, leafing through a new volume of Munch reproductions. "Don't you think he's a little too cheerful?" And then they would both smile at their long-standing joke.

Maija was pleased to see Briitta finally settle down with such a goodnatured and intelligent man. She found it reassuring to see her daughter so happy and secure. Her only regret was the absence of any grandchildren, but this was not a subject she ever mentioned—even to Leena.

Briitta sighed. She had been sorely tempted to accept Max's offer to come home for the funeral. She wanted to sink into his comforting embrace and listen to words of sympathy whispered in her ear. She wanted to lapse into a state of lethargy and torpor and block out all her grief, letting him attend to the necessary plans and arrangements. She wanted to cling to his arm and let him deal with all the condolences offered by acquaintances and friends. But in the end, she had told him not to come.

"Are you sure?" Max repeated, feeling himself torn by the pain he could hear in his wife's voice but wanting to honor her decision.

"Yes. I'll be OK. Besides, you know you shouldn't leave the film right now. And Maija would understand. She was so proud when she heard you were finally going to direct a real movie. She wouldn't want you to interrupt your work.

"And Robert and Leena are both coming. I think Joel will be here too. I don't know if Elly or Kirsti can make it, but a lot of Maija's friends will probably be at the funeral. It's going to be a simple affair. Maija left instructions about what she wanted—that makes things a lot easier.

"Don't worry. I'm fine. Really I am."

So Max told her to call him the following morning, and then he said he loved her, and he hung up.

Briitta had put down the phone, all at once feeling desperately alone. The emptiness of the house suddenly overwhelmed her, and she decided she had to leave. When Max called, she had been in the midst of cleaning up the house, which was in disarray from the general commotion of the morning.

The medics—four genuinely kind and sympathetic young men—had moved some of the furniture when they brought the stretcher into the house. And when they left with her mother's body, Briitta couldn't bear to watch. She fixed her eyes on the dents in the gray carpet where the hall table normally stood, and rushed to move it back in place as soon as everyone was gone. Then she put clean sheets on the beds, did a load of wash, and straightened up the house. On the floor in Maija's room, she found a volume of poems by Edith Södergran. Briitta picked up the book and was about to put it back on the shelf, but instead took it into her own bedroom and slid it into the side pocket of her briefcase.

She made herself eat a piece of toast and drink a glass of orange juice, even though she had no appetite at all. But she didn't want to faint from low blood sugar when there were so many things she had to think about.

Thank God for her mother's foresightedness. A few years back Maija had arranged to have the legal ownership of her house transferred to Briitta so there would be no problems with probate court when she died. And only a couple of weeks ago, right after the big windstorm in Seattle, Maija had called Briitta to remind her that all her important papers were in the top drawer of her desk. "Just in case something happens to me," she had said in that voice full of foreboding that always made Briitta secretly smile. She was used to her mother's superstitions and seldom took them too seriously. But this time Maija's presentiments had turned out to be right.

Briitta felt tired and anxious to leave, but she still had several more things to take care of before she could go. She canceled the rest of her Seattle business appointments and called her office to say she would be taking a week off. She talked to the funeral home and told them there would be no casket or burial. Maija had been quite adamant about that.

"Don't put me in one of those horrible boxes," she would say to Briitta whenever she was in a particularly gloomy mood. "I can't stand the thought of lying next to all those strangers in some desolate cemetery without a tree in sight. And all those awful monuments and artificial flowers—they're just too gruesome." Then Maija would make her daughter promise to scatter her ashes in the woods when she died. And Briitta intended to honor her mother's wishes.

She was quite surprised to find the name of a pastor among Maija's papers and to read her mother's request that the memorial service be held at St. John's Church.

Maija had always dismissed organized religion as too narrow and limited, too dictatorial and confining. She once told Briitta that she wished she could share the animistic beliefs of her ancestors—regrettably, she had been born several centuries too late. Maija always insisted on attending services on Christmas and Easter, but she had no affiliation with any particular church, and it was more a matter of carrying out a ritual than any expression of piety. In fact, Maija seldom attended the same church twice, a practice that made Briitta wonder whether her mother wasn't still hoping to find a modern-day shaman in the guise of some minister or priest.

When Briitta called Pastor Hansson, she was glad that she got his answering machine. She didn't think he would find her sudden burst of laughter entirely appropriate, under the circumstances. But she couldn't help laughing at the sound of his voice. His accent was exactly like her mother's. The heavy rolled "r's" and long vowel sounds told her at once that he was a Finn, and that was why he had been chosen. When she finally reached him, the pastor murmured his condolences, and then they agreed on Wednesday afternoon for the funeral. He said he was aware of Maija's wishes for the service and offered to meet with Briitta on Tuesday to discuss the details.

A few hours later, Briitta left the house, having gathered up her overnight bag, her briefcase, Maija's folder of important papers, and a box full of family photos. She locked the front door with trembling fingers. The emotional turmoil of the day was suddenly too much for her, and she didn't have the strength to head back home to Portland. Friday morning would be soon enough for that. Instead, she drove downtown and checked into the Sorrento, deciding she needed the comfort of a gracefully old-fashioned luxury hotel. She ordered a light dinner from room service: poached salmon with rice, and a small fruit salad. But when the food came, she just sat and stared at it, unable to eat a thing. Then she got out of her clothes and crawled under the eiderdown cover, leaving the bedside light turned on. And even though it was only nine o'clock, she fell fast asleep and didn't wake up until seven the next morning.

Briitta put the little gold ring and her other talismans back into the velvet pouch and pulled the drawstrings tight. She placed the pouch in her leather bag and picked up the key from the step. Until this very moment, she had planned on going inside to air out the house and prepare things for the reception following the funeral. It was her childhood home, after all, and as familiar to her as any lifelong friend. But now she had changed her mind. They would hold the reception somewhere else.

This was more Maija's house than hers. And Briitta suddenly felt that the presence of a large group of people, even though they were family and close friends, would be an unbearable intrusion. This house was her mother's private sanctum, and even though they had all spent time with Maija here, it had always been at her invitation and on her terms. Now Briitta had the strong sense that this house was temporarily closed to them. And she had to respect that feeling.

In a week or two she would be able to come back. She could envision herself sitting on the sofa, looking at Maija's glass candleholders on the coffee table, and browsing through Pentti's book on symbolist painters that he managed to finish before he died. She could imagine sitting at the kitchen table and drinking a cup of Earl Grey tea from a white china teacup, remembering other occasions when she had sat there having a companionable talk with her mother. And she could even picture herself sorting through Maija's things, putting aside small mementos for her cousins.

She would come back, and the house would welcome her once again. But not today.

Briitta slipped the house key into her jacket pocket and slowly got to her feet. She walked down the path to her car, got into the driver's seat, and turned on the noisy engine. For a moment she stared at the yellow house with its rhododendron bushes and the two Douglas firs. Then she backed the Toyota into the street and drove away.

Seven

"Gate 7," announced Robert, leaning down to pick up his garment bag and briefcase, which he had left with Leena while he checked on the boarding gate. "We have to hurry. The flight leaves in twenty minutes." He started off toward the United concourse, but Leena didn't move. "Leena? Are you coming?" he asked anxiously, looking over his shoulder.

Robert was more worried than ever about his wife. She hadn't shed a single tear since the brief moment of surrender on Thursday when he held her in his arms after the telegram arrived. Since then Leena had been unusually quiet and withdrawn, and it was this uncanny composure that concerned Robert most.

Leena was normally a cheerful person who always tried to look on the bright side of things. She had little adages for every occasion, and when one of the kids was feeling blue, she always used to say "keep your tail up," and then propose some kind of project as a distraction. Kirsti once tried to convince her mother that the proper expression was "keep your *chin* up," but Leena continued to use her own variation, unabashed.

She hated conflict and would avoid it at all costs, which frequently meant swallowing her own opinion or caving in to someone else's decision—usually Robert's. In the beginning he had found it frustrating that his wife was so ready to relinquish her own views in favor of his, but he soon got used to it. By now, he would have been sincerely startled to learn that Leena differed with him on any matter of importance. Every so often, some totally unpredictable issue or situation would dredge up Leena's deeply embedded streak of stubbornness, and she would refuse to budge. On those occasions, Robert knew it was futile to argue or to try to impose his own will. But normally Leena was an amiable and obliging person.

He was grateful to Leena for her lighthearted spirit and cheery disposition. He loved her bright clothes, and he admired her weavings, although he had no real sense of design himself. His appreciation of art was dictated more by convention than by any personal preferences. In fact, Robert was quite often completely unaware of his surroundings, and it was only at Leena's prompting that he would notice some new knickknack on the sideboard or a recently finished weaving now hanging over the bed. Robert's university life consumed most of his thoughts, and he counted on Leena to provide a congenial home for him to retreat to at the end of the day. And for forty-seven years she had done just that.

But Leena was never very good in a family crisis.

She would attempt to maintain a sunny outlook in the face of whatever disaster had struck, but her panic was always clearly evident beneath the façade. When Joel disappeared, she was in such a jittery state that Robert finally urged her to ask the doctor for some tranquilizers to calm her nerves. But Leena insisted she was perfectly fine. When Elly revealed that she was pregnant, Leena assumed such an air of officious concern that Elly couldn't stand to be in the same room with her. And when Kirsti called to tell them of her impending divorce, Leena chattered on and on about the latest dramatic reconciliation on "As The World Turns," as if a soap opera could offer her daughter any realistic comfort or advice.

Eventually the strain of her charade would prove too great for Leena, and Robert would find her sobbing into her pillow when he came to bed. Then he would wrap his arms around her and hold her tight. After a few more weepy days, Leena would be her old self again.

This time Leena was too subdued and calm. Robert intended to keep a close eye on her, wanting to be there to console her if she suddenly fell apart—and he assumed that eventually she would.

Leena picked up her large handcarry bag and followed Robert through the airport terminal. She was still debating with herself about what she should wear to the funeral. She hadn't been able to decide between her favorite red dress and the one somber outfit that she owned—a light-gray linen suit. In the end she had impatiently stuffed both of them into her bag, along with a random assortment of toilet articles and two changes of underwear. Whenever they traveled, she usually made careful lists of everything she wanted to take along. This time she couldn't be bothered. She felt irritable and depressed, and this morning she had almost told Robert that she wasn't going to go. But then she gave herself a little shake and muttered, "Don't be silly. Of course you have to go." At the last minute, she grabbed the Walkman that Elly had given her last Christmas and a couple of cassette tapes and put them in her purse.

Two seconds after Leena got in the car, she told Robert she had forgotten something and ran back into the house. She pulled the manila envelope with the old photograph out of her button box, hurriedly relocked the front door, and jumped back into the car. Robert was getting anxious about the time, but he didn't say a word.

They finally made it to the airport, after fighting the fierce rush-hour traffic. Robert was cursing under his breath as he drove through the parking garage, looking for a vacant slot. At last he found one on the top floor, but he was still trying to contain his temper as they waited for the elevator that would take them to the main terminal. Leena seemed unperturbed.

Now they were putting their bags on the belt at the security checkpoint, and Robert had to give Leena's arm a little squeeze to get her moving again. She was staring at the security monitor, mesmerized by the x-ray image of the contents of her purse. Robert picked up his bags and set off at a healthy pace, keeping an eye on his wife as she trailed along beside him.

Every time he came out to the airport, he couldn't help thinking about the way things had changed—all this glass and gleaming construction replacing the humble brick building of the old days, back when no one worried about hijackings or concealed weapons. When the kids were small, he often brought them out here to watch the planes take off and land. It was one of their favorite Sunday afternoon excursions.

In those days, Billy Mitchell Field was an exciting place, and air travel was an exotic adventure beyond their wildest imagination or meager income. Robert's salary as an assistant professor didn't stretch very far, and he seldom had even a spare nickel for the mechanical horse that the kids always wanted to ride in the airport terminal. He would lift them up onto the shiny red horse with the flaring nostrils and tell them to pretend they were galloping off into the sunset. And he would attempt a few horse-like whinnies, say "giddy-up," and then glance around to see whether anyone besides the kids had heard him. He was always a little worried about undermining his professional image.

When Robert and Leena reached Gate 7, the boarding had already started, and they joined the short line of passengers heading down the jetway. The flight was apparently only half full, and Robert was looking forward to having extra room on board. He hated being cramped up next to some stranger. And on full flights an obnoxious toddler would inevitably be kicking the back of his seat. Ten minutes later, the plane took off and they were on their way.

Leena pushed the button in the armrest to tilt her seat all the way back. Then she put on the headset of her Walkman and closed her eyes. Robert placed his briefcase on his knees, snapped open the lid, and pulled out the most recent issue of the *Journal of American Psychology*. There was an article by J. S. Aimsworth that was supposed to be interesting. He placed the briefcase on the empty seat next to him and opened the journal to page 52. But the type seemed to blur before his eyes, and he found his mind wandering.

He couldn't stop thinking about the last time he visited his mother in Tennessee.

That was ten years ago, and Sarah Anne Martin was in her early eighties, but she hadn't lost her imperious bearing or her commanding tongue. Robert had taken to visiting her every few months since the doctors told him that she was slowly declining in strength, in spite of her claims to the contrary.

"Those young docs don't know what they're talking about," Sarah Anne would tell her son when he queried her about her latest medical tests. "You can see for yourself that I'm fit as a fiddle. I haven't been sick a day in my life, and I don't intend to start ailing now."

Then Robert would set up the cribbage board or take out the ancient Scrabble game, and they would spend the next few hours bickering over the score or quarreling about Sarah Anne's faulty spelling. She seemed to suffer from little lapses of memory, and halfway through the game her spelling would start to deteriorate. If Robert challenged a word, she would insist on looking it up in the dictionary. When she realized her mistake, her dismay would automatically give way to impatience, and she would announce that she was bored with the stupid game anyway. And then they would switch to backgammon or gin rummy or crazy eights.

Robert's father had died fifteen years earlier of a heart condition complicated by a serious drinking problem that Sarah Anne never was willing to acknowledge, even to her son.

One day she simply moved all of her personal belongings into the back bedroom upstairs. In every other way, her attitude toward her husband remained unchanged. She was still the charming hostess whenever William Martin invited some of his former business cronies over for dinner, and she never uttered a word of protest as the liquor flowed freely during the course of an evening. She continued to address her husband affectionately as "Pappy," and she would gently tuck a light blanket around him whenever he fell asleep in his old brown recliner. She loved her husband, and she would always regard him with tenderness, but she could no longer share his bed. The hazy stupor of liquor frequently made him a stranger to her, and she had to retreat to her own room on the second floor. It would never have occurred to her to confront her husband or demand that he change his ways.

William, for his part, was initially puzzled by his wife's sudden withdrawal to the upstairs bedroom, but he never associated it with his own behavior. He assumed it was one of Sarah Anne's peculiar whims, and he resigned himself to waiting it out, as he had done so many times before during their long years together. He had married a strong-willed woman, and he was used to her spirited opinions and odd caprices.

Neither one of them was in the habit of examining or discussing their relationship.

The last time Robert visited his mother, she seemed as feisty as ever, and she put up a steadfast resistance when he tried to persuade her to rent out a room to a nurse or a university student. She was even more averse to the idea of moving to a smaller place or to some kind of retirement home. Robert was worried about her living all alone in that enormous old house, and Mrs. Tulley, the cleaning woman, had told him that Sarah Anne had started sleeping with a loaded shotgun under her bed. She was afraid of burglars.

"There are too many criminals on the loose these days," she

told her son when he brought up the subject of the gun. "A lady doesn't feel safe anymore, even in her own bed. I'm just taking a necessary precaution—and I won't be afraid to use it if I have to. I'm not a bad shot, you know."

Sarah Anne looked at Robert with steely eyes. "I'm perfectly capable of taking care of myself. I don't want some stranger living in my house and making a lot of racket. I need my peace and quiet, and I don't like being disturbed. I've lived in this house for fifty-five years, and I'll stay here until I die."

Three weeks later, when Mrs. Tulley arrived on Monday morning to clean the house, she found Sarah Anne sitting in William's old recliner, a crocheted afghan thrown over her legs. She was wearing a brown silk dress and a string of pearls with matching earrings. Her hands were folded in her lap, and she had a stern but dignified look on her face. It took a few minutes before Mrs. Tulley realized that Sarah Anne was dead.

☙

Robert refocused his gaze on the pages of the psychology journal he was holding in front of him. He suddenly missed his mother terribly, and he had to swallow hard to hold back the sob threatening to escape him. My God, here he was getting all choked up and sentimental when Leena was the one who needed to cry. Robert took a gulp of cold coffee from the plastic cup sitting on his tray and glanced over at his wife. She still had her eyes closed, but he didn't think she was asleep. He could see the little wheel of the cassette in her Walkman slowly turning, and he wondered what she was listening to.

For years the Martins had belonged to a mail-order record club, and they had gradually acquired an extensive collection of American musicals and folksongs. When the kids were small, Mitch Miller was Leena's favorite, and she used to sing along to his records as she cleaned the house. Leena readily admitted that she didn't have much of a voice, but that didn't spoil her enthusiasm, and Robert often found her humming some popular show tune when he came home from the university. Lately, Leena seemed more interested in listening to classical music, especially when she was weaving.

Robert reached across the empty middle seat and patted his wife's hand. Leena opened her eyes, gave him a little smile, and then settled herself more comfortably, leaning her head on the pillow she had propped against the wall of the plane. She always requested a window seat when they traveled, and she loved to watch the shifting patterns of the landscape passing far below. But today she had no interest in the view, so she had pulled the plastic shade all the way down. She was listening to Bach's *Cello Suite*, arranged for guitar and played by Segovia—a beautifully soothing piece.

She saw herself drifting in a gently rocking rowboat on a lake in northern Karelia. She had pulled the oars into the boat and moved into the bow, where she was now sitting on the floorboards, with a dark blue cushion supporting her back. She was twenty years old. She was wearing a long white dress with little cap sleeves and dozens of tiny silver buttons down the front. Her arms were resting along the sides of the boat, and the sun felt warm on her bare skin. She tilted her head back and looked up at the clear sky as she listened to the rippling water lapping against the wooden boat. She was all alone on the lake. She felt peaceful and calm. Her mind was empty and light; she was thinking of nothing. And then she fell asleep.

Cʒ Cʒ Cʒ

Elly tugged on the seat belt strap, trying to pull it loose from where it was lodged between the armrest and her seat cushion. Finally she got it free and slipped it into the metal clasp. Then she leaned back with a sigh of exasperation. She hated flying. She never used to feel that way, but the older she got, the more she dreaded getting into an airplane. Her stomach always churned, her head ached, and her level of anxiety soared. The mere thought of flying made her a nervous wreck, and the reason for this particular trip was making her feel even worse. When she and Rachel had checked in at the ticket counter, most of the seats were already taken, so they weren't even able to sit together. At least they both had aisle seats. Elly liked to know that she could get up and race to the bathroom at a moment's notice if she had to.

Elly leaned over and glanced up the aisle. Three rows ahead, she could see her daughter's long blonde hair trailing over the armrest as she leaned her chin on her hand. She was apparently reading the copy of *SPIN* magazine that she'd bought in the Denver airport. It was hard to believe that Rachel was already twenty-two years old. Her new job as backstage manager at The Club seemed to suit her. And she'd finally given up her standard uniform of torn t-shirt, cut-offs, black tights, and clunky workboots in favor of a more sophisticated, but hip, wardrobe. Elly had been telling her daughter for years that she should show off her figure while she was still young and thin.

"Put on a slinky dress once in a while—you'd look terrific," she'd say. But Rachel would just laugh and tell her mother that she liked the clothes she wore and would feel funny in anything else. Then Elly would bite her tongue to stop herself from voicing any further objections. She already sounded too much like her own mother. Rachel's new job, which gave her high visibility in the local music scene, seemed to have changed her attitude about clothes. Earning a decent salary probably helped too.

When Rachel got into the car that morning, Elly was impressed once again by her daughter's natural poise and air of maturity. She was turning out to be a confident and striking young woman, and Elly had to give a lot of the credit to John. His calm manner and easygoing approach offset her own hot-headed temperament, and he had frequently saved mother and daughter from tearing each other's hair out. Elly couldn't imagine what their lives would have been like without John.

⋘

It was sheer luck that Elly ended up going to the Raymond Dexter concert at the Odd Fellows Hall on Capitol Hill that rainy September night. (Although Maija would later insist that it was fate, and that luck had nothing to do with it.) Rachel had just turned two, and she was going through a cranky stage that was starting to wear down Elly's patience. Their tiny one-bedroom apartment didn't allow much breathing space, and the constant worry about finances was adding to Elly's gloom.

The monthly fee at Rachel's daycare center had just gone up again, and she didn't know how she was going to manage on her salary from the library. She didn't want to take any more money from her father.

When Maija called to ask if she'd like a babysitter for the evening, Elly was feeling so dejected about things that at first she turned down the offer.

"Are you sure you don't want me to take Rachel?" Maija pressed her gently. "It's Friday night, so she could stay here until tomorrow, and you can have some time to yourself."

Elly had to admit that would be nice, so they agreed that Maija would pick Rachel up in half an hour and keep her until the next morning. Elly was grateful for her aunt's generosity and support. Maija never interfered, and she respected Elly's wish to find her own way. But she was always available to offer assistance or advice when asked, and she had been a mediating force between Elly and her parents.

After Maija left with Rachel, who adored her great-aunt, Elly roamed restlessly around the apartment, opening the refrigerator door but finding nothing she wanted to eat, picking up Rachel's toys from the living-room floor, and throwing dirty clothes into the bathroom hamper. When she went through the pockets of her jeans before tossing them in too, she found a flyer that Denise had given her for a concert of new music by Raymond Dexter that was taking place that night.

"You've got to come to it," Denise had urged, her eyes full of ardent admiration for this "great composer," as she called him. Denise was always taking Elly to the weirdest concerts and performances, trying to convince her that Seattle was a hot-bed of avant-garde talent. Elly willingly tagged along, but she remained skeptical about the crowd of artists and musicians that Denise touted so highly. Most of their work seemed more pretentious than innovative, and Elly had a strong feeling that it was the artistic *image* that obsessed them most. Few seemed to have the stamina and discipline required to produce any work of real integrity.

At the last concert she'd attended with Denise, the performer had ended the show by setting fire to all the rice-paper lampshades in the room. This act of spontaneous mischief had sent Elly stomping out in disgust. She told Denise that she didn't see the point of "artistic" vandalism.

But maybe this concert would be different. Raymond Dexter was internationally known on the New Music scene. And besides, she desperately needed to get out of the apartment. So Elly decided to go.

The performance had already started by the time she made her way up the dingy stairway to the second floor of the Odd Fellows Hall, frequently rented out for just such occasions. The large room was packed full, with most people sitting on the floor and gazing raptly at the spotlighted figure of Raymond Dexter. Elly squeezed her way inside and sat down a few feet from the door.

The high-pitched sounds emanating from the small stage were at first excruciating, then bearable, and finally merely tedious. Three or four notes repeated over and over, produced on either a synthesizer or some kind of sitar—Elly couldn't see well enough over the crowd to be sure what the instrument was. She lasted half an hour, then quietly got up, stepped over the people huddled near the door, and slipped out.

"Hard to take, isn't it?" said a voice as she exited. She looked up to see a tall blond man wearing jeans and a heavy blue sweater leaning against the banister out in the hallway. "His compositions are fascinating from a theoretical perspective, but I've never been able to sit through a whole concert. The repetition always fries my brain."

Elly smiled in agreement. "My friend Denise says he's one of the best new composers, but I have to admit this kind of music bores me to tears. When I start getting the urge to stand up and screech, then I know it's time for me to leave. I always feel like the kid in that story about the emperor's new clothes. Everybody is oohing and ahhing about all his jewels and his ermine robe, and I'm the only one who can see that he doesn't have any clothes on."

The blond man laughed. "John Campton," he said, offering Elly his hand. "Nice to meet you."

"Elly Martin," she replied, taking note of the warmth of his handshake.

"I was just thinking of walking over to the B&O for some coffee. They've got great desserts too. Want to come along?" he asked.

Elly hesitated. She hadn't dated anyone since Frank, and the consequences of that affair had made her a little wary of men. But John Campton had a pleasant manner, and she liked the way he laughed. And Elly was sorely in need of more stimulating company than the nice but rather restrained librarians she worked with all day long.

"All right," said Elly. "Sure, let's go."

cs

A flight attendant pushed a rattling cart down the aisle. Elly asked for a Diet Pepsi and then sat back, smiling to herself. Their three-hour conversation at the B&O over coffee and German chocolate cake had led to many more evenings together. John was ten years older and divorced. It turned out that he taught music theory and composition at the same college where Elly worked, but his real passion was the blues. He had an enormous record collection that covered a whole wall of his apartment. And he wasn't a bad piano player himself.

Occasionally Elly would spend the night at John's apartment, and he would play her a marathon of blues records before they finally tumbled into bed together. Elly couldn't believe the raunchy lyrics of some of the tunes they listened to. The bawdy words, driving rhythms, and melancholy notes appealed to her own raucous and moody nature, and she wondered why she'd never listened to the blues before. Elly even persuaded Denise to skip a few New Music concerts and go with her to the one blues club in town. She had finally discovered her kind of music.

John got into the habit of stopping by the library and whisking Elly away for lunch. Her colleagues started teasing her about her professor boyfriend, and eventually she stopped contradicting them.

Three months after they met, John was offered a good teaching position at the university in Denver, and one day he asked Elly to marry him.

When she hesitated, John said quietly, "Come with me, Elly. We don't have to get married right away if you don't want to, but come with me. I can't bear to leave you and Rachel behind. You're my family now, and I need you."

For several days Elly wrestled with her doubts. She had vowed to make it on her own. She wanted to prove to her father and the rest of the family that she was capable of making a comfortable life for herself and her daughter. But she had to admit that the strain of working full-time and trying to raise Rachel alone was more overwhelming than she had thought. The library job earned them just enough money to get by, with nothing left over. Elly was barely coping, and she wasn't happy alone—she was happy when she was with John.

Finally Elly called Maija to ask her advice.

"Forget about your pride," Maija said bluntly. "If you know in your heart that John is the right man for you, don't turn him away. Take a chance, Elly."

That's all she said, but it was enough.

And even though their marriage had had its ups and downs, John's even temper and steady faith in their relationship had seen them through. Elly got involved with a small experimental theater and started taking acting classes at the university. Before she knew it, she had racked up enough credits for a B.A. in theater, and for the past fifteen years she had taught modern drama at a Denver high school, while continuing to act in local productions. Every few years they would go back to Seattle to visit Maija, and Elly had kept in close touch with her aunt by phone.

And now here she was, sitting in this god-awful airplane, going to Maija's funeral. Elly felt sick to her stomach at the sound of that word "funeral." It couldn't be true. It just couldn't. She refused to believe it. She wanted to think of Maija sitting at her kitchen table, sipping a cup of tea, and lamenting the dearth of trees in her neighborhood. Maija couldn't be gone. She just couldn't be.

Elly angrily yanked her Walkman out of the seat pocket in front of her and jammed the headset over her unruly curls. She wasn't going to think about it anymore. She was going to listen to the blues. She put in a cassette of Billie Holiday tunes, pushed the "play" button, and closed her eyes.

ࠃ

Rachel Campton twisted around in her seat and glanced back down the aisle. She saw her mother tapping her fingers on the armrest, keeping time to the tape she was listening to. She had her eyes closed, and she was smiling slightly. Rachel sighed and turned back to her magazine. She tucked a strand of her long hair behind her ear, and gazed at the ad for a new Calvin Klein fragrance on the page in front of her. God, it stinks, she thought. Why do they always have to douse the magazines with such nauseating perfume? She ripped out the entire page and slid it under her seat.

The guy sitting next to her gave her a strange look and then went back to his laptop computer. He'd tried to put the move on her when she first sat down, but one snide remark and an icy glare had stopped his feeble attempts at conversation. She was in no mood to talk to goofy-looking nerds or any other strangers today.

It seemed so unreal that Maija could be dead. Rachel had never imagined the possibility, even though she knew of plenty of other people who had died well before the age of seventy-five.

But Maija was as much a part of her life as her parents or grandparents. And the visits to Seattle over the years had meant a lot to Rachel.

She had been reliving those visits in her mind ever since she heard the news of Maija's death. But the memory of one particular summer kept coming back to her. It was the summer when Maija's cat Edith died.

ೞ

Rachel was eight years old, and she and her mother were spending their three-week vacation in Seattle, staying with Maija. It was a hot July day, and they were all sitting outside around the patio table under the blue-and-white-striped umbrella. Elly was reading a script for a new play, and Maija was going over her notes from the class she had just finished. That summer she had switched from education seminars to art history classes. She had already made her way through the art of antiquity and was now looking forward to the Renaissance. Rachel was poring over a Wonder Woman comic book, but she was feeling restless and thirsty, so she went inside to get some cold juice.

She found Edith stretched out on the kitchen floor. Rachel took one look at her poor body, wheezing and shuddering, and ran back outside to get her aunt. It was obvious that Edith had taken a turn for the worse. She was twenty years old, and Maija called her the "Grande Dame" of the cat world. She told Rachel that in human terms Edith was well over a hundred.

Until recently, Edith had been as alert and curious about things as ever. But she had begun sleeping through more and more of the day, sometimes not budging from her place on the sofa until dinnertime. Then she would jump down onto the floor, stretch her creaking joints, and hover around her empty dish in the kitchen until Maija took notice and opened a can of food.

Edith's fur had lost some of its sheen lately because she just didn't have the energy to finish her usual regimen of washing. The vet said there was nothing really wrong with her; old age was just naturally slowing her down.

Maija hurried into the kitchen with Rachel and Elly close behind. She slid her hands under Edith's quivering body and gently lifted her up. Then Maija went into the living room and sat down on the sofa, stroking her old friend's white fur.

"I think I'll just sit with her for a while," she said quietly. "The vet says there's nothing he can do for her."

Elly took Rachel's hand. They tiptoed out of the room and went back to their reading outdoors. An hour later Maija came out and told them that Edith had died.

Rachel burst into tears, and Elly cried too.

Later that afternoon, Maija held a funeral for Edith. She put her body into a beautiful old hat box lined with a soft wool scarf, and then they buried Edith in her favorite spot under the thick shrubbery in the back yard. Maija read a funny poem about a cat, and then she gave a short speech in Finnish that Elly and Rachel couldn't understand.

Back inside, Maija told them to put on their best clothes—they were going out for dinner. And then she drove them over to a fancy restaurant on Shilshole Bay.

When it was time to order, Rachel was still looking teary-eyed and glum. "I'm not hungry," she told her aunt, biting her lip to keep from crying.

Maija asked the waitress to give them a few more minutes to decide. Then she looked across the table at Rachel.

"I know you're sad about Edith," said Maija. "I'm sad too, and I'm going to miss her a lot. It's important to mourn for her. But she lived a long time, and I think we should celebrate the good life that she had.

"Every time I sit down to watch TV, I'm going to think about Edith jumping up into my lap, and settling herself so she was in the best position to see the screen. She didn't care what was on—she'd watch anything—but she'd prick up her ears at any fast movement. And she loved shows about animals, especially baby bears. She even liked those old Roadrunner cartoons you always used to watch.

"And every time I drive up to the house, I'm going to remember how Edith would be sitting in the window, making that strange juddering noise and eyeing those big old crows on the telephone wires as if she thought she could really catch them.

"When someone dies, Rachel, the important thing is not to forget them."

Rachel looked into Maija's somber but sympathetic eyes. She sniffled a little, nodded, and then picked up the menu.

They all ordered baked salmon for dinner. It was Edith's favorite.

ↄ⒊

The seat belt sign was flashing overhead, and Rachel blinked rapidly. She pulled the paper napkin out from under her glass of orange juice and blew her nose. Then she fastened her seat belt and leafed through the rest of her magazine as the plane began its descent into Seattle.

⊗ ⊗ ⊗

Kirsti's plane had some kind of mechanical problem in Copenhagen that delayed the departure for an interminable eight hours. By the time she arrived in Seattle after a nine-hour flight, she was completely exhausted and out of sorts. She made it through immigration and customs, answering the routine questions in a daze. Then she had to relinquish her bag again, take the airport subway to the main terminal, and wait for her blue suitcase to show up on another baggage carousel. By that time it was already ten p.m., and all she wanted was a hot shower and a comfortable bed.

Kirsti slung her heavy handcarry bag over her shoulder, picked up her laptop in one hand, and took a firm grip on her big suitcase with the other. She was only staying a week, but she had never learned to travel light. She was normally a practical person, and she knew it wasn't sensible to pack so many clothes. But she had finally decided that the comfort of taking along everything she thought she might need was more important than paring her belongings down to a bare minimum. Traveling was stressful enough without worrying in advance about exactly what she would wear each day of the trip. The only time she regretted her indulgence was when she had to haul around her own bags.

She trudged out to the curb and flagged down the Shuttle Express van headed for the U District. She had decided to stay at the Meany Towers so she would be near the university. She was hoping to meet with her old friend Lydia, who taught Women's Studies, and she planned to spend some time in the library too.

Kirsti stared at all the new buildings on the Seattle skyline as they drove past downtown. She hadn't been back here in fourteen years, and things had changed a lot since then. She kept reading articles about Seattle being the "most livable" city in the U.S., but she remembered Maija's comments on the subject the last time they'd talked on the phone a few months back.

"It's nothing but hype dreamed up by some politician to entice people with money to move here. Even Briitta says it's a ridiculous scam, and she's been in the ad business for years. And all those Southern Californians are going to spoil the city. They buy up property, sight unseen, just because it's cheap by L.A. standards. Then they build huge ugly houses and drive around in expensive cars, talking on their car phones and endangering everybody else on the road. They're even starting to move into Ballard—I saw a Mercedes and two BMWs parked right down the block."

Kirsti smiled. She hadn't seen Maija since the spring of 1981 when she'd finished her doctorate and accepted a teaching position in Comp Lit at the University of Minnesota. But every few months they would talk on the phone, and her aunt was always as opinionated as ever.

The van pulled up to the hotel, and Kirsti got out, glad to leave her bags in the hands of the bellhop, who waited for her to check in and then showed her up to her room on the eighth floor. Kirsti gave him a five-dollar tip, too tired to chide herself for being so extravagant. She took a long hot shower, put on her royal-blue cotton nightgown, and climbed into bed.

She lifted her feet to pull the covers out from the end. She hated the way American hotels tucked in the sheet and blanket all around the edge. She didn't like the feeling of snug imprisonment, and hotel blankets gave her the creeps. They were always made of some synthetic fiber that didn't allow your skin to breathe.

Kirsti turned off the reading light and closed her eyes. She was so tired, but her body was suddenly reminded that it was already eight a.m. in Copenhagen, and she couldn't fall asleep.

She was a little surprised to find herself back here in Seattle. At first she hadn't intended on coming to the funeral. The expense of a transatlantic plane ticket was reason enough not to come. And she wasn't sure she could face seeing her entire family gathered in one place, especially on such a sad occasion.

For the past few years, she had felt herself more and more estranged from all of them. There was nothing specific that she could point to and say "that's why I can't talk to them anymore" or "that's what makes me feel so hollow inside." She had simply begun to feel uncomfortable with her accustomed role in the web of family relationships.

Kirsti was fed up with being the sensible and dependable one. She was tired of being the steady, competent, and serious person that her family always counted on. She was tired of being the perennial good student, the dutiful daughter, and the reliable sister.

She was weary of the predictable pattern of their phone conversations: she discussed politics with her father, family news with her mother, and theater or music with Elly. She rarely heard from Joel. When he did call, she could never get beyond his bantering and teasing to have any real conversation. None of them wanted to hear that Kirsti might be unhappy about something or unsure of herself. Maija was the only family member Kirsti felt she could talk to about her worries, without running up against a wall of preconceptions. And her aunt seemed genuinely interested in hearing about her work.

Kirsti was tired of following the expected career route, moving steadily up the university ladder to her present position as department chair. She knew she was well liked and respected by her colleagues, but this didn't give her the same satisfaction that it had in the past. Something was wrong. Something was missing. And that's why she had decided to spend her sabbatical in Copenhagen. She needed to get away from the familiar university environment with all its petty politics and competitive maneuvering. She needed to rid herself of distractions. She needed breathing space and time alone.

Sometimes she wondered if her family regarded her failed marriage to Alan as a mere blip in the otherwise smooth curve of her ascendancy to academic success—a minor episode in an otherwise spotless career. After the divorce, Leena and Robert never once mentioned Alan again. Even Elly seemed reluctant to listen to Kirsti's muted comments on the phone about adjusting to life alone.

"Good riddance," Elly would say. "That guy was such a jerk, and he was a terrible painter too. I always wondered what you saw in him. You're better off without him." And then Elly would change the subject and start telling Kirsti about her acting classes, or about Rachel's progress in school. She rarely asked Kirsti about her teaching or research, although she liked to tease her older sister by calling her "Dr. Martin."

During the past few months, Kirsti had finally come to the conclusion that her marriage to Alan had been an impetuous attempt to break out of the rigid mold that her family had long ago cast for her—with her own willing collusion. Her choice of husband had been misguided and unfortunate, but the flight from the prescribed path was not a mistake. It was the first time in her life that she had followed her heart instead of her head. And even though the marriage had been a disaster, she didn't regret her mutiny.

Now, at the age of forty-two, she had a feeling that she was preparing for another departure from the expected routine of her life.

She was desperately bored with the endless faculty meetings rife with childish backbiting and ill will. She was sick of the mediocre work produced by dull young students, whose only real interest was in making it through college as effortlessly as possible. Kirsti loved literature, but lately she had lost her enthusiasm for teaching.

In the middle of a lecture on German Romanticism, she would feel part of herself splitting away to observe the scene from a far corner of the room: half the students slumped in their chairs, barely conscious, just waiting for the sound of the bell; the other half hunched over their desks, scribbling meaningless notes and wondering which key phrases would be on the next test. And then she would look at herself, standing in front of the chalkboard, methodically delivering the prepared lecture, looking calm, professional, and remote. The whole room seemed under some kind of spell, and she would suddenly have the urge to shriek, to pound on the lectern, or to fling all her papers in the air and watch them rain down like useless confetti. Anything to wake everyone up. Anything to put some life into the room.

When summer quarter was over last August, Kirsti had packed her bags and left for Denmark. She was due back at her teaching post in the fall, but she was already thinking about handing in her resignation. She knew she would go mad if she had to stand in front of all those benumbed faces again.

Kirsti groaned and rolled onto her back. She threw the limp acrylic blanket onto the floor. She had started thinking about what other sweaty bodies had slept under that very blanket, and she finally had to get rid of it. The room was too hot anyway.

Since she had left Alan, Kirsti had had many affairs and one relationship that lasted well over a year, but she seemed destined to be disappointed in love. The men she attracted were either the brilliant, academic types who were dreary in bed, or the smooth-talking PR types that she eventually learned to recognize as mere baggage-handlers. They wanted her body but not her mind. So far, she hadn't found a man who was interested in the "whole package," as she would say to her women friends with a wry smile.

Lately, she had declared a moratorium on dating, and it was with great relief that she threw herself into her research. She was writing a biography of a little-known Danish author who wrote amazingly passionate prose.

It was Elly's husband John who had indirectly introduced her to the works of Jens Peter Jacobsen. Kirsti was visiting her sister's family in Denver one Christmas, and on a snowy afternoon John put on a CD that caught her attention.

"What are we listening to?" Kirsti asked her brother-in-law, intrigued by the power of the music. She didn't usually like such experimental pieces, but this one had a haunting air about it.

"It's one of Schoenberg's most famous compositions. It's called *Gurrelieder*, based on an epic poem by a Danish author. I can't remember his name, but we can check the liner notes."

"J. P. Jacobsen," it said. "Danish writer, born 1847, died 1885." And that's all it said.

When Kirsti returned home to Minneapolis, she couldn't get the strange music out of her mind. She bought a CD of the piece, studied the German translation, and finally went to the library to see what she could find out about this Danish writer. Her search led her to his poetry and three books of fiction, which she was able to decipher with the help of a dictionary. She became so enamored of Jacobsen's lyrical style and psychological insight that she started teaching herself Danish in earnest.

And now she was writing his biography and thinking about staying in Denmark after her sabbatical was up. But she hadn't thought any farther than that—she had no idea what she would do with her life after she resigned.

CB

When Kirsti finally reached her father on the phone last Friday, she was surprised to hear herself say that she would be coming to Maija's funeral.

"I want to be there," she told Robert. "I'll catch a flight on Tuesday. Where is the service going to be held?"

"At St. John's Church in West Seattle," said her father. Then they chatted for a few minutes about unimportant things, and Kirsti hung up.

She realized that both the distance and the cost exempted her from attending, but she suddenly felt it imperative that she go. Her decision was not based on a need to satisfy convention or out of a sense of familial obligation. This was a deeply personal desire to honor Maija's life and to mark her passing. It was too easy to sit down and have a good cry and then get on with everyday routines and concerns. It was too simplistic, too superficial, too cold. Kirsti was not a religious person, but it suddenly seemed to her irreverent to allow Maija to die without formally commemorating her life.

So here she was, tossing and turning in a stuffy hotel room, jet-lagged, irritable, and a little nervous about facing her family the next day. But she had no regrets about her decision. Maija had been an abiding presence in her life, and Kirsti had come to Seattle to say goodbye.

CB CB CB

At seven o'clock on Wednesday morning, Joel Martin was already approaching the U.S. border. He'd been sleeping badly ever since Monique had left, and he usually got up around four to work on a translation or an editing job. Sometimes he'd take a nap in the afternoon, finally overwhelmed by the weariness that eluded him at night. Fortunately, one of the benefits of his freelance life was the ability to arrange his own schedule.

Today he'd gotten an early start from Vancouver, feeling too restless to work and suddenly anxious to get out of his small apartment. The funeral wasn't until two, and he didn't know what he would do before then, but he felt an urgent desire to get out on the road.

As Joel slowly drove toward the immigration and customs booth, he cast an ironic glance at the towering white form of the

Peace Arch with its Canadian and American flags. He knew that no matter how many times he crossed the border, he would never be rid of the mixture of anger and sorrow that always filled him on returning to the United States.

Ↄ

On that October afternoon when Maija miraculously got him across the border and then left him standing behind an old boarded-up gas station, Joel was filled with an overpowering sense of relief. He looked up at the bright sky, astounded that the world was not going to come to an end after all, and then he set off down the road with a confident and buoyant step. His grandfather's *puukko* was carefully stowed away in the small duffel bag that contained one change of clothes and an extra pair of shoes. Joel had been impressed with the gravity of Maija's words as she handed him the family treasure, and he was even more amazed by the sum of money he found in the envelope after she drove away. He vowed that someday he would repay her.

The next few years were not easy ones, and Joel was frequently discouraged, but his youth and his sense of humor gave him a resilience that got him through the low periods. And all trace of Joel's former laziness seemed to have vanished overnight. He couldn't afford to fool around anymore. Tenacity, hard work, and discipline were suddenly necessary if he was going to make it on his own.

The organization of American draft resisters in Vancouver helped Joel find a job on a construction crew, and eventually he started taking night classes at the university. Several years later, with a degree in Romance languages and solid recommendations from his teachers, he found a job with a translation agency, and he'd been doing that kind of work ever since. The hard part was not the job search or finding an apartment or taking care of other practical matters. The hard part was trying to lead a new life without a past.

Joel never talked about his family, and he avoided telling people where he was really from—except in situations that required the truth on official documents. To explain his accent, he made up a story about having a Canadian father but an American mother, and then he'd use his wit to shift the conversation to some other topic far removed from his personal life. After his first few months in Canada, Joel stopped associating with other draft resisters. It made him uneasy to hear their anger, and he was unwilling to respond to their challenge to express his own. He wanted to forget, he wanted to move on, and he didn't want to be bogged down in bitterness and rancor.

When Joel met Monique Devereaux, his determination to conceal his past began to waver for the first time. From the moment he saw her walk into the Winston Translation Agency, delivering a job she had just completed, Joel knew that he wanted to be with her. Her intense brown eyes, thick auburn hair, and lovely French-Canadian accent charmed him at once. He had never believed in love at first sight; he had never really believed in love at all. Joel's joking manner, combined with his reticence to discuss personal feelings, had prevented him from making any close friends. So far, his girlfriends had all been the fun-loving but flighty types who were easily bored and who quickly moved on to the next sexual adventure.

Monique was different. She was a serious and gentle person

with a passion for books and languages. She laughed at Joel's jokes, but she also demanded, in her own quiet way, that he talk to her about matters of importance. When she asked him a serious question, she wouldn't let him get away with a glib reply. "Come on, Joel," she'd say with a smile. "Quit kidding around and tell me what you really think."

Monique found it strange that Joel never talked about his family, and her patient probing eventually broke through his resistance. He realized at last that he *wanted* to tell her about his parents and sisters and about the circumstances of his arrival in Canada. One day Joel told her the whole story, opening himself again to his anger and hurt, and for the first time he cried over what he had lost. Then his defenses closed around him, and he refused to speak of the past again.

When Joel married Monique in 1975, he decided to become a Canadian citizen. He thought it would put to rest his unresolved feelings for the country that had exiled him. He thought it would be a way of publicly stating that he was a new man—he had officially cut his ties to his former life, and he was starting over. But his new status only served to bury his past a little deeper, not to erase it.

Two years later, Joel was caught by surprise when Carter, in an attempt to begin his new role as President with an act of redemption, decided to pardon all draft evaders. The amnesty opened a floodgate of memories, and for the first time Joel realized that in order to move forward, he was going to have to go back. For all these years he had been fooling himself. His attempts to establish a new life, no matter how valid or admirable, were not enough to break the emotional holding pattern that he now realized he was locked into.

He hadn't seen his family in eight years. His only ties to them had been through the postcards he occasionally sent to Maija and the rather formal letters that she sent in return to his post office box. He asked Maija not to give his address to anyone, not even his parents. Maija said he was being too harsh on his family, but she complied with his wishes, although several times she forwarded a letter from Leena along with her own brief note. Joel tossed his mother's letters unopened into the fireplace, afraid that if he kept them around, he would eventually read them. And he wasn't prepared for what they might say. Silence was the only way he could hold his life together. Even his phone number was unlisted.

Joel and Monique were living in Montreal when they read in the paper that Carter had granted amnesty to all those who had resisted the draft or deserted during the Vietnam War. And Joel suddenly realized he needed to go home.

୧

Three weeks later, Leena plucked the usual bundle of letters and academic journals out of the mailbox and tossed everything onto the dining-room table. The red and blue stripes of an airmail envelope caught her eye, and she picked up the letter with the Canadian stamp. When she recognized the handwriting, her heart started beating so fast that she had to sit down on a chair before she could open the envelope. It was a letter from Joel.

"Dear Mom and Dad," it said. "I know it's been a long time since you've heard from me. I'm living in Montreal now, and I'm married to a wonderful woman named Monique. We both work as freelance translators, and we manage to make a comfortable living. I was wondering if we could visit you sometime next month. It would be good to see you again. Love, Joel." That's all it said, although he had carefully printed his address at the bottom of the page.

Leena ran into the study to call Robert at the university, but his secretary said that he was still in class. Leena was so excited that she couldn't resist blurting out the news that their son Joel was coming home at last. Then she called Diane and told her about the letter too.

Robert was equally happy about the upcoming reunion, but there was a touch of acrimony to his thoughts, which he did his best to hide from Leena. Eight years was too long a time to wipe away with a single letter or visit. He wasn't quite sure how he would feel when he actually saw Joel in person.

On a Saturday near the end of March, Joel and Monique flew to Chicago, rented a car at the airport, and drove the sixty miles north to Milwaukee. Joel parked the car in front of his parents' house, pulled the key out of the ignition, and then sat in silence for several minutes, his brow furrowed, his eyes lowered, and the fingers of his right hand mechanically flipping the car key back and forth. Monique gently took the key out of his hand, leaned over to kiss him lightly on the cheek, and then said quietly, "Shall we go in, Joel?"

The meeting turned out to be much easier and far less dramatic than any of them had thought.

When Leena opened the door, she saw an older and more somber-looking Joel. He had cut his hair, grown a mustache, and put on some weight. He had exchanged his ragged jeans and tie-dye shirt for charcoal-gray slacks and a neat green sweater under a brown corduroy sport coat. But his face was so familiar that Leena suddenly felt as if it were only yesterday that she had looked into his eyes.

"Aren't you going to invite us in, Mom?" Joel joked as Leena continued to stare, unusually tongue-tied. Then he gave his mother a quick hug and introduced Monique.

Robert came into the living room as Leena was hanging Monique's coat in the hall closet and Joel was recounting the saga of their plane trip, which had nearly been canceled by a threatening snowstorm. Joel stopped in mid-sentence. He took a step toward his father, but couldn't decide whether to continue, unsure of his reception.

"Welcome home, Joel," said Robert after a moment. And then he shook his son's hand and patted him on the back. At that instant of recognition when he looked into Joel's face, Robert felt such a flood of gratitude at having his son back that all his hostility evaporated. Later, some of Robert's bitterness would return, and over the years there continued to be an unexplored rift between father and son. But on that March day, both were touched by that rare moment of genuine connection.

Monique's presence made the visit less charged and more enjoyable than it might have been if Joel had come alone. Her natural grace and quiet manner put everyone at ease, and before long Joel had returned to his customary joshing and bantering. He was glad to be back in the family.

CB

The U.S. customs official gave Joel's Canadian driver's license a superficial glance and then waved him through without asking a single question. Joel grinned as he shifted into gear and drove into the Evergreen State. Sometimes he still had nightmares about what would have happened if the border guards had opened the trunk of Maija's '53 Plymouth and found him huddled under that prickly blanket. He owed her a lot. But when he tried to repay the money she had given him, Maija refused to take it. Twice he had sent her checks, and both times she had returned them. She told him the money was not meant as a loan, and there was no need for him to repay her.

Three years ago, Joel and Monique had moved back to Vancouver, hoping that a complete change of scene might rejuvenate their foundering marriage. And it was no accident that they decided to return to the city where they had first fallen in love. Every so often they would drive down to Seattle to visit Maija.

It was an overcast Friday afternoon about six months ago when Joel last saw his aunt. He had called Maija in the morning to ask if she would like to meet him for tea at the bookstore café in Pioneer Square. He was in Seattle to talk to some clients, and he thought it would be nice to get together if she had time. Maija told Joel that she would love to see him.

That afternoon she found a secluded table in the popular café in the basement of her favorite bookstore. She got herself a cup of tea, and then sat down and opened the biography of Carson McCullers that she'd started the day before. Maija always carried a book with her in case she had to wait for any length of time, and today Joel was late.

Half an hour after the designated meeting time, Joel rushed into the café, set his briefcase and packages on the floor next to Maija's table, and sank heavily onto the chair across from her. His face was flushed and he was feeling both harried and nervous, knowing how much emphasis his aunt always placed on being prompt.

"I'm really sorry to be late, Maija," he hurried to apologize. "The meeting took longer than I thought, and the traffic from Northgate was atrocious—the freeway was a parking lot, and I had to get off and take the surface streets. Anyway, I'm glad you could come—it's good to see you. Shall I get you some more hot water for your tea? I think I need a triple latte."

When Joel came back with the coffee and tea, they got caught up on family news, and Maija told her nephew about the volunteer work she was doing for the local chapter of the Sierra Club. When she retired from teaching, she finally had time to get involved with the causes she believed in, and the Audubon Society was another group that had attracted Maija's zeal.

Joel talked about a big translation project he was doing for the United Nations (a book on population control in a multitude of languages), but he didn't say a word about the problems in his marriage.

At a pause in the conversation, Joel suddenly reached down, picked up a large, flat package wrapped in brown paper, and handed it to Maija.

"What's this?" she asked in surprise.

"It's a gift," said Joel. "Go ahead and open it."

Maija carefully undid the wrappings and slid out a painting of a woman peacefully sleeping on the bank of a river with laughing fish leaping in her dreams. High overhead, two red dogs were circling around the moon. The colors were vivid, the lines were bold, and there was a certain Chagall-like charm about the overall composition.

"I love it," said Maija, looking up at Joel with an expression of wonderment and pleasure. "What's it called?"

"It's called 'River Dreams,' by Cheri O'Brien—she sometimes has paintings in a gallery just down the street. I've seen her things before, and I was sure that you'd like her work."

"Thank you," said Maija. "It's a beautiful painting, and I know exactly where I'm going to hang it."

A few minutes later they said goodbye. Joel had another meeting to go to, and his thoughts were already focused on what he needed to discuss with his client. He didn't mention to Maija that the painting was his way of thanking her for the money, for the knife, and for all her help; but he thought she probably understood his intention.

❣

Joel slowed down to allow a merging car to slip in front of him. There was surprisingly little traffic on I-5, and it wouldn't be long before he reached Seattle. He was still feeling restless and tense, and Monique's sudden departure only two weeks ago was constantly on his mind. But he didn't want to dwell on that today.

He decided to stop at Green Lake and take a slow stroll around the lake. The hordes of joggers would just have to veer around him; he wasn't prepared for any kind of frenetic activity himself. Later he thought he'd have lunch at the bookstore café where he and Maija had last met. It would be his private salute to his aunt and to the time when she rescued him from the draft. And then he would go to her funeral.

Eight

It turned out to be a brilliantly sunny day without even a wisp of cloud in the sky. It was a little chilly—cool enough to wear a sweater or a light coat—but otherwise it was an unusually benevolent spring day for Seattle.

When Leena looked out the hotel-room window that morning, she wished it was raining instead. She would have preferred dark and miserable weather with torrents of water and a blustery wind. Or better yet, a raging storm. She felt exposed in the glare of all that bright sunshine. And it seemed suddenly unfair that the day should be so lovely when Maija was not there to see it.

CB

When Robert parked their rental car in the lot next to the church later that afternoon, he was grateful to discover the one remaining space marked with a discreet sign: "Reserved for family members." Everyone else seemed to have already arrived, since even the street was lined with parked cars. Robert turned off the engine with a sigh of relief. They had gotten lost on their way through West Seattle and had to stop at a deli on California Avenue to ask directions. By the time they made their way past the wooded expanse of Lincoln Park, swerved around the line of cars heading for the Fauntleroy ferry terminal, and sped up the hill to St. John's Church, it was already 1:45. Robert almost made a joke about what Maija would say if they showed up late for her funeral, but he stopped himself from uttering such an ill-timed remark. Leena was clearly in no mood for humor, even of the most affectionate kind.

All Robert's attempts at conversation that morning had been met with stubborn silence. At eight o'clock he called room service to order breakfast. Robert had his usual oatmeal, toast, and a glass of juice, but Leena refused the English muffin and fruit that he ordered for her, settling for two cups of black coffee instead. Afterwards, Robert suggested that they take a walk, but Leena said she'd rather read for a while, and she sent him off alone. Robert was reluctant to leave his wife behind in the hotel room, but he wanted some exercise and fresh air, and he needed a break from Leena's grim silence.

When he returned just before eleven to take Leena out to lunch, he found her sitting in the armchair by the window with a book in her lap, but she didn't seem to be reading. Robert was startled to see that she was wearing a red dress with pewter buttons and an old Finnish brooch. When he left for his walk, she had been wearing a plain gray suit with a white blouse and a silver necklace. He was about to remark on her change of attire, but just then Leena raised her head and gave him such a defiant look that he decided not to comment.

"Ready to go?" he said instead. "It's a beautiful day, but you might need a sweater. I thought we'd drive over to Lake Union and have lunch in one of those restaurants overlooking the water." The frown on Leena's face told him that she was about to protest, so he added firmly, "You need to have something to eat or you won't make it through the rest of the day."

Leena sighed but then acquiesced. "All right, dear," she said, setting her book on the table. "It'll just take me a minute." She slipped into the bathroom to comb her hair and put on some lipstick. Then she picked up her purse from the bedside table and took a black angora sweater out of the closet where she had hung it the night before. She didn't look happy, but she was ready to go.

Now they were sitting in the parking lot outside St. John's Church, and Robert had the distinct impression that Leena was not going to budge from the car. He reached over and took her hand, but she continued to stare straight ahead. Then Robert got out of the car and went around to the passenger side. He opened the door and simply stood there until Leena finally swung her legs around and stepped out onto the asphalt. Robert closed the car door, took Leena's arm, and they walked up to the entrance of the church.

It was a stark white building, quite new, with a dramatically designed roof that looked like billowing sails. The tall wooden doors, carved with an intricate pattern of interlocking loops, had been flung open, and the familiar strains of a Sibelius piece greeted Leena as she reached the top step. She recognized the emotional tones of the great composer's symphonic poem *Tapiola*, an ode to the forest god of the *Kalevala*, and she was filled with surprise. She was even more astonished when she stepped into the large foyer, flooded with sunlight from a row of oval windows high overhead.

White-painted panels designed like folding screens had been placed along two walls, and they were covered with neatly matted photographs, most of them enlarged family snapshots. Under each one there was a label with the place, date, and names of the people in the photo printed in exquisite calligraphy. In the center of the foyer a large glass vase filled with dozens of red tulips had been placed atop a circular, matte-black pedestal.

Two birch saplings with delicate light-green leaves were set in wooden tubs on either side of the doorway leading into the church itself. To the left of the door, framed posters of three paintings had been hung on the wall: Edvard Munch's "Moonlight," Emily Carr's "Wood Interior," and Vilhelm Hammershøj's "Dust Motes Dancing in the Sun." To the right of the doorway hung a superb print of Hugo Simberg's "The Wounded Angel." Beneath the print stood a small table with an elegant leather-bound registry in which all the guests had signed their names.

And next to the registry was a triptych of black-and-white photos that Briitta had taken on an autumn day, late in the after-noon, just last year: Maija striding along a path in Lincoln Park, wearing a plaid wool skirt and rubber boots, her hands thrust into the pockets of her jacket; Maija stopping to gaze up at an eagle perched in the top of a tall fir; Maija retreating down an avenue of trees, their branches arching overhead, and leaves piled up in great drifts along the path.

Leena stood in the foyer, shocked by the sheer beauty of the room. This was nothing like the weighty, claustrophobic, and self-righteously penitent setting that she had imagined when she heard the service was to be held in a church. Her sense of dread had been growing for days, and this morning at breakfast she felt as if she would suffocate. That's why she decided that she couldn't bear the somber propriety of that awful gray suit. She hadn't felt like herself, and she had to wear the red dress instead.

At Robert's urging, Leena had managed to eat a small salad and half a bowl of soup for lunch, but she hadn't really tasted any of it. And when they got back in the car and finally headed toward the church, she was seized by such a sense of panic that she could hardly breathe. Her hands were clammy, her heart was beating too fast, and everything seemed to be streaming past the car window in a great blur of light.

When Robert stopped to ask for directions, Leena had a wild impulse to leap out of the car and run back down the street the way they had come—away from the church, away from the family, away from all the mournful faces. She gripped the door handle and was just about to get out of the car when Robert jumped back into the driver's seat and reeled off a string of directions. They pulled away from the curb and ten minutes later they finally made it to the church.

Now, standing in the sunlit foyer and listening to the surging music, Leena felt a great wave of warmth pass through her. This was not going to be the empty and impersonal ceremony that she had feared. She had pictured herself sitting in an oppressive sanctuary filled with relics and symbols that meant nothing to her, peering through the dim light at some gesticulating minister who would thunder a message about death and repentance. The mere thought of the funeral had filled her with nausea and horror.

It had never occurred to Leena that Briitta might create such a loving tribute to Maija. The photos of the Lahtinens and Martins were funny and poignant, arousing memories of so many family events over the past forty years.

There was a formal photo of Maija and Pentti, newly married, standing on the steps of the City Hall in Helsinki. And there were lots of pictures of Briitta: five months old and laughing, sitting in her baby buggy that Maija insisted on calling a "perambulator"; Briitta, her hair in pigtails, playing in a sandbox in the park; Briitta as an unsmiling teenager, as a student in art school, and as the proud owner of a graphic design studio, showing Maija around her new offices. There were pictures of Max working on a movie set, and scores of photos of the Martins— Christmas pictures, birthday pictures, and snapshots from Maija's visits to Milwaukee. And there was even a photo of Edith, hunkered down on the living-room floor, her eyes staring alertly into the camera.

The group of three paintings on the wall (so different in style and mood but all strikingly devoid of any people) reminded Leena of her sister's great love for nature and art. But she could hardly bear to look at the print of "The Wounded Angel."

The painting showed a bowed and drooping angel seated on a litter, a bandage covering her eyes, her bare feet dangling, her white gown trailing, a patch of blood marking one wing. But even worse than the sorry figure of the angel was the reproachful gaze of the young stretcher-bearer, staring straight out from the canvas. Leena knew that painting well, and normally she found it intriguing and touching, but today she had to look away.

A man dressed in a dark suit came into the foyer from inside the church and approached Leena and Robert as they studied the family photos.

"Mr. and Mrs. Martin?" he said. "I'm a friend of Briitta's. She asked me to escort you to your seats when you arrived. Everyone else is here. Would you come with me, please?"

As Leena turned to follow the man into the church, her eye was caught by a small framed photo on the wall panel nearest the door. It was that old picture from so long ago, the one taken on the day of her aunt's wedding, the same one that she was carrying in a manila envelope in her purse. Leena stopped and was about to take a closer look, but Robert gave a little tug on her arm, and she followed her husband into the church.

The usher led them down the aisle to the front pew on the right, and as they took their seats, the last notes of the Sibelius piece died away. Elly and Rachel were already sitting in the pew, and they both got up to give Leena and Robert a quick hug. Kirsti, Joel, and Briitta were seated across the aisle, and they all turned their heads to smile and nod.

The rest of the church was filled with Maija's friends, school colleagues, and many former students who remembered their old teacher with affection. Even her aging Finnish mechanic had come to pay his respects. There was not an empty pew in the church.

As the music ended, a hush fell over the room, punctuated by an occasional cough, a rustling of paper, and the sound of someone's foot scraping along the floor. From a door on the right, Pastor Hansson entered the church, dressed in white robes elaborately embroidered in gold. He climbed the steps to the pulpit, put his hands on either side of the lectern, and gazed out over the assembly.

As Leena raised her head to look up at the pastor, she was inexplicably overcome by a feeling of homesickness. There was something about this unusual church that reminded her so much of Finland. The bare white walls, soaring up to the vaulted ceiling, the sleek curve of the light oak pews, and the tasteful design of the wrought-iron candelabra standing at intervals along the side aisles, all had a simplicity and grace that seemed so familiar to Leena. A light-blue *ryijy* rug lay on the polished floor of the chancel. A plain white cross stood on the natural wood of the otherwise unadorned altar. And behind the altar, an entire wall of glass, slightly tinted to block out the heat of the sun, offered the parishioners a breathtaking view of the Sound. A couple of sailboats were skimming across the shimmering water, and the clarity of the day made the snow-capped peaks of the Olympics seem even larger and closer than usual.

"Dear friends," began Pastor Hansson in a resonant voice, "we are gathered here today to honor the life of Maija Lahtinen. Born in Viipuri, Finland, in 1920, Maija came to this country as the wife of Pentti Lahtinen in the fall of 1948. Their daughter Briitta was born a year and a half later. When Pentti's life was so tragically cut short, Maija became a teacher at Queen Anne Elementary, where her intelligence, common sense, and indomitable spirit won the love and respect of students and colleagues alike. In 1985 Maija retired from teaching, but she continued to pursue her interest in art—taking courses and attending lectures—and she volunteered a great deal of her time to organizations seeking to protect and nurture our environment. She was the beloved sister of Leena Martin, and her kindness and strength touched the lives of everyone in the Martin family.

"I too was struck by her calm dignity and warmth, even though I met Maija only twice. The first time was at the midnight service on Christmas Eve last year. And the second time was just a few weeks ago, when she came to see me at my office. She told me that her life would soon be over, and she asked me if I would speak to her family and friends when the day came for her funeral.

"She said, 'Don't make it a gloomy occasion. Don't talk to them about sadness and death. Talk to them of springtime and love.' I found her request compelling, and I told her that I would gladly speak at her funeral.

"And so, for my sermon today, I have chosen the passage from the *Song of Solomon* which begins: 'For lo, the winter is past, the rain is over and gone; the flowers appear on the earth; the time of the singing of birds is come...' "

Leena bowed her head and closed her eyes. She heard no more of the pastor's sermon. She was suddenly carried back to a warm, sunny day at the end of June in 1931. She was six years old and Maija was eleven. They were both wearing new dresses, and they had just posed for a picture, taken by their mother outside their home in Viipuri. It was the day of their aunt's wedding.

03

Leena was sitting on the old wooden swing that hung from a sturdy branch of the big sycamore tree in their back yard. She was holding onto the scratchy ropes of the swing, and tapping the ground with her feet just enough to keep the gentle back-and-forth motion going. It was too hot to put more effort into her swinging, and Maija said that she didn't feel like pushing her. Leena hummed a little tune, feeling the light breeze ruffle her short hair. Out of the corner of her eye, she saw her sister slumped against the faded cushions of the white garden bench with the high back. Maija was in one of her moods, and Leena knew better than to try to talk to her.

When they woke up that morning, all of the adults were already bustling around, getting ready for the celebration feast that was going to be held at their house after the ceremony.

Their mother had been baking and cooking for days, and the whole house smelled of cardamom rolls and fresh bread, of smoked sausage and baked ham. Vases of bright spring flowers stood on the kitchen table, waiting to be placed on the mantelpiece and on the wide windowsills in the living room. Extra leaves had been added to the dining-room table, but it was still going to be a tight squeeze to fit in all the guests invited for the wedding lunch. The good china and silver had been brought out, and their mother's best linen tablecloth had been meticulously starched and pressed for the occasion.

Their aunt had arrived the day before, and she had promised to let Leena carry her bouquet on the way to the church.

That morning, Leena had jumped out of bed with excitement, rushing to put on her new red dress. Maija was sitting on the window seat, still in her nightgown, gazing out at the sunny day. She didn't look happy.

"What's wrong?" asked Leena, fastening the tiny jet buttons of her dress.

"The birds aren't singing," said Maija without turning her head. "I haven't heard a single bird all morning. I'm getting a bad feeling, and I don't like it."

"But I thought the birds always stopped singing before summer came," said Leena, a little puzzled.

"Yes, but not all of a sudden like this—not overnight. Usually one kind of bird stops singing, and then another. But I haven't heard one single bird today, and I don't like it."

Leena frowned. She was always a little in awe of her big sister, but today she was impatient with Maija's bad humor. This was supposed to be a happy day—the weather was perfect, she had a brand-new dress, and she was looking forward to the food and the music and the dancing. She didn't want to get caught up in Maija's mood.

"Could you tie my bow?" Leena asked her sister, turning around so Maija could tie the ribbons of her dress in back. "I'm going to go downstairs and help Äiti with the flowers."

Leena rushed out of the room, as Maija stood up to put on her own new dress, sighing to herself. Something was definitely wrong.

Now they were sitting outside, waiting to leave for the church. After their mother had taken their picture, she told them to stay put, because they would be going soon. She warned them for the umpteenth time not to get their new dresses dirty, and then she hurried off to finish the preparations in the kitchen.

A few minutes later Leena and Maija heard the pounding steps of someone running toward their house. They both turned their heads just in time to catch a glimpse of Mrs. Virtanen's youngest boy, Hannu, racing up the steps to the front door. Mrs. Virtanen was the postmistress and the proud owner of one of the few telephones in the neighborhood. A second later, the girls saw their father, all dressed up in his best black suit, dash out the door and take off down the street toward the Virtanens' house with Hannu right behind him.

When their father returned ten minutes later, he was no longer running. He came walking up to the house with a strange look on his face. His shoulders sagged, and his arms were hanging limply at his sides. The girls thought he seemed suddenly older, and they both stood up and headed for the back door.

They climbed the stairs to the porch, and Maija put out her hand to pull open the screen door. The kitchen was deserted and there was an eerie calm in the room after all the commotion of the morning. The two sisters took a step toward the hallway leading to the rest of the house.

And then a piercing shriek splintered the silence.

Leena and Maija looked at each other in horror and then raced down the hall to the living room. They stopped on the threshold, transfixed by the scene before them. All of the grown-ups were standing in a circle, frozen in poses of anguished disbelief. On the floor in the middle of the room, the girls saw the figure of their aunt huddled on the dark red carpet, her face buried in her hands, the dazzling white satin of her wedding gown spread out around her. No one said a word. No one even seemed to be breathing.

And then the women began to cry, and the men started murmuring and shaking their heads.

The telephone call had come from a cousin in Lappeenranta who had been traveling with the groom. They had caught the ferry boat in Savonlinna the day before, and both had been in splendid spirits, looking forward to the wedding and celebration. They drank a few beers in the bar on the upper deck and got to talking with a couple of salesmen from Helsinki. They stayed up all night, switching from beer to aquavit, and suddenly an argument erupted over some topic no longer worth mentioning. A brawl ensued and two men fell over the side. The salesman was rescued, but the groom had drowned.

Maija and Leena learned the story from their mother, who quickly told them what happened in a hushed voice, her face pinched with the effort of holding back her tears. Then she told the girls to go outside and play. The grown-ups needed to be alone.

Maija took Leena's hand, and the two sisters slowly retreated to the back yard and sat down side by side on the garden bench.

A great sob rose up inside Leena and she buried her head in her sister's lap and wept. Maija stroked her hair and whispered, "Go ahead and cry, Leena. It's all right to cry."

ଓଃ

Leena opened her eyes. She was sitting in the front pew of St. John's Church with tears streaming down her cheeks. Robert had his arm around her shoulders and he was peering at her with a worried look on his face. Leena gave him a little smile and then put her hand in his.

The pastor had finished his sermon, and Briitta was now standing in the front of the church, reading the last lines of a poem by Edith Södergran:

The future casts on me its blissful shadow;
it is nothing but radiant sun:
pierced through by light will I die,
when I have trampled all that is chance,
I shall turn away smiling from life.

A chorus of voices filled the church, singing a song based on an ancient rune and accompanied by the crystalline sound of a *kantele*. When the music ended, the pastor said a prayer in Finnish, then left the pulpit and walked up the aisle toward the foyer. Everyone rose from their seats and stood in silence as Briitta moved toward the door with Joel at her side. Kirsti and Elly were a few steps behind, with Rachel between them. Leena wiped her eyes with a tissue and took two deep breaths. Then she and Robert, hand in hand, followed the rest of the family out into the sunlight.

HOLY SIMPLICITY

HOLY
SIMPLICITY

---

*The Little Way
of Mother Teresa,
Dorothy Day
& Thérèse of Lisieux*

JOEL SCHORN

PUBLISHED BY ST. ANTHONY MESSENGER PRESS
CINCINNATI, OHIO

Excerpts from *A Revolution of Love: The Meaning of Mother Teresa,* by David Scott, ©2005, used by permission of Loyola Press, www.loyolabooks.org. Excerpts from *Mother Teresa of Calcutta: A Complete Authorized Biography,* by Kathryn Spink, ©1997, used by permission of HarperCollins Publishers. Excerpts from *The Long Loneliness,* by Dorothy Day, ©1980, used by permission of HarperCollins Publishers. Excerpts from *The Story of a Life: St. Thérèse of Lisieux,* by Guy Gaucher, ©1982, used by permission of HarperCollins Publishers. Excerpts from *Story of a Soul,* translated by John Clarke, O.C.D., ©1975, 1976, 1996 by Washington Province of Discalced Carmelites, used by permission of ICS Publications, www.icspublications.org.

Every effort has been made to trace and acknowledge the copyright holders of all the material excerpted in this book. The editors apologize for any errors or omissions that may remain and ask that any omissions be brought to our attention so that they may be corrected in future editions.

Scripture passages have been taken from *New Revised Standard Version Bible,* copyright ©1989 by the Division of Christian Education of the National Council of the Churches of Christ in the U.S.A., and used by permission. All rights reserved.

Cover design by Candle Light Studios
Cover image ©Penywise Photography
Book design by Mark Sullivan

LIBRARY OF CONGRESS CATALOGING-IN-PUBLICATION DATA
Schorn, Joel.
Holy simplicity : the little way of Mother Teresa, Dorothy Day and Thérèse of Lisieux / Joel Schorn.
p. cm.
Includes bibliographical references and index.
ISBN 978-0-86716-815-0 (pbk. : alk. paper) 1. Christian life—Catholic authors. 2. Simplicity—Religious aspects—Catholic Church. 3. Teresa, Mother, 1910-1997. 4. Day, Dorothy, 1897-1980. 5. Thérèse, de Lisieux, Saint, 1873-1897. I. Title.

BX2350.3.S36 2008
248.4'82--dc22

2007045255

ISBN 978-0-86716-815-0

Published by Servant Books, an imprint of St. Anthony Messenger Press
28 W. Liberty St.
Cincinnati, OH 45202
www.ServantBooks.org

Printed in the United States of America
Printed on acid-free paper

08 09 10 11 12 5 4 3 2 1

CONTENTS

Not to be encompassed by the greatest, but to let oneself be encompassed by the smallest—the divine.

—FRIEDRICH HÖLDERLIN (1770–1843)

God walks among the pots and pans.
—Saint Teresa of Avila

On many occasions the late Pope John Paul II reminded the church of the universal call to holiness. "Everyone in the Church," he wrote, "precisely because they are members, receive and thereby share in the common vocation to holiness."[1] The Second Vatican Council put it this way: "All Christians in any state or walk of life are called to the fullness of Christian life and to the perfection of love." This holiness, the council said, grows out of giving glory to God, serving others and "doing the will of God in everything."[2]

But what is holiness, and how do we respond to the call? Can we do the will of God *in everything?*

Saint Benedict, the founder of monasticism in Europe, wrote that the keeper of the pots, pans and "all utensils and goods of the monastery" should regard them as "sacred vessels of the altar."[3] The holiness of pots and pans points to the holiness of everyday life. The things we do in everyday life lead us to holiness if we do them with an awareness of the presence of God.

Thérèse of Lisieux, Mother Teresa and Dorothy Day are three modern Catholic women whose lives show us how the

path to holiness is a little way. "We can do no great things—only small things with great love," Mother Teresa said.[4] These words very well describe the way to closeness to God that Thérèse, Mother Teresa and Dorothy followed and offer to us. In littleness we can find beauty and the love of God. Little things, even the least, hold the power of big things, for in them God reveals his presence.

We can respond to this presence with devotion to and love for the ordinary activities and encounters of everyday life. Rather than letting our days fly by, mechanically performing our daily tasks in order to get them over and done with, we can see little drops of grace in all the things we do. We can see in them new opportunities to respond to the ocean of God's love flooding the world.

Seeing God in every moment leads us as well to total reliance on God in every moment. This little way to faith and trust can help us accept ourselves for who we are, redefine how we see success and failure and cope with suffering and the sacrifices of daily life.

Love of God and others in the small things of life: This is the little way that Thérèse, Mother Teresa and Dorothy give us. As Mother Teresa put it, "I think…that we must live life beautifully, we have Jesus with us and he loves us. If we could only remember that God loves us, and we have an opportunity to love others as he loves us, not in big things, but in small things with great love."[5]

NAMES

The little way we are describing is a path, and any path we take requires a first step. In his poem "The Road Not Taken," Robert Frost wrote, "Two roads diverged in a wood, and I—I took the one less traveled by, / And that has made all the difference." Thérèse of Lisieux, Mother Teresa and Dorothy Day decided to take the less-traveled path: Thérèse from a comfortable, middle-class life to the austerity of a Carmelite monastery; Dorothy from a budding career as a journalist to the voluntary poverty and life of service of the Catholic Worker Movement; and Mother Teresa from a stable teaching position with the Sisters of Loreto to the streets of Calcutta. They all followed the path that Thérèse called "my little way."

To make these decidedly "downwardly mobile" moves, these women had to take a first step out of their comfort zones into the new lives to which God was calling them. These first steps were hard for Thérèse, Dorothy and Mother Teresa. But for them—and for others who are contemplating a new spiritual path—the rewards were well worth the risks and the sacrifices involved.

What led them to step out boldly and embrace a new life?

The Big Teresa

One way to understand their motivations is to go back in time 400 years to another spiritual trailblazer, Teresa of Avila, the great sixteenth-century Spanish Carmelite sister, mystic, reformer, writer and spiritual master. From her name and spirit runs a spiritual lineage to Thérèse, Dorothy and Mother Teresa.

In Catholic tradition names are important. We sometimes give children the names of saints, as we do churches, institutions and religious communities. This naming expresses a belief that we are in communion with the saints, who continue to be living presences among us. It also opens us to the patronage of the saints, their inspiration and care.

It was for Teresa of Avila that Thérèse's parents named their daughter, who also became a renowned Carmelite. And it was from Thérèse that Mother Teresa took her religious name.

According to Eileen Egan, friend and biographer of Mother Teresa, a great simplicity characterized Mother Teresa's outlook, words and work. Perhaps the simplicity of Thérèse appealed to her. In the Loreto novitiate the sisters would hear readings from the lives of the saints during dinner. One of those lives, Egan speculates, may have been that of Thérèse of Lisieux. "The story of a French Carmelite nun declared a saint in 1925," Egan writes, "was one of utmost simplicity."[1]

Though Mother Teresa made it clear that she chose "not the big St. Teresa but the little one,"[2] some saw in her "a follower of Saint Teresa of Avila, a dynamic and determined woman who was constantly ready to go out and start new foundations."[3]

Dorothy Day also recognized a kindred spirit in Teresa of Avila, a fact she reflected in giving her daughter the middle name of Teresa. Lying in the maternity ward of New York City's Bellevue Hospital shortly after giving birth, another young mother asked her about the new baby's name. When Dorothy told her that the baby was named Tamar Teresa, the other woman asked if "Teresa" was for the Little Flower. No, Dorothy said, for Teresa of Avila. She had never heard of the Little Flower, and the other woman had never heard of Teresa of Avila.

Dorothy, in fact, had a great affinity for Teresa of Avila. She had read the life of the saint, and the contrasts in Teresa's life appealed to Dorothy: The Carmelite was mystical and practical, reclusive and well traveled, cloistered and active. Then there was the attraction of Teresa's unconventional spirit. Dorothy had picked up on "delightful little touches to the story of her life which made me love her and feel close to her."[4] As a young girl Teresa read novels, and when she entered the convent she wore a red dress. Dorothy particularly enjoyed the account of Teresa's conversation with God after the donkey she was riding threw her into a stream. "The story goes that our Lord said to her, 'That is how I treat my friends.' And she replied, 'And that is why You have so few of them.'"[5]

To Teresa life was a "night spent at an uncomfortable inn." She once tried to enliven the sisters' recreation hour by dancing with castanets, saying, "One must do things sometimes to make life more bearable." As a religious superior she ordered melancholy sisters to eat steak. For these and other reasons, Dorothy "decided to name my daughter after her. That is why

my neighbor offered me a medal of St. Thérèse of Lisieux, who is called the little Teresa."[6]

Too Small?

While Dorothy would eventually develop great admiration for Thérèse, her initial exposure to the saint, beyond the gift of the medal, was not exactly positive. After she became a Catholic, her confessor gave her a copy of Thérèse's autobiography, *The Story of a Soul*. Dorothy's thought after reading it was that "men, and priests too, were very insulting to women, . . . handing out what they felt suited their intelligence; in other words, pious pap." She found the book dull and "too small in fact for my notice."

"What kind of a saint was this," she asked, who saw heroic charity in eating the food in front of her, taking medication and putting up with the cold and heat of the cloister? Who called a splash of water to the face when the community was doing the laundry together "a 'mortification' when the very root of the word meant death, and I was reading in my Daily Missal of saints stretched on the rack, burnt by flames, starving themselves in the desert"?[7]

"Too small in fact for my notice." Dorothy's irony may have been intentional, for her words demonstrate her grasp of the little way, an understanding she would later embrace: It is precisely in heroic performance of everyday things and the endurance of little "mortifications" that one can find saintliness.

Thérèse, Dorothy and Mother Teresa shared with the "big" Teresa a gift for leadership and for starting and maintaining new things. Dorothy and Mother Teresa began their work

with an idea and not much else. Thérèse assumed a role of quiet and humble leadership in the convent.

All three women encourage us to step out and, if necessary, to step down in order to find a more satisfying spiritual path. They show how leadership means becoming a servant. To "get ahead," in a sense, you should "fall behind." Just as Jesus "came not to be served but to serve," so "whoever wishes to become great among you must be your servant, and whoever wishes to be first among you must be slave to all" (Mark 10:45, 43–44).

INSPIRATIONAL MOMENTS

Common to many of the saints' lives is a moment of dedication to a future work. Almost a conversion, this experience marks the moment when the person, however religious he or she may be, makes a new commitment to live for God and others. It involves a sense of being absorbed in God, of God's filling up one's being so that the only possible response is to give oneself completely to God and, at the same time, to others.

The need for reconversion and recommitment does not signify that one's earlier faith life was lacking. Rather, this conviction marks the first step in entering more deeply into what one believes.

For Teresa of Avila, this new awareness followed a long struggle to find a deeper and more satisfying way to pray. Looking at an image of the suffering Christ, "I threw myself down beside him," she wrote, "shedding floods of tears and begging Him to give me strength once and for all so that I might not offend Him.... I told Him then that I would not rise from that spot until He had granted me what I was beseeching of Him."[1]

Here again, Thérèse of Lisieux, Dorothy Day and Mother Teresa followed in Teresa of Avila's footsteps: They all had their moments of crisis and conversion in which they found their vocations.

HEALED BY LOVE

Beginning when Thérèse was still a child, she experienced a number of crises, both physical and spiritual, that plunged her into misery but also led her to new life, joy and a sense of her true vocation.

On Easter Sunday night of 1883, when her sister Pauline was in the process of becoming a member of the Lisieux Carmel that Thérèse later would enter, Thérèse became severely ill with flulike symptoms and delirium. She took to her bed, continuing in this state until the day Pauline took the Carmelite habit. At that point she strangely came out of her illness, only to relapse when the event was over.

The condition puzzled the doctor, and Thérèse's family feared she would never recover. They placed a family statue of the Virgin Mary in her room. They also began praying a novena to Our Lady of Victories, whose shrine in Paris was beloved by the family.

On Pentecost, during the novena, Thérèse's three sisters who were still in the Martin home were praying to Our Lady in the presence of the statue, and Thérèse, to the extent she was able, joined in. She later reported: "All of a sudden the blessed Virgin appeared to me beautiful....Her face expressed an ineffable goodness and tenderness, but what went right to the depths of my soul was THE BLESSED VIRGIN'S RAVISHING

SMILE. Then all my pain vanished."[2] The next day Thérèse returned to her normal life as if nothing had happened.

But something had happened. She had experienced a singular grace that demonstrated God's care for her.

Another turning point came three years later, on Christmas night. Thérèse heard her weary father say to her sister Céline, "Well, fortunately this will be the last year!"—meaning the last Christmas he would have to put the customary gifts in anyone's shoes. Thérèse went upstairs, and Céline advised her not to go back down to open her gifts, as that would upset her more.

Suddenly, however, Thérèse felt a change surge through her; a strength entered into her that would never leave. Jesus had changed her heart, she would say later. She said that she "recovered the strength of soul" that she had lost when her mother died. At this moment she ceased to be a hypersensitive girl who was prone to tears. Now she was ready to embark on the next, mature phase of her life.[3]

The Spirit must have been moving across France that night. In Paris, at Notre Dame Cathedral's vespers liturgy, a young atheist named Paul Claudel converted to Catholicism; he would become a prominent Catholic writer and diplomat. That same year Charles de Foucauld, who would become the hermit and servant of the poor Venerable Charles of Jesus, experienced what he called his "first Christian Christmas."[4]

Thérèse's third crisis began during the Easter season of 1896, after she had joined the Lisieux Carmel. She had entered into a classic dark night of the soul experience, in which she felt her faith had left her, and she questioned her

vocation. She pondered other vocations: missionary, warrior, priest, deacon, apostle, doctor of the church (which she would become), martyr.[5]

In September of that year she began her annual private retreat. In an attempt to escape what she called "night" and a "tunnel," she started writing a letter to Jesus. She asked, "O my Jesus! What is your answer to all this foolishness? Is there a soul more *little*, more powerless than mine?"

For an answer she turned to Scripture. She opened the New Testament at random and found the thirteenth chapter of 1 Corinthians on faith, hope and love. After reading this passage, she wrote:

> I finally had rest.... I understood that LOVE COMPRISED ALL VOCATIONS, THAT LOVE WAS EVERYTHING, THAT IT EMBRACED ALL TIMES AND PLACES....IN A WORD, THAT IT WAS ETERNAL!.. My vocation, at last I have found it.... MY VOCATION IS LOVE!
>
> Yes, I have found my place in the Church.... In the heart of the Church, my Mother, I shall be *Love*.[6]

This experience she called a conversion.

INSPIRATION DAY

Mother Teresa's moment of decision came in 1947. Her reading of Matthew 25:40, "Truly I tell you, just as you did it to one of the least of these,...you did it to me," planted an idea in her mind and heart. While on a train ride to the Indian city of Darjeeling—the "City of the Thunderbolt"—to make a retreat, she became aware of a new calling, a new vocation: to

leave the Sisters of Loreto community, dedicate herself to the poor and live among them.

"It was on that train that I heard the call to give up all and follow Him into the slums," Mother Teresa said, "to serve Him in the poorest of the poor. I knew it was His will and that I had to follow Him. There was no doubt that it was to be His work. The message was quite clear.... It was an order."[7] Every year the Missionaries of Charity and their Coworkers celebrate this day, September 10, as "Inspiration Day."

At a retreat following this experience, Mother Teresa was even more absorbed than usual. From time to time she wrote notes on slips of paper. Later she gave these slips to her friend and adviser, the Belgian Jesuit priest Celeste Van Exem. When he looked at the notes later, he found Mother Teresa's vision for a new task.

> She was to leave Loreto but she was to keep her vows. She was to start a new congregation. That congregation would work for the poorest of the poor in the slums in a spirit of poverty and cheerfulness. There would be a special vow of charity for the poor.... The work was to be among the abandoned, those with nobody, the very poorest.[8]

Sister Teresa eventually received permission to leave Loreto and begin her new work. She asked Van Exem, "Father, can I go to the slums now?"[9] She had showed extraordinary patience and discretion in waiting for her new life to begin; now she was obviously anxious to start as soon as possible.

At the beginning of her new work, Sister Teresa had almost nothing. The "school" she started was an open space in which

she taught the children the letters of the Bengali alphabet by scratching them in the mud with a stick. Visiting the site years later, she pointed out the exact place where she had done this, a spot under a plum tree. This patch of ground held the roots of the Missionaries of Charity.

A few students from the Loreto school followed Mother Teresa into the slums, where they began teaching children the basics of reading, writing and personal hygiene. After this small group of women received a donation, they rented two nearby huts with dirt floors.[10]

One day Mother Teresa found a woman dying in the street. The hospital would not accept this abandoned person, so Mother took her back to where she was staying and gave her a bed in which to die with dignity. From this one small action would grow the Missionaries of Charity's homes for those society had cast off: the dying, abandoned children, lepers, AIDS sufferers and unwed mothers.

This step into the unknown world of ministry to the poorest of the poor seems like a frightening leap into an abyss of insecurity. How would she live? *Where* would she live? What if her mission failed and all her long and careful preparations to leave Loreto came to nothing?

The conviction of her calling sustained Sister Teresa in those intimidating first days. We can see her strength of faith as a special grace God gave in order to raise up a modern saint. And God gives all of us a similar gift. Even in the least sure situations, putting ourselves totally in the hands of God will see us through.

TEARS AND ANGUISH

Dorothy's moment of crisis led her to pray and then to trust that God would lead her to a new calling. She was in Washington, D.C., covering a workers' rally. A Catholic for three years, she was questioning what effect her joining the church was having on her life and work. Comparing herself to the workers who were demonstrating for beneficial laws, unemployment insurance, pensions and relief for women and children, she thought, "How little, how puny my work had been since becoming a Catholic…. How self-centered, how ingrown, how lacking in sense of community! My summer of quiet reading and prayer, my self-absorption seemed sinful as I watched my brothers in their struggle, not for themselves but for others."[11]

It was the Solemnity of the Immaculate Conception, and after the rally was over and Dorothy had written her story, she went to the National Shrine of the Immaculate Conception, then still under construction. "There," she wrote, "I offered up a special prayer, a prayer which came with tears and with anguish, that some way would open up for me to use what talents I possessed for my fellow workers, for the poor."[12]

A moment of anguish, prayer, an offering of self—and thus direction. God answered Dorothy's prayer in an immediate if unexpected way.

Returning to New York, she found waiting in her apartment a "short, stocky man in his mid-fifties, as ragged and rugged as any of the marchers I had left."[13] It was Peter Maurin, with whom she would cofound the Catholic Worker Movement. Dorothy recalled later that "the collar of his shirt

was dirty, but he had tried to dress up by wearing a tie and a suit which looked as though he had slept in it." As she found out later, he had.[14] Someone had told Peter to track Dorothy down because "we think alike."[15]

Peter—"the peasant-intellectual"[16] and a "troubadour of Christ"[17]—was born in a small French village in the Pyrenees mountains to a family that included twenty-three children. He went to a Christian Brothers school in Paris and eventually became a teacher there. Peter associated himself with various political movements, and later he became an itinerant laborer, traveling from job to job in Europe, Canada and the United States.

"As Peter was fond of saying," Dorothy wrote, "he earned his living by the sweat of *his* brow, rather than by the sweat of someone else's brow."[18] Part of the program of life Peter would recommend to others included daily manual labor.

Peter was a philosopher. He read constantly and thought deeply about social problems and the Catholic answers to them. He could talk to people—"indoctrinate" them, as he put it—for hours. On that day he told Dorothy that her education lacked a Catholic background. He began to rectify that situation by telling her about the history of the church, the fathers of the church and the prophets of Israel.[19]

Peter believed that the modern world had given itself over to the "spirit of acquisitive materialism"—what we might also call consumerism—in large part because it had lost its moorings in the sacred, which had guided and in some ways restrained it from its excesses.[20]

The answer to the problems of the modern world, Peter thought, "had to be a community answer, a community bound to the truths of eternity. Only in the Church, Maurin believed, existed the intellectual tradition, the theoretical framework, and the passion for life that took account of the entire equation."[21]

Borrowing a phrase from the Industrial Workers of the World labor union, Peter emphasized "the need of building a new society within the shell of the old," one "in which it is easier for people to be good." He believed that humanity was on earth to exercise its abilities and to be happy. It was a life, Dorothy wrote, that would let all people find self-fulfillment, support themselves by producing their own basic necessities and be able to develop their capacity for love and worship through the arts.[22]

Peter told Dorothy of his desire to found houses of hospitality in which people would live in voluntary poverty, practice the works of mercy with the guests they welcomed—most of them off the street—and converse about the ideas and issues that concerned them—what Peter called "clarification of thought." The latter would involve publication of a newspaper to advance his ideas and publicize the activities of the movement. He also wanted to establish farms, because he thought a return to the land to be the best way for people to regain their Christian humanity. Peter's plans would eventually come to be, in one form or another, with Dorothy's help.

She described Peter's vision this way: "We were to reach the people by practicing the works of mercy, which meant feeding the hungry, clothing the naked, visiting the prisoner,

sheltering the harborless, and so on. We were to do this by being poor ourselves, giving everything we had; then others would give, too. Voluntary poverty and the works of mercy were the things he stressed above all. This was the core of his message."[23]

In a few short years, Dorothy would move from a lonely moment in the crypt of a basilica to a vital role in the Catholic Worker, a movement that believed in the church's vision for renewing the world. The project was an experiment based on community, works of mercy, work and Catholic doctrine and worship, all for the purpose of bringing abundant life to the world and, with God's help, restoring creation.

For Thérèse, Dorothy and Mother Teresa, a moment came when they realized that they needed to do something more for God. Theirs was the sense that maybe their faith was too self-satisfied or self-contained, too routine or easy. A greater sense of need pressed in on them. They emerged from these experiences with a dedication to give themselves completely to something new.

Our own rededication involves entering more deeply into our faith and ourselves. In so doing we open ourselves decisively to God's love and to the service of others as a way of life. How to begin?

The Little Way

In seeking to grow spiritually, we might sometimes think that we need something big to happen. While dramatic changes have often accompanied spiritual growth, holiness does not always take big steps. "The older I get," Dorothy wrote, "the more I see that life is made up of many steps, and they are very small affairs, not giant strides."[1]

Little steps work just as well as big ones, sometimes better. Yes, the first actions Thérèse of Lisieux, Dorothy Day and Mother Teresa took were in some ways dramatic. But before too long they found their new vocations to be made up of small things: serving the "little ones" of God; doing small, everyday acts of faith, hope and love over and over again; pouring love and devotion into everything they did—in short, seeing the connection between the ordinary activities of life and the presence of God.

Why should the everyday tasks of life not reveal the divine any less than larger and more dramatic spiritual gestures do? The world tends to measure success and effectiveness in terms of big numbers: how much money someone makes, how much a person owns, how much they do and so on. But the little way gauges success much differently.

THE VOCATION OF LOVE

Thérèse's very life stands as a kind of monument to smallness. She lived only to the age of twenty-four, spending nine of her years in a Carmelite monastery that was itself small and poor. She marked her accomplishments in small favors she performed and little sacrifices she made, many of them invisible to others. One may wonder whether these sacrifices really amounted to much. But within the limited horizons of her convent she found a connection with the infinite love of God.

Eventually the small horizon within which she operated embraced the whole world. She became a popular saint and a doctor of the church. Her memoir sold 1,000,000 copies by the time of her canonization in 1925, and it has been translated into every major language. Millions of people have benefited from the little way of holiness she espoused.

The Catholicism in which Thérèse grew up came under the influence of a movement called Jansenism, which grew out of the thought of Cornelius Jansen (1585–1638), the Catholic bishop of Ypres in Belgium. Jansenism emphasized a kind of predestination, the thought that God had chosen those who would respond to his grace and those who wouldn't. The task of earthly life, then, involved demonstrating that one was among the saved by trying to achieve moral perfection, staying aloof from the world and its temptations and longing and preparing for life in heaven.

Looking at Thérèse's focus on doing small things well, it is easy to think that she had absorbed something of the spirit of the age. But it would be an error to think that Jansenism dominated her. On the contrary, Thérèse's spirituality showed how

God's love, not only his judgment, triumphs in the end. It did not take her away from the world but engaged her more deeply in everyday life and relationships.

In wanting to give little things her attention and do them well, she sought to reach heaven not by outward perfection but by letting God's love flow into even the most ordinary tasks. Whereas perfectionism is a malady of the soul that stresses doing things without making mistakes, the little way demands that we do things for the sake of love. The heart of Thérèse's life was "to live in one single act of perfect love.... For love is to give all and to give oneself."[2]

Love: giving oneself for the good of another. By doing things lovingly, we return God's love and care for creation to God. The way we work and relate to one another ripples outward in ever larger circles and eventually reaches all the way to God. God created us to do "small things with great love," Mother Teresa said.[3]

And she believed that this great love should start at home. "I want you to go and find the poor in your homes," she said. "Above all, your love has to start there. I want you to be the good news to those around you. I want you to be concerned about your next-door neighbor. Do you know who your neighbor is?"[4] Thus devotion begins with the love God places in our hearts. To love is to devote oneself to the art of relationships and doing things well. In the little way, who and what we can love are all around us, all the time.

CHILDREN OF GOD

Dorothy thought Thérèse had found a secret, perhaps *the* secret. "She knew with a certainty that is heaven itself, or a foretaste of heaven, that she had been taught the secret, the 'science of love.'... Her secret is generally called the Little Way, and is so known by the Catholic World."[5]

Dorothy experienced this change in how she looked at things and how she saw God working in her life. Reflecting on her spiritual life around the beginning of World War II, a few years after the beginning of the Catholic Worker, she wrote that she had always felt that God had guided her and would reveal his will in the events of her life. At first she had looked for the divine will in "some big happening, some unmistakable sign." She "disregarded all the little signs." Then in those little things she began to see the signs she wanted, "and with such clearness that I have to beg not to be shown too much, for fear I cannot bear it. I need strength to do what I have to do—strength and joy and peace and vision."[6]

But if the little way unlocks the mystery of love, how do we open this door and walk through it? By embracing spiritual childhood. "[Thérèse] called it little," Dorothy wrote, "because it partakes of the simplicity of a child, a very little child, in its attitude of abandonment, of acceptance."[7]

Thérèse was indeed Sister Thérèse *of the Child Jesus* and of the Holy Face. A few months before her death, she told her sister, "I feel that my mission is about to begin, my mission to make God loved as I love Him, to teach souls my little way." When her sister asked what this little way was, Thérèse replied, "It is the way of spiritual childhood, the way of trust and

absolute surrender."[8] When Pauline asked how difficult it was for Thérèse to achieve perfection, the Little Flower replied, "Oh, that's nothing," and, "Sanctity...means being ready at heart to become small and humble in the arms of God, acknowledging our own weakness and trusting in His fatherly goodness to the point of audacity."[9]

Three quarters of a century later, Pope John Paul II, during a pilgrimage to Lisieux, would describe the little way as "the way of 'holy childhood.'...What truth of the Gospel message is indeed more fundamental and more universal than this: God is our Father and we are his children?"[10] Thérèse's grasp of basic gospel truths explains why in 1997 the pope named her a doctor of the church, the official honor for greatness in theology and holiness.

Even in small things, Thérèse taught us, we can find the love of God in the presence of Jesus. "You know very well," she wrote in a prayer, "that never would I be able to love my Sisters as You love them, unless *You,* O my Jesus, *loved them in me....* Yes, I feel it, when I am charitable, it is Jesus alone who is acting in me, and the more united I am to Him, the more also do I love my Sisters."[11]

TEACHING THE LITTLE WAY

Thérèse felt she had a mission to teach others her little way to love God. "I would show them the little method I have found so perfectly successful and tell them there is but one thing to do on earth; to cast before Jesus the flowers of little sacrifices. That is what I have done and that is why I shall be so well received."[12] She liked to quote Matthew 18:3: "Amen I say to

you, unless you turn and become like little children, you will not enter the kingdom of heaven."

But what kind of "childhood" are we to obtain? To become helpless and dependent on others? In the words of Catholic psychoanalyst Karl Stern, for an adult to "regress" to a childlike state "in our relationships with people is a most serious form of neurosis." We all probably know grown men and women who have damaged themselves and their relationships by acting like children. But we call this behavior *childishness*.

What Thérèse meant was childlikeness. To find our way back to childlikeness "on the supernatural plane, in our relationship with God," Stern says, "is the highest degree of maturity. 'As one whom the mother caresses, so will I comfort you,' says God (Is 66:13). But for this to be possible there has to be a child on the receiving end."[13]

"Thérèse's childlikeness" another commentator writes, "has nothing to do with infantilism. It is practice in simplicity, obedience, and satisfaction with the little things and hidden work of everyday."[14] The very fact that serious minds have expounded on Thérèse's idea of childhood testifies to its depth.

It is this spiritual childhood that the popes who confirmed the advance of Thérèse's journey to canonization emphasized. Catechist and author Father John Hardon said that this childhood takes the form of humility: It "knows nothing of spiritual pride," realizes the need for supernatural help to be holy, relies totally on God for help in times of temptation, believes God's presence is in everything, trusts God's power and mercy and has faith in providence, the guiding hand of God behind everything.[15] These are not new spiritual ideas. What the little

way brings to these values is their practice in the ordinariness and hiddenness of everyday life.

"[This] meant living with a childlike sense of wonder at God's gifts, with a child's sense of dependence and trust," author David Scott wrote. "It meant, Thérèse said, finding the true divine significance 'in the least action done out of love.'"[16]

Childlike dependence on God, Karl Stern said, "sounds easy. Depend on God like a little child. Trust him blindly no matter what happens. Use the inconspicuous events and situations of everyday life as material for sanctification. Do it in obscurity." It is, however, "just about the most difficult thing to do."[17]

"The final word is love," Dorothy wrote, and she knew that love is not child's play. "At times it has been, in the words of Father Zossima [in Fyodor Dostoevsky's *The Brothers Karamazov*], a harsh and dreadful thing, and our very faith in love has been tried through fire."[18] "Love in action is a harsh and dreadful thing compared to love in dreams."[19]

GOD'S PENCIL

Mother Teresa too lived the little way. She said that "all of us are but [God's] instruments, who do our little bit and pass by,"[20] and she conveyed this ideal to her fellow workers. When she disbanded the Missionaries of Charity Coworkers as an organization, their spiritual adviser, Father Paul Chetcuti, wrote:

> We have said so often in the past that we are all Co-Workers of Jesus. Mother is just a small pencil in the hands

of the Lord. With this small pencil Jesus has called us to serve and love him. With this same pencil he is calling us to concentrate more on him. Perhaps we have forgotten the hand that has been writing all these years and concentrated too much on the pencil. So the difficult and hard words that pencil has just written may be an invitation to look a bit higher up and see the Author of Life calling us closer to Him, for his own sake and nothing else.... Let us continue to be Co-Workers of Jesus. No single act of love and of service to the needy must be stopped.[21]

Mother Teresa's smallness—both her spirituality and her physical size—made an impression on many, especially in their contrast to the greatness of her person. "She is tiny to look at," said Indira Gandhi, the late prime minister of India, "but there is nothing small about her."[22] A man who lived in the Missionaries' New York home for people dying of AIDS said that Mother Teresa was "like a quiet storm that will shake you. She says little things—but from them come oak trees."[23]

Have not all of us felt the desire to give ourselves completely for something greater than ourselves? We too can be God's small pencils, with which he will write an invitation of salvation to the world.

Strength and joy come when we focus our attention on the matter at hand. Such focus is an antidote to the "continuous partial attention" disorder that journalist Thomas Friedman sees to be the "disease of our age."[24] In the midst of our endless stream of cell phone calls, e-mails, text messages and television channel options, we humans are having more

and more trouble focusing on what is right in front of us. Adjusting our vision to the small things around us can put the big things in perspective.

The first step of the little way is to see God in every moment. As the eighteenth-century Jesuit spiritual writer Jean-Pierre de Caussade said, "Embrace the present moment as an ever-flowing source of holiness."[25] In every step we take after that first one, we commit ourselves to finding God. It is a path of contemplation in action: seeing God's presence and letting that awareness shape what we do.

It is a paradox of Christian faith that God is revealed especially in the little—the poor in both material goods and in spirit. In the humbleness, limitations and imperfections of life, we can contemplate the presence of God. The life of Christ shows a concern for the small: the sick in body and soul, the disenfranchised, the forgotten and abandoned, the lost sheep.

Christ's attitude offers us an example. "When we meditate on Our Lord's life we are meditating on our own," Dorothy observed. "God is to be found in what appears to be the little and the unimportant. Don't look back 1900 years. Look around us today."[26]

All Are Called

When someone at a news conference asked Mother Teresa what being a living saint was, she said, "I'm very happy if you can see Jesus in me, because I can see Jesus in you. Holiness is not just for a few people. It's for everyone, including you, sir."[1]

The holiness of saints comes from their closeness to God. Saints draw close to God because they give themselves completely to him, to others and to their work. In doing so they imitate Jesus' self-sacrifice for the salvation of the world and unleash a spiritual power that transforms lives. When we let the saints influence us, they inspire us to the same imitation of Christ—putting on Christ like a holy garment, offering ourselves to God. This is the key to saintliness. And it's something all of us can do.

Thérèse of Lisieux, Dorothy Day and Mother Teresa believed that the call to sainthood goes out to all, not only a few. All people have not only the *possibility* to be saints but also the *responsibility* to be saints according to their gifts.

CHRIST'S EXAMPLE

A big part of the holy garment that we are to don is Christ's passion and resurrection. Christ's passion gives value to all suf-

fering and death. Every person must experience suffering and death in his or her own way, and Christ gathers up all these experiences in his own. And death is not the end.

The passion and resurrection of Jesus forever ended meaningless suffering and death. All sacrifice, all loss, even and especially of the innocent, now have ultimate value because Christ offered himself and rose again. In confronting and trying to heal others' pain, we may have to endure some pain ourselves, but this pain leads to redemption. It is not an end in itself but a means to let loose through sacrificial love a healing power upon the Earth.

The little way helps us receive two great mysteries of the Christian faith—the Incarnation and the Passion and Resurrection—and see the connection between them. The Incarnation makes it possible for us to see Jesus in every person, but so does his passion. Mother Teresa said that if Christ's becoming a human being "was not enough…he died on the cross to show that greater love, and he died for you and for me and for that leper and for that man dying of hunger and that naked person lying in the street not only of Calcutta, but of Africa, and New York, and London, and Oslo."[2] Through his suffering we notice the suffering of others, especially the most vulnerable.

Mother Teresa took up this sacrificial and saving love in her work in the slums. "The care with which Mother Teresa gathered up scraps of humanity from Calcutta's streets was a startling sight. The love lavished on men and women abandoned by all, covered with loathsome sores and unable to take care even of their bodily functions," demonstrated the

Christian view "that each person's life and death are unique" because each life is "related always to the life and death of the person Jesus the Christ."[3]

For Dorothy "the consolation is this—and this is our faith too: By our suffering and our failures, by our acceptance of the Cross, by our struggle to grow in faith, hope, and charity, we unleash forces that help to overcome the evil in the world."[4] We offer all to God, including the sufferings and failures of others and of ourselves, in the glorious hope and faith that God does not forget them and in fact uses them to transform creation.

Saintliness does not depend on our doing something superhuman. It need not come from the extraordinary; it can come from the ordinary and the everyday. Many saints did mighty works: they became great missionaries; they founded schools, hospitals, religious orders and other institutions; they even performed miracles, among other things. While these achievements make saints worthy of acclaim, none of us need to do something "big" to answer the call to sainthood. What is extraordinary in both "big" and "little" sainthood is the commitment to give oneself to God in whatever the circumstances may be.

Dorothy wrote, "We are all called to be saints, Saint Paul says....We might also get used to recognizing the fact that there is some of the saint in all of us."[5] Each person carries the seeds of sainthood, which, though small like a mustard seed, can grow into a great tree if properly tended (see Matthew 13:31–32).

Dorothy also wrote, "We are put here to become saints. Every life should be dedicated to [God].... God has invited us to a union with himself. We must combat the idea that only a few are called to sanctity. We are all called to be saints. God expects something from each of us that no one else can do. If we don't, it will not be done."[6]

To grow into holiness is more than something that happens along the way; it is the central task of life. Each person has a unique vocation and responsibility to devote his or her life to God and to all that flows from that dedication.

"Holiness is not the luxury of the few," Mother Teresa reminded us. "It is a simple duty for you and for me."[7] A simple duty: something we undertake every day without thinking that we are undertaking some gargantuan task, though it might be quietly heroic. Mother Teresa recognized this daily vocation to holiness in offering herself. She saw the universal call to sainthood in her vision for the Missionaries of Charity, telling her sisters that "she had...promised to give saints to Mother Church and she was rigorous in forming them with that intention. She would not be satisfied with their just being good religious. She wanted to be able to offer God a perfect sacrifice and, as far as she was concerned, only holiness perfected the gift."[8]

A LITTLE SAINT

When the sisters of Carmel asked Thérèse whether she thought she was a saint, she admitted that she must be "a very little saint." She told them, "But you are saints, too."[9] Thérèse's words went to both the little circle of religious sisters gathered around her deathbed and the legions who would hear in her story the

same nearness to the holy. We are called to be saints. We already have the seeds of saintliness sown in our everyday lives.

Thérèse's road to sainthood—and her idea of how to walk that road—reveals an interesting tension. On the one hand she felt a strong desire to be a saint and nothing less. She was a highly precocious, emotional and charismatic child. When she entered the monastery, the prioress wrote of her, "This angelic seventeen-year-old has the judgment of a thirty-year-old, the religious perfection of an old and accomplished novice, and self-mastery. She is a perfect nun."[10] The priest at the abbey school she attended called her "my little Church doctor"[11]— an interesting premonition. God led her to understand that her glory "would consist in becoming a great *saint!*"[12]

"I have always wanted to be a saint," Thérèse said. This desire was consuming: "I don't want to be a *saint by halves*."[13] Reading the lives of heroic French women, especially Joan of Arc, about whom Thérèse would write a play for the convent, taking the starring role, led her to believe that "I was born for *glory*."[14]

On the other hand, Thérèse did not exactly see herself as saint material. In measuring herself against the saints, she felt like "an obscure grain of sand"[15] in comparison to a mountain. She felt a similar inferiority when reading "spiritual treatises," when "my poor little mind is very quickly wearied." At these times she would close the book and open Scripture. "Then everything seems so clear.... I see that it is enough to recognise one's nothingness and abandon oneself, like a child, into the arms of God."[16] It is evident that her desire for glory did not grow out of vanity or arrogance.

Thérèse also believed, though, that God would not have given her a desire for sainthood without making it in some way possible. How then did she resolve the conflict between wanting to do great spiritual things but not thinking she was able to?

She drew on an insight she received from Saint John of the Cross, the great Carmelite spiritual writer who was Teresa of Avila's colleague. "I can," she said, "despite my littleness, aspire to sanctity."[17] This idea would open a way to holiness for both herself and generations to come. We can say that she—and all of us—could aspire to sanctity *because* of littleness. Drawing on the then recent invention of the mechanical elevator, she likened her discovery of her little way to a "lift to take me up to Jesus; because I am too little to climb the stairway of perfection."[18]

Thérèse read Scripture and was very familiar with it. She was fond of a passage from the Book of Wisdom: "For to him that is little, mercy will be shown" (see Wisdom 6:6). Here, she felt, she had found a key to her doubts about her own abilities. Before, holiness had appeared impossible to her. Now she had a way she could travel with confidence and love.[19]

What was her way? First of all, trust and faith. "I always feel," she wrote, "the same bold confidence of becoming a great saint because I don't count on my merits since I have *none,* but I trust in Him who is Virtue and Holiness."[20]

Another key lay in beginning with and accepting herself. "I've got to take myself just as I am, with all my imperfections," she wrote, "but somehow I shall have to find out a little way, all of my own."[21]

LOVING THE LITTLE FLOWER

Dorothy too thought that God expects something from each of us. He knows our gifts, abilities and even our limitations, and he calls us to grow in holiness out of our uniqueness. So it is possible to be "great" by being small. In fact, for those not destined for "greatness"—and that's most of us—we do best when we start small and for the most part remain that way.

Dorothy pointed out how devotion to Thérèse appealed to "the 'worker,' the common man.... It was the masses who first proclaimed her a saint. It was the 'people.'" In their daily lives the little way found fertile ground: "When we think of the people we think of the child at school, the housewife at her dishpan, the mother working, the mother sick, the man traveling, the migrant worker, the craftsman, the factory worker, the soldier, the rich, the bourgeois, the poor in tenements, the destitute man in the street. To a great extent she has made her appeal to all of these."[22]

One way Thérèse expressed her approach of littleness was through the metaphor of flowers, which she loved. She compared souls, especially what she saw as her own small soul, to flowers. Jesus, she wrote, "willed to create great souls comparable to lilies and roses, but He has created smaller ones and these must be content to be daisies or violets.... I understood, too, that Our Lord's love is revealed as perfectly in the most simple soul that resists His grace in nothing as in the most excellent soul."[23] In seeing herself as one of these smaller blooms, she gave herself the name by which millions would know her: "the *little flower* gathered by Jesus."[24]

Thérèse's appeal is not surprising when you consider how she saw the power of littleness in others. Speaking of her sister Céline, for example, she "remarks that 'He is prouder of what he has done in her soul, of her littleness and poverty, than of having created millions of suns and the whole expanse of the heavens….' It should be noted that on such occasions she speaks no longer in clichés but in a daring and, in a sense, shocking language."[25] The "shocking" language Karl Stern noted amounts to speaking of Céline—and as we have seen, of herself—in great and even cosmic terms.

Some critics of Thérèse have seen in these kinds of statements an immature inflation of self, like a child fantasizing about some grown-up exploit. Rather, Thérèse was expressing her belief in the value of the human person: In littleness we have not human souls that are insignificant, that people can throw away for their own aggrandizement; each soul, though little, has an infinite value.

In speaking of the worth of human beings, we move into a different realm. Our language expands to meet the many threats to life and its value. And in affirming human worth, "the 'sweet' and 'little' French girl," Thérèse, "disappears, and before you stands an immense, awe-inspiring timeless figure, a companion of the prophets, the apostles, the Fathers of the Church, and of the great mystics of the Middle Ages."[26]

God Is Easy to Please

Having a grandiose sense of oneself would be contradictory to the little way. At the other extreme, and similarly hostile to the little way, is not enough self-worth: self-abasement rather than

humility. The road to holiness does not have to begin with condemnation. Rather, this pilgrimage begins by accepting one's limitations in humility.

While Thérèse understood that "to become *a saint* one had to suffer much, seek out always the most perfect thing to do, and forget self," she also realized that "there were many degrees of perfection and each soul was free to respond to…Our Lord."[27]

However great her desire for spiritual greatness, Thérèse's way, "a little way," would follow a path of knowing her limitations but still giving as sacrificially as she could within the horizons of her life.

A small, simple soul pleases God as well as a "great" one. "How easy it is to please Jesus, to delight his heart," Thérèse wrote to Céline. "All we have to do is to love him without looking at ourselves, not examining our faults too closely."[28]

Following the little way, then, means starting with oneself, accepting oneself and doing the things that present themselves as well as one can. Thérèse recalled the words of her sister Marie, who was also her godmother: "She spoke…about the eternal riches that one can so easily amass each day, and what a misfortune it was to pass by without so much as stretching forth one's hand to take them. She explained the way of becoming *holy* through fidelity in little things."[29]

The mandate to see the light of God in everyone, including the least, leads us to love the person. We start by loving the poor for Jesus, Dorothy Day thought, but we soon love them for themselves and see each one to be special. If we go to those in need because they are beloved children of God, serve them

and live with them, we come to love them as human children too. Thérèse said:

> To be little...is...not to attribute to ourselves the virtues we practice, nor to believe ourselves capable of practicing virtue at all. It is rather to recognize the fact that God puts treasures of virtue into the hands of his little children to make use of them in time of need, but they remain always treasures of the good God.... To be little means that we must never be discouraged over our faults, for children often fall but they are too small to harm themselves very much.[30]

Where can we find holiness? In ourselves and in our daily lives, with all their small activities and gestures; in those around us, especially people experiencing deprivation or other limitations—and all of us are limited in some way. We honor the holy in God's creation when we treat others and the tasks of life with respect.

Friends of God

Besides showing us a little way we all can follow to saintliness, Thérèse, Dorothy and Mother Teresa also point out some important things about saints.

We find great comfort in thinking of saints as people of tremendous commitment and strength whom God chose for special missions. We can go to them and ask them to intercede for us precisely because they exist on a higher level. From heaven they continually contemplate and praise God, and from this place they care for us.

At the same time the saints lead us to imitate them in their

compassion, works of mercy, fortitude and prayerfulness, just as they imitated Christ. They walk with us as our friends in heaven; they are close to us, just as God is. Whether through intercession or imitation, saints bring us closer to God.

We have to be careful not to put saints only on pedestals. While we may look to them for help in one way or another, we must remember to see them in another dimension. Like Christianity as a whole—like the cross—our way of relating to the saints has both a *vertical* and a *horizontal* dimension: vertical in relating to the majesty of God, horizontal in relating to one another as members of the body of Christ. These two dimensions are distinct but not separate. On every moment of faith falls the shadow of the cross, on which Christ stretches his arms between heaven and earth and draws the two together.

The great spiritual power and glory of saints give people much-needed supernatural helpers. If we see saints only as intercessors, however, we miss other important things to which they call us. We may lose sight of their personal histories and the things they have said and done that make us uncomfortable. It may be hard to find them inspiring for our own lives. Dorothy was aware of this possibility when she responded to suggestions of her own sainthood by saying, "Don't call me a saint. I don't want to be dismissed so easily."[31]

As a group, Thérèse, Mother Teresa and Dorothy illustrate both the vertical and horizontal directions of sainthood. Thérèse has become one of the most popular saints ever in the time since her death, more than demonstrating the promise she made not long before her death: "If God answers my requests, my heaven will be spent on earth up until the end of

the world. Yes, I want to spend my heaven in doing good on earth."[32]

At the same time Thérèse gives us an example to follow in daily life. The naming of her as a doctor of the church drew attention to her "earthly" philosophy of living the little way. The widespread reading of *The Story of a Soul* did the same thing.

With Mother Teresa and Dorothy, we come at the matter from a different angle. They too serve as examples and inspirations to dedicate ourselves to God and others for the sake of God. As practitioners of the little way, they stand for the power of smallness as a spiritual path and a way of life. In looking at them, we move from the holiness of what they did on Earth to the possibility of their power as intercessors. Indeed, many people already pray to them.

To let these three holy women inspire us is to turn to them as both guides and sources of spiritual power. We can call on them to pray for us, and their example can strengthen us to follow the little way with attention and determination.

PRAYER

Thérèse of Lisieux, Dorothy Day and Mother Teresa knew the importance of prayer. Here was the source of the strength and inspiration they manifested in their public lives.

Speaking of the work and life and the Catholic Worker communities, Dorothy wrote, "Here is the way—or rather here is *a* way—for those who love God and their neighbor to try to live by the two great commandments. The frustrations that we experience are exercises in faith and hope, which are supernatural virtues. With prayer, one can go on cheerfully and even happily. Without prayer, how grim a journey!"[1]

Mother Teresa said to a new and nervous helper, "I don't want you to go to the home for the dying feeling sad. Pray and ask God to lift up your heart because whatever you see there, I want you to transmit joy." And on receiving the Nobel Peace Prize she said, "Let us keep that joy of loving Jesus in our hearts, and share that joy with all that we come in touch with. That radiating joy is real, for we have no reason not to be happy because we have Christ with us. Christ in our hearts, Christ in the poor that we meet, Christ in the smile that we give and the smile that we receive."[2]

We see here an illustration of how faith and works need each other. Doing good works without prayer is not futile, but it can be a joyless grind and perhaps a misguided one. Faith that does not express itself in good works, on the other hand, "is dead" (James 2:26). We do not merely do or merely believe; we do because our faith compels us, and we believe more because we do.

BE STILL

The contemplative tradition teaches that the first "language" of God was—and is—silence. Before God created anything, there was the silence of God. "Be still, and know that I am God!" says Psalm 46:10.

Contemplation seeks to connect with the silence at the heart of creation by getting behind the noise of the world and the thoughts and images that crowd our minds. To do so is to get in touch with God, and therefore it's not surprising that silence has much to do with prayer.

Silence lay at the heart of the spirituality Mother Teresa recommended for her Missionaries of Charity—for both the regular sisters and the contemplative branch of the order she established later. "God is the friend of silence," she wrote. "If we really want to pray we must first learn to listen, for in the silence of the heart God speaks." Her famous formulation was "The fruit of silence is prayer, the fruit of prayer is faith, the fruit of faith is love, and the fruit of love is silence."[3] Prayer, faith and love begin and end in silence.

Dorothy as well saw the value of silence, though this appreciation did not come automatically. Her first retreat,

made just a few years after she became Catholic, found her "not ready for the long days of silence, of reading, of intimate colloquy with one of the nuns."[4] A later retreat experience was quite different: "The five days of complete silence...were a feast indeed."[5]

As for Thérèse, silence was built into her Carmelite life. Within the walls of her monastery at Lisieux, "my desires were at last accomplished; my soul experienced a *PEACE* so sweet, so deep, it would be impossible to express it."[6]

THE PRAYER OF THE CHURCH

While personal prayer was an important part of spiritual growth and strength for each of these women, so was the prayer of the church. For Dorothy, "The Mass, high or low, is glorious and I feel that though we know we are but dust, at the same time we know too, and most surely through the Mass, that we are little less than the angels, and that it is indeed not I but Christ in me worshipping, and in Him I can do all things, though without Him I am nothing." The Mass made all the difference for her: "I would not dare to write or speak or try to follow the vocation God has given me to work for the poor and for peace if I did not have this constant reassurance of the Mass."[7]

The Mass was also the key to understanding love in community. "We cannot love God unless we love each other, and to love we must know each other. We know Him in the breaking of bread, and we know each other in the breaking of bread, and we are not alone any more. Heaven is a banquet and life is a banquet, too, even with a crust, where there is companionship."[8]

Thérèse spoke of "the tremendous consolation of daily Holy Communion" during three weeks of an influenza epidemic that devastated Carmel. "I was most happy to be united each day with my Beloved," she wrote. She described her thanksgiving after Communion:

> I picture my soul as a piece of land and I beg the Blessed Virgin to remove from it any *rubbish* that would prevent it from being *free;* and then I ask her to set up a huge tent worthy of *heaven,* adorning it with *her own* jewelry; finally, I invite all the angels and saints to come and conduct a magnificent concert there. It seems to me that when Jesus descends into my heart He is content to find Himself so well received and I, too, am content.[9]

Yet true to her little way, Thérèse admitted that even this glorious experience did not prevent distraction and sleepiness. "At the end of the thanksgiving when I see that I've made it so badly I make a resolution to then be thankful all through the rest of the day."[10]

Daily Mass, Communion and eucharistic adoration are central to the life of the Missionaries of Charity. Mother Teresa always spent an hour of her day in adoration of the Blessed Sacrament, no matter how busy she was and even when she was ill. She wrote to the archbishop of Calcutta in the late forties: "One thing I request you, your Grace, to give us all the spiritual help we need. If we have our Lord in the midst of us, with daily Mass and Holy Communion, I fear nothing for the Sisters, nor for myself. He will look after us. But without Him I cannot. I am helpless."[11]

Mother Teresa knew well the words of Jesus: "My flesh is true food and my blood is true drink. Those who eat my flesh and drink my blood abide in me, and I in them.... Whoever eats me will live because of me" (John 6:55–57).

THE DARK NIGHT

These three women of the little way cherished the hidden, obscure life of the Son of God. But could too much obscurity lead to despair?

Near her death it seemed to Thérèse as if her last days were receding into nothingness, like a vanishing point. Looking out into the garden from her bed, she said, "Look! Do you see the black hole [under some trees near the cemetery] where we can see nothing; I am in a hole like that as far as my body and soul are concerned. Ah, yes, what darkness! But I am at peace there."[12]

How to be at peace there? In spiritual terms we can think of darkness, nothingness, in two ways. One has to do with the "dark night of the soul," an experience of the seeming absence of God, dryness of prayer, hopelessness. Nothingness also can be an experience of the *presence* of God, as the contemplative tradition teaches. In nothingness we can feel empty and almost obliterated; we can also enter into the silence of God. Perhaps these two experiences, one negative and the other positive, do indeed meet at some mysterious point. In the very sense of being little or nothing, we find the God who always reaches out to us.

On the cross it seemed that all that Jesus had been working for was nothing. His persecutors had caught up with him

and condemned him to an inescapable death. All the teaching and healing he had done, all his efforts to lead people to believe in him, seemed to have ground to a halt. In that moment he cried out with a loud voice, "My God, my God, why have you forsaken me?" (Matthew 27:46; Mark 15:34). "It is finished," he says in John's Gospel (19:30); some translations say, "It is completed," or, "It is accomplished"—not over but fulfilled.

The Gospels tell the whole story of Christ with the end in mind, and Jesus' passion and death were not the end. Out of the despair of the cross grew the possibility of resurrection. In the stillest moment, when all grew dark, Jesus encountered the silence of death and the tomb and complete union with the Father. As Mother Teresa wrote to a priest who had entered into a dark night of the soul, "In you, today, He wants to relive his complete submission to His Father. It does not matter what you feel, but what He feels in you....You and I must let Him live in us and through us in this world."[13]

In the end hiddenness, smallness, even darkness, is a gift. It can be where we encounter God and where God touches us. It is a place that affirms the holiness of our littleness and the little things we do. The vigil of darkness gives way to light and to a transformed life. The moment of abandonment becomes the first taste of glory.

And so it is with the little way. Many people do not know Thérèse's full religious name: Thérèse of the Child Jesus *and the Holy Face*. In her time there was a devotion to the suffering face of Christ. It had its roots in the tradition that Christ's image remained on the cloth that Veronica used to wipe his

face while he carried his cross. An official Confraternity of the Holy Face was formed in Tours, France, in 1884 for the purpose of encouraging people to make prayerful reparation for blasphemies uttered against Christ.

Thérèse's participation in the devotion to the Holy Face did much to popularize it. In contemplating the Holy Face, she would confront suffering: Christ's, her own, her community's, the world's. "Thérèse," Hans Urs von Balthasar wrote, "wishes all her life long to be doing what Veronica did once: to console Our Lord, and lighten his burden by her boundless self-surrender."[14]

In seeking the Holy Face of the suffering one, Thérèse also found a way through that suffering. She could be at peace in the darkness because she knew that the only way to get to the light was to go through the darkness.

"CONVICTING EMPTINESS"

Only after Mother Teresa's death did the world come to know that she who throughout her life was such a rock of faith underwent her own dark night. A person always sensitive to the movements of God's spirit in her own soul, she had written about her experience:

> In the darkness…Lord, my God, who am I that You should forsake me? The child of Your love—and now become as the most hated one. The one—You have thrown away as unwanted—unloved. I call, I cling, I want, and there is no one to answer…. Where I try to raise my thoughts to heaven, there is such convicting emptiness that those very

thoughts return like sharp knives and hurt my very soul. Love—the word—it brings nothing. I am told God lives in me—and yet the reality of darkness and coldness and emptiness is so great that nothing touches my soul.[15]

It may come as a bit of a shock to hear someone like Mother Teresa say that she felt God hated and had abandoned her, that heaven was empty and that her prayers came back at her like weapons. This side of Mother Teresa's experience, however, uncovers several spiritual truths.

First, doubt is not always the opposite or the absence of faith. The Christian spiritual tradition over and over again attests to the importance—even the necessity—of doubt. A person of faith who has never doubted is a person who has received a rare blessing. It is a hallmark of a mature faith to acknowledge doubt in one's faith life, engage it and emerge with strengthened faith. The trappist monk Thomas Merton wrote, "We too often forget that faith is a matter of questioning and struggle before it becomes one of certitude and peace. You have to doubt and reject everything else in order to believe firmly in Christ, and after you have begun to believe, your faith itself must be tested and purified."[16]

We can see in Mother Teresa's dark night that even saints go through major spiritual crises. To have heroic faith does not mean having a perfect spiritual life, if by "perfect" we mean flawless. The strength Mother Teresa showed leads us to aspire not to an unrealistic perfection but to perseverance through dark times in the hope that we will come out in the light.

Finally, a sense of abandonment sensitizes us to the aban-

doned. As Thérèse said of the Holy Face: "His look was as it were hidden!... [I]t is still hidden today...for who comprehends the tears of Jesus?... He makes Himself poor so that we may be able to do Him charity; He stretches out His hand to us like a *beggar*, that upon the sunlit day of judgment.... He may be able to utter... *'Come, blessed of My Father.'*"[17]

"Following Thérèse into this night of nothingness, Mother Teresa too sought the Holy Face of the Crucified in the crushed and the dying, walked the path of spiritual childhood in the small, ordinary realities of her days, and lived life one little act of love at a time."[18]

This movement turns the margins into the center. Instead of centering on competition for wealth, power and advantage, we hold first the value that all people have as God's beloved children. Here the poor and the resourced join hands and pull one another to the same level of value and justice.

The journey through darkness leads us nearer to God, not further away, because we draw close to the poverty of which the gospel speaks. Sometimes to feel the presence of God we have to experience its absence; to feel full of God's spirit, at times we need to feel empty.

"God has shown his greatness by using nothingness," Mother Teresa wrote in a letter to all the Missionaries of Charity sisters, priests, brothers and Coworkers, "so let us always remain in our nothingness—so as to give God free hand to use us without consulting us. Let us accept whatever he gives and give whatever he takes with a big smile."[19]

HIDDEN TREASURES

In the Gospel of Matthew, Jesus likens the kingdom of God to "treasure hidden in a field, which someone found and hid; then in his joy he goes and sells all that he has and buys that field" (13:44). We are to treasure the kingdom as something of the highest value, such that we would give everything we have for it.

For Thérèse of Lisieux, Mother Teresa and Dorothy Day, the kingdom was hidden in the little, like treasure buried in a field. Though these women eventually attained fame, their ministries began in "hidden" places: convents, slums and inner-city storefronts. In places many people refused to go and did not even see, they found the presence of Christ hidden in sick and abandoned people, in small tasks, in the people around them.

Karl Stern wrote, "It is [her] hiddenness which is so important in the picture of St. Thérèse.... Hiddenness, for some reason, seems to be an essential element in the economy of salvation." Abraham and the Israelites were "inconspicuous.... The Blessed Virgin was an unknown and hidden girl when she received the salutation from the angel. People often do not realize that Christ himself, in terms of temporal fame and in terms of political history, was quite unknown."[1]

Of course all these figures—Abraham, Mary and Jesus—emerged from hiddenness. God plucked Abram from his homeland and made him a father of faith. Through her openness to the will of God, Mary became the Mother of God and the Queen of Heaven. Jesus founded a way that in time shook an empire. In one way, however, Jesus still remains hidden: in the poor to whom people like Dorothy and Mother Teresa devoted their lives; in our loved ones and family; in our friends, neighbors and coworkers; in strangers and in all the little things that make up our days.

A KINGDOM PRINCIPLE

In Matthew 25 Jesus tells the story of how God will judge us at the end of the world. He will look at how we treated the least among us: whether we gave food to the hungry and drink to the thirsty, clothed the naked and visited the sick and imprisoned. Why? Because how we treat these is how we treat the Lord himself. He is in them, and they are in him. If we see the presence of God in Jesus, then we should be able to see that same presence in the people and activities of our lives.

The kingdom of God works by reverse logic. "Greatness" hides in the little, while what the world considers great is, in the end, rather small. It is the logic of the Beatitudes and the Magnificat.

> Blessed are the poor in spirit, for theirs is the kingdom of heaven.
> Blessed are those who mourn, for they will be comforted.
> Blessed are the meek, for they will inherit the earth.

Blessed are those who hunger and thirst for righteousness, for they will be filled.

Blessed are the merciful, for they will receive mercy.

Blessed are the pure in heart, for they will see God.

Blessed are the peacemakers, for they will be called children of God.

Blessed are those who are persecuted for righteousness' sake, for theirs is the kingdom of heaven.

Blessed are you when people revile you and persecute you and utter all kinds of evil against you falsely on my account. Rejoice and be glad, for your reward is great in heaven. (Matthew 5:3–12)

My soul magnifies the Lord,
 and my spirit rejoices in God my Savior,
for he has looked with favor on the lowliness of his servant.
 Surely, from now on all generations will call me blessed;
for the Mighty One has done great things for me,
 and holy is his name.
His mercy is for those who fear him
 from generation to generation.
He has shown strength with his arm;
 he has scattered the proud in the thoughts of their hearts.
He has brought down the powerful from their thrones,
 and lifted up the lowly;
he has filled the hungry with good things,
 and sent the rich away empty.
He has helped his servant Israel,
 in remembrance of his mercy,

> according to the promise he made to our ancestors,
>
> to Abraham and to his descendants forever.

(Luke 1:46–55)

As Dorothy put it, "Worldly justice and unworldly justice are quite different things. The supernatural approach when understood is to turn the other cheek, to give up what one has, willingly, gladly, with no spirit of martyrdom, to rejoice in being the least, to be unrecognized, the slighted."[2] The kingdom of God is full of these reversals. The foolish are wise, the defeated are victorious, the poor are rich.

TREASURES OF CREATION

The message of the little way does not condemn power and wealth in themselves. But it does reveal something of the mind of God on how human beings are to use their resources. We need to do everything with the awareness that the Earth is not a fluke of the universe but the creation of God. God made the entire universe out of love, so that he could share his divine life. God loves all of creation and its creatures. The human response is gratitude, respect and love of our own.

The abuse of creation—which can take many forms— throws God's love back in his face, so to speak, or at least ignores it. It is a turning away from God. In *that* situation power and wealth can become sinful. To produce and consume with a blind eye to the survival of the environment, to accumulate and use our financial resources for our own benefit and without regard for the good of all: These actions are a kind of selfishness. More than that, they amount to idolatry: doing

things, in the words of the Second Vatican Council, "without any reference to [the] Creator."[3] To spend billions on office complexes and sports stadiums while schools deteriorate and people go homeless, hungry and without enough health care is a sin against God.

The little way offers a proper vision of creation: It leads us to see everything with reference to God. The little way brings our attention to the small things, things from which the glamour and allure of the big, sleek and glorious can distract us. It corrects our vision.

Often we don't recognize the divine that is right in front of us—whether in the poor, in our daily work, in our communications with others, in a book we are reading, even in a room we are cleaning. We tend to see value only in the events of politics, business, sports and other spectacles of this world. This narrowness of vision is also idolatry: We see only the created, not the Creator.

The greatness of the small—in contrast sometimes to the pettiness of the large—permeates the gospel, where "the last will be first" and "the meek…will inherit the earth" (Matthew 19:30; 5:5; see Psalm 37:11). Karl Stern saw this backward logic of the kingdom of God in writing about Thérèse: "We see that a curious incongruity exists between the political and the spiritual history of mankind. It seems almost as if a thing to be world-shaking in spiritual terms had to be inconspicuous and unknown in temporal terms."[4] That faith and virtue lay in the small, hidden and even invisible was certainly a truth Thérèse, Mother Teresa and Dorothy Day knew.

The Little Flower's Example

When Saint Thérèse lay sick and dying, she overheard two novices whom she directed chatting outside her window. They were speculating about the death notice that the mother superior would send to the other Carmelite communities, as was customary on the death of a sister. "I really wonder sometimes what our Mother Prioress will find to say about Sister Thérèse when she dies," one of the novices said. "She has certainly never done anything worth speaking of."[5]

Imagine Thérèse lying there in pain, trying to collect her spiritual and emotional resources to face her approaching death, only to hear this quaint speculation about whether her memory would amount to anything. Did she feel the anguish of wounded pride? On the contrary, the words of this young sister did not seem to trouble her.

In fact, she was probably pleased. "Complete and utter anonymity was one of the essential features of her 'way.' It is one of the elements of 'littleness,' that concept of hers which often leads to so much misunderstanding. The idea was precious to her 'that no one may think of me, that I may be forgotten and trodden underfoot as a grain of salt.'"[6]

While Thérèse enjoyed the satisfaction of knowing that her intense spiritual work was, at the time, unappreciated, in the long run her wish to be forgotten was not granted. Rather she has had "a spectacular career" as a saint. The church both canonized her and declared her a doctor of the church. Millions of people have prayed to her. Her statues stand in thousands of churches. All this for someone whose life ended in young adulthood and who spent most of it in cloistered

surroundings. She founded no institutions. Though she desired to become a missionary to the Far East, she did not travel after becoming a Carmelite. She was not responsible for great undertakings. She did not face martyrdom, unless one considers the way she endured her illness a form of martyrdom.

Why are such power, devotion and interest connected to so seemingly insignificant a figure? What would be the reply to those naïve novices outside Thérèse's window?

Mother Teresa answered this question. "'For what will Holy Father canonize her?' they asked. 'She has not done anything.' And the Holy Father wrote one sentence: 'I will canonize her because she did ordinary things with extraordinary love.'"[7]

In similar words Dorothy asked about Thérèse, "What did she do? She practiced the presence of God and did all things—all the little things that make up our daily life and contact with others—for His honor and glory."[8] Dorothy concluded, "I began to understand the greatness of the Little Flower. By doing nothing she did everything. She let loose powers, consolations, a stream of faith, hope and love that will never cease to flow. How much richer we are because of her."[9]

DOWNWARDLY MOBILE

The little way invites a certain amount of "downsizing." Thérèse of Lisieux, Dorothy Day and Mother Teresa all chose to marginalize themselves in terms of wealth, possessions and status. One of the reasons Dorothy and Mother Teresa did so was to be able to see those on the margins and therefore serve them. To "make" oneself one of the abandoned creates a situation where it is easier to see others as one's own people.

Thérèse stated her motivation clearly: "That shall be my life…to miss no single opportunity of making some small sacrifice…always doing the tiniest things right, and doing it for love."[1] In this brief statement she condenses the meaning of the little way to its essence.

A PERMANENT NOVICE

In 1893 Thérèse asked for and received permission to remain a novice. Normally a Carmelite moved out of this phase of religious life after three years, but Thérèse wanted to remain in it permanently. For the rest of her life, the community would expect her to live under the principles of the novitiate—never to become a sister in full standing.

What a decision! From childhood Thérèse had yearned and struggled to enter the Carmel of Lisieux. Now she was giving up forever the possibility of higher status. While she would be a full member of the community, her work would remain tied to those just starting religious life. Though spiritually mature, "she was always to be the youngest, always the last."[2]

Part of this decision grew out of the fact that because two of Thérèse's sisters were part of the chapter, the general meetings of the community, Thérèse could never, according to the rules, sit on the chapter or be elected to a major office in the community. Her decision, however, was not merely a matter of following regulations. It was Thérèse's choice to eschew honor, derail ambition and limit her scope of action. By confining herself to a low station in the community, she presented herself with the challenge of being holy with the least means.

In her permanent novitiate she became the mistress of novices. For help in her task, she prayed, "Lord, I am too little to nourish your children; if you wish to give them through me what is suitable for each one, fill my small hand, and without leaving your arms or turning away my head, I will give your treasures to the soul who will come and ask me for nourishment."[3]

Might we too enter into a "permanent novitiate"? Not necessarily rejecting all opportunities for advancement in our lives, but striving to do everything and relate to everyone by devoting ourselves without thought of praise or blame? Strength of character follows from being able to do the right thing without regard for how others may interpret our actions. It includes a willingness to forgo congratulations and not let

fear of shame inhibit us. A "permanent novitiate" would mean accepting our limits, even our failures, and concentrating on the possible and the good that are right in front of us.

If the little way takes this one step, in a sense it stays here. "If I am ever inclined," Thérèse said, "to get worried because of some misguided words or thoughts, I turn towards myself and say, 'Ah, still standing in the same spot as at the beginning!' But I say it to myself very peacefully, and without sadness. It is so good to feel one's weakness and littleness."[4]

In December 1894 Thérèse's sister Pauline, who had become prioress of the Lisieux Carmel community, instructed her sister to write down her childhood memories. She wanted her sister to write of "'*my little* doctrine' as you call it."[5]

The text that became *The Story of Soul*, however, was more for Thérèse than an escape into a happier past. It came to be part of her growing realization that holiness lay not in martyrdom, as it did for Joan of Arc, or life in a distant mission, to which she had aspired. Thérèse realized that she would find sanctity within the walls of Carmel and in the daily round of prayer and work, silence and conversation, difficulties and consolations.

Thérèse's writing presented her with a dilemma. "It seemed to me it would distract my heart by too much concentration on myself." Jesus reassured her that she would please him by obedience in this matter. "Besides," she said, "I'm going to be doing only one thing: I shall begin to sing what I must sing eternally: '*The Mercies of the Lord*.'"[6]

Dorothy would experience a similar reservation in her profession and a similar acceptance of it. "The sustained effort

of writing, of putting pen to paper so many hours a day when there are human beings around who need me, when there is sickness, and hunger, and sorrow, is a harrowingly painful job. I feel that I have done nothing well. But I have done what I could."[7]

DO ALL THINGS WELL

Eileen Egan made a connection between the spirituality of Thérèse of Lisieux and the isolation Mother Teresa must have felt when teaching alone in the slums. Mother's "new solitude was accepted in the spirit of the patron she had chosen, the 'little' Saint Thérèse whose 'way' emphasized the acceptance of the monotony of obscure sacrifices." While "the great way of heroic martyrdom was not open to many, [the] slow, secret…'little way' [was] open to the generality of folk"[8]—that is, all of us.

Thérèse, Mother Teresa and Dorothy Day all started small, and smallness continued to guide their lives and work. In their valuing of small things, they transformed the little into the great—without losing the humble character of the little things. Littleness became greatness because it remained little. They lived the words of the Gospel: "Whoever wishes to be great among you must be your servant, and whoever wishes to be first among you must be your slave; just as the Son of Man came not to be served but to serve" (Matthew 20:26–28), and, "Many who are first will be last, and the last will be first" (Mark 10:31).

We must be careful not to see in Thérèse's intent of "always doing the tiniest things right" a recommendation of perfectionism or a constant fear of making mistakes. Rather

she meant to give herself to every task or encounter with another and to do things well for the sake of generosity and love. Her life—and the example she offers—meant first of all paying attention to the small tasks that make up a day.

Mother Teresa had a similar sense of doing things well and so glorifying God. Moreover, she did not reserve this awareness to works of mercy or spiritual pursuits.

> Her life was made up of doing…small things…. These weren't chores for her, but little gifts of herself, things she did for Jesus. Everything we do, she said,…can be done for the love of Jesus, can be offered as something beautiful for God. The whole day can be a prayer, a dialogue with God. She asked, "Do you play well? Sleep well? Eat well? These are duties. Nothing is small for God."[9]

When she met the English cricket player Bob Taylor, she told him, "You must play this game of yours simply to the best of your ability, for if you are doing your best you are pleasing mankind and thus you too are doing God's work."[10]

Dorothy Day also recognized the importance of doing small, everyday things well, and she came to this notion—and Thérèse's little way—from her contemplation of the great mass of human problems and sins. What to do under the crushing weight of the world's troubles, on which the efforts of those seeking the good do not seem to have much effect?

"I was all the more confirmed in my faith in the little way of St. Thérèse," Dorothy wrote. "We do the things that come to hand, we pray our prayers and beg also for an increase of faith—and God will do the rest."[11] The way to deal with big

problems was not with big solutions but by doing little things that add up to big things.

Attentiveness to the value of investing small tasks with care means a different view of time as well. We tend to think of time as a commodity—and a very limited one at that. We try to cram as many activities as we can into our waking hours, and the clock is always ticking. But if we look at time as holy time, our use of it changes. We can "invest" it rather than just use it up. Giving a worthy task the time it needs, or doing something that may seem like a "waste" of time, can produce surprising results.

"The same principle always worked," Dorothy wrote:

> If we are rushed for time, sow time and we will reap time. Go to church and spend a quiet hour in prayer. You will have more time than ever and your work will get done. Sow time with the poor. Sit and listen to them, give them your time lavishly. You will reap time a hundredfold. Sow kindness and you will reap kindness. Sow love, you will reap love.[12]

SMALL MARTYRDOMS

Like Dorothy's insight about time, the little way itself presents a paradox: Little things seem to have small effects, but they are absolutely necessary to keep love moving through the system of the world and carrying away the toxins of suffering. Thérèse's life in a Carmelite convent presented her with numerous opportunities to follow the little way of love: taking care of the chapel, working in the dining hall, writing and act-

ing in plays for the community, caring for the ill and going out of her way to treat the more difficult sisters with concern. In fact, one could say that almost her whole life was made up of little things. And she found the spiritual significance of this life.

Difficult or unpleasant tasks presented chances to do small things with love and a spirit of sacrifice. One sister in the convent had "the faculty of displeasing me in everything." Thérèse wrote, "Not wishing to give in to the natural antipathy I was experiencing, I told myself that charity must not consist in feelings but in works; then I set myself to doing for this Sister what I would do for the person I loved the most."[13]

Thérèse offers an interesting insight: Treat a person you dislike as if that person were the one you liked the most. "I say to you, love your enemies and pray for those who persecute you" (Matthew 5:44). In fact, she made a point of seeking out "the Sisters who are the least agreeable to me," so she could offer them a kind word, a smile and a "spiritual banquet of loving and joyful charity."[14]

Thérèse "loved to render [the sisters] all sorts of little services."[15] She accepted blame for things others had done wrong, cleaned up after other people and ate the food others did not want. When sisters borrowed books from her, she did not ask for their return.

We might think this behavior strange. It is certainly not the kind of thing many people in our self-centered society would do, let alone consider. Thérèse, however, was not doing these things for their own sake or to bring pain upon herself. She saw these as sacrifices for God and a means of loving others and perfecting herself in virtue.

When helping a frail sister one evening, Thérèse heard music coming from the distance. She immediately imagined "a well-lighted drawing room, brilliantly gilded, filled with elegantly dressed young ladies conversing together and conferring upon each other all sorts of compliments and other worldly remarks." It's clear that Thérèse could have seen herself, lively and attractive as she was, in such company. Instead she was helping an infirm elderly person down the cold, dimly lit corridor of a cloister. But something "happened in my soul; what I know is that the Lord illumined it with rays of *truth* which so surpassed the dark brilliance of earthly feasts that I could not believe my happiness."[16]

In this moment Thérèse was not simply rationalizing her disappointment and self-sacrifice. She was positively joyful about what she was doing. The dim light of the cloister surpassed the brightness of the more glamorous life that an attractive and talented person such as she could have been leading.

The value of what we do and experience is reckoned not only in our material world. Though we live in the world, we are not of it. We belong to the kingdom of God, which is among us now and is to come in its fullness. We are citizens of heaven, and we walk the path to heaven on our earthly pilgrimage. God reaps what we sow, and the harvest God wants is one of love for one another, of seeking the good of the other ahead of our own good.

The satisfaction of such love may not be apparent at first. But it is a deeper contentment and delight than what self-centeredness brings. Our acts of generosity register in a place and in a way we do not always see, but we hope and

believe that God is pleased with them.

Numerous other opportunities for small sacrifices presented themselves to Thérèse, like not looking at the clock during prayer time and avoiding unnecessary words during recreation periods with the other sisters. She endured without complaint the distracting rattle of rosary beads during prayer and the splash of dirty laundry water from a novice. As one biographer wrote, "No one noticed the heroism of these little things."[17]

Well, perhaps not at the time. But in her book on Thérèse, Dorothy Day wrote, "One needs to have gone through these small martyrdoms to understand them."[18] These little events may seem insignificant—not the stuff of sainthood—but are they not the kinds of things that make up most of our lives?

Like Thérèse, Dorothy did not feel she measured up to the "great" saints, so she had to try another path to holiness. "When I say mortification," she said, "I do not mean the sort of penance the saints undertake. I was not like those grand souls who practice all kinds of penance from childhood. My mortification consisted in checking my self-will, keeping back an impatient word, doing little things for those around me without their knowing it, and countless things like that."[19] We see in these women that a lifetime of "countless things like that" add up to the making of a "great" soul.

JESUS' KIND OF LOVE

A "hidden and ordinary life" appealed as well to Mother Teresa, who pointed to the thirty years Jesus spent in Nazareth before embarking on his public ministry.[20] She also found

ways to do small things that meant a lot for her sisters. One Missionary of Charity, recalling her first Christmas in the order, told of how Mother Teresa stayed up the night before decorating the dining room and placing at each sister's place a small bag of gifts, on which were written the words, "Happy Christmas to dear Sister...from Mother."[21]

But Christmas served as an occasion to ask for sacrifices too. In Advent an empty crib and a box of straw stood in the sisters' chapel. In the weeks before Christmas, whenever a sister would make even a small personal sacrifice, she would go discreetly to the chapel and put a piece of straw in the crib. "Thus when the infant Jesus was laid in the manger at Christmas it would be in a crib warmed by [the sisters'] love and sacrifice."[22] Christmas for the missionaries meant "a time to welcome Jesus, not in a cold manger of our hearts but in a heart full of love and humility, in a heart so pure, so immaculate, so warm with love for one another."[23]

A life of love and service may gain us little recognition and prestige. It might not add up to much according to society's standards of success. It could, in the eyes of some, seem bizarre. Dorothy was aware that some would consider the Catholic Worker lifestyle to be "craziness." In her 1945 Christmas appeal, she wrote, "If we hadn't got Christ's own words for it, it would seem raving lunacy to believe that if I offer a bed and food and hospitality to some man, woman or child...that my guest is Christ."[24]

In fact, the strangeness of the way of sacrifice and service not only contrasts with more "successful" pursuits; it is also in a sense a higher path. Like Thérèse, who preferred to care for

an ailing sister rather than be at a glittering party, Dorothy, while acknowledging the difficulty of the Catholic Worker life, favored walking this road because in doing so she did not tread on others. "Daily, hourly, to give up our own possessions and especially to subordinate our own impulses and wishes to others—these are hard, hard things; and I don't think they ever get any easier.... At least we can avoid being comfortable through the exploitation of others."[25]

To sacrifice one's interests for the good of another, whether that means helping someone or taking care not to hurt someone, may be the perfect expression of Christian love. It is the kind of love Jesus preached and lived, even to the point of giving his life. The everyday forms of these sacrifices, these small martyrdoms and daily witnesses to faith, can seem like craziness and failure—like a humble pile of straw. In the light of a gospel faith, they make for sanity and success.

"Day after day," Dorothy said, "we accept our failure, but we accept it because of our knowledge of the victory of the Cross. God has given us our vocation, as He gave it to the small boy who contributed his few loaves and fishes to help feed the multitude, and which Jesus multiplied so that He fed five thousand people."[26] The poor widow too gave all she had to the temple treasury, in contrast to the rich people who gave out of their abundance: "Truly I tell you, this poor widow has put in more than all of them" (Luke 21:3).

On the little way, "failure" is success, and "loss" is gain. You might also say, as Saint Paul did, that foolishness is wisdom (see 1 Corinthians 1:18–25).

Dorothy wrote in a 1972 issue of the *Catholic Worker:* "The work is hard.... But if God is with us who can be against us? In Him we can do all things. We do know that God has chosen the foolish of this world to confound the wise. So please help us to continue in our folly, in the 'Little Way' of Saint Thérèse."[27]

ONE PERSON AT A TIME

The little way's reversal of values also shows itself in its measure of effectiveness. Not surprisingly, effectiveness starts not with big numbers of people or problems but with one at a time. "*Ek, Ek, Ek,* as Mother Teresa would say in Bengali, 'One by one by one.'"[1]

Thérèse of Lisieux, Dorothy Day and Mother Teresa knew that every life has absolute value. Save only one life, and you have done something of absolute value. Do something to make a life better, and what you do lays up permanent treasure.

Dorothy worked to relieve suffering on the individual level and to change the systems that impoverished and brutalized people. But did the social change efforts of the Catholic Worker shorten the lines of those waiting for soup, coffee and a piece of bread at the hospitality houses? Did the relief it brought to many make a difference to the millions it never reached? It's difficult to say. But in an important way it doesn't matter.

William D. Miller, a historian of the movement, wrote that each Worker house merited its own history, "because each story is the drama of a few people who were convinced that the doomfelt shaking of an increasingly eccentric universe

could, through active love, be brought into harmony; that one could begin this reconstruction only in the 'little' way of St. Thérèse of Lisieux and with a few of the most woebegotten of men; and that, indeed, to 'succeed' would be to fail."[2]

THE ARITHMETIC OF LOVE

By 1984 the Missionaries of Charity and their collaborators had treated 4,000,000 leprosy patients, provided food to over 150,000 hungry people, served more than 13,000 in homes for the poor dying and cared for 6,000 children in over 100 children's homes.[3] At this time the population of Calcutta was between six and eight million, of which more than 200,000 lived on the street.

With these large numbers in mind, Eileen Egan thought about the sixty children in the Missionaries' home for children. "Mother Teresa seemed to follow an old maxim that the good that is possible is obligatory. She and her Sisters were obliged to do everything possible for the poorest and weakest; they were not paralyzed by the thought of what they could not do."[4] If the Missionaries thought they could subtract even one person from the number of those suffering, they did. In fact, they believed they *had* to. The awareness of the numbers they could not reach did not serve as an excuse to ignore the good they could do.

On several occasions Mother Teresa had to answer the charge that she and the sisters were responding to only a tiny fraction of the need. "I do not add up," she would say. "I only subtract from the total number of poor or dying....We use ourselves to save what we can."[5] Subtracting one life from mis-

ery or a lonely death is God's arithmetic of love. Think of the Gospel story of the lost coin: "What woman having ten silver coins, if she loses one of them, does not light a lamp, sweep the house, and search carefully until she finds it? When she has found it, she calls together her friends and neighbors, saying, 'Rejoice with me, for I have found the coin that I had lost'" (Luke 15:8–9).

Mother Teresa said that the work of the Missionaries of Charity was a drop in the ocean but a drop that still made a difference. The Missionaries' primary schools helped only a fraction of the children in need of basic education, but they made a tremendous difference for the thousands who otherwise would have been left in the street.

If when visiting the Missionaries' Calcutta children's home, Mother Teresa saw an infant likely to die soon, "she would wrap it in a blanket and give it to one of the helpers to hold, with the instruction simply to love that child until it died."[6] This action encapsulated her whole value system: A person, no matter how small and vulnerable and even without much chance of survival, is worthy of love. Whether that individual is dying, poor, unwanted, sick or outcast, that person deserves love because he or she is a human being who is a child of God. If Mother Teresa could not save a person's life, she at least could make him or her feel loved and wanted for the time left. She loved to say, "It is not success that is important but our faithfulness."[7]

"It is the same thing for our Home for the Dying and our home for the children," she said. "If we didn't have that home, those people we have picked up, they would have died in the

street. I think it is worth while having that home even for those few people to die beautifully, with God and in peace."[8]

The Missionaries of Charity do not give homes to every last abandoned dying person, AIDS sufferer, sick child or single mother, just as the Catholic Worker did not feed all the homeless. But both these groups have continued their work because they know that doing even a little bit of good has infinite possibilities, and this good echoes in the courts of heaven.

Smallness means serving all those in need who ask for it, even the terminally ill and those who do not improve with treatment. Smallness includes sometimes primitive and imperfect methods of caring for the masses. This was especially true at the beginning of Mother Teresa's mission, when the order did not have many supplies. Basic care is better than none at all.

THE LAW OF CHARITY

For her part, Dorothy knew that it would be hard for a handful of Catholic Workers to transform the world. Single acts, however, have multiple values. First, they add up. In addition, they are all one can do at a given time. And in the spiritual realm they have a power many times their size.

"What good can one person do?" Dorothy asked.

What is the sense of our small effort?... We must lay one brick at a time, take one step at a time; we can be responsible only for the one action of the present moment. But we can beg for an increase of love in our hearts that will vitalize and transform all our individual actions, and know that God will take them and multiply them, as Jesus multiplied the loaves and fishes.[9]

Karl Stern described what he termed Thérèse's "Law of the Conservation of Charity":

> Nothing which is directed either toward or away from God can ever be lost.... In the economy of the universe...[an] inestimable preciousness...[exists in] every hidden movement of the soul. Compared with people in her and our century, Thérèse had a peculiar sense of statistics. "Zero, by itself, has no value, but put alongside *one* it becomes potent, always provided it is put on the *proper* side, after, and not before...." With this goes an immediate, almost natural, awareness of the infinite value of each single person.[10]

The point does not lie in statistics. Mother Teresa could have been speaking for Thérèse and Dorothy when she said, "Don't look for numbers. Every small act of love for the unwanted and the poor is important to Jesus.... Every human being comes from the hand of God and we all know what is the love of God for us."[11]

As one writer observed of the work of the Missionary Brothers, if they ever felt "that what they were achieving was so little in relation to the magnitude of the need, the boys and young men who found a home, companionship, clean clothes, a warm meal or simply a sofa on which to snooze undoubtedly had a different estimate."[12]

The work of the kingdom of God proceeds one person at a time. Mother Teresa was famous for giving the person she was talking to at a given moment her full attention. Photos of her with others bear out this quality. "I believe," she said, "in person to person contact. Every person is Christ for me and

since there is only one Jesus, the person I am meeting is the one person in the world at that moment."[13]

It would appear that Mother Teresa cared more for the individual person than for the system. But it would be more accurate to say that she believed in changing systems by changing people. On one hand she described her philosophy as thus: "We all have a duty to serve God where we feel called. I feel called to help individuals, not to interest myself in structures or institutions."[14] At the same time she believed that starting with individuals would add up to a much different world.

Her distrust of institutions grew out of a fear of what "bigness" could do. "The system is all too big, too ponderous, too unwieldy," she said. "Everything needs to be decentralized, into many smaller institutions, smaller hospitals, courts and so on. I wonder that there is ever any unemployment, with all the work that needs to be done in the world."[15] So much work remained, but vast numbers of able-bodied people were idle, and "the system" could not bring the two together.

LOVE BEGINS AT HOME

Besides being cumbersome, social service institutions also could serve as dumping grounds for those who were difficult to care for. On a visit to a church in Ireland, Mother Teresa expressed her concern about the practice of institutionalizing the vulnerable. "If you really love God begin by loving your child, your husband, your wife. The old people, where are they? They are in some institution. Why are they not with you? Where is the crippled child? In some institution. Why is that child not with you? That child, young

mothers and fathers, is a gift from God."[16]

Love does begin at home, where we are, and in a sense it should stay there. Mother Teresa saw this in her childhood, when her mother, Drana, opened the family home to the poor. One elderly woman was a regular guest for meals. Drana told her daughter: "Welcome her warmly, with love. My child, never eat a single mouthful unless you are sharing it with others."[17]

Mother Teresa recalled: "We had guests at table every day. At first I used to ask: 'Who are they?' and Mother would answer: 'Some are our relatives, but all of them are our people.' When I was older, I realized that the strangers were poor people who had nothing and whom my mother was feeding."[18]

What a wonderful way to present this act of hospitality. First, to put it in terms a child could understand. Then to have the words really explain what was going on: the welcoming of poor people to the family table.

There was an elderly, sick, alcoholic woman, File, whose family had abandoned her. Drana would go to File every week and bring her food, bathe her and clean her house. On one occasion Drana brought into the family six children when their mother, a poor widow, died. Live "only, all for God and Jesus," Drana told the young Agnes.[19]

Years later Drana would receive a letter from her daughter describing the fine school where she was teaching. She wrote about the fact that everyone liked her and appreciated her work.

"Do not forget," Drana wrote Teresa in reply, "that you went to India for the sake of the poor. Do you remember our File? She was covered in sores, but what caused her far more

suffering was the knowledge that she was all alone in the world. We did what we could for her but the worst thing was not the sores but the fact that her family has forgotten her."[20]

Mother Teresa felt that helping people on a mass scale might make it too easy to overlook the presence of Christ in each person. This presence called for a reverence and devotion similar to the attention we give the real presence of Christ in the Eucharist. Each individual is a kind of tabernacle, deserving our full and undivided compassion. The Jesus we encounter in the Eucharist is the same Lord we meet in other people. "They are one and the same Jesus; at the altar and in the streets. Neither exists without the other."[21] As the *Catechism of the Catholic Church* says, "The Eucharist commits us to the poor" (1397).

A PERSONAL REVOLUTION

In 1947 the *Catholic Worker* newspaper marked the beginning of its fifteenth year by printing on its first page the "much-quoted statement of [Pope] Pius XI: 'Let us thank God that He makes us live among the present problems. It is no longer permitted to anyone to be mediocre.' Dorothy Day added the personalist injunction: 'The coat which hangs in your closet belongs to the poor…. It is you yourself who must perform the works of mercy.'"[22]

Personal involvement grows out of a Christian personal revolution. To articulate this point of view, Peter Maurin and the Catholic Worker drew on the philosophy of personalism (a philosophical tradition that also influenced Pope John Paul II). In the words of Catholic Worker historian and Dorothy Day

biographer William Miller, "The theme of the personalist idea held...by...the Catholic Worker was that the primacy of Christian love should be brought from its position of limbo where human affairs are concerned and infused into the process of history."[23]

In other words, Christian love should not be a feel-good ideal or something confined to church buildings on Sundays. Every Christian is to embrace love as a personal vocation and bring it to bear on how we live. We are to be evangelists of love, witnesses of a Christian-informed love in all our relationships.

To take on this calling requires great optimism about people in general and about ourselves in particular. Peter Maurin had this optimism. "He made you feel that you and all men had great and generous hearts with which to love God," Dorothy wrote. "If you once recognized this fact in yourself you would expect and find it in others. 'The art of human contacts,' Peter called it happily. But it was seeing Christ in others, loving the Christ you saw in others. Greater than this, it was having faith in the Christ in others without being able to see Him. Blessed is he that believes without seeing."[24] The responsibility to see and act on love was at the heart of the Catholic Worker's personalism.

THE WORK OF THE CHURCH

Soon after her baptism a priest approached Dorothy and asked her about how the social teaching of the church had led her to become Catholic. At the time she knew nothing of the church's social teachings and the social encyclicals, but a factor that had influenced her decision to enter the Catholic church

was that it "was the Church of the poor, that St. Patrick's [Cathedral in New York City] had been built from the pennies of servant girls, that it cared for the emigrant, it established hospitals, orphanages, day nurseries, houses of the Good Shepherd, homes for the aged."

At the same time Dorothy thought that the church did not do enough to address the underlying causes of the misery it worked to alleviate. "I felt that it did not set its face against a social order which made so much charity in the present sense of the word necessary."[25]

Peter Maurin did much to enlighten Dorothy about the broad reach of the church's social teaching, though he believed the church had yet to realize the full power of that teaching. He likened this teaching to dynamite that Catholics needed to ignite in order to make the church a true agent of transformation.

Dorothy came to agree with Peter that it was up to people working as the body of Christ, not the state, to do the work of social healing and change. She did not want to turn people over to a city or state agency, even to Catholic charities. Each one of us, she thought, needed to perform works of mercy ourselves, not relying on others to do so. Jesus gave *us* this task to do, not aid institutions. Dorothy said of a longtime friend, Ammon Hennacy, "He recognized the importance of beginning with oneself, starting here and now, and not waiting for someone else to start the revolution."[26]

Dorothy and Peter called the Catholic Worker a permanent revolution. It was also a personal revolution: Each member of

Christ's body, the church, was to take responsibility to do what she or he could to remake the social order in Christ's image.

No Room for Judgment

Dorothy and Mother Teresa were not only trying to do good. They took Matthew 25 literally: "Truly I tell you, just as you did it to one of the least of these who are members of my family, you did it to me." Because they believed Christ showed himself in the poor and in their sufferings, Dorothy and Mother Teresa felt compelled to respond as a matter of faith. "Christ is with us today, not only in the Blessed Sacrament, and where two or three are gathered together in His Name, but also in the poor."[27]

The discovery of God's love in and for each person did not allow for moral judgments. Like Dorothy, Mother Teresa was not in the slums to judge the people she served or the other people serving. "I do not feel like judging or condemning," she said. [28]

Just as Mother Teresa saw the living Christ here and now in other people, especially the poor, and responded to them, so Dorothy said,

> We can do it too.... We are not born too late. We do it by seeing Christ and serving Christ in friends and strangers, in everyone we come in contact with.... For He said that a glass of water given to a beggar was given to Him. He made heaven hinge on the way we act toward Him in His disguise of commonplace, frail, ordinary humanity.[29]

We do it too. By looking to the tasks before us, we imitate the saints and partake of holiness. "It is we ourselves that we have to think about, no one else," Dorothy said. "That is the way the saints worked. They paid attention to what they were doing and if others were attracted to them by their enterprise, why, well and good. But they looked to themselves first of all."[30]

WORKS OF PEACE

We have seen how Dorothy Day looked to Thérèse of Lisieux for guidance. She even invoked Thérèse as a kind of patron saint of the Catholic Worker: "We should look to St. [Thérèse], the Little Flower, to walk her little way, her way of love."[1] Dorothy also believed that the answer to violence and the destruction of modern war lay with little Thérèse, whose tuberculosis-wracked body had been resting in its grave for half a century when Dorothy wrote, "On the frail battleground of her flesh was fought the wars of today."[2]

The little way is the way of peace, Dorothy believed. "Paperwork, cleaning the house, dealing with the innumerable visitors who come all through the day, answering the phone, keeping patience and acting intelligently, which is to find some meaning in all that happens—these things, too, are the works of peace, and often seem like a very little way."[3]

We can see the importance of finding meaning in everything that happens, of seeing the presence of God in all people and things, but how could Dorothy describe these tasks as "works of peace"? How could such a huge problem as the violence in the world find itself laid at the door of a house of hospitality? Even more, how could Dorothy make the connection

between the violence of the day and the life of Thérèse? What did she mean when she said, "In these days of fear and trembling of what man has wrought on earth in destructiveness and hate, Thérèse is the saint we need"?[4]

CHRISTIAN WEAPONS

To answer these questions, we can look to an idea Dorothy brought from her retreat with Father John Hugo, a retreat experience that Dorothy called a "second conversion."[5] From Father Hugo she learned to oppose weapons of destruction with "weapons of the Spirit." "Prayer and penance! There are indeed spiritual works, spiritual weapons to save souls, penance for luxury when the destitute suffer, a work to increase the sum total of love and peace in the world."[6]

As Karl Stern pointed out, in modern times "the potential power of one single individual has increased to an incredible degree."[7] In this age of nuclear weapons, one person could start a conflagration that could destroy millions of lives and possibly the world itself. Thérèse, Dorothy Day wrote, "speaks to our condition. Is the atom a small thing? And yet what havoc it has wrought. Is her little way a small contribution to the life of the spirit? It has all the power of the spirit of Christianity behind it. It is an explosive force that can transform our lives and the life of the world, once put into effect."[8]

Just like the extremely small atom, whose complexity and potential power almost defy human comprehension, a little thing done with love holds an infinite potential for power. We Christians hold the power to remake the world, one person and one deed at a time. Pope Pius XI said in his homily at the

Mass of Thérèse's canonization: "If the way of spiritual childhood became general, who does not see how easily would be realized the reformation of human society."[9]

Thérèse liked to take up "the pet names given her by her companions: little lamb, Jesus' toy, little ball, little reed, *atom*" (emphasis added). Obviously these names were "an invitation" not to the power of bombs but to "the hidden life, to littleness, to abandonment, to silence."[10] Thérèse had a fighting spirit, but the sword she grasped was one of love. "Let us always grasp the sword of the spirit," she wrote, "let us never simply allow matters to take their own course for the sake of our own peace."[11]

The hate and destruction Dorothy saw in the world, its "convulsions," are what Karl Stern called "Big Stuff." Here Christians encounter the challenge to do something to stem the tide of evil. But do we counter Big Stuff with Big Stuff of our own? Do we fight fire with fire in some sort of massive retaliation?

No. The church no longer fights wars in the name of God. In fact, it is dangerous for Christians to dabble in earthly power, lest that power possess us and lead us into the temptation of using it for selfish and un-Christian purposes.

The power of God is absolute, of course, and is greater than any earthly power. As Pope Pius XI wrote when he instituted the Solemnity of Christ the King in 1925,

> When once men recognize, both in private and in public life, that Christ is King, society will at last receive the great blessings of real liberty, well-ordered discipline, peace and

harmony.... For with the spread and the universal extent of the kingdom of Christ men will become more and more conscious of the link that binds them together, and thus many conflicts will be either prevented entirely or at least their bitterness will be diminished.[12]

Christ's power works indirectly. Like a mustard seed, it grows into a mighty work (see Matthew 13:31–32). We oppose the violence of the world by refusing to participate in it, by instead doing small acts of good at every opportunity, by continually increasing the total of good. Then we will see the flood of evil recede.

And this, Karl Stern said, "is where we come back to Thérèse's plan. Point number one, she would say if she were here with us right now: Don't use any Big Stuff, use Little Stuff.... There is in everybody's life, in every place and at every moment, a lot of Small Stuff around which would provide excellent material for sanctity if one only exploited it." Thérèse's sister Céline said, "She revealed her strength 'in a multitude of slight, almost microscopic, acts.'" These acts were "the raw material out of which, miraculously, she made her 'little, nameless, unremembered acts of kindness and of love.'"[13]

THE WAY OF LOVE

For Dorothy Day the small acts of mercy the Catholic Worker practiced opened the road to peace, for the way of peace is a little way. "Year upon year of serving meals, making beds, cleaning, and conversing with destitute, outcast people," Catholic Worker historian James Allaire wrote, "provided

Dorothy with 'schooling' in the Little Way. Added to this daily routine were her writing and publishing the *Catholic Worker* newspaper, speaking around the country, praying, fasting, protesting, and enduring jail on behalf of peace and justice....

"The Little Way is the way of Gospel nonviolence because it invites us to love one another as Jesus loved us (Jn 13:34), an unrestricted love that brings mercy and compassion to all people. Jesus' nonviolent love extended even to giving his life in redemptive suffering on the cross."[14]

While she was visiting the Calcutta Missionaries of Charity in 1970, Dorothy

> told of her refusal and the refusal of other Catholic Workers to interrupt the works of mercy even in wartime, when Jesus' command to "love the enemy" was replaced by the command of the state to kill, starve, and maim the enemy. She explained that her manifesto when the Second World War was declared was the Sermon on the Mount. The Catholic Worker movement, she went on, took Jesus at His word when He told His followers to do good in return for evil, thus overcoming evil by good not by violence.[15]

Dorothy's admission that she had gone to jail for protesting war and war preparations "created a stir" among the sisters. The Indian sisters knew of women who had gone to jail as part of Mahatma Gandhi's campaigns of nonviolence, "but for a Catholic woman to go to jail for the Sermon on the Mount was another matter."[16]

Mother Teresa had her own version of weapons of the Spirit. Like Dorothy and the Catholic Workers, she had a

personalist approach both to people and to the problems of the world. "A smile is the beginning of love," she would say. "Let us not use bombs and guns to overcome the world. Let us use love and compassion. Peace begins with a smile. Smile five times a day at someone you don't really want to smile at all. Do it for peace."[17]

With its unprecedented catastrophic wars, genocides and offenses against God's creation, the twentieth century needed a saint like Mother Teresa, who defended the absolute value of life even in its most fragile and unwanted forms. Though she received the Nobel Peace Prize, it may not be obvious to people what her acts of mercy had to do with peace. One admirer, the British author and commentator Malcolm Muggeridge, had a reply to those who wondered about this connection. "By dedicating her life wholly to Christ, by seeing in every suffering soul her Saviour and treating them accordingly, by being, along with her Missionaries of Charity, a sort of power-house of love in the world, she was a counterforce to the power mania, cupidity and egotistic pursuits, out of which violence, individual and collective, in all its forms, comes."[18]

Brother Andrew, the founder of the Missionaries of Charity Brothers, spoke of the ministry of the Missionaries in El Salvador during the height of the civil war in that country: "It seems that God calls them to this and other violent places to be a little center of love, peace, joy, and prayer. There is no hope here of a solution from arms or politics or ideologies of the right or of the left. These Sisters and Brothers are so weak, so small. They only have God—His love and His power."[19]

When it came to weapons that destroyed human life, Mother Teresa could only express her incomprehension. "The fruit of war is so terrible.... How any human being can do that to another—and for what?"[20] Looking over scenes of destruction in Beirut, she said, "'I don't understand it. They are all children of God.' When asked about capital punishment, she had also said, 'I don't understand it.' She could not understand how any human being could dare take life since all life is a gift of God."[21] This concern for human life extended to that of the unborn, the war victim and the prisoner on death row.

Mother Teresa also ministered to civilian victims of war. Often these are war's forgotten victims. A member of the Missionary Brothers was in Los Angeles when the Persian Gulf War ended. He observed, "While we in America were busy getting ready for our parades and festivities, Mother headed in the opposite direction. She had managed to get herself and the Sisters into Baghdad, setting up facilities for the malnourished and crippled children, and mobile clinics for the sick and wounded."[22]

In 1976 Dorothy Day and Mother Teresa attended the Eucharistic Congress in Philadelphia. They were invited to speak on the topic of "Woman and the Eucharist" on August 6, the anniversary of the atomic bombing of Hiroshima. Dorothy, at seventy-nine years of age, in what would be her last public speech, chided the congress organizers for overlooking the anniversary of the atomic bombing and holding instead a Mass for the military. "Our Creator gave us life and the Eucharist to sustain life," she told the assembly, who interrupted her speech with applause. "But we have given the

world instruments of death of inconceivable magnitude.... Women are born to nourish, not to destroy life."[23]

Again, the small ways to love and life stand in opposition to the big ways of destruction, like David before Goliath. "You come to me with sword and spear and javelin," David said to the giant, "but I come to you in the name of the LORD of hosts" (1 Samuel 17:45).

THE EMBRACE OF SUFFERING

A strength of the Christian faith is that it is not afraid to see suffering in the world and even embrace it if necessary. It recognizes suffering to be part of the human condition and instructs us to make suffering a holy thing by joining it to that of Christ, who in being human willingly exposed himself to pain and death.

But suffering is never an end in itself or inherently good. To seek it for its own sake can be a distortion of faith; it can damage us and others. We should not fail to alleviate pain and deprivation in some misplaced hope of drawing closer to Christ on the cross. The paschal mystery does not end with the crucifixion of Jesus; it *goes on* with his resurrection. The ultimate meaning of this mystery is that Christ won the victory over sin and death, as Christians have proclaimed since the earliest days of the church.

Sometimes suffering is unavoidable, and sometimes it can be avoided but should not be. Part of living in Christ's redemption is showing the mercy and compassion Christ showed us. Like the Good Samaritan who crossed the road to help an injured person, if I have the choice to suffer in order to help another, my faith calls me to say yes and act as Jesus did.

The challenge is to find meaning in suffering. As one Missionary of Charity Brother wrote, "Pope John XXIII, speaking on suffering, stressed the need to find a purpose in it. In the love of Christ there is no life without suffering…. So we cannot escape it and we must do all we can to help one another find a purpose in it. If we can find a purpose for accepting his cross as Jesus Christ accepted his own then one will never feel alone."[1]

To find purpose in it: That is the key to uncovering meaning in suffering. "Suffering in itself is nothing," said Mother Teresa, "but suffering shared with Christ's passion is a wonderful gift. Man's most beautiful gift is that he can share in the passion of Christ."[2]

Offering Illness

Thérèse made an offering of her suffering in the midst of her final illness. She gave her suffering to Jesus and asked him to stamp his pain on her heart, if such an exchange would bring people to him and bring him consolation. "I am willing with all my heart to suffer all that I suffer. Your happiness is all that I want…. I have begun to love my darkness, for I believe now that it is part, a very small part, of Jesus' darkness and pain on the earth."[3]

"It is no longer I who live, but it is Christ who lives in me," Saint Paul wrote (Galatians 2:20). We can let Christ live in us by joining our sufferings to his in prayer.

Jacqueline de Decker was a Belgian woman who went to India to serve the poor. Like Mother Teresa, she began her work there with next to nothing. While she had wished to join

a religious order, including the newly founded Missionaries of Charity, poor health intervened. An early diving accident developed into a severe spinal disease that several surgeries could not alleviate. Jacqueline would have to give up her desire to work with the Indian poor and return to Europe.

In 1952 Mother Teresa sent a letter proposing to Jacqueline a spiritual connection to the Missionaries of Charity. "I need souls like yours to pray and suffer for the work," Mother wrote. "You'll be in body in Belgium but in soul in India where there are souls longing for our Lord, but for want of someone to pay the debt for them, they cannot move towards him. You'll be a true Missionary of Charity if you pay the debt while the Sisters—your Sisters—help them to come to God in body."[4]

As usual, Mother Teresa's simple and direct way of speaking expressed some deep and agile thinking. These suffering Coworkers could do the spiritual work of prayer and sacrifice while the sisters, bolstered by their prayers, would be physically present to the poor. So was born the idea for the "Link for Sick and Suffering Co-Workers" of the Missionaries of Charity. "I am very happy," Mother Teresa wrote Jacqueline de Decker the following January, "that you are willing to join the suffering members of the Missionaries of Charity.... You and others who will join will share in all our prayers, works and whatever we do for souls, and you do the same for us with your prayers and sufferings."

In another piece of imagination, Mother Teresa saw the suffering and prayers of these Coworkers as "the chalice in which we the working members will pour in the love of souls

we gather round." Into this spiritual chalice—a powerful symbol of both suffering *and* love—the sisters would pour the wine of their work. "In reality," Mother Teresa wrote, "you can do much more while on your bed of pain than I running on my feet, but you and I together can do all things in him who strengthens me." In such a union of spirit and body, Mother asked, "What would we not do, what can't we do for Him?"[5]

SUFFERING WITH PURPOSE

In offering our suffering for another, we find purpose in that suffering. And by working directly with others to alleviate suffering, we help to transform people and the world through the power of the gospel, especially for those most in need. We help others find purpose in *their* suffering by giving them hope that they can find relief from their pain and deprivation.

The material and spiritual. Active and contemplative. Change and acceptance. We see in the work of Thérèse of Lisieux, Mother Teresa and Dorothy Day how these apparent opposites are two sides of the same reality. All three prayed and worked. They ministered to both body and soul. They suffered and embraced the sufferings of others in order to accept what could not be changed and to bring comfort and betterment where possible.

We do everything for a purpose, they tell us. We should not close in on ourselves, around our own difficulties. The little way embraces the way of suffering. We can offer our sufferings for our own good and that of others, in acceptance and spiritual sacrifice. And our own pains and anxieties and discomforts can help us see the same things in others and so impel us to do what we can to ease them.

Dorothy saw the value of suffering in the hospitality the Catholic Worker extended, both to guests and to the Workers themselves. In a letter Dorothy sent to the other Worker houses, she said that "whenever anyone came into the group, he was to be accepted fully as a brother. Problems should not be solved by an imposed order; they should be suffered.…'The more we suffer…the more we learn. Infinite patience, suffering is needed. And it is never-ending.'"[6]

The Catholic Worker movement started from one house. And the story of the movement, especially of the New York Worker houses and farms, tells of how the Workers had to move from location to location every few years because of lost leases, space concerns, financial crises and other problems. Situations varied, but the desire of the Workers to choose poverty and live as the people they served frequently put them in poor conditions.

In accepting the vulnerable on a personal level, the Workers challenged stereotypical images of poor people. Dorothy tried to change people's awareness of the bread lines, to change their conception of what it means to be poor. The poor have a right to eat and to have a roof over their heads, she believed, to have what the rest of us have, to love as the rest of us do. She represented the claims of the dispossessed.

Bearing one another's crosses—putting up with and even lifting others' burdens—such is Christian love and community. Thérèse wrote, "I understand now that perfect charity consists in bearing with others' faults, in not being surprised at their weakness, in being edified by the smallest acts of virtue we see them practise."[7]

The Poverty Around Us

Like suffering, poverty is not good in itself. But we can find some valuable things in it, like hope, simplicity and an appreciation for the basics of life. Mother Teresa said:

> The beauty is not in poverty but in the courage that the poor still smile and have hope, in spite of everything. I do not admire hunger, damp or cold, but the disposition to face them, to smile and live on. I admire their love of life, the capacity to discover richness in the smaller things—like a piece of bread that I gave to a boy which he ate crumb by crumb, thinking it was better so. While the poorest of the poor are free, we are excessively worried about the house, money. The poor represent the greatest human richness this world possesses and yet we despise them, behave as if they were garbage.[8]

Whatever some of the positive effects of poverty may be, we must never forget that it is a crushing condition in which people are deprived of what they need to live as human beings. Poverty robs people of their basic human dignity. Our first task when faced with poverty, then, is to try to do something to ease it. We might provide the poor with immediate assistance, work to change the conditions that contribute to their poverty or do both.

When Mother Teresa was journeying east as a young Sister of Loreto, her first stop was at Colombo in Sri Lanka, then on to Madras on the Indian mainland. She found the poverty "indescribable." After a brief stay in the Loreto house in Calcutta, the order assigned her to teach in the convent school

in the city of Darjeeling and also at a small medical mission. There she saw more of the Indian poor.

Returning to Calcutta, she began teaching at one of the Loreto schools, where the classroom was primitive. Sometimes she had to start the day by cleaning. Other times she conducted class outside in a courtyard or in what she said bore resemblance to a stable. "It is not possible to find worse poverty,"[9] she said of the children's living conditions.

Sister Teresa's devotion to these children and her small gestures of care for them earned her the title "Ma," "Mother."[10] At this time she began visiting the poor in the slums of Calcutta, the *bustees*. Many of the sick poor she encountered had walked for miles. They suffered from sores and other lesions, and some were dying from tuberculosis. They needed medications but did not understand how to take them. Later Sister Teresa would equip herself to serve these people. After leaving Loreto she spent some time with the Medical Mission Sisters at a hospital in Patna, where she received medical training.

Voluntary Poverty

Thérèse, Mother Teresa and Dorothy embraced suffering and at the same time worked to alleviate it, through living at the heart of the spiritual and material poverty they saw around them. And just as suffering has two sides—the involuntary and the purposefully chosen—so does poverty. One can choose poverty *with a purpose*.

Voluntary poverty is a vocation involving a commitment to serve the poor and to become one of the poor, to know the

life of the poor as one of them, not from afar. It means embracing poverty as both a virtue—not only a hardship but also a joy, a profound freedom—and an evil to combat. It is an exercise in *compassion,* in suffering in solidarity with another.

Through true personal sacrifice, through giving ourselves—not only our charity—we make ourselves poor, and in so doing we increase our participation in love. Love for the poor, those who have nothing or not enough, means not only "us for them" but also "us with them." It breaks down barriers and inequities between us and them.

Dorothy shared the French Catholic writer Léon Bloy's idea of "the mystery of poverty": "that voluntarily embraced, it can be a freeing and purifying force; that suffered, it is a hellish thing."[11] She recognized poverty as a paradox:

> I condemn poverty and I advocate it; poverty is simple and complex at once; it is a social phenomenon and a personal matter.... People do not understand the difference between inflicted poverty and voluntary poverty; between being the victims and champions of poverty. I prefer to call the one kind *destitution*, reserving the word *poverty* for what St. Francis called "Lady Poverty."[12]

She noted with approval the philosopher William James's thoughts about voluntary poverty. He wondered whether the revival of the religious vocation of poverty "may not be the...spiritual reform which our time stands most in need of." James believed that poverty needed greater praise. He noted people's fear of the poor and of poverty, including voluntary poverty. "We despise anyone who elects to be poor in

order to simplify and save his inner life."[13]

James recognized another paradox of poverty. Yes, it can be both a curse and a blessing, but few choose to embrace its liberating power. It is inconceivable for most of us to imagine how poverty voluntarily chosen could mean a life of simplicity and freedom. But as James pointed out, when people push away the virtue of poverty, they push away the poor as well.

Mother Teresa did not want the Missionaries of Charity to become an institution themselves—a permanent and effective community, yes, but not an institution that would begin to try to move up the social and economic ladder. She thought the poverty of the order would preserve the spirit of the work and keep its members close to those they serve.

"Our rigorous poverty is our safeguard," she said. "We do not want to do what other religious orders have done throughout history, and begin by serving the poor only to end up unconsciously serving the rich. In order to understand and help those who have nothing, we must live like them.... The only difference is that these people are poor by birth, and we are poor by choice."[14]

In the 1990s Mother Teresa went so far as to disband the Coworkers as an organization. This painful decision, which came as a shock to many, seemed to grow out of Mother's concern that the Coworkers maintain the simplicity and joy that they had when they began their work.[15] To the Coworkers she wrote, "I want you to work with Sisters, Brothers and Fathers directly—the humble work, beginning in your own homes, neighbourhood, your parish, your city; and where there are no Missionaries of Charity, to work in that same spirit wherever

you may be. It is this that will transform the world. If you pray, God will give a clean heart and a clean heart can see the Face of God in the Poor you serve."[16]

RICH AND POOR

The tension between wealth and poverty was a concern for Mother Teresa and Dorothy Day. Both were wary of the danger wealth presents in allowing people to forget the poor and neglect their Christian responsibility to care for them. Mother Teresa firmly believed that poverty did not just happen: It existed because people let it happen. Human beings have enough resources to eliminate poverty if they want to. "If there are poor in the world it is because you and I don't give enough" was her simple way of putting it.[17]

In a similar vein Dorothy wrote: "We need always to be thinking and writing about [poverty], for if we are not among its victims its reality fades from us. We must talk about poverty because people insulated by their own comfort lose sight of it."[18]

What are the more well-off to give? Mother Teresa told a convention of Rotary International that the Missionaries needed not their money but their time and their very selves. "We want all of you to donate *yourselves* to the poor people.... I think that all of you and I myself should start sharing what we have got. This attitude would certainly beget a better understanding between nations."[19]

While people might not embrace poverty in order to serve the poor, they still have a vocation when it comes to their resources. Mother Teresa perceived yet another paradox:

"She had seen the poverty of the rich and wealth of the poor." She did not see the rich to be bad in themselves. "They were rich for a purpose." In fact, she strove to bring together the rich with the poor.[20] "She wanted the rich to save the poor and the poor to save the rich."[21]

Just as poverty is both a burden and a vocation, so wealth is a gift that can also be a danger. "There must be a reason why some people can afford to live well. But I tell you, this provokes avarice, and there comes the sin. Richness is given by God, and it is our duty to divide it with those less favored."[22]

Those with abundant resources have a dual responsibility: to see their wealth as a gift from God and, because it is a gift, to express their gratitude by sharing with those who have less than they need or nothing at all. Dorothy wrote, "There is money...for all sorts of nonsensical expenditures, but none for these least of God's children suffering in the midst of millions of people who are scarcely aware of their existence."[23]

Mother Teresa called upon those who live in a world caught up in the race to be rich, powerful and effective to be aware of their own poverty, to make themselves weak with the weak and seek to do not big things but only "small things with great love."[24]

SPIRITUAL POVERTY

Responding to the material poverty around us is one thing. But the spiritual poverty in our midst can be harder to see and thus respond to. Those who suffer from spiritual poverty are under our roofs, in our workplaces or among our friends.

"Do we know the poor in our own homes?" Mother Teresa asked. "Sometimes people can hunger for more than bread. It is possible that our children, our husband, our wife, do not hunger for bread, do not need clothes, do not lack a house. But are we equally sure that none of them feels alone, abandoned, neglected, needing some affection? That, too, is poverty."[1]

Mother Teresa observed this spiritual poverty on her visits to New York. In that city, she reported, "the Sisters are doing small things…helping the children, visiting the lonely, the sick, the unwanted. We know now that being unwanted is the greatest disease of all. That is the poverty we find around us here."[2] In the West, she said, "there is a different poverty. The poverty of the spirit, of loneliness and being unwanted."[3]

Do we recognize this loneliness? "We have all known the long loneliness," Dorothy Day wrote in the famous conclusion

to her memoir, "and we have learned that the only solution is love and that love comes with community."[4]

PRESERVING DIGNITY

The task of helping these poor begins in our everyday lives. Saint Thomas Aquinas defined Christian love as willing the good of another. What can we do to love those around us? What do our loved ones, friends and coworkers need from us? How about the other people we encounter—those who stand behind cash registers, wait on us at restaurants or help us find something in a store? Do we treat them as beloved children of God, just as we want others to treat us?

Then come those we find most difficult to love: people with whom we are in conflict, whom we dislike, who trouble us with their inconsiderateness and selfishness, their bad habits or destructive behavior. Jesus was clear about such relationships:

> Love your enemies, do good to those who hate you, bless those who curse you, pray for those who abuse you.... Give to everyone who begs from you; and if anyone takes away your goods, do not ask for them again. Do to others as you would have them do to you.... Love your enemies, do good, and lend, expecting nothing in return. Your reward will be great.... Be merciful, just as your Father is merciful. (Luke 6:27–28, 30–31, 35, 36)

Whether we are dealing with the materially or the spiritually poor—those in our homes or those outside our homes, loved ones, strangers or enemies—God calls us, the little way says, to see the dignity of every person and to take steps to build up

that dignity. For example, Mother Teresa's care for lepers and other sick people involved not only dispensing anti-leprosy sulphone drugs, physical treatment and giving free rice and milk. The sisters also sought to give those in their care the dignity their situations had damaged.

Dorothy painted a picture of the unemployed and sick people the Catholic Worker served in its bread lines: "They are stripped then, not only of all earthly goods, but of spiritual goods, their sense of human dignity. When they are forced into line at municipal lodging houses, in clinics, in our houses of hospitality, they are then the truly destitute."[5]

The Worker sought to provide sustenance while preserving dignity. "We only tried to fulfill their immediate needs without probing, and to make them feel at home, and try to help them in regaining some measure of self-respect."[6] A jail stay later in life helped Dorothy "see how much we accomplish at the Catholic Worker by not asking questions or doing any investigating but by cultivating a spirit of trust."[7]

IN HIS PRESENCE

This desire to care for souls as well as bodies comes from an all-embracing spirituality of God's presence in oneself, in every person, rich or poor, and in the whole world. Mother Teresa did not want her sisters to be only "social workers"[8] or teachers or caregivers. Their work came from their desire to practice their faith: They were to be contemplatives in the world and prayer professionals whose mission grew out of finding God's presence in their surroundings. Mother asked the sisters to have "the constant awareness of the Divine

Presence everywhere and in everyone, especially in our own hearts and in the hearts of our Sisters with whom we live, and in the poorest of the poor."[9]

Trying to always have an awareness of the presence of God cultivates God's presence in oneself and the ability to see the image of God in others. Take Matthew 25 literally, as Dorothy and Mother Teresa did, and we see that the poor are Jesus.

> "Lord, when was it that we saw you hungry and gave you food, or thirsty and gave you something to drink? And when was it that we saw you a stranger and welcomed you, or naked and gave you clothing? And when was it that we saw you sick or in prison and visited you?"... "Truly I tell you, just as you did it to one of the least of these who are members of my family, you did it to me." (Matthew 25:37–40)

Christ, Mother Teresa said when she received the Nobel Prize, "makes himself the hungry one, the naked one, the homeless one, the sick one, the one in prison, the lonely one, the unwanted one, and he says: 'You did it to me.' He is hungry for our love, and this is the hunger of our poor people. This is the hunger that you and I must find. It may be in our own home."[10]

In the end, Mother Teresa thought, material and spiritual poverty are two sides of the same reality:

> Today, the Poor are hungry for bread and rice—and for love and the living word of God; the Poor are thirsty—for water and for peace, truth and justice; the Poor are naked—

for clothes, for human dignity and compassion for the naked sinner. The Poor are homeless—for a shelter made of bricks, and for a joyful heart that understands, covers, loves. They are sick—for medical care—and for that gentle touch and a warm smile.

The "shut-in," the unwanted, the unloved, the alcoholics, the dying destitutes, the abandoned and the lonely, the outcasts and the untouchables, the leprosy sufferers—all those who are a burden to human society—who have lost all hope and faith in life—who have forgotten how to smile—who have lost the sensibility of the warm hand touch of love and friendship—they look to us for comfort—if we turn our back on them, we turn it on Christ, and at the hour of our death we will be judged if we have recognized Christ in them, and on what we have done for and to them. There will be only two ways: "come" or "go."[11]

When Dorothy addressed the Missionaries of Charity in Calcutta in 1970, she said of the efforts of the Catholic Worker: "We keep repeating the message of Gospel non-violence and the importance of voluntary poverty in serving the poor. For us, everything depends on seeing the poor as ambassadors of Christ, and of keeping open our Houses of Hospitality for those against whom other doors are shut."[12]

Dorothy's use of the word *ambassador*, drawing on Saint Paul (see 2 Corinthians 5:20; Ephesians 6:19–20), says much about poor and vulnerable people. In a special way they represent Christ, because he is present in them. For the rest of us, they also carry his message.

During this same visit Brother Andrew visited Dorothy. He had first heard of the *Catholic Worker* when he received a copy of the newspaper meant for someone who had moved— not an unusual occurrence in the paper's history. He kept reading it for twenty years. The idea of extending hospitality to the poor and lonely inspired him in his work with the Missionary Brothers.

Thus in London the ministry of the Missionaries of Charity included founding homes of hospitality for the homeless, much like Catholic Worker houses of hospitality, and visiting the lonely and elderly. The brothers lived in the places from which they offered hospitality, to any who came to the door, regardless of whether they were people the brothers had set out to serve.[13] "A thing I learned from you," Brother Andrew told Dorothy, "is to give hospitality to the visitor. We can put people up, since young people just sleep on the floor, in the refectory, or anywhere."[14]

Following the path of the works of mercy offers a sure way to faithfulness and holiness. If we do such works in Jesus' name, we know that we are following him in a way that is pleasing to God. Despite the difficulties of leading the Catholic Worker, Dorothy knew that she was doing the right thing. "One reason I feel sure of the rightness of the path we are traveling in our work is that we did not pick it out ourselves. . . . We cannot feel too satisfied with the way we are doing our work—there is too much of it; we have more than our share, you might say. Yet we can say, 'If that's the way He wants it—'"[15]

And Jesus does want it that way. Jesus wants to come to us and invite us to follow him, just as he did in choosing his first

disciples. How do we meet him? In the poor, of course. As Peter Maurin believed, the poor are the first children of the church, and so the poor should come first—a point he made in parishes where he observed houses for priests and facilities for educational, social and recreational purposes but no houses of hospitality for the poor.

Dorothy Day shared this concern. Her spiritual mentor, Father John Hugo,

> knew very well the importance of Catholic social teaching, and he was close to those struggling to make correct social structures more just. But he knew well also that an unconverted heart is a dull instrument for seeking justice. Hearts must change if society is to be changed. Compassion for the suffering must drive us to be more than good social workers. For the poor ones Christ loved need more than economic advancement.[16]

THE OPPORTUNITY TO LOVE

Like Mother Teresa and Dorothy Day, Thérèse of Lisieux found inspiration from Jesus among the "least of these." On one occasion she volunteered to help a frail sister walk to and from meals and prayer. This sister "was not easy to please," and assisting her could be a difficult experience. But Thérèse offered herself because "I did not want to lose such a beautiful opportunity for exercising charity, remembering the words of Jesus: 'Whatever you do to the least of my brothers, you do to me.'"[17]

Each of us needs to take personal responsibility to love others, especially those whom poverty and deprivation make

especially dear to God. While Dorothy was active both at the systemic and the personal level, her focus was on the person at her door. She advised the Workers to thank the person in the soup line, because he or she was giving them the chance to perform the works of mercy.

If we take advantage of opportunities to help others, especially when being of service means sacrificing our own pleasure, comfort or convenience, we can experience what we are doing in a spirit of joy, not a pain to be endured because we want to do the right thing. Giving ourselves to a task, even an unpleasant one, uncovers the secret joy and deep satisfaction hidden in every act.

During her 1971 visit to the United States, Mother Teresa addressed the teaching sisters of the diocese of Scranton, Pennsylvania:

> We are all working together to bring Christ to the university or high school or right down to the slums. We are doing it together. The work that you do is His gift to you. Today, talking about the poor is in fashion. Knowing, loving, and serving the poor is quite another matter. The little St. Thérèse said, "In the heart of the Church, I will be love." That is what we are, love in the heart of the church. The password of the early Christians was joy. Serve the Lord with joy.[18]

A CHALLENGE TO CHRISTIANS

Ｉf we could sum up the Christian faith in a phrase, it might be "Live for the glory of God in Jesus and the service of others." Or as Jesus said, "'You shall love the Lord your God with all your heart, and with all your soul, and with all your mind…. And…you shall love your neighbor as yourself'" (Matthew 22:37, 39; quoting Deuteronomy 6:5; Leviticus 19:18).

Because this theme is so basic to Christian faith, it appears often in the history of Christian spirituality. For example, the spiritual tradition Saint Ignatius of Loyola established called on people to live for the greater glory of God (*Ad majorem Dei gloriam*), to seek God in all things and to be a person for others. Faith centers us on other people, not ourselves. We start not with our own needs and desires but with those of others. Faith forms people into a community that lives to serve God and neighbor.

Thérèse of Lisieux, Mother Teresa and Dorothy Day embodied these values. Prayer and worship were part of their daily lives. They saw the presence of God in the "littlest" people and the smallest tasks. And they lived to serve those in need and lead others to that service.

One of the first Missionaries of Charity said that it was the "little people" of the Missionaries, rather than the leaders, who exercised a crucial role. Mother Teresa "had learned to value the importance of the smallest brick in the construction of a building.... Thanks to the combined efforts of small people prepared at her inspiration to give their all, thousands of lives had been saved."[1]

CONFRONTING THE HIDDEN EVIL

Evil, whether small or great, grows out of selfishness, putting one's interests ahead of what others need and ahead of what is good. Evil varies in degree, but the source of all evil is the same.

It is bad enough when people turn away from one another and in on themselves. Worse is when people of faith do so under the guise of religion, hiding behind their faith and using it to mask their selfishness. The sin of hypocrisy is that of creating an appearance of righteousness while other parts of one's life betray something very different.

When one plays with one's faith, the most important thing in the world, the stakes are high. As the theologian Hans Urs von Balthasar put it, Thérèse's "battle is to wipe out the hard core of Pharisaism which persists in the midst of Christianity; that will-to-power disguised in the mantle of religion, that drives one to assert one's own greatness instead of acknowledging that God alone is great."[2]

Dorothy quoted François Mauriac, the French novelist: "There is a kind of hypocrisy which is worse than that of the Pharisees; it is to hide behind Christ's example in order to follow one's own lustful desires and to seek the company of the dissolute."[3]

She referred to the words of two priests who were influential in her life. Father John Hugo was a young priest of the diocese of Pittsburgh who gave retreats for the Workers. For him the "great enemy was a worldly, a pharisaical Christianity."[4] And Father Pacifique Roy, a Josephite priest and friend of the Catholic Worker, told Dorothy and her colleagues that "if we did our works of mercy to be praised by men, or from pride and vanity and sense of power, then we had had our reward. If we did them for the love of God, in whose image man had been made, then God would reward us; then we were doing them for a supernatural motive."[5]

PRAY FOR HOLY PRIESTS

Thérèse, Mother Teresa and Dorothy had particular concern for the holiness of priests. They all had friendships with and deep respect for priests, but they were not blind to the failings to which priests, like the rest of us, are susceptible.

Perhaps characteristic of her time—and of her convert's zeal—Dorothy had an admiration for priests bordering on the reverent. Yet she also bemoaned those who seemed to be going through the motions and who lacked concern for social issues:

> The scandal of businesslike priests, of collective wealth, the lack of a sense of responsibility for the poor, the worker, the Negro, the Mexican, the Filipino, and even the oppression of these, and the consenting to the oppression of them by our industrialist-capitalist order—these made me feel often that priests were more like Cain than Abel. "Am I my brother's keeper?" they seemed to say in respect to the

social order. There was plenty of charity but too little justice.[6]

By *charity* Dorothy meant the type of financial giving that serves as an excuse to distance oneself from Christ's poor. Writing a check can help a worthy cause, but personal involvement is key. Peter Maurin reminded her "that we must have a sense of personal responsibility to take care of our own, and our neighbor, at a personal sacrifice."[7] Dorothy wrote: "We *are* our brother's keeper. Whatever we have beyond our own needs belongs to the poor.... And it is sad but true that we must give far more than bread, than shelter."[8] We must give *ourselves*.

Her friend Father Hugo would say that "the Gospels are a flaming fire. They invite ordinary men and women to intense love of God and of one another. The Gospels in no way suggest that Christianity is a flabby life, or that one who wishes to be a good friend of Christ can avoid the Cross."[9]

Mother Teresa too wanted priests to be holy, though "she had no illusions about the human nature to which even priests were susceptible—Jesus, she once pointed out, handpicked twelve disciples, one of whom proved to be a crook and the others ran away."[10]

As for Thérèse, "one of the principal duties of a Carmelite nun is to pray for priests, a duty which [she] discharged with great fervour at all times." She was aware of the pitfalls these men faced, praying in particular for "the good estate" of a former Carmelite priest who was a well-known apostate.[11]

THE CALL TO HOLINESS

In the early 1960s Jean Vanier, a former naval officer and philosophy professor, decided to do something about the conditions he saw in institutions for the developmentally disabled. He made a home for two men who had disabilities. Naming their house "L'Arche," after Noah's Ark, he and the two men lived as a family, sharing daily tasks and relaxing together. Since then L'Arche communities, embracing people of different abilities and disabilities, have sprung up throughout the world.

The kind of life and attitudes of which Vanier spoke in describing what led him to commit himself to the disabled express very well the little way:

> My life is to live with them, to be fragile, vulnerable and weak. I'm not sure that we can really understand the message of Jesus if we haven't listened to the weak.... We can love people who have been pushed aside, humiliated, seen as having no value. And then we see that they are changed. And at the same time, we discover that we too are broken, that we have our handicaps. And our handicaps are... about elitism, about power, around feeling that value is just to have power.[12]

We can hear an echo of Dorothy Day's voluntary poverty, of Mother Teresa's life in the slums, of Thérèse of Lisieux's casting her lot with a small Carmelite community and going out of her way to be kind to her infirm, difficult and inexperienced sisters. These women, all talented and able, stepped out of their comfort zones to become one of—and one with—the people they served.

For them, and for everyone who takes such a step, embracing a life with fragile and distressed people allows for acceptance of one's own limitations. This life sees success not in money, power, comfort and security but in generosity, sacrifice and commitment to others.

"The quest is not just believing in God, but believing in other people," Vanier said. "Believing in ourselves as children of God, and that we are called to see other people as God sees them, not as we would like them to be....You see, the whole of the Christian message is that we have to change to see people as God sees them. We have to have our eyes changed. We have to have attitudes that are changed. It begins...with listening."[13]

When you listen—to God, to others and to your own desire for holiness—you begin to see God in every moment and person or, as Vanier put it, to see every moment and person as God does. Such seeing means trusting completely in God; of this Thérèse, Mother Teresa and Dorothy reminded the world.

"We're caught up in a culture where we have to do, where we have to run, where we have to have projects and more projects," Vanier said. "Discover what it means to be human, to listen to each other, to love each other."[14]

The theologian Hans Urs von Balthasar saw the little way like this:

There are many reasons for this epithet "little." In the first place, because it bypasses extraordinary methods with a warning against them, and, like the Gospel itself, presupposes everyday life as its field of application. Again, because

it can find no better picture to express the soul's eagerness to receive God's love than that of a little child aware of its littleness before God. Lastly, because it is a short way: it eliminates all measurable distances and, if it is really followed, keeps one in immediate contact with one's goal.[15]

In the end the little way invites us to find the big in the small, God in the pots, pans and every other thing and every other person in daily life and to respond with love and devotion, in a spirit of childlike trust and faith. This "direct route" is a call and way to holiness—a call all of us can answer.

SAINT THÉRÈSE OF LISIEUX

1873 Born Marie-Françoise-Thérèse Martin, the ninth and last child of Zélie and Louis Martin in Alençon, France

1875 First thinks of being a religious sister when she grows up

1877 Martin family moves to Lisieux; death of her mother Zélie

1882–1883 Suffers from severe nervous illness; cured during prayer to the Blessed Virgin Mary

1886 Has experience she calls a "conversion"

1888 Enters Carmelite community at Lisieux

1889 Becomes a Carmelite novice

1890 Makes solemn vows as a Carmelite and takes the name Sister Thérèse of the Child Jesus and of the Holy Face

1893 Becomes assistant novice mistress

1897 Dies of tuberculosis on September 30 at age twenty-four

1898 First publication of *The Story of a Soul*

1923 Beatified

1925 Canonized

SERVANT OF GOD DOROTHY DAY

1897 Born in New York City

1903 Family moves to California, where journalist father gets a job in Oakland

1906 After San Francisco earthquake, experiences the hospitality her mother and neighbors extend to those the disaster made homeless; family moves to Chicago

1914–1916 Attends University of Illinois and joins the Socialist Party

1916 Begins working for socialist newspapers in New York

1926 Birth of daughter Tamar Teresa

1927 Becomes a Roman Catholic, an act that alienates many of her radical associates

1933 With Peter Maurin founds the *Catholic Worker* newspaper and the first Catholic Worker house of hospitality for the urban poor in New York

1936 Thirty-three Catholic Worker houses of hospitality in operation in the United States; today there are about 130 houses in thirty-two states and eight foreign countries

1936–1945 Advocates pacifist position during Spanish Civil War and World War II and supports Catholic conscientious objectors

1952 Publishes her autobiography *The Long Loneliness*

1956 Arrested for opposing compulsory civil defense drill in New York City

1962 Helps found American PAX, which will become the Pax Christi Catholic peace organization

1973 Jailed at age seventy-six for taking part in a banned picket line with Cesar Chavez in support of farmworkers

1980 Dies in New York City

2000 Canonization cause officially opens, named a Servant of God

BLESSED TERESA OF CALCUTTA

1910 Born Agnes Gonxha Bojaxhiu in Skopje, in the former Yugoslavia

1928 Becomes a Sister of Loreto and begins novitiate in Dublin, Ireland; takes name Sister Teresa

1929 Arrives in Calcutta, India; teaches geography at St. Mary's High School

1937 Makes solemn vows

1946 On a train to Darjeeling receives calling to serve among the poorest of the poor

1947 Permitted to leave Loreto community, moves to slums to start school

1948 Receives medical training

1950 Founds the Missionaries of Charity

1952 Opens Nirmal Hriday ("Pure Heart") home for the dying

1953 Opens orphanage

1957 Begins work with lepers

1958 Missionaries of Charity's first community outside Calcutta opens in Drachi, India

1965 Receives permission to open missions outside India; first one opens in Venezuela

1979 Awarded Nobel Peace Prize

1990 Reelected superior general of Missionaries of Charity, despite her wish to step down

1997 Steps down as head of Missionaries of Charity on March 13 and is succeeded by Sister Nirmala

1997 Dies of a heart attack in Calcutta on September 5 at the age of eighty-seven

2003 Beatified

INTRODUCTION

1. John Paul II, *Christifidelies Laici*, Apostolic Exhortation on the Vocation and the Mission of the Lay Faithful in the Church and in the World, December 30, 1988, no. 16.

2. *Dogmatic Constitution on the Church*, no. 40, in Austin P. Flannery, ed., *The Documents of Vatican II: The Conciliar and Post Conciliar Documents* (Northport, N.Y.: Costello, 1998), vol. 1, p. 397.

3. Rule of Benedict 31:10, in Timothy Fry, ed., *The Rule of St. Benedict in English* (Collegeville, Minn.: Liturgical, 1981), p. 55.

4. Quoted in David James Duncan, "No Great Things," *Orion*, January/February 2006, http://www.oriononline.org.

5. Quoted in Kathryn Spink, *Mother Teresa: A Complete Authorized Biography* (San Francisco: Harper, 1997), p. 302.

CHAPTER ONE: NAMES

1. Eileen Egan, *Such a Vision of the Street: Mother Teresa—The Spirit and the Work* (Garden City, N.Y.: Doubleday, 1985), p. 17.

2. Quoted in David Scott, *A Revolution of Love: The Meaning of Mother Teresa* (Chicago: Loyola, 2005), p. 47.

3. Spink, p. 235.

4. Dorothy Day, *The Long Loneliness* (San Francisco: HarperCollins, 1997), p. 141.

5. Day, *Long Loneliness*, p. 140.

6. Day, *Long Loneliness*, pp. 140, 141.

7. Dorothy Day, *Thérèse: A Life of Thérèse of Lisieux*, reprinted in *Communio*, Fall 1997, p. 596.

CHAPTER TWO: INSPIRATIONAL MOMENTS

1. Quoted in Shirley du Boulay, *Teresa of Avila: An Extraordinary Life* (New York: BlueBridge, 2004), p. 42.

2. Quoted in Guy Gaucher, *The Story of a Life: St. Thérèse of Lisieux,* Anne Marie Brennan, trans. (San Francisco: Harper and Row, 1987), p. 48.

3. Gaucher, p. 61.

4. Gaucher, p. 62.

5. Gaucher, p. 169.

6. Thérèse of Lisieux, *Story of a Soul: The Autobiography of St. Thérèse of Lisieux,* John Clarke, O.C.D., trans. (Westminster, Md.: Christian Classics, 1976), p. 194.

7. Quoted in Egan, p. 25.

8. Spink, p. 23.

9. Spink, p 31.

10. Egan, p. 55.

11. Day, *Long Loneliness*, p. 165.

12. Day, *Long Loneliness*, p. 166.

13. Day, *Long Loneliness*, p. 169.

14. Dorothy Day, "Peter Maurin 1877–1977," *The Catholic Worker*, May 1977, www.sbcw.org.

15. Day, *Long Loneliness*, p. 169.

16. William D. Miller, *All Is Grace: The Spirituality of Dorothy Day* (Garden City, N.Y.: Doubleday, 1987), p. 20.

17. Day, *Long Loneliness*, p. 172.

18. Dorothy Day, *Loaves and Fishes* (New York: Orbis Books, 1963), p. 96.

19. Day, *Long Loneliness*, p. 170.

20. Miller, *All Is Grace*, p. 28.

21. Miller, *All Is Grace*, p. 24.

22. Day, *Long Loneliness*, pp. 170, 171.

23. Day, *Loaves and Fishes*, p. 97.

CHAPTER THREE: THE LITTLE WAY

1. Quoted in Miller, *All Is Grace*, p. 114.

2. Gaucher, 148.

3. Spink, p. 131.

4. Mother Teresa, *One Heart Full of Love,* Jose Luis Gonzalez-Balado, ed. (Ann Arbor, Mich.: Servant, 1984), p. 84.

5. James Allaire, "Saint Thérèse of Lisieux Inspired Dorothy Day," www.cjd.org.

6. Miller, *All Is Grace*, p. 4.

7. Allaire.

8. *Story of a Soul*, p. vii.

9. Quoted in Hans Urs von Balthasar, *Thérèse of Lisieux,* http://carmelite.com.

10. Quoted in Gaucher, 217.

11. *Story of a Soul*, p. 221.

12. Day, *Thérèse*, p. 606.

13. Karl Stern, "St. Thérèse of Lisieux," www.cin.org.

14. Thomas Schmitt, "John Paul II and Thérèse of Lisieux," in *Communio,* Fall 1997, p. 544.

15. John A. Hardon, S.J., "St. Thérèse of Lisieux," www.catholic.net.

16. Scott, p. 49.

17. Stern.

18. Day, *Long Loneliness,* p. 285.

19. William D. Miller, *A Harsh and Dreadful Love: Dorothy Day*

and the Catholic Worker Movement (Garden City, N.Y.: Doubleday, 1974), p. 25.

20. Malcolm Muggeridge, *Something Beautiful for God: Mother Teresa of Calcutta* (San Francisco: Harper and Row, 1971), p. 15.

21. Quoted in Spink, p. 273.

22. Quoted in Spink, p. 162.

23. Quoted in Spink, p. 210.

24. Thomas Friedman, "The Age of Interruption," *Oakland Tribune,* July 8, 2006, http://findarticles.com.

25. Jean-Pierre de Caussade, *Abandonment to Divine Providence,* John Beevers, trans. (Manila: Sinag-tala, 1988), p. 36.

26. Quoted in Miller, *All Is Grace*, p. 68.

CHAPTER FOUR: ALL ARE CALLED

1. Quoted in Egan, p. 382.

2. Quoted in Spink, p. 295.

3. Egan, p. 71.

4. Day, *Loaves and Fishes*, p. 209.

5. Quoted in Allaire.

6. Quoted in Miller, *All Is Grace*, p. 102.

7. Spink, p. xiii.

8. Spink, p. 72.

9. Quoted in Monica Furlong, *Thérèse of Lisieux* (New York: Pantheon Books, 1987), pp. 116, 117.

10. Gaucher, p. 112.

11. von Balthasar.

12. *Story of a Soul*, p. 72.

13. *Story of a Soul*, pp. 207, 27.

14. *Story of a Soul,* p. 72.

15. Gaucher, p. 139.

16. Quoted in Gaucher, p. 183.

17. Gaucher, p. 139.

18. Quoted in von Balthasar.

19. *Story of a Soul,* p. 188.

20. *Story of a Soul*, p. 72.

21. "Saint Thérèse's Little Way Demands Love in Action," excerpts from Thérèse of Lisieux, *Story of a Soul,* http://www.cjd.org.

22. Day, *Thérèse*, p. 609.

23. *Story of a Soul*, p. 14.

24. *Story of a Soul*, p. 15.

25. Stern.

26. Stern.

27. *Story of a Soul*, p. 27.

28. Gaucher, p. 128.

29. *Story of a Soul*, p. 74.

30. Day, *Thérèse*, p. 607.

31. Jim Forest, "A Biography of Dorothy Day," http://www.catholicworker.com.

32. *Story of a Soul*, epilogue, p. 263.

CHAPTER FIVE: PRAYER

1. Day, *Loaves and Fishes*, p. 206.

2. Quoted in Spink, pp. 124, 301.

3. Quoted in Spink, pp. 172–173.

4. Day, *Long Loneliness*, p. 244.

5. Day, *Long Loneliness*, p. 255.

6. *Story of a Soul*, p. 148.

7. Quoted in Miller, *All Is Grace*, p. 83.

8. Day, *Long Loneliness*, p. 285.

9. *Story of a Soul*, p. 172.

10. *Story of a Soul*, p. 173.

11. Sebastian Vazhakala, M.C., *Life with Mother Teresa: My Thirty-Year Friendship with the Mother of the Poor* (Cincinnati: Servant, 2004), p. 91.

12. Quoted in Gaucher, p. 202.

13. Quoted in Scott, p. 155.

14. von Balthasar.

15. Quoted in Scott, p. 152.

16. Quoted at http://www1.bbiq.jp/quotations/merton.htm.

17. von Balthasar.

18. Scott, p. 158.

19. Quoted in Spink, p. 225.

CHAPTER SIX: HIDDEN TREASURES

1. Stern.

2. Day, *Long Loneliness*, p. 59.

3. *Pastoral Constitution on the Church in the Modern World*, no. 36, http://www.rc.net.

4. Stern.

5. Stern.

6. Stern.

7. Quoted in Spink, p. 132.

8. Day, *Thérèse,* p. 609.

9. Quoted in Miller, *All Is Grace*, p. 106.

CHAPTER SEVEN: DOWNWARDLY MOBILE

1. Quoted in "Roots of the Catholic Worker Movement: Saint Therese's Little Way Demands Love in Action," www.cjd.org.

2. Gaucher, p. 129.

3. Quoted in Gaucher, p. 156.

4. Quoted in von Balthasar.

5. *Story of a Soul,* p. 189.

6. *Story of a Soul*, p. 13.

7. Day, *Long Loneliness*, p. 11.

8. Egan, p. 55.

9. Scott, p. 52.

10. Quoted in Spink, p. 179.

11. Day, *Loaves and Fishes*, p. 176.

12. Day, *Long Loneliness,* p. 252.

13. *Story of a Soul*, p. 222.

14. *Story of a Soul*, pp. 246–247.

15. *Story of a Soul*, p. 159.

16. *Story of a Soul*, p. 248.

17. Gaucher, pp. 144–145.

18. Quoted in Allaire.

19. Quoted in Peter Casarella, "Sisters in Doing the Truth: Dorothy Day and St. Thérèse of Lisieux," *Communio,* Fall 1997, p. 494.

20. Spink, p. 3.

21. Spink, p, 50.

22. Spink, p. 75.

23. Quoted in Spink, p. 205.

24. Jose Rueda, "Seminarian Discovers Dorothy Day," *Houston Catholic Worker*, vol. XXIII, no. 2 (March-April 2003),

http://www.cjd.org.

25. Day, *Loaves and Fishes*, pp. 84, 86.

26. Day, *Loaves and Fishes*, p. 215.

27. Mark and Louise Zwick, "Dorothy Day and St. Thérèse of Lisieux Respond to the Despair of Our Time," *Houston Catholic Worker*, vol. XXII, no. 6 (November 2001), www.cjd.org.

CHAPTER EIGHT: ONE PERSON AT A TIME

1. Spink, p. 257.

2. Miller, *Harsh and Dreadful Love*, pp. 121–122.

3. Spink, p. 203.

4. Egan, p. 49.

5. Quoted in Spink, p. 87.

6. Spink, p. 124.

7. Quoted in Vazhakala, p. 28.

8. Muggeridge, p. 119.

9. Day, *Loaves and Fishes*, p. 176.

10. The author owes his awareness of Stern's essay to David Scott, who quotes it on p. 57 of his book.

11. Quoted in Spink, p. 88.

12. Spink, p. 233.

13. Spink, p. xi.

14. Quoted in Spink, p. 247.

15. Day, *Loaves and Fishes*, pp. 190–191.

16. Quoted in Spink, p. 133.

17. Spink, p. 6.

18. Quoted in Scott, p. 41.

19. Spink, p. 11.

20. Quoted in Spink, pp. 19–20.

21. Muggeridge, p. 130.

22. Miller, *Harsh and Dreadful Love*, p. 217.

23. Miller, *Harsh and Dreadful Love*, p. 21.

24. Day, *Long Loneliness*, p. 171.

25. Day, *Long Loneliness*, pp. 150.

26. Day, *Long Loneliness*, p. 265.

27. Day, *Loaves and Fishes*, p. 177.

28. Quoted in Spink, p. 247.

29. Dorothy Day, "Room for Christ," *Houston Catholic Worker*, vol. XV, no. 8 (December 1995), reprinted from *The Catholic Worker*, www.cjd.org.

30. Quoted in Mark and Louise Zwick, "Dorothy Day and the Catholic Worker Movement," *Communio*, Fall 1997, p. 431.

CHAPTER NINE: WORKS OF PEACE

1. Dorothy Day, "House of Hospitality, Chapter Four," Dorothy Day Library on the Web, http://www.catholic-worker.org.

2. Zwick, "Dorothy Day and St. Thérèse of Lisieux Respond to the Despair of Our Time."

3. Quoted in Jim Forest, "What I Learned about Justice from Dorothy Day," *Salt of the Earth* (Claretian, 1996), http://salt.claretianpubs.org.

4. Dorothy Day, *Thérèse: A Life of Thérèse of Lisieux* (Springfield, Ill.: Temple-gate, 1991), p. xii, as quoted in Allaire.

5. Ronald Lawler, "John Hugo's *Weapons of the Spirit*," *Communio,* Fall 1997, p. 635.

6. Quoted in Casarella, p. 493.

7. Stern.

8. Dorothy Day, *Thérèse*, reprinted in *Communio*, p. 610.

9. Quoted in Day, *Thérèse*, reprinted in *Communio*, p. 610.

10. Gaucher, p. 98.

11. Quoted in von Balthasar.

12. Pope Pius XI, *Quas Primas,* Encyclical on the Declaration of the Feast of Christ the King, December 11, 1925, no. 19, www.dailycatholic.org.

13. Stern.

14. Allaire.

15. Egan, p. 185.

16. Egan, p. 185.

17. Quoted in Scott, p. 54.

18. Quoted in Spink, p. 166.

19. Quoted in Egan, p. 309.

20. Quoted in Spink, p. 242.

21. Egan, p. 407.

22. Quoted in Spink, p. 241.

23. Quoted in Egan, p. 283.

CHAPTER TEN: THE EMBRACE OF SUFFERING

1. Quoted in Spink, p. 144.

2. Quoted in Spink, p. 144.

3. Quoted in Scott, p. 157.

4. Quoted in Spink, p. 140.

5. Quoted in Spink, pp. 141, 142.

6. Miller, *Harsh and Dreadful Love*, p. 118.

7. Quoted in Gaucher, p. 189.

8. Quoted in Spink, p. 251.

9. Spink, p. 17.

10. Spink, p. 17.

11. Miller, *Harsh and Dreadful Love*, p. 45.

12. Day, *Loaves and Fishes*, pp. 71, 82.

13. Day, *Long Loneliness*, p. 119.

14. Spink, p. 44.

15. Spink, p. 265.

16. Quoted in Spink, p. 269.

17. Spink, p. xiii.

18. Day, *Loaves and Fishes*, p. 71.

19. Quoted in Spink, p. 184.

20. Spink, p. 150.

21. Spink, p. 247.

22. Quoted in Egan, p. 409.

23. Day, *Loaves and Fishes*, pp. 176–177.

24. Spink, p. 131.

CHAPTER ELEVEN: SPIRITUAL POVERTY

1. "Mother's Wisdom," Mother Teresa: The Path of Love Homepage, http://home.comcast.net.

2. Quoted in Spink, p. 87.

3. Quoted in Spink, p. 86.

4. Day, *Long Loneliness*, p. 286.

5. Day, *Long Loneliness*, p. 215.

6. Day, *Loaves and Fishes*, pp. 64–65.

7. Day, *Loaves and Fishes*, p. 177.

8. Spink, p. 70.

9. Quoted in Spink, p. 74.

10. Quoted in Spink, p. 296.

11. Quoted in Spink, pp. 258–259

12. Quoted in Egan, p. 185.

13. Spink, p. 111.

14. Egan, p. 183.

15. Day, *Loaves and Fishes*, p. 198.

16. Lawler, pp. 635–636.

17. *Story of a Soul*, p. 247.

18. Quoted in Egan, p. 261.

CHAPTER TWELVE: A CHALLENGE TO CHRISTIANS

1. Spink, pp. 225, 257.

2. von Balthasar.

3. Day, *Long Loneliness*, p. 59.

4. Lawler, p. 635.

5. Day, *Long Loneliness*, p. 247.

6. Day, *Long Loneliness,* p. 150.

7. Day, *Long Loneliness*, p. 179.

8. Day, *Loaves and Fishes*, p. 92.

9. Lawler, p. 635.

10. Spink, p. 106.

11. Michael Walsh, ed., *Butler's Lives of the Saints* (San Francisco: Harper and Row, 1985), p. 312.

12. "Feature: Jean Vanier," *Religion & Ethics Newsletter*, May 26, 2006, www.pbs.org.

13. Cathleen Falsani, "There's No Crying in Journalism Except …," *Chicago Sun-Times*, May 5, 2006, p. 38, www.suntimes.com.

14. Falsani.

15. von Balthasar.

About the Author

Tiina Nunnally is known for her translations of novels and short stories from Danish, Norwegian, and Swedish. She has published fifteen books in translation and has received numerous awards. In 1992 she decided to give up her office job and make her living as a freelance editor and translator. She lives in Seattle with her editor husband and their cat Amalie.